A COMBAT-K NOVEL
CLONEWORLD
ANDY REMIC

SOLARIS

First published 2011 by Solaris
an imprint of Rebellion Publishing Ltd,
Riverside House, Osney Mead,
Oxford, OX1 0ES, UK

www.solarisbooks.com

ISBN: 978 1 906735 58 6

10 9 8 7 6 5 4 3 2 1

A CIP catalogue record for this book is available from the
British Library.

Designed & typeset by Rebellion Publishing

Printed in the US

This one's for Kevin Blades.
For lost friendship found again...
and I'm *the Monopoly Master, Matey!! Reet??*

TORTURE

Franco Haggis was in the shit.

Now admittedly, Franco Haggis spent most of his waking life "in the shit," and it should have come as no surprise to the hardy Combat K squaddie that, as he regained consciousness and swam languorously up a familiar blurred tunnel of mental honey-mucus towards bitter wakefulness – and, no doubt, an accompanying agony/torture/misery of body, mind and spirit – that he was indeed once again taking a huge chomp from the ripe shit pie. However, upon inspection, this time it certainly appeared to be an even *bigger* dunking in the faecal-tank of *life* than that to which he was normally accustomed. In at the deep end, so to speak.

Franco groaned, and the first thing that hit him was

the stench. It was bad. Made him gag. It reminded him of a barrel of ten-week rotted fish-heads. He heard a voice, then, a low, masculine rumble. The sort that promoted bad B-movie trailers. It growled, boomed and reverberated in its quavering celluloid uncool:

"The little bastard's awake."

Uh-oh, thought Franco. *That's not promising, is it? What happened, eh? Just what the hell happened? How did I get here? What's that funny smell? And more importantly, why am I all itchy-scratchy and surrounded by deep macho masculine voices?*

Franco opened one eye, experimentally. He saw five huge men walking towards him with the swaggering gait of those in assured control. They wore suits that were far too tight, because of all those bulging muscles. It was like an explosion in a steroid factory for deviant mutations. They carried an array of what could only be described as "torture implements": one had a pair of laser shears, another a digital scalpel, yet another an iron bar with holes in it hissing some kind of gas; a fourth carried what looked like a spiked ball on a chain, glimmering like a holoproj whip; and the fifth carried just his fists, adorned with shiny brass knuckle-dusters, which he flexed and cracked in an alarming manner.

Franco closed his squinting eye. *Damn and bloody bollocks! What now? What now? Shit and greasy fried chicken! I don't remember how I got here, or what I did wrong. Did I do something wrong?* His mind tried a replay of recent events, but there was a big blank STOP sign – probably with a middle finger raised.

Franco struggled, raising a clatter, but his hands were manacled to a steel chair, which in turn was bolted firmly to the solid titaniumconcrete floor. He struggled hard, and his round, and some would say slightly *chubby*, face grew red with exertion. His powerfully muscled, and some would say *rotund*, barrel of a body squirmed and flexed and fought the steel. Sweat ran down his shaved head, through his ginger goatee beard, and glistened on his tattooed body. But steel was steel, and Franco was Franco, and one was definitely harder than the other.

Franco slumped in defeat, and opened his eyes. *Okay then. Let's get this done.*

One of the large men sniggered, in a slow, cruel way.

"Alreet, guys," sighed Franco, with the kind of resigned sigh that suggested he'd experienced many similar predicaments before. This should have provided a gentle warning to any thug approaching the incarcerated CK soldier with brass dusters. On this occasion, it served no such purpose. "What's the gig, then?"

One large man, a beefcake subtly larger than the other bulging beefcakes, stepped forward. He carried the digital scalpel. He looked meaner than mean, madder than mad, harder than hard. He was a regular kick-ass bad-boy. Ex-police. Ex-military. Ex-exorcist. Probably with a price on his head. And something bionic. "You are Franco Haggis!" he bellowed, spittle foaming at his lips and enunciating each word with care, as if memorised from cardboard pages. "You *will* tell us everything!" He spoke with total confidence. Like a man who got answers.

Franco thought about this. He was, as previously indicated, Franco Haggis; but Franco Haggis was Combat K, an elite detonations expert with finely honed military combat skills and the ability to fight all day and sleep all night. Franco had, in fact, once been incarcerated for being a little bit insane. Not all the time – oh no! – but a goodly amount of his *life cycle* was spent not operating on the same plane of reality as other, more normal, people. Indeed, Franco sometimes didn't operate in the same *life bubble*. The same damn *galaxy shadow*.

Franco had taken bucketfuls of rainbow coloured pills during his time at The Mount Pleasant Hilltop Institution, the "nice and caring and friendly home for the mentally challenged," had drunk enough ale and liquor during his life to fill a small lagoon, was obsessed with breasts, ate copious amounts of Pre-Cheese, Cube Sausage and dodgy tubs of horseradish, and was what could be generously described as *unstable*. His powers of recollection were woeful at best, and he was indeed blank right back to the point where he'd been sat on the SLAM DropShip heading for an important mission which, now he thought about, he'd misplaced.

So Franco grinned, and nodded, and frowned,

and said, "Yeah mate, no worries," because Franco didn't, in fact, remember anything worth telling.

"You'll spill the data, dickhead," said another beefcake, stepping forward with his iron bar.

"Yeah. Or we'll beat the fucking mission out of you!"

"Er," said Franco. "It would seem we have a problem."

"Which is?"

"Er. I got drunk? I don't remember much. In fact, lads, I was so pissed I seem to have contracted this strange itching sensation down... below, so if you'd just, you know, undo these shackles so I can have a bit of a root around..."

"Silence!"

The voice was very powerful and very female. She strode through the – Franco blinked, his senses swirling into some semblance of comprehension – *shit*, he thought, *I'm in a dungeon!* Franco gulped. Then gulped again. The woman strode through the dungeon. She was tall, and stocky, and looked as if she was very, *very* strong. She was black, with a long luscious pelt of shining curled hair, and her make-up gleamed and her simple white dress contrasted beautifully with her ebony skin. She looked more like a rockstar – no, looked more like a *goddess* – than somebody who would imprison poor little helpless Franco.

She stepped across pools of stagnant water and stopped, very much out of place against the black and grey stone. The walls were lined with rusted iron chains. Franco glanced about some more, like a man probing a wound with a finger, not really wanting to do it, but curious as to the real damage inside. All around were chairs with spikes, racks with spikes, and tables with spikes; the spiked theme made Franco shiver, and wish fervently he was back home with his mum.

"Er," he said, again, realising he wasn't making much sense.

"Do you know who I am?" boomed the woman, and Franco's eyes dropped in degrees, from her shockingly beautiful face to her shockingly huge bosom, and finally to the shockingly lethal *laser chainsaw* which she held with the sort of practised ease which only came to people proficient with laser chainsaws.

"Somebody who's come to undo my shackles, pat me on the bottom, call me a naughty boy, and send me home with a stern letter of telling off?"

"I am Opera," said the woman, and smiled, and her smile shone like diamonds. In fact, her teeth really *were* inset with diamonds, which caught strands of light and glittered as she spoke.

"Never heard of you," said Franco. He noticed her stiffen a little, and frowned. That was odd. Should he have heard of her? *Opera?* It was more the kind of reaction he'd expect from a movie star than a gangster with a portable killing machine.

Franco was fully awake, now, and fully aware. He was frowning. Memories sleeted back into his brain like Space Worms eating through the hull of a floating Ion Platform. He remembered being fully armed and armoured. SLAM Dropship. A FAST fast drop to... where? *Come on, come on, remember your mission, dickhead. Where are you? What are you doing?* He glanced down. His Kekra quad-barrel machine pistols were gone. As was his Permatex electronic WarSuit, which had been stripped from his body, leaving him sat forlornly in big white underpants and scruffy boots.

Opera moved close. There came a *click*, and a *hiss*, and the digital chainsaw ignited with flickers of blue and gold light. Franco watched the chainsaw's digital teeth spin at high speed and a noise rose from the machine, a machine used on forest worlds like Tetunga and Dago to chop down hundreds of thousands of trees but which here, it would seem, was about to be implemented in chopping down Franco Haggis.

"Wait," said Franco weakly, rattling his arms against the shackles holding him tight. "Surely, we can come to some arrangement?"

"Yes," beamed Opera, with that glittering diamond smile, "surely we can. I will cut, and you will scream." And the beautiful glow of the chainsaw moved ever closer to Franco's squirming body...

THE FAST ATTACK Hornet *Metallika* hung immobile in the fluttering hydrogen streams fifty klicks above the glowing, swirling panorama of the Ganger World – known by its official Quad-Gal-imposed title of *Cloneworld*. Pippa sat at the Hornet's console, staring down at the world below and fighting a peculiar feeling of vertigo. Her hands skimmed the console, activating air and light sensors, and the HUD scanned and searched the vast, slow-turning, beautiful world below.

"I cannot locate him," came the soft, soothing and maternal voice of Alice, the ship's computer.

Pippa snorted in annoyance, and ran both hands through her bobbed brown hair. "That's impossible. The ginger bastard has logic cubes implanted in his spine. With the right codes he should light up like a damn global-net firework!"

"Even so," said Alice, "I have conducted a full continent-by-continent global search. On all channels. Fifty times. Franco Haggis has, to all intents and purposes, vanished."

"The *bitch*."

Pippa rubbed at her chin, eyes staring into the distant blue glow of the planet, swirling with white masses of cloud cover. It had been a simple mission. Using previously gathered intelligence, Franco's aim was to visit the planet covertly in order to determine the whereabouts of something called the *Junkala Soul*. An ancient planetary being named VOLOS had directed Combat K to Cloneworld; Franco's job was to get in via a high-dive SLAM drop, sniff around, and get out again. No fuss. No drama. But now he'd vanished, and Pippa had to decide how long to leave it before revealing her cloaked Hornet and attracting unwanted interest from Cloneworld's authorities. And Pippa knew, both dominant factions on the planet – the orgs and the gangers – had little or no love for QGM, the Quad-Gal Military. In fact, the orgs and gangers were downright hostile and suspicious of all things QGM; they saw them as interfering, meddling bureaucrats. Which they no doubt were.

"Shit."

"Your tension levels are running at 97%." Alice released a gentle aroma of orange blossom. "I suggest a hot bath and a beaker of alcoholic depressant."

"No. No, I'm going to have to fly in after the simpleton, aren't I? If I find out..."

"Yes?" enquired Alice, politely.

"No, no, it's okay. I was about to say that if I find out this mission has been compromised because of Franco's incurable love of beer, brothels and nasty alien cuisine... but then, no, that wouldn't happen, would it? Even Franco's not *that damn stupid* to risk the entire future of the Quad-Gal under an onslaught of invading junk armies like a toxic plague, even *he's* not that fucking dumb to risk it all for gambling, booze and cheap sex."

Pippa and Alice considered this.

"Is he?" said Pippa, eyebrows arching over beautiful green eyes.

"I think we should go in," said Alice, making a calculated decision.

"Shit. Yeah, so do I. Prime the engines…"

"Engines primed," said Alice, and deep in the belly of the Fast Attack Hornet *Metallika*, slick neutron engines fired into life with a tremble of anticipation. "SLAM drop commencing in five, four, three…"

"STOP!" SHOUTED FRANCO, suddenly, and from the corner of his eye he caught a glimpse of four or five QuickRepair PopBots fluttering near the dungeon ceiling amidst the mould and dripping water. Again, he frowned at the context, and his eyes met Opera's and there was a bright, sparkling intelligence there. Something was deeply wrong. This whole thing stunk like a rancid dead donkey.

"One last request?" smiled Opera.

"Yes. This." Franco's boot lashed out, slamming Opera in the crotch. She grunted, taking a step back, and the digital chainsaw hit the ground, buzzing as it cut a stream of sparks through stone. There came a squawk, and the five men started forward with torture implements raised. Franco's boots clamped the chainsaw's flanks and kicked it up into the air, where it spun for a moment and fell to earth in an arc, shearing neatly through one of Franco's hand shackles – and the arm of the steel chair itself – before skittering off across the floor, leaving a trail of molten stone. Franco wrenched his right arms free, just as the first bulky beefcake struck with the iron bar. Franco took the blow on his arm, twisted his wrist, and took the bar neatly from the man, who stood for a moment, hands empty, a confused expression rioting across his flat features. The look vanished as the bar hit him between the eyes with a meaty *thunk*. He dropped, and Franco levered the bar under the shackle on his left wrist, popping it with a squeal, and stood. The other four men attacked, screaming, and Franco ducked the whirring mace, planted a left punch in its owner's belly, backhanded the iron bar across Scalpel's face, front-kicked Shears in the balls, and slammed the iron bar across Knuckle-Duster's temple. Franco grabbed Mace, who was doubled over, wheezing, by the hair at his temples with both hands, and rammed his knee into his nose three times. The thug dropped, bleeding, to the dungeon floor. The beefcake with the digital scalpel threw the buzzing weapon, and Franco swayed, the blade flashing past his face and embedding in the wall. *This is getting serious*, thought Franco with a frown, and he leapt forward with a grunt and shoved the iron bar up the man's nose so hard it wedged into his skull, and he hit the floor, screaming and trying to pull it out with blood- and snot-slippery hands.

"Wait," came Opera's soothing voice. She had collected the digital chainsaw and held it in front of her, weaving a gentle figure of eight as she advanced on Franco with purposeful steps.

"Don't do it," snapped Franco, fists clenching. "I am not," he preened, "as shit as I look."

"You come in here, messing everything up with your fucking *combat training*, you little fat bastard...!"

The chainsaw swung for him, and Franco skipped back. The spinning, glowing chainsaw blade caught the wall and left a long glowing streak of molten stone.

"I'm warning you," said Franco, face grim, voice dropping to a dull monotone, "if you don't put down the pretty toy, I'm going to have to get nasty. And if there's one thing I really hate, it's killing a beautiful woman with a bosom like yours."

"You bastard, you ruined my show!" howled Opera, charging forward, but Franco had ducked to the right, back towards the groaning heavies, and as she swung the buzzing chainsaw Franco spun away, Opera tripped over the fallen body of one of her men, and the chainsaw blade fell back, cutting neatly through her own neck. Opera's head rolled across the floor like a deflating football. Blood trickled from the neatly cauterised neck stump. Everything was still, tense, a frozen moment in time, and Franco uncoiled from his fighter's crouch and looked around warily.

"Cut! Cut! Cut!"

And suddenly there were blinding floodlights blazing from every angle, along with mechanical roars and grinding and the thumping of heavy ratchets filling the world as two of the very *walls* were lifted on huge mechanical arms, and Franco turned around, dazed and confused, a mixture of horror and wonder on his goatee-bearded face as, as, as... as he realised he was in a fucking *television studio*.

"Cut! I said stop the fucking cameras!" squealed a small, frizzy-haired man, as he came stomping towards Franco, and Franco simply gawped with a stupid look as he took in the dollies and cranes and jib-arms, the plethora of sound engineers and runners and a *studio audience who were sat, mouths open in shock at the sight of their favourite, funny, brilliant TV star Opera with her head now twelve metres from her body.*

"Franco, you stupid little bastard, you just went and killed Opera! She's the biggest TV star in *the whole damn world!* What were you thinking? What were you doing? Oh my Green Gods, we're gonna be so in the shit-oven over this fiasco, and I ask again, WHAT WERE YOU EVEN THINKING OF, YOU STUPID LITTLE GINGER TWAT? YOU WERE ON FUCKING TV FOR ALL THAT'S HOLY, YOU WERE ON A LIVE TV SHOW!"

Franco considered this. "Actually," he said, looking around for the exit, fists still clenched, mind working fast, "if I was being pedantic, I'd say that a) I didn't know I was on TV, b) Opera *technically* cut off her own fat head, and c) what kind of insane TV show has you pretending to torture people in a torture dungeon? Eh? I said eh?"

The producer seemed to fill up with a crimson rage. "It's TORTURE, the numero uno most popular and well-loved reality TV show in the whole of fucking QUAD-GAL, you chump! It's beamed through all Four Galaxies, is watched by fifteen *billion* Blobbers, and *YOU JUST KILLED THE BLOODY STAR! THE*

PRIME OF CORE GOVERNMENT WILL HAVE YOUR HEAD ON A SILVER PLATTER FOR THIS ATROCITY!"

Franco looked around. He scratched his beard. He looked around again. "Er," he said. Then shrugged. "I'm. Er. Sorry?"

There was a commotion, and fifty heavily armed police officers stormed through a variety of doors and studio entrances. They carried state-of-the-art MPK sub-machine guns and D5 Shotguns used for riots and crowd control (and the controlling slaughter of rioting crowds). And... Franco blinked. Every single member of the Royal Ganger Police Force looked *exactly the same*. They were the same build, the same height, and had the same facial features – that of a thirty-year-old man in his prime, with neat dark hair and purple rings under the eyes from too many late nights drinking coffee and eating donuts.

"Throw down your weapons!" came a crackly voice through a loud-hailer.

"Put your hands in the air!"

"Lie on the floor!"

"Hands behind your back!"

"Don't move, sucker!"

"I'm not carrying a weapon," said Franco, helpfully.

"He can't put his hands in the air *and* lie on the floor, you idiot," crackled the loud-hailer.

"Er, just kneel down then, with your hands in the air. And throw down your weapons, mister!"

At that point, Franco's earlobe comm gave a tiny

buzz. In his ear, Franco heard Pippa's voice. "At last, we've found the bugger. Franco? Franco, what are you – oh, no, tell me this is a joke, a bad dream, a slap in the face with a portable bloody nuke! You've *killed Opera?* Holy shit! She's a public *phenomenon* and you've just decapitated her on live TV! Oh, *no...*"

"I didn't kill her," said Franco through gritted teeth. "She sort of cut off her own head with a digital chainsaw during a fight. I was the completely innocent party, I was."

"Listen, just hang tight," snapped Pippa. "Do not fight these goons. I repeat, do not fight..."

The RGPF waded into Franco, and he slammed a right hook, a right straight, a left hook, another right straight, breaking jaws and cheekbones on that perfectly gangered face before the sheer weight of cloned police and batons clubbed him to the ground in a flurry of eagerness and Franco entered yet another blissful state of dreamless euphoria.

CHAPTER ONE

PUBLIC ENEMA NO. 1

SHE LAY ON a cold slab. It was uncomfortable, pressing against her shoulder blades, coccyx and ankles. She was naked. She shivered, but relished the feeling. Goosebumps rippled along her flesh. Pain teased her. But then – that was okay. Pain meant life. Pain meant *existence*. She opened her eyes. The world was grey. The world was black. Swirling whorls, a fluid jigsaw. And she remembered – *no colour*. Everything was black and white. Like an old filmy. Like the P-Earth-History books. She released a breath. A breath held in a cage for a million years. She sat up. Looked around. Her eyes settled on a table. On the table there was a photograph. Next to the photograph was a gun. She took the gun. It nestled in her palm, like metal flesh. She licked her lips. Studied the face in the photo. And instinctively, because she was programmed to, she knew what she must do.

FRANCO GROANED, LONG and low, and realised he was in the shit. This was going to be a week of being in the shit, he understood that now, and somehow it made him reticent to open his eyes because everything would be brown. *I'll just lie here for a while. It's cool. No new violences are being visited upon my organs, and despite a rumbling in my belly and the craving for a few stiff whiskies, I think I could just get used to this.*

"Oy!"

Franco remained stoically calm, and stubbornly refused to open his eyes. A distant pounding drummed through his skull from rough treatment at the hands and clubs of the Royal Ganger Police Force. The ends of his fingers tingled, signifying some element of nerve stress, and Franco tried hard not to imagine what would happen when Pippa finally turned up... and yet! Yet it had been going so well. And what happened when things were going so well, was that they usually *stopped* going so well, and then kicked a man in the balls – or if one didn't have balls, the nearest damn equivalent...

"Oy! You there!"

Franco gave in. He opened his eyes. He gazed up at cold grey steel. It was a cold grey steel ceiling attached to cold grey steel walls. A cool breeze washed over him. *Aircon? A drink, sir? Maybe you'd like to retire to your room for a massage...?* Franco clicked his brain into gear and ran a physical diagnostic. He wiggled everything. Everything seemed to work. His eyes were going in and out of focus, and he tenderly touched his head where a lump the size of an egg was threatening to crack open and spill yolk across the... yep, he checked, across the cold grey steel floor. So then! Police cell. Ganger police cell. A ganger police cell fashioned from, Franco blinked and checked around, a solid cube of grey cold steel. Shit. *Shit*. How did one escape from a cube? And more importantly, how did they *feed you*?

"I said oy, you, bastad!"

There came a *whirring* sound, followed by several clunks, and Franco shuffled into a sitting position on his cold grey steel bunk. From the steel gloom came a woman, a little old woman, and *awww*, Franco liked little old women because they reminded him of his mum, and Franco loved his mum, but this little old woman *leered* and *loomed* from the gloom because, because... the clanking stopped. She had splayed metal toes at the end of what could only be described as robot legs.

"Er," began Franco.

"What you in for?"

"Excuse me?"

"You, you bastad. What you in for?"

Franco eyed the woman up and down. She looked perhaps eighty years old, assuming an old-hume lifespan. She was bent over, stooped, almost hunch-backed in that perennial display of the aged: weighed down by a great pressure of years. Her skin was wrinkled, and Franco stared for a while, fascinated by this phenomenon. After all, in most corners of Quad-Gal the QG Cosmetica Syndicate, one of the most affluent, powerful and influential of galaxy-wide corporations, had pretty much eradicated old age. Or at least, the *appearance* of old age. "*Why Grow Old!*" proclaimed the marketing slogans, with blatant disregard for correct punctuation. "*Why Wrinkle and Prune!*" spat aggressive marketing splats 24/7 on all available channels. "*Let the Cosmetica Syndicate help you beat those ageing blues... We make the Old New, we make the Crone Beautiful, our simple course of phenuclearaxiate injections make the Dead Alive...! Only a simple remortgage required!!! @ggg.iwanttobeyoungagain.com.*"

"Er." Franco stared hard at her. Understanding clicked with a tiny *click*. The old woman was an *org*. Distant phrases from the "Infiltration Sheet" drifted like wedding confetti in the vacuous caverns of Franco's mind... Franco never read his infil. literature. *What's the point,* he reasoned, *when I'll be on the job soon enough? Eh? I ask you?* In reality, it sometimes made Franco Haggis a liability best avoided.

Anyway, in this instance he *had* read some of the infil.literature (at Pippa's 9mm-pistol-prodding insistence), whilst perched on the alutitanium auto-flush toilet, pants round his ankles, vacating himself of the previous evening's vindaloo:

The Org – Upgrade Information
An ORG INC. Pamphlet

GENERAL

The orgs are a species who have evolved from a basic human construct/shell with the addition of mechanical and bio-mechanical aids. The orgs' religion is based on the premise "Thou Shalt Improve Thyself" and any org who does not wholly embrace such technological splicing – indeed, the art of mechanical self-improvement in its entirety – is thus exterminated as deviant to the core species. Here is the latest SALES PACK from ORG INC. [Upgrades Division/ Cloneworld East Sec].

UPGRADE TECHNOLOGY: BASIC PACKAGES

[1] Core Power

The human "heart" is always the first unit to be replaced, and replace it you should! Why perambulate along like a bowl of sushi, when you can FLY... This is obviously the most expensive unit to be incorporated, as on its energy input/

output/capability rests the operation of the complete org construct. One must carefully decide as to other requirements before choosing a heart unit (or 4-valve supply, as it has become trendily known). Basic 4-valvers will accommodate most normal augmentations, but for our "extra-special" special models, 8-valvers and even *16-valvers* can be employed after special artery-rerouting organic circuitry. You'll have to dig deep in those deep pockets for the latest tech! But hell, for any org true to his/her roots, IT'S WORTH IT! A bargain! – $117.99.

[2] Arms and Legs

These are considered the "back-bone" upgrade (along with the *real* backbone, a-ha-ha-ha). Arm and leg upgrades (orgspeak for beginners: mods/ augmentations) give increased strength/ stamina/speed, allowing any happy org much increased power in all athletic events! Want to win that race? Win that girl/boy? Woo that mutant? You need the basic ARMALEG units! Soft! Strong! And very, very durable! A special "FIGHT PACK" can also be ordered for all you budding ORG COMBATANTS (and let's face it, who doesn't like the odd punch-up, eh?), which substitutes carbontitanium bones and enlarged knuckles for those all-important fist-fights to the death. If you want to bludgeon your enemy to death, the FIGHT PACK is a must! Only – $55.99.

[3] Armour

Fed up with being shot in the face? Annoyed when a more powerful org kicks in your breast bone, splintering fragments into your woefully inadequate 4-valver and causing a temporary death sequence? Do not fret! Armour can be applied to ANY area of the org construct. Breast plates, joint plates, face plates. Hell, you can even encase those precious testicles in tiny solid balls of steel – or even better, have them removed entirely! [recommended for PIT SLAB FIGHTERS]. Special pink units can be ordered for the ladies, as can protective head-shells for the kiddies! Never again worry when little Charlie org falls down the stairs, gets crushed in the KITCHEN MINCER, or is attacked by a violent DOG ORG with his irresponsible dumb owner (but aren't they all these days, eh? Heh, heh, heh). Protect your children. Protect your genitals. Get our ARMOUR PACK TODAY! A snip at – $38.99.

[4]Sexual Upgrades

Hey there, sexy lady/ man/ mutant/ nudge-nudge-wink-wink, fancy giving your org partner a little bit of spice-up? Sexual upgrades are a popular augmentation for all you happily married orgs/ lotharios/ sexual predators/ femaleORGpower junkies! We have the obvious penis and clitoral upgrades, with added biomechanical vibrating stimulation for those lonely nights all on your lonesome! Guys! – Don't ever miss that opportunity with your best friend's wife EVER AGAIN! Get yourself a THROBBING EXTENSION™ (comes in five hundred and fifteen different size/ colour/ alloy configurations – It's the Quad-Gal's first ever "Pick & Mix Cock"!). And *ladeees!* – Don't ever let him get away with cutting you short of a good time! With our TEETH+SPIKE inserts, you can gently prod him into yet more energetic work and eager efforts – with the simplest of mental impulses! Don't be cheated ever again, buy our wonderful VAGINA DENTATA mods.

:SPECIAL LOVE-DAY OFFER:

Go on, guys, treat the woman org of your dreams to a combo MULTI-ORGASM INSERT combined with the MEGAVIOLENCE™ pack for some awesome sex in the sack!! You know it makes sense... All sexual upgrades at the wonderfully low but sexually stimulating – $89.99.

[5] *SPECIAL* Upgrades

- Ever wanted to BECOME a fifty-foot-tall MECH?
- Ever wanted to CRUSH buildings with a single swipe of a car-sized fist?
- Ever wanted HELICOPTER ROTORS on your back? So you can FLY?
- Ever wanted A JET ENGINE up your ass?

Call one of our special ORG INC. salesorgs for the latest deals. Special rates for the military and teachers!

At this point, Franco had stopped reading. *Hey,* he reasoned, *one robot man is the same as the next? Reet?* And he'd moved onto his hacked PAD to check the latest Arsebook updates (Welcome to Arsebook – Arsebook helps you connect and share with the arses in your life...).

Now, here and now, Franco was frowning hard and starting to wonder (not for the first time) at his lack of research prior to an infiltration in enemy territory. *But it was just such an easy gig,* he reasoned to himself. *It was simply a search and sniff mission, yeah? A take-it-from-behind mission. A lame-ass gig with no worries, baby, no drama!*

The old woman had stopped and was staring at him. Franco swallowed hard as he analysed her close-up in the gloom of the confined cubic cell. She was small, and bent, and wrinkled, yes. But she had bone-grafted spikes along her arms that looked pretty mean. Her legs from the knees down where pure mechanical, and clicked and *whirred* with every subtle shift of weight. Her face was wrinkled like an old woman, but now Franco studied her, he noted her eyes *glowed* green, with a deep and worrying malevolence. And her teeth were chromed like the finest of Franco's motorcycle accessories.

"I said," and she reached out, and prodded

Franco with an alloy finger that clicked and hissed on hydraulic joints, "what you in for? You deaf or something?"

"I, um, got into a spot of bother, old crone," said Franco, smiling optimistically. The "old crone" stepped backwards and, with a clanking and grinding of metal, rose on hissing hydraulics until her legs were ten foot long, and her midriff separated from her pelvis on a fat greased piston that took her head all the way up to the ceiling. With *clicks* and *clacks* her shoulders opened, revealing tiny mounted lasers that focused, and locked red dots, one on Franco's face, the second over his heart...

"Er?" said Franco, eyes wide.

"Old crone, is it, fat boy?"

"Er," and Franco held up his hands in supplication. "Wait, wait, I beseech thee! It was all a misunderstanding, I was stuck in this here cell through no bloody trouble on my part, oh no, I was simply walking down the street and next thing I know I'm accused of cutting off Opera's head! Hot damn and dirty donkeys!"

"You – you *cut* off Opera's head?" screeched the old crone org. "I don't fragging believe it!"

"Is that an 'I don't fragging believe it' in a 'thank the gods that really awful TV presenter is finally devoid of her skull and brain innards' sort of way? Or..."

Suddenly, the org dropped and loomed close, and blew foul breath over Franco, stinking of hot oil and melted grease. There came a sound like dry bearings grinding steel shavings. "No, you idiot deviant. I admit I hate gangers on general principle, as is only just and right for an org such as I, but Opera... well, she was something different. Something special. She brought hope to the masses!"

"Ah."

"She brought messages of freedom and ultimate peace between org and ganger kind!"

"Ah. *Aaah.*"

"She was the one hope of uniting the orgs and gangers, of halting the progress towards all-out war, of stopping the rape and mutilation and eventual total destruction of the entire bloody planet of Cloneworld!"

"Shit," said Franco in a little voice.

"And you killed her, you little bastad!"

Lasers tracked again. Franco whimpered. There came a whine, deep down in the old org's belly, like some great and massive power source charging, ready to ignite and *fire*...

Which it did.

"I WAS SIMPLY walking down the street."

Franco Haggis, Combat K, efficient in demolition, detonation and assassination.

Mission: to find the Soul of the Junks, or the Junkala Soul as it is also known. Sent to Cloneworld by VOLOS – an ancient machine-God and also an entire living *planet* – theirs was the mission to end the advance of the junks spreading like a toxic virus across Quad-Gal. With the Junkala Soul, Combat K could potentially re-infect the decadent warmongering species of junks, re-infect them with a digital retrovirus and pacify their hatred; turn them back into a *good* species. Turn them from their path of darkness and abomination. Return them to former nobility and integrity.

Mission: a fast SLAM-drop, with Franco disengaging from the Hornet at two klicks over the surface of Cloneworld and SLAM-diving with his auto-chute. This had been a problem, because a) Franco hated heights, and b) Franco *fucking* hated heights. He screamed like a prepubescent girl from disengagement to his final hard, rolling, coughing landing in the dust of a toxic zone power plant, in what were comically known as the Abandoned Sectors of Cloneworld. Not the sort of place you wanted to back-pack. Not unless you wanted to grow three heads.

Franco stood in the dust, breathing in the tox and staring around. It was night. A cold sour wind blew. It smelt bad. It smelt like... toxic overload.

"Hot damn and bloody bollocks," said Franco, and cut himself free of his SlickChute, rolling it into a ball and stowing it under some nearby dead, skeletal shrubbery, twigs like bony fingers. "So I'm here. And Pippa dropped me in a toxic shithole." He considered this. "So. Some things'll never change, then."

In the distance, the lights of a city glittered. This was Nechudnazzar, one of the twin capital cities on the ganger continent of Clone Terra; it was also the place where Franco was to begin his search for the mythical Junkala Soul artefact.

Instruction: Do not engage in combat. This is a covert mission. Do not make your presence known. Find information on the Junkala Soul – if it exists – and report back to Pippa on the Fast Attack Hornet *Metallika*. From thence, further plans will be formulated. *Sorted*.

Simple. Easy peasy. With a bit of lemon squeezy.

Even Franco couldn't mess it up. Right?

"I'm in. You dropped me in a snot-pit again, Pips."

"Nothing less than you deserve, deviant."

"Well, now I've got a fifty klick hike, thanks to your crap nav skills. Skills, did I say? Your lack thereof!"

"Maybe you'll lose your paunch, gutsy. I'm just looking on the bright side."

"I *do not* have a paunch. I'm just robust. Like a digger. Or a tank. Or something. Anyway, I absolutely refuse to walk."

"You'll have to. No bringing attention to yourself, right?" She sounded annoyed now; which was ironic, as far as Franco could see. "We can do without compromising the mission before it even begins! You know the rules, Franco. The whole planet is in a constant flux of political upheaval, and teetering on the brink of total war. The gangers and orgs hate each other, and need little enough persuasion to fire off a few micronukes or HighJ spikes. The last thing

Quad-Gal and Combat K need is to be caught up in the middle of some dogshit dogfight. So you do what we all do in these situations, Franco, and you bloody well keep a low profile and use your brain. Right?"

"Of course," said Franco, with a slick, easy, ready smile. "I am a total professional." Then he cut the link.

BIG BEN WAS a politician for the New Ganger Freedom Party, a New Party for a New Free Age. He was big, hence the Big, and he was called Ben, hence the Ben. He thought his name gave him the kind of friendly and happy trustworthy persona which other gangers would really dig. And trust. It made him sound friendly. And trustworthy. He hoped it would get him votes. Lots of votes. Enough votes to make *a lot of money!*

The Coolskin Hotel was a class place. A place for the inordinately wealthy. And also the trustworthy. A hive for the morally corrupt. A pleasure palace for those seeking pleasure. A sin-pit for those seeking hedonism. Five hundred floors of plex-glass steel and titaniumIII, it rose like a rocket, a shimmering glittering tower pointing defiance at the gods and screaming wealth and power with just a sprinkling of light decadence sprinkled over the creamy cream. That it was forty nine kilometres from Nechudnazzar was an oversight; or maybe its saviour. For whilst it did not rub brotherly shoulders with other overtly wealthy hotel conglomerates from the sprawling –

some would say bloated – mechanised, over-populated Machine Age nightmare that was Nechudnazzar, it offered a certain *something*. Discretion, indeed. Notoriety, certainly. But away from the core sprawls of the twin ganger capital cities, the Coolskin Hotel offered something much more desirable.

Anonymity.

Big Ben was currently in his hotel suite, although "suite" was perhaps an understatement, as Big Ben had reserved an entire *floor* of the Coolskin Hotel, using funds from the New Ganger Freedom Party's deep and healthy coffers. The way his logic ran was: I am keeping the people happy and serving the people, thus the peoples' money can keep me happy and serve my every whim. It was a good financial policy. It was like taking candy from a kid. A bone from a dog. A slick tongue-twisting kiss from a touting hooker.

The political party's collective funds had been put to other trustworthy and useful pursuits. Big Ben sat on a leather watercouch, bobbing a little with every movement, wearing silver hotpants and an erection you could hang a pervert's mac on. The erection was unwavering, thanks to the drugs. And there were lots of drugs. There were mountains of *Grey*, a hallucinatory narcotic grey powder said to give sexual stimulation *even to those without sex organs!* There were huge jars filled with *Pebbles* and *Skivs*. On a mirror, one of Big Ben's new lady friends was cutting and snorting lines of *Greebo,* which gave the best high and sex and high sex on this or any continent, but had the unfortunate temporary side-effect of making the user turn green.

Big Ben slopped off the watercouch onto carpets so thick they encompassed his ankles and ran static charges up his inner legs to crackle on his already over-charged testicles. "Hey, baby, save some for me," he crooned, slicking one hand through his long slick hair, as he finished the journey towards her on hands and knees, his tongue hanging out.

"I always shoot first," winked the naked lady, and what a naked lady she was! Breasts to her ankles, ripe plump buttocks you could fry an egg on, and a direct Zuiss bank account which charged Big Ben *by the second, baby, by the second!*

Big Ben reached the mirror, faltered, and ploughed his nose into a pile of Greebo. It got caught up in his whiskers and he giggled, snorting out a puff of powder worth thirty of his constituents' annual salaries.

"Oh, Ben," said Rebecca, giggling coquettishly. She wore her brown hair in a fashionable basin haircut, and her podgy squidgy face had been gangered to mimic the greatest actress of the Ganger Age, Rebecca Rebecca, star of screen and stage, warrior actress and unreservedly best shot with the Bausch & Harris Sniper Rifles, models KZ1526 and KZ1527. "Don't snort it everywhere! You know how hard it is to come by! And we have so much fun planned!"

They did indeed. As the buzz took Big Ben, he gazed around at the thirty other hookers in the suite of apartments. They were caught in myriad poses and gestures and acts, and his mind swam with the perfect base *beauty* of the scene.

"Come to me!" cried Big Ben, opening wide his arms, his silver pants glittering, and the thirty women (with a couple of men thrown in for sheer variety) ran to Big Ben, and smothered him with their nakedness, with their soft bits and hard bits, with their floppy bits and hairy bits. *I just fucking love expenses,* Big Ben revelled, falling onto his back as he was swamped, tickled, and caressed, and a squirming orgy encompassed him...

"Ahem."

The cough was the sort of cough coughed by somebody who knew he shouldn't be interrupting Big Ben's multiple carnal pleasures, but had indeed something of great importance to impart. When the first cough went unnoticed amongst the huge breasts, the slathering flesh, and the moans reverberating from the organic pink SuckPaper™ wallpaper, the man coughed again. Only this time a little louder.

"AHEM."

"Yes, yes, yes, what is it, why am I being interrupted, is there no bloody privacy in this whole damn place? I'm having the time of my life here and you have to come coughing your guts up all over my lovely naked men and women... oh, it's you, what do you want? Can't you bloody see I'm bloody busy?"

Johnson, Head of Private Security, was a sensible man. You had to be a sensible man when working for insane narcissistic-types, like politicians, rockstars and head teachers. Johnson gave a thin smile from his black bearded face, and smoothed out an imaginary crease on his perfectly pressed black uniform. "Mr Ben. Sorry to intrude on your..." – the pause was calculated – "*business meeting,* but it would appear somebody is trying to steal your motorcycle."

Big Ben gawped at Johnson for a moment, mouth opening and closing, flapping like a guppy fish. "Well... well... well..." he spluttered, clambering over three buxom hookers who squealed in delight. He managed to get to his feet, sliding in something slick and juicy. "*Do something about it!* Shoot the bastard! That's what I pay you for!"

"Perhaps that could be considered a tad excessive? After all, if we kill a man, the Royal Ganger Police Force will be here in a few short minutes. And I thought you were supposed to be dutifully engaged in a month-long off-world conference on ecology and the saving of the planet." He gave a brittle smile. *And not,* he added mentally, *living it up with decadents whilst snorting enough puff to put a strap-on rocket into space.*

"Yes. Yes. Well, er, send some men. Bring him down, then bring him to me."

Johnson departed the business-meeting-which-resembled-an-orgy, and Big Ben slapped off several questing fingers and rushed to the window. He peered down. And there – by all the gods indeed! – there was a short stocky fellow, a little stick man in the distance, fumbling with the mechanical innards of *Grace*.

"Enhance," snapped Big Ben, and the window hissed softly to enhance his view, tracking Ben's eye movements. There! A bastard with a shaved head and an untidy ginger goatee beard! Not a man who would be hard to forget, since due to the hot climate of Cloneworld most people, gangers and orgs included, were of darker skin and hair colouring. (Yes, some gangers had gone to extremes, but the ginger gangers were something of a rarity – indeed, a cult! It was something which never seemed to catch on in the clone community.) As a result, the shaven-headed ginger-bearded thief stood out like an org at a ganger SF convention.

Ben shifted his perspective. He saw a group of men running across the car park. Aha! They would have him now! His view shifted back to the thief, but there came the roar of a HondaHarley V24 even from this distance, and a massive burst of black fumes, and the *maniac* opened the throttle wide, leaving a twenty-inch streak of molten rubber across the alloyconcrete as he powered off, veering and swerving, and the security men grabbed frantically and pointlessly for the fast-disappearing thief.

"Baby, come back and do that thing with your tongue," crooned Rebecca, cupping her ankle-length stretched breasts with a grunt, her bowl haircut wobbling sexily.

"Johnson!" screamed Big Ben, and ran out into the corridor. "Johnson!" He was in the shuttlelift, thumping buttons, and sprinting out into the lobby before anybody could mutter "*Bastard bike thief...*"

"Sir," said Johnson, smiling a narrow smile. He seemed calm, unruffled, in perfect control. He was always calm, unruffled, and in perfect control.

"Get after him! Call the RGPF! Get in the gunships! Blow the motherfucker into a steaming puddle of motherfucking oilgrease!"

"Sir. I think, first, you need some pants."

Big Ben looked down. He was still proud. And he was definitely naked.

Big Ben looked up. A glittering crystal room crammed with succulent diners had paused, forks to mouths, spoons in soup, glasses to lips, to observe his outburst. Suddenly, there came a *click* and a *flash*. Kunta, the worst of the worst global tabloid paparazzi, gave him a big grin and a thumbs-up, and slid out of the revolving hotel doors before Big Ben realised what was happening...

Big Ben lifted his hand. His face was covered in Greebo.

He looked down. His skin was as green as his erection was hard.

Shit. Shit and damn! Shit and bastard bloody buggering bastards!

Cursing in yet more languages, Big Ben hurried back to his flesh-filled hotel suites, already wording apologies, hypothesising his explanations on *News*

At Eleven as he stood on the podium, a stricken-looking harrowed wife on one arm, happy smiling children gambolling at his feet – and he would wail as to how he had become a slave to the drugs, and the drugs made him do it, and his wife was strong and stood by his side, and how all he needed was time, and hope, and the trust and honour and belief of his constituents and the Prime Manager!

His eyes glittered with hatred and rage. Once again, he pictured the ginger bearded one.

"It's all your fault! You've ruined me! Ruined my political career! Ruined my funtime!" It didn't occur to Big Ben that, in fact, it was his own doing. The logic of the politician clicked neatly into place. "You've got a micronuke up the arse coming real soon, my friend," he muttered.

"I WAS SIMPLY walking down the street."

Franco enjoyed the rush of the HondaHarley V24 over the rough, dusty and pretty much deserted roads which led, like gently curving tributaries, to the distant, glowing, and slowly *growing* city of Nechudnazzar.

As the klicks clicked down, Nechudnazzar grew alarmingly, until its towers towered over Franco, its ramparts glistened like black oil, its mammoth walls and buildings and temples and factories formed a huge and towering blur, its vastness and sheer *height* almost beyond comprehension. Now, Franco was a veteran of big cities, of vast cities, of cities so titanic they inspired new cultures and species within their urban sprawls. Franco was a denizen of every sleazy pub, bar, brothel and gambling den it was possible to be a denizen *of*. But Nechudnazzar was different. It looked like a vast and unforgiving mountain range. It filled his vision like the frightening and near-mythical Black Pike Mountains of distant legend. It ran from horizon to horizon, from corner to corner. Nechudnazzar seemed to *fill* the world. It certainly filled Franco's head, with the glimmer of... *possibilities*.

He pulled the HondaHarley into the side of the road with a rumble, and sat there, twenty-four pistons thumping and idling, as he gazed with slack jaw and possibly slack *brain* at the massiveness before him. It reached all the way up to the sky. It stunk like a corpse pit, waves of stench rolling out over Franco as his palms grew sweaty in agitation and his mind started to do strange things, to tread well-known paths of terrible imagination.

Do nothing, touch nothing, fuck nothing, came Pippa's echoing, long-distant, unbidden words.

Ahead, Nechudnazzar seemed to *breathe*, like some huge, decadent, dying beast.

This was the largest capital city of the gangers.

This was the core of the cloning civilisation.

No drinking! No bars! No women! You're there to do a job, and do a job you shall!

"Bah," said Franco, kicked the bike into second, and roared towards the behemoth that filled his world, and now his imagination. He zipped past a battered titaniumII sign which read:

> WELCOME TO NECHUDNAZZAR
> YOU'LL NEVER, EVER LEAVE!

Franco grinned. They were probably right.

"I WAS SIMPLY walking down the street."

It was 3AM. Franco sat on the bar stool and glared blearily at the line of shimmering bottles lining the back of the bar.

"Are you okay?" asked the barmaid. She had a dumpy basin haircut which had, at first, made Franco laugh. A lot. Until it was pointed out that this was, in fact, a cool *ganger look*, mimicking the greatest of filmy and TV goddesses, Rebecca Rebecca.

"S'fine. Drink."

"What would you like?"

"S'whiskey."

"Single? Double?"

"S'bottle."

"Are you sure you're fit for a *whole* bottle?"

"S'listen here, Rebecca, can I call you Rebecca, oh yes you said I could call you Rebecca, well I is Franco Haggis and I'm here on this mission and oh dearie me I can't be talking about all that. Still, nice to meet you, and be ashured I can take my spill. My s'drink. You know it. What I mean, I mean."

"Sure, sugar." Rebecca passed him a bottle of whiskey, and Franco poured himself a pint. He squinted at the label. SCROTUM'S OLD TODGE CLOGGER – FINEST SINGLE MALT.

"Good stuff," said Franco, without irony, as it left a burning trail from his tongue to his arsehole. "Never had it so good."

"Good, sugar. Glad you like it."

Another barmaid appeared. She looked exactly like the first one, and for a few moments Franco thought it was SCROTUM'S OLD TODGE CLOGGER – FINEST SINGLE MALT playing games with his clogged old todge. But it wasn't. She was a ganger. They all were. That's why it was called Cloneworld. It was full of clones. *Hot shit.*

"So tell me," he drooled, leaning in his own spit. "Why are you called gangers? Eh?"

"Because we have the ability to *ganger,*" said Rebecca, clone of Rebecca Rebecca, and sister to her fellow barmaid, also a clone, a ganger, and also called Rebecca, named after Rebecca Rebecca and all the other Rebeccas. "We can clone ourselves, copy ourselves, or *shift* ourselves. We can only do it so many times during a cycle, but we can *change* to resemble other people, or, using blank body shells, make another version of our person. Our reality. We can shift to look like people we find attractive, or alluring, or just downright fashionable, for example. Or we can make multiple gangers."

Franco could see this might get complicated, and

his mind twisted and curled like a twisted neutron core. "Er," he said.

"It comes from *doppelgänger*... we are the *double walkers,* my ever-so-slightly drunk friend; we can change to look like any other living person in existence with only the slightest genetic sample. It's part of our heritage, as finely ingrained in the cultural psyche as sausages, horseradish, leather shorts, large glasses of beer and slapping our thighs when we dance. We are proud of our ability to mimic, to copy, to clone. It's an ability unique to our human pro-species."

Franco's lips twitched. "Did you say sausages and horseradish?"

"Ah, so we have a cultural awakening!"

"I'm hungry."

"I'll bet you are, soldier. Listen. Take this card" – she slipped him a glossy business card on wafer thin alloy – "then head out of here, turn right, and half a klick through the neon bustle, there's a place on the right called *Van Gok's.* You'll find everything you need right there."

"S'everything?"

"Trust me," smiled the ganger, and her teeth were perfectly straight, in a genetically modified kind of way.

Franco nodded, and stumbled out into the night. This was Downtown Nechudnazzar, otherwise known as *Party Town*, or *The Streets That Never Sleep*. It was a bustling maze of neon and flesh and drugs. It was a labyrinth of decadence, of hedonism, of violence, of pleasure. It was Franco's kind of place.

As he wandered through a violently colourful maze and haze, his mind swam. *Mission?* queried his inner guilt. *Aah, fuck it, what mission? What difference would one night make? After all*, insisted Franco's internal lack of logic, *if you keep a Combat K squaddie, one so rampant and horny and downright exuberant as I, locked away like a fish in a bowl, like a tiger in a cage, like a like a like a like a* STAG *in a* SHED, *then you can't expect anything else than a blowout when I go on R&R, reet? Stands to reason. Like night follows day. Like salmon swim in ponds. Like octopi have nine legs and a beak. Or something. Thus, so, when Pippa sent me on this mission, alone, on my billy-o, after such a long, long, long lockdown, then she must have,* MUST HAVE *known I'd go a bit loopy the first night, stands to reason, that's what I always do, and even though she said not to, that's what she'd would have to say, standard procedure, but she'd know I'd do the opposite and so that's okay, because she knows, so I can do it, and not get into trouble, as long as I do the mission tomorrow, and nobody'll ever be the wiser. Reet?*

Franco stopped, and blinked, and placed his hands on his hips. The thick flesh snake flowed around him, a million party people going about the business of pleasure. Franco blinked. Clarity flooded him. An epiphany took him in its fist and squeezed harder than hard. *I can party. Party, baby! After all, I'm the party boy, all right!*

Franco swaggered down the street, leering at pretty

women (and a few pretty aliens). As a rule, most of the gangers avoided him. It was obvious he was an off-worlder. His clothing, for a start, proclaimed him an alien to Cloneworld. And then there were the subtle pheromones that gangers exuded to attract either sexual mates, or ganger mates. On certain drugs, gangers could get *high* just from cloning one another...

Franco squinted again at the alloy business card. *Van Gok's.* Wasn't he that bloke who cut off his nose? Or something? A poet, or summat? Used to paint poems? Or was it the one who helped fat women disguise the wobbles? And wrote that bestselling celebrity navel: *Hide the Fatty?* Or maybe it was a celebrity shit? I mean, *chef?*

Franco stopped. He could see *Van Gok's* up ahead, through the haze of sweat and heat. And gods, it was hot. Like a furnace. Hotter than Hell. But a damn sight more fun...

Purple neon glittered. *Come to Momma,* said the neon letters.

Franco tottered forward like a baby taking its first steps.

Pippa would beat him for being such a Bad Boy!

He brightened. Hell yes!

Outside *Van Gok's* stood three tall gangers. They were identical. They had the same fluorescent purple hair, the same silvered breasts, the same powerful, beautiful features. One moved to Franco, and touched him lightly on the arm.

"We have many pleasures inside," she said.

"Pleasures of body, mind and soul, pleasures of which you could never dream, pleasures only allowable to *gangers* but here, you can have anything and everything, anything filtered from the magic of an infinite mind, anything you can *dream,* we can provide..." She licked glistening, moist lips.

"Anything?" breathed Franco, hoarsely.

"Anything," she crooned, her voice music.

"Can I have sausage and horseradish?" he said, almost whimpering like a naughty little schoolboy.

"As much as you can spread across your mighty, hairy body!"

"That'll do. I'm home, chicken, I'm home..."

The three gangers led Franco under a dark archway, and into *Van Gok's*. The last one halted on the threshold, turned, and made eye contact with a woman across the street. She was tall, and thin, and gangly, and looked like a man. She wore simple black clothes and hair like a fused tangle of lightning-struck barbed-wire.

Their eyes remained locked for a few moments, and the watching woman gave a nod, as if dismissing the ganger. The ganger promptly disappeared from sight, leaving an open archway: like a maw leading straight down into Hell.

With a sound, the woman shifted, merged with the crowd, and disappeared into the heaving mass of Downtown Nechudnazzar.

*   *   *

"AND SO YOU see, technically, I was simply walking down the street. Yes, I did get dragged drunkenly in Van Gok's weird and wonderful emporium, but then it went black, and that can't be my fault, right? I mean, how can it be my fault that everything went black? I'm just an honest geezer, a lad, a bloke, a dude, and I'm riding through life on the bubble of chance that is my existence. Yes, I'd had a few whiskies, but who doesn't? One certainly doesn't expect to be kidnapped and put into a kidnap situation and then brutally abused to the extent where you think, y'know, that your very existence is threatened and so you get a bit violent, in a purely self-defending kind of violent way, and Opera accidentally cuts off her own head in the kerfuffle and BAM! You're in a cell with an enraged but *deactivated* org who thinks she's the shit, but, no offence meant, crone, she's not. Because she's been deactivated. *Made safe.* You see what I'm saying?"

"Do you ever shut up?" said the old org who had, indeed, been deactivated. Yes, her lasers targeted, but there was no laser in the laser. It had been a very tense few moments when Franco Haggis had thought he was about to become a Franco Haggis *kebab.* But no lasers came. No burning red purification emerged, and the clanking old org had sighed and grumbled and muttered and consigned herself to the corner of the cell cube, as far away from Franco as she could get. Unfortunately for her, it wasn't far enough. Franco could talk for the Quad-Gal board.

Or bored. He prided himself in it. He'd won medals. Or at least, time in the brig.

"Actually, I have been known for my scintillating conversations," said Franco, primly, puffing out his chest, which was currently naked, as befitted his prisoner status. He had been allowed to wear only his Big White ASDA Underpants (BWAUs). And flip flops.

"You got any more gifts, wanker?"

Franco completely ignored, or was simply oblivious to, any form of sarcasm. "Actually, yes. I am considered a sexual athlete." His eyes gleamed. Then they fell on the mechanised *mess* that was the old org. She was indeed an old model. One of the first. What flesh hadn't been replaced by metal and machine had been replaced with bad skin graft. She was like a merged explosion of car factory and female sex doll.

"A sexual athlete?" She sounded interested.

Uh-oh.

"Er, ahem. I'm married, you know."

"You look like the divorced sort, to me."

Franco reddened. How did she know that? How *could* she know that? The bitch! The bugger! Franco was indeed divorced. He had married the girl of his dreams, but through a very strange set of esoteric circumstances, his bride-to-be had transmogrified into a kind of zombie genetic super-soldier – a one-way process, which left her eight feet in height, mucus of skin, disgusting of flesh, an eight foot monster who looked like she was inside-out. Doing the right thing, the best thing, the *honourable thing*, Franco had indeed married his betrothed – and gone through with the evil deed. Several times, if he remembered right. Often in his nightmares. However, after a further series of adventures, Mel – for thus was her name – had filed for divorce. She cited reasons such as Franco being unreasonable to live with. And lusting after other women... which wasn't *that* surprising when you considered his wife was a zombie, and Franco would lust after a one-legged whore in a vat of supermodels. He was *that kind of dude*.

"Actually, I *am* divorced," Franco said primly, "but I have a long line of women lining up to be the next Mrs Haggis."

"So that's your name? Haggis?"

"Yes. Haggis. Franco Haggis. Shaken, not stirred. Except, you know, when I've been shaken."

"Which would be right now?"

"Er, yes. Opera decapitating herself, that was hardcore shit. Left me a bit rattled. After all, I'm here to, er, yes, well. I've said enough."

"And killed enough, by all the sounds of it." The old org started to cackle, rocking backwards and forwards. Her machinery hissed and spat occasionally, and she belched old oil smoke, and Franco stared at her, as he would a particularly mangy dog.

"So then," said Franco, conversationally. "What you in for?"

"Murder."

"Aaah."

"Well, they call it murder, but I call it self-defence. After all, they was only gangers, they was. And we're practically at war. Damn police shouldn't have come poking around my neighbourhood. We have walls and things. And gates. Their disguises didn't stand up to much."

"So you killed the Royal Ganger Police? Wowsers. How many?"

The old org shrugged. "Thirty, forty. It's hard to count when they all get mashed up in a slurry pulp of severed limbs."

Franco shuffled along his bunk, until he was as far away from the aged psycho as was humanly possible without actually merging into the steel of the cube prison's wall. He felt suddenly, deeply vulnerable in his BWAUs and flip flops. It wasn't exactly War Grade Armour. It wasn't exactly nuke-proof *Permatex*.

"Wonderful," he said. *Shit. Just my luck. Put in a cell with a police-murdering metal psychopath machine-woman! Hot damn and bloody hot bollocks. How does I get myself into these damn situations, eh? I ask you, eh?*

AND FRANCO SLEPT.

In his sleep, he dreamed. He dreamed Pippa came to him, naked and voluptuous, and his hands ran down her naked flanks, along the powerful muscles of her arms and belly, and she smiled at him, and there was love in her eyes, and Franco chuckled to himself because this was just natural, and normal, and good, and the way it should be. She moved into him, pressing her body against his, and he groaned in longing and lust, but something more, something deeper, for he had always loved Pippa, always been addicted to her worse than any injected narcotic, or even a lightly fried sausage/horseradish muffin.

"Franco," she said, and kissed him, and their mouths pressed and her breath was sweet and their tongues entwined, and she groaned in fast-rising lust, and need, and hot bubbling ecstasy – and Franco's eyes flared open in sudden, wild, hard, insane panic, as "Franco," she said, and kissed him, and their mouths pressed, but her lips were metal, and her breath was foul like broken old engines, and their tongues entwined and her tongue was scaled, metal, like a robot snake, and she groaned in fast-rising lust, and need, and hot bubbling ecstasy –

"Get off!" screeched Franco, shoving the old org away. She clanked back, leg hydraulics hissing, and grinned at him, licking her lips.

"You taste real fine, wanker!"

"Eurch! Ouerch! How could you do that? How could you take such advantage? I feel," he pouted, "quite abused." He spat out a mouthful of black engine oil. "Yeuch!"

"An old gal has to take what she can get." The org retired to her own bunk, and was soon snoring, oil bubbles frothing at her lips. Her mechanicals made whirring and grinding noises deep in her machine bowels.

Rubbing his lips on his arm at least a hundred times, Franco retired back on his own bunk, grumbling, and casting many a suspicious glance at the old crone. "Cheeky git," he muttered, and pressed his earlobe comm in a vain attempt at communicating with Pippa.

There was nothing but a muted, static hiss. Obviously, here in the cell, signals were blocked.

"Bugger," said Franco, and tried hard not to fall asleep.

"GOOD MORNING!"

She stood in the doorway to the cell, and she was smiling a Big Smile. Franco groaned, and sat up, rubbing at his tousled beard and scratching his shaved head. *Where am I? What's going on? What happened?* Consciousness gave him a kick. *I'm in prison. I'm a prisoner. Ah, shit,* that *happened...*

Franco squinted at the woman. She was tall and thin and gangly, and wore an asexual simple black outfit Franco had seen on all prison warders. She had a mass, a mop, a tangle of frizzy black curly hair, a mass so amassed it towered over her head by a good foot, and fell away down her back like a plate of chaos-spilled barbed-wire spaghetti. The hair was a mess. It was more than a mess. Franco scowled at the hair. It was a fucking *abomination*. And yet there was something different about this woman, despite the bad hair, the narrow, cruel eyes, the weird nervous ticks when she spoke or smiled. She carried a strange little air of authority. As if she was important: Or *as if she thought she was important,* which could amount to the same thing when applied to any individual's behaviour.

"I," said the frizzy woman, with an air of dignity, "am Theresa Sourballs. Teddy, to my enemies. A-ha. Ha."

"So?"

"I am Governor of the Nechudnazzar Correctional and Reintegration Facility."

"So?"

"You may address me as *Ma'am*."

"Fuck off."

Sourballs stared hard at Franco Haggis. "You will pay me some respect, young man!"

"Or what you gonna do? Put me in prison?" He sniggered. Nobody else did. He realised Sourballs was backed up by about six hefty guards with steel truncheons and Steyr laser cannons. Franco clamped his mouth shut. If he'd had a hammer and nails, he would have nailed it shut.

Sourballs's eyes had narrowed, and she turned, and waved to two guards. They wheeled in a terrible and frightening contraption, a huge black cube with trailing cables and weird sharpened spikes. Franco gave a little whimper as his mind tumbled back through the years to his incarceration as a mental patient at The Mount Pleasant Hilltop Institution, the "nice and caring and friendly home for the mentally challenged." This all felt terribly real and horrible, and Franco regressed, Franco mumbled, Franco shivered, and Franco realised that everybody was staring at him.

"Not the electrodes," he blurted.

"Pardon?" said Sourballs, frizzy hair bobbing.

"Don't stick 'em in me! I beg you! I'll tell you everything... not that I bloody know anything, nobody round here tells me nuffink."

"Haggis, this is a TV."

"Eh?"

"A TV. It shows TV pictures. Shows and filmys and the best show ever created: *Torture!* Until you killed the star, that is..."

"Ahh. Yes. That little misunderstanding."

"No misunderstanding, I believe, although we'll let the judge sort that one out. I think you'll find she'll find you guilty. And then it's the death penalty for you." Sourballs smiled. Her teeth were small, yellow and crooked.

"Who's the judge?" said Franco, scowling.

"The Mistress. My boss. She's also the Prime of Core Government, and owns the TV network that employed Miss Opera, the woman whom you decapitated. Switch on the TV!"

The TV, which was indeed a TV and not a torture contraption, was switched on.

Franco blinked, at an enlarged photograph of his very own face. At the bottom of the screen scrolled other news items – gang rapes, murders, false gangers, breach of gangercide, the impending war with the orgs, an earthquake in northern Clone Terra that killed one thousand, five hundred and eighty seven gangers – but here and now, Franco Haggis was *the* most important item of news.

Franco paled. This didn't look good.

The newscaster was speaking. Sourballs turned up the volume. "And as can be seen by this photograph, Franco Haggis, most abusive murderer of the lovely, talented and beautiful Opera, erstwhile TV presenter on the Quad-Gal phenomenon *Torture!* will go on trial tomorrow, but we all know how that one should go, heh, heh, heh, after all, look at the evil weaselly little bastard... And it has been confirmed that Franco Haggis was also responsible for the earthquake in northern Clone Terra with his illegal offworld spaceship landing, and thus directly responsible for the one thousand, five hundred and eighty-seven deaths... it can be deduced that Franco Haggis was an ASSASSIN sent especially to execute our lovely Opera, and so tomorrow be ready with your voting panels during the trial, as we wouldn't like the little bastard to get off with anything other than THE DEATH PENALTY AFTER MONTHS OF TORTURE..."

"I love a fair trial," mumbled Franco, dejectedly.

"...it has been officially announced, FRANCO HAGGIS IS PUBLIC ENEMY NUMBER ONE – AND ON THE OFF-CHANCE THAT HE ESCAPES, EVERY MEMBER OF THE PUBLIC HAS A RIGHT TO EXECUTE HIM ON SIGHT! Now, let's pray that he escapes, folks, so we can prime those high-powered rifles and get partying down on the range..."

Sourballs switched off the TV.

Franco held his head in his hands. Pippa's words rang in his ears like the screech of a military drill instructor.

No bringing attention to yourself, right? We can do without compromising the mission before it even begins! The last thing Quad-Gal and Combat K need is to be caught up in the middle of some dogshit dogfight.

And his response? *Of course. I am a total professional.*

Oh, how those words were biting him on the arse right now! He considered his face, beamed out all over Cloneworld, to gangers and orgs alike. So what, that they were about to go to war – if the truth be told, they were about to go to war on HIM!

Franco rubbed at his face as Sourballs wheeled out the TV and left. In the corner, the old org cackled.

"You're in the shit, dear boy," she grinned.

"You don't say."

"What you need to do is *escape*."

"You reckon? I hadn't fucking *thought* of that one."

"If you're nice to me, I'll tell you where the tunnel is."

Franco considered this. "Nice?" he said, squinting at the old cyborg and covering his nuptials with both cupped hands in a protective and defensive manner.

"Real nice," she said, licking her oily lips and advancing with hisses and clanks of org hydraulics.

CHAPTER TWO

HARD TIMES

THE ROOM WAS bare, except for a table and a wardrobe of steel. She opened the steel wardrobe and took out the WarSuit. Standard QGM issue. It was her size. She pulled it on, activated the Permatex protection controls. The WarSuit gave a tiny whine, a buzz, a reassuring hum. It felt like regressing; becoming an embryo, safe in a womb. She pulled on her boots. Tied back her hair in a tight tail. She weighed the gun thoughtfully. Took up the photo. Studied it, and placed it back on the table. With a *click,* she removed the mag from the gun. Fifty rounds. Then she drew her sword with a *hiss.* She stared at the gleaming dark blade, forged from a single molecule. She weighed the blade thoughtfully, then very carefully – so as not to slice off her own fingers – re-sheathed the weapon. She stared at the gun – it was a special gun. Very special. Nothing like it had ever been seen in Quad-Gal – it came from way beyond the Four Galaxies. Beyond the known Life Bubbles. The gun was alive. And it spoke to her. She nodded. She accepted the mission. It was why she was born. Why she was *created*. Why she breathed, why she ate. She tucked the gun into a holster at her belt. Walked to the door, paused. Studied the door. She felt *new*. Like everything was unique. Many past memories were gone; she had to make new ones. She reached out, opened the door. Rain was pouring from purple bruised skies. She stepped out into the rain.

The Mistress was made of snakes. Currently, she was enjoying a hot bath in a pit of molten honey-oil. The Mistress had broken into her many component parts, at least a hundred pink-white, writhing, snake-like individual entities, each one as thick as a man's wrist and a metre long, each with tiny black eyes and a flickering, cherry-red tongue. They squirmed, the snakes, squirmed in the oil, a blur of constant movement like a bucket of albino eels. The backing track was a gentle hissing, with an occasional slop of bath oil.

The Monastery was a huge edifice at the heart of Nechudnazzar. It sat atop a steel and glass tower and was fitted out with marble tiles, million-piece jigsaw mosaics, white stone statues and heavy velvet drapes. A cool breeze blew through the chamber, bringing with it the low-level drone of heaving city life below; indeed, all around. This was the Mistress's home, seat of business, seat of *power*.

There was a similar building at the twin Clone Terra capital city of Raifnazzar, two hundred klicks southwest, over the Bastard Straits as the crow flies. A third – making up the Mistress's triumvirate of Clone Terra Headquarters – was located in the city of TV, the heart of her media empire, some six hundred kilometres north of Nechudnazzar, and just east of the mammoth Wooky Peaks which cut across the continent like broken teeth, spilled from a World Leviathan.

There came a *click* as the door opened, and a small, wizened man hobbled into the bath chambers of the Monastery. He closed the door behind himself, and worked his way forward with the curious ambling of the hunchback. He halted a respectful distance from the bath, and watched as the snakes squirmed and writhed, glistening.

"I have brought a message, Mistress," he said finally, his voice very low, very quiet, his eyes small black pebbles in a dark-skinned face that hadn't been shaved in a week.

The snakes writhed faster, then merged into what appeared, for just an instant, as a bloody mash of pulped muscle – before *shifting* and becoming one. Becoming whole. Becoming what appeared, to the naked *human* eye, a woman.

The Mistress surged from the bath, her eyes a solid black, the only feature that set her apart from her human counterparts. She took a white silk robe and draped it over her shoulders. She had shoulder length, perfectly straight black hair, and pale white skin – almost translucent in its perfection. She moved slowly, languorously, sexually; always poised, always... alluring. She stopped before the hunchback and reached down to pat him on the head. He began to purr.

Finally, she turned to a drinks cabinet and poured out a small glass of something black, oily and foul smelling. The hunchback knew better than to interrupt this ritual, for it was part of the *binding*, part of the Mistress shifting from her myriad snake form to the human. He waited patiently, one leg throbbing, his hump itching terribly, but he resisted the urge to squirm around and try to reach the itch – he never could – and instead simply squinted at the Mistress through eyes which were not just different colours, but different shapes and sizes.

She drank the black goo, which was so thick she had to coax it from the glass with a finger. Then she shuddered, and stood for a moment with her eyes closed. Finally, she blinked, and placed the glass down with a tiny *clack*.

"Ziggurat. My faithful friend." She moved to him, and knelt by the tiny hunchback man. She took him in her arms, and they embraced, and then she stood and moved back to the cabinet, pouring another drink, a *normal* drink to wash down the binding tonic. "What is the message?"

"He is here."

"At last! He has come!" The Mistress's eyes gleamed. "I knew he would. It was only a matter of time before they sent somebody sniffing around. Does he know what he's looking for?"

"I believe he does," said Ziggurat, shaping each word with care, for his mouth was slightly upturned at one side and could give him great difficulty in forming some words. "Sourballs has him. He has caused quite a stir! Did you not see the reports concerning Opera?"

The Mistress tilted her head to one side. "No. Speak on, what has happened to Opera?"

"Somehow, this man, this..." Ziggurat framed the name carefully, as if it was an alien taste on his lips, "this *Franco Haggis,* managed to get caught up in the Snare Nets. He must have done something bad, or given the drones cause to think he was a degenerate vagrant. Whatever. The drones thought he would not be missed, picked him up from a club, and he was filtered through the TV producers and placed on *Torture!*"

"And?" The Mistress's voice was suddenly icy. She could sense impending bad news, and like all egotistical power junkies, she did not *like* bad news.

"Well, the dumb bastard *really thought he was about to be tortured.* And, unbeknownst to us until now, he turned out to be *Combat K.*"

"Quad-Gal's elite."

"Yes," nodded Ziggurat.

"What did he do?"

"He killed the thug-like actors, and according to reports – for the live footage is a crazy piece of panic shit that veers all over the place – well, he cut off Opera's head with a laser chainsaw."

The Mistress did not groan, but she performed the nearest visual equivalent. She moved slowly, gracefully, to the window and peered out over her domain. Her dominion. She peered out over Nechudnazzar, but more, she peered out over the continent of Clone Terra, and onto the occasionally war-ravaged planet of Cloneworld.

"She is dead?"

"Dead as an org with a nuke up its arse."

"What about the SlushPits?"

"Tried it. We were too late. Ahh... Sourballs was more intent on arresting and incarcerating Haggis than saving Opera. Or so it would seem. There were mistakes made. There were... errors."

The Mistress considered these problems for a while, fingers steepled, dark eyes glowering. Then she said, "Do you think he knows? Do you think he was sent here by Quad-Gal Military to find out... well, our *plans,* shall we say, concerning the orgs? About our little..." she paused, considering. "About Live TV? About the Disintegrator?"

"It's impossible he, or QGM, could know our extended plans," said Ziggurat smugly.

"I disagree. QGM are more resourceful than you think, despite being distracted by the invading junks.

I don't like this." She tapped her lower lip with her index finger. "I don't want him here. I don't want a TV trial. No judges. No voting panels. No. I want him dead. Tell Sourballs to kill Franco Haggis. Tell her to kill him *now*."

"Of course."

Ziggurat turned to leave, then stopped. He looked back, instinctively realising there was something else to come. Ziggurat had known the Mistress for too long. After all, he had been her sexual plaything for... *millennia*.

"Make sure Sourballs keeps it quiet, totally covert, and she follows this Haggis infiltrator on his grunge path to the Smelting Halls and SlushPits. I want him pulverised into smush and fed back into the genetic tanks as a liquid dribble."

"My pleasure," said Ziggurat, with a cold smile, and hobbled away.

"*Nooo!*" SQUEALED FRANCO, holding up his hands as the ancient org slipped from her oil-stained underwear, trying desperately to act seductive. Then there came a *clank*, and the door slid open, and there stood the barbed-wire head of Sourballs, hands on hips, a sour slick smile on her excuse for a face.

"What are you two lovebirds up to?" She waved away the guards, who retreated uncertainly, lowering their Steyr laser cannons. "It's okay. I have this pussycat under control, isn't that right, little man who's about to receive a publicly-voted death penalty followed by genetic pulping?" The door closed with a *click*.

"Well," said Franco, swaggering close to Sourballs, panting, weak, deranged from being locked away with a mad, sexually-deviant org, still stinking of whiskey and *still as cunning as a fox's cunning uncle*, and he launched himself at the ganger quicker than a striking cobra, his right fist slamming into her jaw, his left knee coming up hard into her groin with a *crunch* which suggested a hefty bulge of wedding tackle, and as she doubled forward, eyes crossing and tongue lolling, his forehead slapped her straight on the nose. She dropped with a grunt and a splatter of blood, and Franco was out the door, wearing just his big white ASDA underpants. The two guards stood, wearing leather armour, their Steyr laser cannons pointing at the ground, their mouths slowly dropping open as they saw the frantic ginger squaddie emerge like a tsunami, Sourballs's blood gleaming on his knuckles. Before they could even *shift*, Franco was on them. He kicked one in the crotch, thumped the second in the helmet, side-kicked the first in the head, and slammed both fists on top of the second guard's head. They both dropped, howling, and Franco stooped, hefting the two laser cannons thoughtfully. Despite being an occasional drunkard and, to superficial glances, an aimless, useless pile of shit, Franco was stunningly proficient with explosives, closely followed by his knowledge of armaments. He might look like a stocky pugilist with a bad haircut and a love of pies, but he was a damn sight more dangerous than he first appeared, which usually led to gross underestimation on the part of his enemies. Which was just fine, by Franco's twisted logic.

His eyes scanned the laser cannons. He made a few minor tweaks to dials. They whined as he eked out 25% more power, and he grinned, showing his missing tooth – or *tuff,* as he liked to call it. "Right, baby," he said. "Time to escape."

Clanking and whining, the old clattering org emerged from her cell, and Franco whirled, both cannons levelled at the cell doorway which had, until a few moments ago, been his pit of incarceration. The old org staggered out, leaking a puddle of hot oil like brown piss, and she grinned at him with metal teeth as her shoulder cannons waved around manically but uselessly.

"You'll never find your way out without me," she croaked.

"I get the feeling you'll be more of a hindrance," muttered Franco, eyeing her with suspicious, beady eyes.

"No, I know the prison, Nechudnazzar, and indeed the whole of Clone Terra like the back of my cyborg hand appendage. I used to work spy missions for The Org States, running shit out of Outpost 9 and Zeg. Trust me, I am your best chance of escape."

"Bets?"

"I promise not to molest you."

Franco sighed. "Okay." He pointed a laser cannon between her eyes. "But don't get any frisky ideas, reet? The last thing I need in a firefight is the hand of an ancient metal crone on my arse cheek."

"Really?" muttered the org, as Franco padded forward down a steel corridor. "I find it helps immensely."

Behind, Theresa Sourballs, Governor of the Nechudnazzar Correctional and Reintegration Facility, staggered to the door, her face coated in a slick of blood, eyes wild beneath her frizzy bobbing mop. On the ground, the two guards – *sans* weapons – were groaning and gradually reintegrating into a world of consciousness. One thing could be said for Franco Haggis; he had a right hook like a hydraulic piston.

"You two!"

"Yes, ma'am?" they groaned, staggering to their feet. Their helmets were dented. Their faces were bruised. They winced and minced, and looked suddenly extremely unhappy to be part of the Nechudnazzar Correctional and Reintegration Facility.

"Get after him! Capture him! Shoot off his legs! But *do not kill him...*"

"Yes, ma'am," they grumbled miserably, and, bearing nothing but truncheons, set off in the kind of weary jog which illustrated more clearly than neon lights that they really did not *want* to catch up with their "prey."

Sourballs pulled out a PAD. She hit a button.

Throughout the Nechudnazzar Correctional

and Reintegration Facility, alarms screeched, red stroboscopic lights flickered, and certain heavily barred doors dropped and locked in place. She gave a narrow, blood-slick smile. "Let's see you get out of this, you little maggot," she snarled through spittle and blood.

FRANCO JOGGED, AND the old org clanked after him, her metal feet occasionally leaving imprints in the alloyconcrete floor. Franco stopped at a junction, just as the alarms sounded and red lights strobed and, before him, a gate whizzed shut with a *clank*.

"Great," said Franco, scratching his beard.

A guard appeared to his right, bearing a Sphinx AT laser cannon and a gormless expression. He stopped when he saw Franco, and turned to run, and Franco coolly gave him a blast of green laser up his pumping, retreating arse. The guard slithered along the ground on his belly, arse-cheeks a smoking mash of charred flesh, unconscious. Franco walked over, stooped, and took the guard's weapon, casually handing it to the old org woman. She grasped the gun in metal fingers, leaving imprints in the alloy.

"You're pretty strong," observed Franco.

"Better believe it, bastad."

"What's your name? I can't keep calling you old org crone. It's bad for my karma sutra." He paused, seeing a rage like a thunderstorm pass across her face. Casually, he continued, "Not that I think you're old, nor a crone. Indeed, I think out of all the orgs I've ever met, you're probably the most..." he groped for a word, "mechanised?"

The org settled down a little, and her face – part old crone flesh, part metal – relaxed. "I am Strogger 7576889," she said.

Franco chortled. "What, that's your fucking... na..." He closed his mouth with a clack. "I like it. Nice. Sexy. Has a certain quick-fire ring to it, you know, like the kind of sort of chick you'd find dancing in a warehouse nightclub with greased poles..." He saw her face darken again, wrinkling, tiny pistons *whumping* in her cheeks. "Or, you know, maybe the name for a waitress working in a cocktail bar..." – her face darkened further – "A sexy nurse in a rubber outfit?" he suggested, and the thunderstorm crowded overhead, as Franco's voice went up yet another octave. "Maybe, you know, some top-brass secret service assassin who always overcomes insurmountable odds?" He paused for breath, and Strogger 7576889 relaxed a little again, nodding in approval, her wrinkled face breaking into a smile that had nothing to do with her eyes.

"Hmm. Yes. I like that, you little bastad."

"I'm Franco. Franco Haggis. I think I already said."

"You did," wheezed Strogger 7576889. "What I suggest, though, is that you call me what my children call me."

"You have children?" blurted Franco, strobing red light glistening in his beard.

"Oh yes. Five hundred and thirty three of the little bastads. Never stop bloody arguing, they don't."

Franco groped for words, aware he wasn't just out of his league, he was bloody Captain Nemo, twenty thousand leagues out of his fucking *depth*. "Er," he managed, looking around as if for some moral *or at least* social support, and finally settled for scratching under one armpit. "Er, you look *very slim for it*," he said.

"You can call me Mrs Strogger," she said.

"Okay. Mrs Strogger. Got it. I'm on the money. Now, you say you know the way out of here?"

"I do. And I'll get you out, on one condition."

"Name it. As long as it's nothing rude."

"You look like the sort of guy who has air support."

"Er." Franco looked suddenly shifty. He shrugged. "You know as well as I that aircraft are banned all across Cloneworld. You know as well as I, that the rampant rogue AI AA mechs that roam the planet would take down any aircraft I had, if I had aircraft, which I don't."

"How did you get in then?"

"Freefall."

"What, from outer space?" snapped the org. "Listen. You're special ops. I ain't that stupid. With age comes wisdom, and all that. Now. Without airlifts, we'll never get off Clone Terra. It's a damn long trek through enemy territory, and an even longer sea voyage either through The Squeeze or the Mek Straits which border the vertical stretch of

The Teeth like a frozen chastity belt. Cloneworld is terraformed, yeah? Two continents, split down the middle – with the aim that never the twain shall meet. We need an airlift if I'm ever going home. Can you help with that, little bastad?"

Franco shrugged. "I'll see what I can do," he said.

"Don't mess with me," said Mrs Strogger. "Don't betray me. Don't make me angry. You wouldn't like me when I'm angry."

"I'm pretty sure I don't like it when you're happy, either." Her face darkened. *Gods,* he thought, *here we go again! Is there nothing a rampant switch-on cool-dude Combat K squaddie can say that doesn't rub this org chick up the wrong way?* He changed tactics. "Listen. Listen. We are, you know, symbi... sybet... we need to rely on each other, reet? You scratch my back, and I'll, er, rub my nails down your scaled iron exoskeleton. Get me out of this damn and bloody bullocks prison complex, and I'll guarantee you a flight home."

"Done," said Mrs Strogger, and held out a mechanised claw. Franco shook it, aware she could probably rip out all his fingers with one wrench.

"Agreed. Now, which way?"

"First, I need to reactivate and recharge my weapons. There are many gates and bars between here and the outside world."

"Are your weapons that hardy?" said Franco.

"Oh yes," said Mrs Strogger, and gave him a dazzling smile full of machinery.

*   *   *

THE TWO PURSUING guards crawled along the corridor, truncheons raised, showing willing but knowing their hearts weren't really in it. After all, in terms of ganger employment, they were pretty near the bottom of the scummy heap. The Nechudnazzar Correctional and Reintegration Facility wasn't renowned for paying good wages. In fact, it was known as being *a really shit employer.*

"There they are," said Grandall, stopping. His friend, Bebooz, bumped into him from behind.

"Shit. We caught them up. What're they doing?"

"Talking."

"Arguing, more like."

"Hey, maybe they'll shoot each other?"

"We could hang on a few moments, see if they throttle each another?"

"Sounds like a plan."

They waited, stepping impatiently from one foot to the other to the other.

"Hey, if one kills the other, there'll still be one left."

The guards considered this.

"Yeah," said Grandall, "but he, or she, will presumably be weakened. Maybe even *wounded.*"

They brightened at this concept.

They waited some more. They could see the big one, the old org blend, getting madder and madder. Then the little one, that Sourballs had called a "human intruder," pacified her. Grandall and Bebooz grumbled to one another, and further down the corridor heard Teddy Sourballs screaming orders at what they assumed were guards come to back them up. Backup! Their faces soured further. What they had to do now was perform a delicate balancing act; they had to approach the escapees, so that they were in the act of confrontation when Sourballs arrived with the troops. Do it too late, and Sourballs would sniff out their cowardly ruse and demote them to the slush bins. But attack too soon and they'd have to face the horrible pair...

FRANCO HOISTED HIS two laser cannons, and whilst they didn't have the same sturdy weight and killing smash as Kekra quad-barrel machine pistols, they felt better than using his hands against guards armed with guns. *Gangers,* he corrected himself. These were all clones.

Franco scowled, and at that moment a pair of guards shuffled unhurriedly into view, looking nervously over their shoulders. They seemed to be whimpering. They stood in the shadows, illuminated by the flickering red prison panic lights, and stared uneasily at Franco as if hoping he wouldn't spot them. But he did. He grinned at them, as behind him Mrs Strogger rose threateningly on her core waist-piston with a sound like an industrial ratchet.

The guards ambled forward, looking again over their shoulders, and Franco snapped, "Drop your weapons!"

Obediently, they dropped their weapons. Franco approached, laser cannon aimed, and said, "Throw me your keys, key cards, and any other entry devices we need to access the gates."

"Please don't shoot!" wailed Grandall.

"We have wives! Families!" blubbed Bebooz.

"Rubbish," clanked Mrs Strogger, grinding forward. "Your families are from the clone vats, picked out to look like whatever deviant sexual fantasy you had on the day! Your children are slush grown puppies designed to give you a hard time! So stop your whining, you sadomasochistic wriggling maggots!"

"Hey, it's easy for you to criticise, you mechanised heap of junk! Get back to the fucking scrapyard!" shouted Grandall.

"Keys!" hissed Franco, prodding the cannon into Grandall's face. The guards both fumbled and produced hefty bunches of digital card keys. Franco looked around for a pocket to stow them in, realised his underpants had no such compartment, and handed the keys to Mrs Strogger, who slipped them neatly into a battered alloy drawer, scarred by fire and bullets.

"Don't kill us!" mumbled Grandall.

"Don't hit us!" whined Bebooz.

Franco knocked Bebooz out with a straight right, and Grandall froze, his steel truncheon half raised. He was like a rabbit caught in the glare of headlights. Like a SPAW caught in a helium-blasted meteor storm.

"It's either my fist, or answering to Sourballs," grinned Franco, toothily.

Grandall closed his eyes, and made an impatient gesture.

Franco whacked him, and Mrs Strogger opened the gate, which buzzed and shunted open. They moved through, and Mrs Strogger closed the gate behind them, pulling a thick-bladed drill on a long, black, rubber cable from a compartment in her chest. The drillbit *whizzed,* and Mrs Strogger plunged it into the slick door control panel. Sparks erupted, and thick oil flooded out, staining the alloyconcrete floor.

"To stop them following?" said Franco, raising his eyebrows.

"Yar," said Mrs Strogger, stowing away her flexi-drill beneath an alloy tit.

"Let's go."

Sourballs and twenty guards emerged from the corridor. She grabbed the bars and howled after her quarry, as her guards opened fire and green laser pulses slammed down the corridors, scorching alloy and steel. Franco and Mrs Strogger ducked and ran, and then were gone...

THE NECHUDNAZZAR CORRECTIONAL and Reintegration Facility was a vast and incomprehensible maze. Mrs Strogger, despite claiming to know the way, seemed to have got them lost and Franco was grinding his teeth in annoyance, trying not to lose his temper.

They stopped at a sixteen-point junction. Around them, the screeching alarms had quietened. Only the red stroboscopic lights flickered, casting eerie shadows and underlining to the prison authorities that they were still in a state of high alert, and that fleeing fugitives were still on the run.

"Which way?" said Franco.

"Give me a minute. I must orientate."

"Orientate? Why don't you just pull out your MonkeyMan satnav, that should guide us through the damn place..."

"Do not be criticising," said Mrs Strogger primly. "I am simply working out the best route."

"Stuff the best route," snapped Franco. "Just get us out of this shithole!"

Guards tramped past the end of one corridor, boots slapping dully on the alloyconcrete floor. But they did not turn. Franco hunched, waiting, then relaxed as the threat passed. He turned, and caught a glimpse of what looked like paper. He gaped at the old org mech.

"Are you *really* looking at a map?"

"No!" snapped Mrs Strogger.

"What's that? There? In your claws?"

"It's paper."

"And what's on the paper?"

"Um. A map. But listen, it's reliable, it was drawn by an old inmate I met, before you arrived. He sold it me for a carton of puffweeds."

"Give me that!" snapped Franco, snatching the

paper from Mrs Strogger. Now, Franco was no genius, but he could see the actual structure of the map was an impossibility: corridors crossed one another, or occupied the same time/space. He snorted. "This is crap. This is a map of your own arsehole. I thought you were going to get us out of here in exchange for an airlift to The Org States? Eh?"

"What I *said* was that I knew the prison and Nechudnazzar well. You extrapolated what you wanted to hear from my dialogue. As I said before, there is definitely a tunnel, way down in the bowels of the prison. We have to head down, looking for our means of escape."

"Hmm," frowned Franco, unconvinced, and handed the absurd map back to Mrs Strogger. "Go on, then. Looks like I haven't got much of a bloody option, do I?" *Except maybe breaking away on my own, carrying out mass slaughter and escaping into the wilds without the ball and chain of Mrs-bloody-Strogger round my constricted throat.* "You lead the way."

With a hiss of hydraulics, Mrs Strogger led the way.

THEY'D TRAVELLED DOWN endless corridors, through endless gates and barriers. It was hot. Unbearably hot. And getting hotter. Franco, despite being in underpants and flip flops, wiped sweat from his brow and flicked it to the steel and alloyconcrete floor.

"By all the gods, it's like a furnace down here!"

"It's going to get hotter," said Mrs Strogger.

"Why's that?"

"We've got to pass through the kitchens."

"Is that a good thing or a bad thing?"

Mrs Strogger gave Franco a sideways look. "Have you ever eaten prison food?"

"Er. Yes. But how is that relevant?"

"Well, you should know the sheer amount of toxins floating around make any prison kitchen more lethal than the core of an active volcano."

"Ah."

"And the prison chefs are pretty good shots with a thrown cleaver."

"Ah. Can the kitchens be avoided?"

"Not according to my map."

Franco stared at Mrs Strogger. She clanked to a stop, hydraulics hissing and machines whirring, and her metal toes flexed, chipping the concrete. Franco acknowledged to himself, there and then, that there were indeed people in the world who were a damn sight more insane than he. Mrs Strogger, third human, third machine, third... *something else,* was one oil-fed nutjob.

They moved on, dropping down deep stairwells into shadowed gloom. High above, large extraction fans spun in eerie silence. Down they moved, laser cannons poised for combat, Franco's head twitching left and right as he scanned for enemies. But there were none. Curiously, the Nechudnazzar Correctional and

Reintegration Facility seemed deserted. And Franco realised: *they think we're trying to escape. Heading upwards... and so concentrating their searches that way! Nobody tries to escape by heading down into the bowels – but they'll catch on, soon enough, and then we'll be flooded and overrun by the bad guys.*

It would seem time was of the essence.

After yet more stairs, that saw Mrs Strogger clanking and moaning and groaning, and occasionally leaning against the wall to puff and pant, and allow oily clouds of steam to ooze from her mechanical vents and orifices, they reached a long, straight corridor. It was lined entirely in steel and gleamed with the sort of shine given by chefs with a particularly anal obsessive compulsive disorder.

Franco stared at the steel. Floor, walls and ceiling gleamed. At the far end of the corridor were large double doors, also of polished stainless steel. Somewhere, echoes of red stroboscopic light gave the scene an eerie cast.

"I don't like this."

"This is our route," said Mrs Strogger.

Franco felt like saying, *Go on, show me the bloody route on the bloody map then, because it's more like a tracing of your mad cyborg arterial system than any damn map of a prison I've ever seen,* but he didn't. He acknowledged, deep down somewhere, that maybe – *just maybe* – this org, in all her insanity, could read an insane map – as if both insanities cancelled one another out, making the end product whole and normal and understandable. *Yeah, right.*

"You lead the way," said Franco through gritted teeth, and pressed his implanted earlobe comm in the hope that Pippa and that Fast Attack Hornet were on their way with a few 65 Stroke Missiles to rescue his ass from this shit. But the comm was dead. Pippa wasn't there. There would be no rescue. "Damn and bloody bollocks," muttered Franco as his situation went from worse to worse to bad to *serious shit, brother.* And it was about to get a whole lot badder...

Mrs Strogger seemed to be using some kind of stealth mode. She hunkered down, her body compressing and hydraulics gliding, and she moved sideways, feet not so much *clanking* as sliding. She obviously thought something bad was beyond those double doors. Franco wiped his sweating hands on the only bit of cloth available; his underpants. *Shit. What I'd give for a decent Permatex WarSuit right now! And a Bausch & Harris Sniper Rifle with SSGK digital sights. And a D5 shotgun! Oh, for a D5 shotgun!*

As they reached the doors, Mrs Strogger suddenly stopped. She glanced at Franco. "Lots of chefs beyond," she said. "Bad ganger chefs, if I'm not very much mistaken, and they're all fast and tough, and jabber-jabber when they attack. I am not at full power; I need a recharge socket. There will be a recharge socket in the prison kitchens."

Franco nodded. "Let's do it," he said.

Mrs Strogger suddenly reared up, and slammed both fists against the doors, wrenching them from their hinges and catapulting them across the prison kitchens. The doors *whammed*, spinning and crashing through pans of bubbling soup and a hundred steel plates and trays and pans, and the air was filled with an eruptive, explosive cacophony of clattering metal, of screaming steel, of raining kitchen appliances. In the midst of this sudden chaos, Franco saw about twenty chefs, identifiable by their trademark starched white uniforms and their cheery tall chef's hats. Each chef was a big, cheery-looking chap, with a bearded, happy, fat face, wobbling jowls, and a serious overhang of gut from maybe ten thousand excessive tasting sessions. In any other setting, the whole scene would have appeared friendly, convivial, a jolly jaunt into the world of prison cooking; but within the blink of an eye, the cheery plump chefs had armed themselves with knives and cleavers, machetes and skewers, and a hail of weapons flashed through the air like the deadliest of archery fire...

Franco unleashed a burst of green laser bolts, which fizzed across the kitchen expanse, blackening steel, knocking over pans of bubbling broth, and knocking two chefs backwards with chomping, hate-filled faces and waving machetes. They disappeared behind the steel cupboards as Franco grunted and hit the ground fast. Knives and skewers clattered overhead, falling around him with a musical tinkling of steel. Franco glanced left, at the razor-sharp cleaver. His eyes narrowed. "The cheeky bastards," he said, reaching up to grab a steel tray from the work surface. He stood, holding the tray up as a makeshift shield, and looked down to where Mrs Strogger was cowering behind a large cupboard. "A bit of help wouldn't go amiss, you big quivering pussy!" he snarled.

"I need my recharge socket!" she whimpered. "I need more power, more energy, more zaza*zoomph!*"

Franco stared at her, then sighed. "Great," he muttered. "Stuck in a firefight with a useless bloody pacifist pussy org!" Something heavy bounced off his tray with a mammoth CLANG! and Franco cursed, raised his laser cannon, and shot a chef in the chest, blowing the hapless culinary maestro backwards through the swing doors and out of sight. "That's for making fucking celebrity TV programs," he muttered, and ducked as another chef appeared, this one with a rifle.

There came a *whiz* and *ping* as a projectile ricocheted off the wall behind Franco and embedded itself in Mrs Strogger's thigh. She didn't seem to notice.

Franco aimed his laser cannon over the steel cupboard, watched the chef reloading an ancient battered Crack Rifle, and Franco shot him in the stomach. "That's for flooding the Festive Market with shite cookery books," he snarled, spittle launching from his aggravated lips.

"Aaah," said Mrs Strogger, as if taking a huge and relieving dump, as Franco watched, nervous now, as fifteen chefs appeared carrying Crack Rifles. They started to load the weapons, hunkering down behind steel benches, their tall white hats wavering.

Franco glanced down. Mrs Strogger had slumped down, opened a flap at her groin, and extracted a long thick black cable, which she'd plugged into an IWS – Industrial Wall Socket.

"Er," said Franco.

"Yes?" said Mrs Strogger, staring at him.

"You got shot then, you realise?"

"So?"

"Didn't it hurt?"

"Should it?"

"Hmm," said Franco. He stared at her recharge socket. "So, that thing, then."

"What thing?"

"That, er, that big tube coming from your groin."

"My recharge cable."

"Odd place to put it."

"Your meaning?"

"A-ha-ha," said Franco. "What I'm meaning to say, is that you're a, y'know, female org. A girlie. And that there big sausage thing, well, it looks a bit like a…"

"Yes?" Each letter contained knives.

"What I mean to say is, somebody, a pervert or something, or a comedian, might say it looks like you've got a massive black…"

"Yes?"

"Nothing," said Franco, and smiled, clenching his teeth.

At that moment, a volley of ammunition slammed across the prison kitchens, and Franco cowered on the floor, tray held over his head as bullets *pinged* and *clanged*, and one neatly removed the bottom inch of his little finger.

"*AARGH!*" screamed Franco, staring in disbelief at the minor amputation. Blood pumped from the wound, and Franco's instant reaction was to put it in his mouth.

Mrs Strogger suddenly reached over, her face a scowl, and grabbed Franco's arm. He struggled for a moment, like a fish on a hook, as she dragged him towards her and produced, from a flap in her belly, what turned out to be a glowing soldering iron. Holding Franco in an unbreakable grip, Mrs Strogger cauterised the stump of Franco's little finger as he screamed again, gnashing his teeth as the stench of frying pork filled the air.

Strogger abruptly let Franco go and he slapped back onto his arse – as another volley whirred overhead. The chefs had organised themselves into two fighting lines, one line reloading ancient Crack Rifles whilst the other took aim and fired. Franco grabbed his laser cannon, his movements fired up by the pain not just in his finger, but in his pride, and started blasting away like a cowboy madman with pistols at a disco.

Chefs were slammed backwards, left and right, leaving trails of steaming cabbage soup, sending platters of rotten vegetables into the air, sending bowls of black braised beef scattering across the steel floor with dry, hard, drumming sounds. Another line of bullets whined across the kitchen, puncturing bubbling pans of donkey stew, and suddenly the air was filled with screaming alarms and more red strobes flickered into life. Behind them, in the corridor leading to the kitchens, Sourballs appeared with a squad of ten prison guards.

"Found you! At last!" she screeched, barbed-wire hair bobbing madly. "Kill them!"

Lasers whined from the corridor, and Franco scrambled sideways across the cupboards, miraculously missing a combined crossfire of laser blasts and ancient steel shells. He dived, slamming into a cupboard, and fired his laser cannon down the corridor without looking, squeezing off twenty bursts of crackling energy. When he peered round, three guards were dead, their corpses smoking, and the rest had fled for cover.

Franco glanced at Mrs Strogger. "We're in the shit!" he snapped, pain in his finger giving him an urgency he hadn't felt in a long, long time. "I could do with some FUCKING HELP, YOU OLD HAG!"

"Almost charged," smiled the old org, her wrinkled face relaxed into the euphoria of a terminal Crack67 sniffer.

Franco started to crawl along a line of cupboards.

His idea was simple: flank the chefs, take them out in a hail of laser fire, then get the hell out of the kitchens and away before Sourballs and her laser-shooting chumps caught up with him. To Hell with Mrs Strogger! The ancient mechanised bitch was too busy getting juiced up!

"I would call a ceasefire, if I was you," came the trembling voice of Teddy Sourballs.

Franco halted. He didn't speak; to make a sound would be to give away his new position. And he liked it just fine that nobody now knew where he was. Franco listened. The chefs had ceased their fire; obviously they recognised their illustrious Governor Sourballs and were loathe to fill her full of lead. Although Franco couldn't think of a better ending for the irascible bitch.

"I have a deal! You've run down here, thinking there is a way out, but you are mistaken! You're trapped! You are pincered down with pincered claws! As if caught by a crab! Ha-ha. You cannot ever leave here without my help! Well, what I offer is for you to come on trial, on TV, and get a fair trial, and we will get good TV ratings right across Quad-Gal and we'll all be winners. I can..." she paused, as if listening to commands through an earpiece. "*What? You'd give the little fucker those terms – oh, oh, sorry,* yes, I am now in a position to offer you a *guaranteed safety clause.* You are Franco Haggis, Combat K, and this will get us better viewings than *Torture!* In fact, the episode where you decapitated Opera – well, it appears my, *er*, boss and superior, the Mistress, has received the viewing figures. You are a star, Franco Haggis! By your act of violence, you have earned our TV network *more commissions, advertising revenue and new subscribers* in one day than we've had in the last three years!"

She paused, out of breath from gabbling. Franco considered this.

There came a *bang*, the whine of a discharged round, and a shot that nearly took Sourballs's head clean off. It parted her hair in a rush of spinning steel. Theresa scowled, and one of her guards lasered the chef in the face, leaving him burnt and broken and twitching.

"I said *ceasefire!*" screeched Sourballs. Here was a woman used to getting what she wanted via screeching. It was quite worrying.

Franco scratched his stubble.

"Well, what do you say? You are a Quad-Gal phenomenon, Franco Haggis! Okay, the people hate you for what you did to Opera, but in terms of monetary value, you are going to be... rich! Very rich. In fact, one of the richest individuals on the planet!"

"You want me to work for you?" said Franco, frowning as understanding bit his balls.

"Yes!" beamed Theresa. She had strode forward, and stood in the doorway, her confidence growing with each passing second that no bullet or laser round removed her head. "You can come, act on our network. We'll have a trial, milk it out, play to the media for months and months – it will be most lucrative for all of us!"

Franco stood up. The guards had followed Sourballs, and were crowding round her in the doorway. Everybody seemed to be smiling. From some dregs of distant memory, Franco remember watching filmy on how the gangers were *obsessed* with TV, with digMEDIA, with stars and reality shows and all manner of extreme digital entertainment. They had taken it to such an extreme that some gangers had, by a combination of genetic modification and basic evolutionary necessity, become huge mounds of flesh which sat in an armchair all day, one short arm used for the remote, the other for feeding food into a hole in their chest, alongside eyes and nose. *Blobbers*, they were called, and they existed simply to eat and shit and watch. Now, a little of the obsession started to dredge through into Franco's confused mind. These bastards were willing to give him a *reprieve*. Willing to let him go. And he could play along, if he was wily and cunning like a wily cunning fox – until he found a moment to either contact Pippa, or do a runner.

Franco rubbed his bristly beard. "Well, that sounds like a great deal to me," he said, and he was the sort of man who, if the truth be known, would trade in his old granny for a crate of PreCheese and a barrel of pungent horseradish. "Would I need an agent? What percentage would I get? Net, not gross, unless maybe I don't have to pay Quad-Gal tax because I'm, you know, exempt for being sometimes mad. I've had a few bad run-ins with the Quad-Gal Revenue." He twitched, remembering his ex-wife Mel, one time tax inspector and later zombie super-soldier. It hadn't turned out well – either in marital terms, or in terms of Quad-Gal Revenue fines. He was still making the repayments. And would be, for the next one thousand and eighty years.

"I am sure," said Teddy Sourballs, holding her arms wide apart, "that we can come to some kind of wonderful arrangement."

Through the silence of minds working out figures, there was a tiny *click*.

"Aaah," said Mrs Strogger, and with various clanks and clonks, she stood up. She looked around. "AAAAHH!" she said, and unplugged her groinal cable. There came a *phuzzz* noise as it retracted into her groin like a cheap spring-loaded lead from a vacuum sucker. "AAAAHH! That felt wonderful, brilliant; a full fast-recharge, and now I'm ready for battle." She squinted myopically. "Right, Franco. Where're the bad guys?"

"No!" said Franco, smiling frantically. "Wait!"

There came a huge roar, clanking sounds and ratchet thumps. Mrs Strogger suddenly seemed to EXPAND as her cyborg upgrades, now fully charged and armed, came into existence. Guns sprouted along her arms, her legs beefed out with armoured plating, her midriff shot up on its piston so she towered over proceedings, and her shoulder-mounted lasers spun around, locating targets and locking on with tiny red beams.

"Happy days," said the old org, in a quiet little voice... as all Hell seemed to break loose. Lasers whined and spat, and Mrs Strogger picked up a *whole row* of benches and threw them at the gawping chefs. Guards returned fire, criss-crossing the room with red and green laser flashes, and Franco ran for it, diving behind a bank of steel cabinets as bullets filled the air from the chefs and Sourballs was screaming for another ceasefire and Mrs Strogger crunched over to her, legs whining and clacking, and reaching out with steel mandibles which seemed suddenly larger to Franco than before. She picked Teddy Sourballs up with a growl and threw her sideways down the corridor. Sourballs, whirling, limbs flailing like a ragdoll's, bounced from the wall and cannoned into six guards, taking them all out in a mash of tangled broken limbs. Mrs Strogger whirled back, legs hissing and clanking, and strode forward through the kitchen – quite literally *through* it – stomping steel cabinets down into platters, slamming through ovens, ignoring the bullets of the now frantically firing and reloading chefs until she reached the cowering, chubby, happy men with wobbling jowls and fat fingers, blasting them off their feet with her lasers as her claws lashed out on huge steel tentacles, grabbing chefs and tossing them around, flesh crunching against walls, bodies slamming into steel, bones breaking and skulls cracking.

Then silence followed, amidst the steam of spilled cabbage.

Franco Haggis uncurled, stood up, and stared hard at Mrs Strogger. "You ruined that deal, didn't you?"

"What deal?"

"My TV-being-famous-and-making-lots-of-money deal. Look! You squashed everybody! Or shot them!" Franco stared up at the huge, heavily armoured war org, and frowned. "What the bloody buggering hell happened to you? I thought you were a little old lady?"

"I've had upgrades," said Mrs Strogger, somewhat smugly.

"I can see that. You look like, like a, like a, I don't *know* what you look like, but you look like a big one!"

Mrs Strogger clanked forward, five tonnes of war-grade steel tenuously attached to the deranged mind of a little old woman. She leered down at Franco. Lasers aligned, and six red dots appeared over Franco's near-naked body. Suddenly, the laser cannon in Franco's hands felt like a toy. He licked his lips nervously.

"I think our situation has changed," said Mrs Strogger, voice growing stronger by the second.

"Er," said Franco, uneasily. "Meaning?"

"I think you're a pulpy little pathetic human, just like these pulpy little pathetic gangers. You're the same breed, aren't you, bastad? Little sacks of pissy shit, held together by nothing more than stretchy flesh all willing to break apart under my org claws. Well..."

Franco's eyes widened. *No*, he thought. *This can't be happening... I'm just about to bloody escape this carnage, and make a pretty penny into the bargain, and my enemies turn out to be my friends and my friend turns out to be my enemy and what's the whole bloody world coming to, eh? I ask you, eh?*

"Can't we talk about this?" said Franco, stalling for time. He was good at that.

"Orgs hate gangers," said Mrs Strogger, bright teeth gleaming, drool drooling from ancient jaws. "We are superior. We are more powerful. We are at war! Or we should be... and you are just another insignificant organic blob to be squashed out of existence..."

With a whine, and a clank, Mrs Strogger attacked...

CHAPTER THREE
CHASE ME

SHE HAD PERFORMED missions before. A thousand missions. She'd killed men, women, children, of every colour and "alien" species to walk the multiple exotic soils of the thousands of worlds of Quad-Gal. She'd blown up factories, oil rigs, military installations, tank depots, politicians' headquarters, schools, and hospitals; she knew no mercy, had no empathy, felt no remorse. She knew the myriad memories would have blurred into one, if they'd not been forcibly erased. They were erased to protect her. If tortured, her pain tolerance was incredibly high, but without memories, she could not talk at all. But then, she had never been caught. She was efficient. She was... *perfect.*

Now, she walked through the rainswept city. The

streets were deserted. She stopped at an intersection, glanced up and down the gleaming black roads, and considered. She knew where she must go. She knew where her target would go. After all – she smiled – they had something very important in common. Something more intimate than a shared lover, a childhood memory, a death-defying experience, a bonding of drug-minds. Yes. They had something *perfect* linking them... She glanced down. Saw her reflection in a puddle. And the shimmering, ghostly, almost *metallic* face of Pippa stared back.

PIPPA WAS NOT in the best of moods. She sat watching the TV, as all manner of images flashed and flickered across at first one, then five, then twenty, then *every single channel* (which was a lot) being beamed throughout the Quad-Gal and Super High-UF Frequency Light Electron TV carrier signals (SHUFFLE TV, they called it). And the longer Pippa watched, from the pilot's crib of the Fast Attack Hornet *Metallika,* the more her colour miraculously shifted. First, she turned from pink to a deep, rich pink, then from a deep, rich pink to red, then from red to purple, and finally she finished her chameleonic display by turning a furious *white.*

"Franco," she muttered, as yet another report slammed across the SHUFFLE. In the report, *there* was Franco's beaming face, *there* was Franco's gurning face, *there* was Franco's shouting face, *there* was Franco wandering the streets, *there* was Franco drinking in a bar, all caught on GLOBAL CAMS, and finally, *there* was Franco Haggis, covert Combat K operative, cutting off the head of Opera, Quad-Gal's most famous reality TV host, on the live TV show *Torture!* Well, it didn't exactly show him cutting off her head, but in the confusion of bobbing cameras and pandemonium, Opera collapsed to the floor with her head rolling away and blood gouting from her neck stump, and Franco was in the midst of the mess being beaten by the over-zealous RGPF.

Pippa lowered her face into her hands and groaned.

"How are you feeling?" said Alice, the ship computer, her voice – as usual – calm and soothing.

"That little bastard has killed our mission."

"Are you sure of that?"

"Well, it looks to me like he dropped in via chute and, instead of following our leads in Nechudnazzar, decided to go on a drinking spree which led to his arrest and placement on the TV show *Torture!*"

"That's a good show," observed Alice.

"Not any more. Franco cut off Opera's head."

"That's yet to be proved."

Pippa eyed the glittering computer banks with narrowed eyes. "Oh yeah? Well, I know Franco Haggis, and I know what the mad little ginger bastard is capable of. I can't *believe* I trusted him, I can't believe I allowed him to persuade me to let him go in. I thought he was grief-stricken because of Keenan's death. I thought he was a changed character. But oh, no, not Franco bloody Haggis, how can I have been so stupid, Alice? You'd think I would have learnt my lesson. I swear, when I get my hands on him, I'm going to beat him till he squeals like a pig on the end of a spear."

"Beat him?"

"Yes," snarled Pippa, fists clenched. "But first we've got to rescue him. We'll rescue him, then I'll batter him like a plate of stinking fish. What's the situation with the AAMs?"

"You know what the situation is," said Alice, soothingly.

The problem was, Cloneworld was a seething pit of violence and warfare. Centuries earlier, the Quad-Gal Peace Unification Army had imposed certain rules and restrictions on the planet in order to try and halt its seemingly permanently escalating violence spilling out and polluting the rest of the Quad-Gal territories. Now, Cloneworld was a zero-trade zone. And Cloneworld was prohibited for all forms of aircraft. This, reasoned QGM, would cut down on the gangers' and orgs' ability to wage war against one another. After all, the terraformed planet was two vast continents separated by the most huge and terrible mountain range ever built by man or alien: The Teeth, an eight-thousand-kilometre stretch of mountain range sitting on its own discrete island, and pretty much impassable except by the most foolhardy of climbers. Yes, there were two sea passages through The Teeth – the northern, and aptly named, *The*

Squeeze, and the southern *Mek Straits*, which were easily patrolled by both races and spent at least eight months of the year clogged with ice chunks. To enforce with zero tolerance the restrictions on all forms of aircraft, QGM had installed several thousand automated AI Anti-Aircraft gunbots – also known as Quad-Gal GASGAMs. These highly intelligent and highly proficient machines had space-grade armour and the intelligence to be self-repairing and self-sustaining, with sufficient weaponry to bring down anything as small as a P Class Hunter, a fast one-man spacecraft, all the way up to Class III Bombers and Offense Frigates.

The problem was, if Pippa took their ship in, looking for Franco, there was a chance she'd get blown from the sky by a rogue wandering GASGAM. Pippa was the best pilot in Quad-Gal, without a shadow of a doubt; but she'd been saving her skills only in the case of emergency – not a Franco exfil necessitated by a screwed-up mission after a heavy drinking session. Pippa was not a happy bunny.

"Can't we target the AIs using brain scans? They show up as advanced cerebral activity."

"They can cloak activity," said Alice. "You know this. We can go in, but it'll be dangerous. The only thing we've got going for us is *speed*. Unfortunately, we don't know what weapons the gunbots are carrying, and in that kind of situation... Goodbye, cruel world."

"Hmm."

Pippa put her chin on her fist and brooded. She knew what she'd have to do, and as she stared from the portal at the slowly spinning world below, a wealth of green and blue and amber scattered with millions of square miles of cloud cover, filled with millions of gangers and orgs – all of which loathed humans, and especially QGM, *especially Combat K* because of sanctions imposed on their particular strain of humanity – well, Pippa loathed the idea of putting her neck on the line for Franco's ten pints of Guinness.

"Ship requesting permission to dock."

"*What?*" snapped Pippa, leaping from her crib. "Alice – I'm amazed! No proximity warnings? No registration idents?"

"I am sorry," said Alice, and to her credit, she sounded ashamed. "I was given strict orders. From the top. Only now was I allowed to break silence. Truly, Pippa, I did not enjoy the subterfuge."

"Who is it?"

"General Tarly Winters."

"The Ice Queen?"

"That would be common derogatory slang in your soldiery ranks, yes; I will advise you she does not take kindly to the term. After all, she is a ranking QGM general."

"Who's with her?" said Pippa, eyes hooded. She did not get on well with other women. In fact, she did not get on well with *people*. Full stop.

"She is alone," said Alice. "I have granted docking clearances. Three minutes until she steps on board."

"Alone?" said Pippa. "A *general,* coming here, alone..." and then it dawned on her. "This is because of Franco, is it not?"

"I have no knowledge of the general's intentions," said Alice, soothingly.

"Ha, yeah, like you'd fucking tell *me.*"

"That hurts, Pippa. Truly, it hurts."

"Well keep me in the damn loop then!" she snapped, and slumped back to her crib. "And – tell Her *Highness* that I'm not in the fucking mood for visitors. And if she doesn't like it, she can fuck off back to whatever Class X disgorged her fat frumpy arse."

There came a *clunk,* and a shudder as the two Hornets connected via fluid umbilical.

Below, Cloneworld spun.

Eventually, the door slid open with a hiss and Pippa was aware of a presence entering *Metallika.* She did not turn, but studiously kept her back to the general and her hand on the pistol in her belt. *Let her fucking push me,* she thought. *I dare her. Double dare!*

Without a word, the figure moved through the Hornet; when finally Pippa did turn, eaten by curiosity, Tarly Winters had gone. Frowning, Pippa stood and moved down the narrow corridor to the four sleeping quarters. She stopped. Standing in one of the rooms, unpacking a small kit-bag, was a tall, lithe woman with a tumble of curled red hair.

Pippa coughed.

Tarly Winters turned, and smiled at Pippa: a cold

smile, from a china-white face, piercing green eyes boring into and *through* Pippa like titaniumIII drill-bits through diamond.

"You would be Pippa, Combat K operative under Section 57 of QGM. I thank you for your cooperation."

"I'm cooperating?" said Pippa, her own voice cold as the grave.

"Oh yes," said the general, and turned back to her unpacking. With a *clack*, she placed a sniper rifle case on the high shelf above her bunk.

"Why are you unpacking?" said Pippa, frowning despite herself.

Tarly stopped, and turned. Again, her smile was frosty, and Pippa recalled a hundred stories of *The Ice Queen* from her days in the canteens of a hundred different bases across a scatter of random planets.

"Well," she said, and ran a hand through her long, deeply luscious red hair, "I have to unpack my clothes if I am to be sleeping here for a while – or else, how would I be able to find them to dress?"

"You're not staying here," snapped Pippa, too quickly.

"Really?"

"Er, what I meant to say, Tarly..."

"General Winters," said General Winters. Again, that thin-lipped smile.

"What I meant to say, was..."

"I have been assigned to assist you concerning the 'Franco Haggis Situation.'"

"The 'Franco Haggis Situation'?" Pippa gave a bitter smile.

"Hey, lady, don't act like a naïve whore the first time a sailor gets his cock out. You fucked up, soldier. You both fucked up *bad*. In fact, you both fucked up *so bad* I can guarantee your arses will be slung in the brig when we hit Realtime Bigshow out of here. You hearing me, little lady?"

Pippa growled, but held her tongue.

"You are dismissed," said Tarly, turning her back on Pippa.

Pippa stood for a moment, face burning, *furious* at being spoken to in such a way. If anybody else had done it, they'd be wearing their spine as a necklace. In fact...

Pippa's hand touched her pistol.

"Do that, and I'll remove your hand at the wrist," said Tarly, softly, her words barely audible.

Pippa disappeared.

Tarly smiled, and finished unpacking.

"WHAT A FUCKING bitch," said Pippa, strapping on yet another weapon from the armoury. Her bunk was strewn with kit, guns and knives and her twin *yukana* swords capable of slicing hull steel. Her kit bag was filled with field rations, med kits, her PAD computer with a billion different functions and several tools and gun tools.

"I advise caution," said Alice, ever the diplomat.

Pippa cast an eye skywards, a movement she saved for when she fancied she was eyeing the seemingly omniscient ship computer. "Oh yeah? Is that because you're contracted to report back on my every word?"

"I am, yet again, deeply offended."

"Well she's a fucking scrote bitch. She's sucked and fucked her way up the ladder, taking it up the arse all the way to the top. I know that sort of bitch, and I'll be damned if I'm working under her, taking orders from her, or lying on my back with my legs spread wide for her. Tarly Ice Queen is a slap bitch of the lowest order, and I'm going after Franco whether she likes it or not."

"She'll place you under house arrest," warned Alice.

"Well, she'll have to kill me to stop me."

"That can be arranged," came Tarly's smooth, silky voice. She stood in the doorway to Pippa's quarters. Pippa didn't demean herself by looking back.

"Yeah, well, better do it from where you're standing, bitch, 'cos the only way you'll ever take me is from behind. Better believe it."

"I worked my way up through the ranks," said Tarly, her voice still soft, distant almost, as if recollecting a dream, or a nightmare. When Pippa did look back, Tarly had her eyes closed. "I was married once. I had two boys, lovely little creatures; my babies. But I loved the job too much, was married to the job, and when Jonny filed for divorce and custody, my scrawled *'yes'* was the first non-mil contact I'd had for two years."

"So?" Pippa was used to sob stories. It took more than a broken family to bring out her tears. Despite describing Tarly Winters as an *Ice Queen, Ice Bitch* and *Mrs Nitrogen*, Pippa had something of a similar reputation in Quad-Gal military circles. One frisky young man ended up with his SMKK shoved so far up his arse he had to have it medically removed. News like Pippa travelled fast.

"Well, I worked my way up the ranks," said Tarly, and her eyes flicked open, like a robot's. "I carried out infiltrations, demolitions, and assassinations before I went pro-pol and spook. I carried out three hundred and seventy four hits – solo. I never missed my fucking target."

"And your point is?"

Tarly stepped close, so the two women were only inches apart. The atmosphere could have been cut with a laser. Sliced with a digital chainsaw. Spliced by cankers. Pippa's hand was on her *yukana*, lifting the weapon by instinct, with no thought to the consequences; only what she *had* to do.

"You will follow my orders," said Tarly, "or die for insubordination. We're at war with the junks. We have no time for slackers, no time for cowards, no time for fucking *wildcards.*"

"I'm going after Franco Haggis," snapped Pippa, and they were nose to nose now. "He might be a sodomising, womanising pain in the rectum, but he's *my* sodomising, womanising pain in the rectum. I sent him in there, and yeah he fucked up, but I'm going to get him out. Shoot me in the back of the skull for looking out for my friends if you like, *General*, but believe me, if that's your angle then with generals like you, the junks will eat us for breakfast and shit out our devolved remains."

There came a hiatus; a splinter in time.

Aeons passed, stars formed and died, galaxies spiralled into oblivion...

"Good," said Tarly, eventually, and forced a smile. "Because that's our mission."

"*What?*"

"Three hours. I've primed Alice. We're dropping vertical, slamming in low under the gunbots arcs – or at least, that's the theory. We're going after Franco Haggis. That's why I'm here. That's why I was sent. To dig you out of your shit puddle. To take you two back to Steinhauer."

Pippa stepped back. She observed Tarly for a while. "There would have been a lot less aggravation if you'd just said that to begin with."

Tarly, still smiling, gave a modest shrug. "I like to know the sort of people I'm working with."

"And what kind of person am I?"

"Somebody who'd kill and die to save their friends. I like that. It's so... retro."

"Yeah, well, don't get too comfy, *General*, I've yet to decide whether you're friend or foe."

"Don't worry about me," smiled Tarly, easing back out of Pippa's quarters. She stopped, and again their eyes were locked. Neither looked away. Neither submitted. "But if you threaten me again, you will be wearing your spleen as a fob."

And Tarly was gone, leaving a subtle scent of sweat and gun-oil in her wake.

Pippa scowled, and continued to pack her kit, with jerky, violent movements. Alice gave a polite cough.

"Yeah, fucker?"

"No need to vent your anger on me, Pippa. I'm your friend, remember?"

"I'm sorry, Alice. She got to me."

"Not hard these days."

"Meaning?"

"There you go again."

"I miss Keenan, Alice. I miss his hands, his face. His scent."

"I know that, Pippa. And there's nothing anybody can do. You have to be strong. You have to move on; savour what you have, move forward, do your best. That's what Keenan would have wanted."

"It's all my fault. If it wasn't for his dead girls, he wouldn't have felt the need to sacrifice himself to VOLOS. To merge with that machine motherfucker. He showed... showed he loved his dead babies more than he loved me. More than he loved life."

"Do you understand that?" asked Alice, her voice gentle.

Pippa gave a shake of her head. "I'll never have

children. It's something I know I'll never truly understand."

"Better get some sleep," said Alice, and Pippa realised she'd dimmed the lights. Her voice was soothing, hypnotic. "We're going after Franco in two hours, if my predictions of when and where he'll pop back onto the grid are accurate. You get some rest. You'll need your strength. This is going to be a tough one."

Wiping away tears, Pippa nodded. "Aren't they all?" she said.

MRS STROGGER ATTACKED, and Franco held up his arms over his face as a rampaging wall of steel and flesh and org flailed at him, and he had to admit, he might have screamed like a little girl. Strogger halted inches from Franco's soft human flesh and flexing human toes. Steam ejected, and thick black fumes belched over him, making him choke and gag, and then came silence, then a slow churn of pistons and machinery in reverse. Mrs Strogger took a step back. She looked almost sheepish.

"Sorry about that," she said.

"What? You're sorry about almost mashing me into a pulp with your mechanised appendages?"

"Yes. Sorry. It happens sometimes. Too much evolution."

"Evolution? Or devolution?"

"There you go again," said the old org. "Being

smart. Being clever. Being *human*. You need to stop with the quips and the whines. I'm an org, and we orgs don't have no sense of humour."

"I can see that," muttered Franco, and slowly lowered his arms. "Er. So you're not going to kill me?"

"You're too valuable. And if we run into more trouble, the Mistress obviously wants your skinny arse for her shows. You might be a valuable bartering tool."

"So I'm your prisoner?" said Franco, incredulously.

"Not quite," said Mrs Strogger, smiling with her metal teeth. "But let's just say you've lost your right to party, Party Boy."

Franco scowled, and nodded, and hoisted his laser cannon. He toyed with shooting her in the face, but recognised she was as much use to him as he was to her. Together, they might get out of this shit alive. Maybe not with all their limbs – he wiggled what remained of his little finger – but at least with their spines in the same damn line of vertical.

"Okay. We can help each other," said Franco.

"Deal," said Mrs Strogger.

Franco didn't point out they'd already made a deal, and she'd broken it. Which made her as slippery as a turd in a bucket of shitty eels. As dodgy as a five-week raw kebab.

Suddenly, gunfire erupted behind them. This was laser cannons, as used by the prison guards; this was heavy shit. Military ordnance. SMKK and D5 shotguns and Kekra quads and railguns. Franco knew the sounds, the tones, the symphony. He'd used them often enough himself...

He pounded along, blind for a moment, pain firing up his arm, panicking. This was bad shit. Real shit. He needed to focus – to keep calm. Franco slid to a halt by a corridor intersection, and Mrs Strogger pounded along, skidding behind him with a squeal and shower of sparks. There came some grinding sounds, and a minigun ejected from one arm. It whined and sent a mammoth volley of firepower screeching down the corridor whilst Franco watched, tongue hanging out like a warporn porn hound. He suddenly realised. The stakes had stepped up a notch. Before, with the guards, it had almost felt like... *playtime.* Now, however, this Sourballs, or the Mistress or whoever the fuck was in charge, had called in the heavy guns. With heavy guns. This was the army. The ganger army. The clones had moved in to take out the org... and Franco was in the middle of the shit. *Shit,* he thought. *It's always the same shit!*

And so he ran. He ran down alloy corridors, across thick steel gratings with rivers of murky effluent speeding below. Bullets sniped after him, *ping*ing and *drring*ing from metalwork. It grew warmer. Always behind him as he ran was the old wrinkled org, terrifying in her mechanical magnificence, pounding along, hydraulics hissing, mechanics booming like some disgusting old faulty diesel engine in need of a service and new pistons rings. Occasionally, she'd halt and her hydraulic legs would eject, stabilising her as the minigun roared and sent a warning jab to the nose of their pursuit. Franco didn't stop to watch or listen. He knew what a minigun could do to flesh, and he knew what the mad bitch of an org could do to gangers; more twisted than a bucket of snakes, she was. Franco thought he'd touched madness in his life, but realised that some forms of madness transcended understanding. Madness which transcended madness! Such as the constant obsession to upgrade. Mrs Strogger had gone beyond the pale. Beyond the event horizon of personal "improvement," dragged ever on and on and on, a pull so powerful she could not head back to the light.

Mrs Strogger had gone one upgrade too far.

She was *heavy metal*.

Franco sprinted like his life depended on it. Which it did. Up and down spiral staircases he ran, through a wonderland-like labyrinthine hell of prison corridors. Over high bridges he ran, sandals flipping and flopping like useless shitty bits of rubber. His underpants chafed. His finger and arm throbbed. Franco had *lost his sense of humour*.

He stopped by a high tower of a ravine, a chasm, an abyss. Franco looked down into an infinite *blackness*. Panting, chest heaving, he fought to regain his breath and realised he might – the horror! – have to lay off the Guinness for a while.

"What kind of shitty hell hole is this place?" he managed, once he'd regained his breath.

"Hell hole is a right description, bastad," said Strogger, pounding to a halt. Her minigun whirred, and her shoulder-mounted lasers targeted, but there was no pursuit. They seemed, for the moment, to have lost the soldiers.

Franco stood up, panting, bathed in sweat, and peered over the narrow rail and down into an abyss. "I mean, that's deep," he muttered, and frowned. "Hey, if there is a tunnel, where would it come out? I mean, we must be right down under the sea by now! Yeah?"

"To the west of Nechudnazzar there is the Symmetrical Canyon. We will emerge there."

"Hmm. And have guards lining every side with high-powered rifles? I know the stench of an ambush when I smell one. Is like bad CubeCheese, you getting me? And *that's* a fucking chemical cheese that takes some rotting! Although to be fair, it's rotted my guts on a few occasions, and I could spin you stories about some of the ladies back on The City, har-har-har, well, we had this big pot of melted cheese right, and these three drunken Astros came in, looking for trouble as Astros tend to, with their big pot bellies and wallets so bulging with Mine Pay they didn't know whether to fuck-a-ho or a diddle-eye-do."

"Maybe another time," said Mrs Strogger, voice level.

"Oh yeah? Why's that?"

Bullets screamed across the black space and spat sparks along the rail where Franco nonchalantly rested. He eyed the sparks flickering past his face, and – cool now, mad now, pissed now – he levelled his laser cannon and sent shafts of green fire lighting up the abyss. Across the way, on a narrow stone ledge, an ejaculation of rock from a hidden tunnel, three Clone Terra soldiers were punched backwards, chests and faces on fire, skin burning, voices screaming. As one, they buckled and fell forwards, diving, flaming, into the void, lighting it all the way down to its nadir.

Franco stood up. He glanced at Mrs Strogger. "I'm getting fed up of this shit."

"You going soft, boy?"

"Just tired of the killing," said Franco, dejectedly. "It never seems to end."

"There's always some bad sort needs a bullet in the cunt."

"Er. Where's you sense of optimism? Where's your positivity on the nature of the human beast?"

"I ain't no human beast," said Mrs Strogger, and glared at him, eyes glowing green and feral.

"Yeah. I see that. Shall we... move on?"

"After you."

"You sure you're happy behind me?"

"You sure you're happy me being behind?"

Franco smirked. "Well, at least you ain't got no rogue dick!"

There was a whirring sound, and Franco caught a glimpse of shining steel spikes, gears, meshing cogs, thumping pistons. He looked away hurriedly and started to run. He felt it was the best course of action.

"Wouldn't bet on it," muttered Mrs Strogger, following at a secure, sedate pace.

"LOOKS LIKE A castle to me," said Franco, peering down from a high arched walkway, only a foot wide and perhaps two kilometres high. It was playing havoc with his vertigo. He was just glad his underpants weren't white. Well, not any more.

Stretching away into infinity were curved walkways, gleaming like black steel. Huge twisted portcullis irons dominated the walkways. Franco could see guards patrolling the walkways. It seemed the alarms hadn't reached this far down.

Even as he thought the thought, alarms rang out across the vast, subterranean caverns and red lights flashed. Franco cursed and kicked the steel wall, then cursed again as he cracked his toe. "Damn all flip flops to Hades and back!" he snarled.

"We'll have to ride it," said Mrs Strogger.

"Eh?"

"Ride it. Like a rollercoaster."

"Well," said Franco, curling his lips into a snarl, "life's like that, ain't it? Life's a rollercoaster. Na-na-na-na-na-na. An' all that. I remember the dude, with his pink quiff. Whatever."

Mrs Strogger stared at him, then shrugged with a clanking of machinery. "I'm going to do something now. Something to save our lives. But you must promise me you will never speak of it."

"Er," said Franco, taking a step back and gripping his laser cannon in ever-more-sweating hands. "Okay."

"You ready?"

"This ain't sexual, is it?"

Mrs Strogger frowned. "No. Should it be?"

"It's just, with you tonguing me back in that there cell, and getting all frisky like; well, I know I'm a sexual athlete," he puffed out his chest, "but as a dirty Harry once said, a man needs to know his limitations."

"No, no, nothing like that. This is... a transformation."

"Another upgrade?"

"V1.7 metalbot," smiled Mrs Strogger.

"Ahh," said Franco, and watched as Mrs Strogger did weird and wonderful things, and pistons slid, and covers clanked, and machines moaned, and machines groaned, and flesh *twanged* and *popped* and metal stretched and screeched and Mrs Strogger bent over, and wheels emerged, and grew, and her head became a big flat steel battering ram – with eyes.

"Er," said Franco.

"Don't say anything."

"So you've transformed?" said Franco.

"Yes."

"You're a transformer?"

"Shut up."

"But look! You transformed! Into a transformer! Into a kind of, well fuck me, what the fuck are you, love? A kind of old-woman car-tank thing with a steel hammerhead shark thing thrown in, for ramming things, I presume? Er..."

"Shut up."

"That's pretty cool. You should be called Mrs Transformer."

"Are you going to get on so we can ram our way out of this shit, or should I leave you behind to rot and get shot?"

"No, no, no, I'll, ah, climb aboard, shall I?" He looked around, frowning. "But... where?"

"You sit on the twin mound command centre."

Franco stared, blank. "You mean your arse?"

"No, it's a *fucking* twin mound command centre, and if I fucking *say* it's a twin mound command centre, then a *fucking* twin mound command centre it is. Right?"

"Er. Okay. No need to lose your gerbils."

Tentatively, he climbed aboard. Mrs Strogger was much bigger now. There was more steel. More machinery. Franco cautiously sat himself down amidst the twin mound command centre, namely her *arse cheeks,* and looked around, warily.

I'm sat up her arse, he thought. And felt a giggle coming on.

"You comfy?" said Mrs Strogger, head revolving a hundred and eighty degrees.

"Er."

"Just grasp the twin circular joysticks."

Franco stared. "They's your tits, right?" he said.

"No," said Mrs Strogger, voice level, face starting to scowl. "They're the twin circular joysticks that control me, in this mode."

"If I touch your .tits," said Franco, squinting, "well, does that mean you're going to get all frisky again?"

"THEY'RE FUCKING TWIN CIRCULAR JOYSTICKS, SO GET HOLD OF THE BASTADS BEFORE I EJECT YOUR ASS AND RAM MY OWN FUCKING WAY CLEAR OF THIS PRISON SHITHOLE!"

"Okay. Okay. No need to get tetchy."

Franco· grabbed the twin mounds/joysticks. He squinted again. "They feel like tits," he said, and chewed his lip, "and, as it is well documented, I certainly *like* tits, and indeed believe that there's *nothing nice as tits,* however, in this particular environ and in this particular situation I believe that I have a certain right, nay, I have a certain predisposition to understanding the precise..."

"Shut up."

Jets roared, and Mrs Strogger set off at an incredible rate. Her wheels squealed. She cannoned down the narrow steel walkway, flames ejecting from her boots like Robby RocketBoy on crack. Franco clung on for dear life, cheeks flapping, g-force ripping at him like an atomic blast through flesh.

"Aaaaaaaaaaaaaarrrrrgh!" screeched Franco, in one long ululation any vocalist would have been proud of. Wheels squealed. Jets roared. Alarms chimed.

Red lights flickered. It was a surreal nightmare filled with surreal nightmares. Franco kept his head down, and his beard whipped his cheeks with a violence to which he would have protested, if he'd been in any position to protest. Which he wasn't.

The first gate was guarded by two guards, who levelled their laser cannons and started firing. Green bursts cut across the darkness, a bright clarity, a stunning contrast. The laser light was deflected from Mrs Strogger's flattened hammerhead. Her speed increased, as did the roar of the jets.

Unable to do *anything*, Franco simply prayed from his seat scooped out of her arse –

And as the guards leapt from the walkway, falling, screaming to their deaths, and Mrs Strogger rammed through the semi-electronic semi-gothic portcullis, sending steel blades whirling and skittering off into enveloping blackness, so Franco buried his head in her twin circular joysticks and pretended, prayed, and deeply fantasised that he was somewhere else entirely...

IT WAS QUIET. A cold wind blew. Franco looked up, shivering, and realised for the first time in what felt like hours that they'd *stopped* moving. Like a clam releasing its grip on a rock after a storm, Franco unclawed his rigid claws from Mrs Strogger's metal tits.

He looked up. And saw daylight!

"Daylight!" he croaked, like a dying man crawling through a desert in pursuit of water.

"Time to move," said Mrs Strogger, and with bangs and whirrs and *cracks,* transformed into her former, aged cyborg self, her legs wrapping up and over and around herself, her torso turning inside out, with the mechanical seeming to take very little care of the flesh yolk inside.

Franco felt suddenly very odd.

Franco felt suddenly very *sick.*

I mean, it's just not natural, reet? I mean, splicing and merging all that flesh together like some kind of human-metal omelette! It's a mish-mash of titanium and pulpy liver and squashed brains and stretched skin, all bolted into steel and plastic and run by tiny machines inside. Urgh.

He shivered, and caught Mrs Strogger staring at him. He coughed. "Okay, okay. I'm moving."

Franco composed himself, and jogged through the tunnel, which grew ever-more rough-hewn and jagged. And, like a triumphant maggot bursting from over-ripe corpse-bloat, Franco emerged into sunlight. It caressed his battered face like a languorous lover with an oiled feather. Franco basked in this unexpected glory, breathing deeply, just damn and glad to be out of the Nechudnazzar Prison complex. "I love the smell of sunshine in the morning," he breathed, huskily. "It smells like... freedom!"

"We're not free yet," scowled Mrs Strogger.

Franco frowned at her. "Just stop. Stop with your pedantic negativity. You've done nothing but bloody

moan since I met you. And I, my dear, am a man of"
– he puffed out his chest – "principles."

"Look." Strogger gestured through an alloy crack
to the vast canyon beyond.

They stood in a tiny gulley, shielded from view by
natural stone clefts. Shifting to the right, Franco got
his first view, his first *full view* of the Symmetrical
Canyon.

The first thing he noticed was its sheer *size*, its
vast *scale*, like some alien god had swept down and
scooped free a long narrow defile with a starship-
sized spade. It was big. It was the sort of canyon
that made other canyons run home to their mummy
canyons.

The second thing Franco noticed was that the
Symmetrical Canyon was filled with war machines.
From flank to gill, from arse to tit, wall to wall
bristled with metal upon metal upon crammed metal.
Tanks and tracks, trucks and infantry transport,
mounted guns and choppers, a hundred thousand
vehicles squeezed like squashed sardines in a bulging
tin, filling the canyon for as far as the eye could see
– and all eerily silent.

"That's a lot of metal," said Franco, eyes wide shut.

"A lot of killing power," nodded the old org,
her own orbs narrowed, her face twisted into an
expression Franco could not at first read. Then he
understood; this hardware was destined to be used
against the orgs. This was part of their eternal,
ongoing war. This new, crisp, tarpaulin-covered

fresh-greased designer killware was created with one purpose: to remove all orgs from the face of Cloneworld.

The machines gleamed.

Mrs Strogger stared, face curled in metal hatred.

"Let's go," said Franco, eventually, uneasily, and started forward. Mrs Strogger stopped him.

"We should be quiet. There will be guards. Lots of guards."

"Great!"

"And, er, other *things...*"

Franco nodded and, grasping his Steyr laser cannon, and cursing the heat of the sun and his lack of not just armour, but *clothing,* he led the way through the sand-rimed rocks, out into the utter silence of the Symmetrical Canyon, out into the silent, still battlefield of waiting metal death.

"OKAY," SAID ALICE. "I've got locks on three hundred AI AA GASGAM gunbots in the immediate vicinity. They don't seem to move about, do they? They are, on the whole, stationary."

Tarly Winters leaned forward over the console, then sat back. She glanced at Pippa, who did not meet her gaze, but stared forward, face set in iron. A rigid mask. "They sit like a lizard on a stone, absorbing energy, waiting – ready to pounce. Believe me, Alice, I've seen these bastards in action. When there's a threat, a hive call goes out and all others within charging distance come in as back up. It's a terrifying proposition. They are very, very dangerous."

"And that makes me feel better how, exactly?" Alice's voice was sweet, for a ship's computer, but carried a sliver of implied menace.

"What sets us apart," said Tarly, "is that QGM put these machines in place to stop the orgs and gangers fighting; to try and bring a bit of sanity to the dinner table of the insane. To halt the escalation of their war! Now, they have pitched battles, and some small naval skirmishes, but it stopped their millions of cowardly air attacks on one another's civilian targets. Spared a lot of lives."

"How humanitarian of them," said Pippa, voice low, tone neutral.

"The point is," said Tarly, reclining like a cat, hands behind her head, her shower of red curls crawling down her back like live biowire, "they were designed to take on enemy aircraft – all forms of aircraft, certainly, but they don't *expect* something like a Hornet to come crashing through the party. Yes, they are capable of taking us out – but they're looking for their enemy below. With a certain amount of stealth, we should be able to sneak through."

"I love your certainty," smiled Pippa, grimly. "Remember, Franco's life depends on this."

"As does finding the Soul of the Junks. This mission is about more than one man, Pippa, and you're best remembering it. After all," their eyes met, "you're as expendable as every other motherfucker in QGM."

"Cheers," muttered Pippa, and slid her seat forward.

Beneath, Cloneworld was getting bigger. Alice was bringing the Fast Attack Hornet in high and fast, but slowing even as Pippa watched. The plan was simple – a near vertical drop, pretty much to ground level, with burners rammed up to full in an attempt to imitate a small meteor strike. Alice had estimated the safest LZ was over the Northern Ice Fields at the northern pole. Not a place the orgs and gangers traditionally fought, due to extremes of temperature and a predilection for most war machines to *freeze*.

As the clouds parted, and the world rearranged itself into a dizzying vista, the engines screamed and howled and the Hornet, normally something sleek and beautiful, was pushed to its limit and began to vibrate with alarming violence.

The nose dipped, and Alice aligned the ship.

"Diving in three, two, one..." and *Metallika* bucked, jets howled and they roared towards the icy surface of Cloneworld's northern ice shelf.

Pippa, strapped in tight, gritted her teeth and gripped the restraints with white knuckles. She glanced across at Tarly, and was annoyed to see the pretty general casually reclining, eyes closed, face serene as if listening to a particularly fine piece of music.

Alice accelerated the ship. Pippa felt her stomach try and crawl out through her open, panting mouth. Engines hissed and ticked, and motors whined as they stabilised the interior. Ahead, Cloneworld was thrown at the ship like a hardball, and green-and-blue flickered through to white as clouds rushed and heaved at them and Alice, with digital precision, levelled them out and neatly applied the brakes.

They hung, immobile, engines hissing with matrix gas, and Pippa released a long slow breath. Yes, she was one of the most skilled pilots in Quad-Gal Military; but no human could pull off a stunt like that. She took control from Alice, and lowered the Hornet to the hard-packed ice.

"What are you doing?" said Tarly, glancing at her.

Pippa rolled her neck, easing tension. "Getting a breath of fresh air."

She moved to the door, hit the ramp button and was blinded for a moment. She stepped out onto the unfolding alloy and walked down the ramp, boots thumping. A biting cold wind nipped at her and, shielding her eyes, Pippa gazed left, then right, across an endless, rippling landscape of ice and powdered snow. Against the glow of an early morning sun, she saw distant mountains, huge towering peaks edging the skyline in black. *They're The Teeth*, she thought sombrely, and knew, deep down in her heart, that they would one day provide her with a terrible challenge. She could sense it. Sense a strange, evil presence there.

"Alice?"

"Yes, Pippa?"

"Have you scanned that horrible, ugly mountain range for activity?"

"Of course. There is no life."

"What, nothing at all?"

"Nothing at all. It's as dead as a dead dog."

"Curious."

"Why so?" asked Alice, voice inflection changing a little.

"You'd expect... *something.* Plant life, snow leopards, hulking yetis, that sort of thing. *Something.*"

"Not necessarily. What's on your mind, Pippa?"

"I've just got a bad feeling. Like it's a really good place for an ambush. But it doesn't matter, does it? Because we're not going there."

"Correct," said Alice.

Pippa gave a shiver. "But I've got a real bad feeling about The Teeth."

Tarly stepped out behind her, boots clacking on the iced ramp. "You okay?"

"I'm just appreciating some real air for a change. No offence to Alice, but after a while stuck in that damn ship, well, the bloody recyc is like breathing noxious toilet fumes."

"I heard that," came Alice's dulcet tones.

Smiling, Pippa moved down the ramp and stepped onto Cloneworld. She dropped to one knee and ran her fingers through the powdery snow. *It's real. A real world. Soft and cold under my fingers.* She breathed deeply, and rubbed at her eyes, then stood and composed her face into an iron mask as she shifted to face Tarly.

"Let's go find Franco," she said.

*   *   *

THE FAST ATTACK Hornet cruised down the western flanks of the narrow barrier-continent known as The Teeth. Crossing the sea seemed the safest option, as the AA gunbots were mostly ground-based. Alice scanned continually, giving Pippa and Tarly updates on military movements across both massive continents, Clone Terra and The Org States. It seemed both countries were ramping up military activity, and it seemed likely they were preparing for one of their regular and predictable battles – although Alice did remind them of the fact that *Opera* had been murdered, and this might be taken as an aggressive military act by The Org States against Clone Terra, thus initiating increased military activity. In response to this, both factions would continually ramp up their own operations, thus creating a self-perpetuating state of escalating high alert and strike probability.

Pippa studied a map on the console screen. Occasionally, she spun it around, zoomed in, switched to vertical fly-by, and committed the landscape of Clone Terra to memory.

"So, he's in the Symmetrical Canyon?" said Pippa.

"Yes," said Alice. "There's a lot of activity down there."

"What kind of activity?"

"Fighting activity."

"Hmm. Any groundbots?"

"I register five. That doesn't mean there's *only* five. Only that I can *see* five. Some of them are craftier than a deviant PopBot on MercuryCrack."

"ETA?"

"Ten minutes. I'd say 'tool up,' but that would be both predictable and slightly cringeworthy. I'd certainly suggest getting yourself heavily armed. I think we're going in fighting, and I think we'll be lucky to bring your, ah, *companion* out in one whole piece."

Pippa smiled, but her humour had gone. Now was not a time for humour. Now was a time for battle.

She pictured Keenan in her mind. She missed him desperately. He had been the glue that bound the Combat K team together; the wire that *connected* them in place. A unit. Yes, individually they were a bunch of psychopathic nutjobs; but without Keenan at the helm, the world seemed to be crumbling apart. A gradual disintegration. His ability to lead them had been invisible, a background skill, the sort you only ever really missed when it was gone. Well, Keenan was dead, and Franco and Pippa were doing a good job of fucking everything else up by themselves.

Tarly touched her shoulder. "I'm coming in with you."

"No, you're not."

"Yes. I am. Orders." She sighed, smiled resignedly. But her eyes were hard. Like flint.

Pippa's jaw muscles clenched. "It seems... *silly* to risk one so exalted as yourself, General, on such a lowbrow, arsewide mission. Maybe you should stay here and continue... checking maps, inventing tactics, winning the war for *hearts and minds*." She waved a mock triumphant fist. "I, on the other hand, am dropping into the real shit."

Tarly shrugged. "I'm coming. End of tale. Accept it, or I'll have Alice confine you to quarters."

Pippa stared at her, then clacked her teeth, spun on her heel, and moved to the doors. They were preparing for a fast SLAM drop, after which Alice would get the Hornet out vertical and fast, and they'd have a window of five minutes to pull Franco before she circled and dropped again, hauling them out on biobilicals. It would be tricky. Dangerous. And all so Franco could get his spot on TV...

"You're risking a lot for somebody who fucked up," said Tarly, moving in behind Pippa at the SLAM door.

"It's Franco. I love him."

"Even though he's a liability?"

"I trust him with my life. I'd kill for him. And I'd die for him." She stared hard at Tarly. "And there ain't many people in this life who get that sort of loyalty from me. You understand that, career-girl-with-a-spotless-fucking-CV?"

Tarly stared hard at Pippa.

"Don't push it, Pippa. My tolerance only stretches so far. And I'm considered a reasonable woman."

"If you don't want fucking answers, don't ask fucking questions!" snarled Pippa. She glanced up. "We at the SLAM zone, Alice?"

"Ten seconds."

The doors opened. Wind buffeted Pippa, and she stepped to the edge and looked down on a semi-arid landscape. She could smell sea. And salt. Hear the whine and deep throb of engines. The snap of flapping straps from her pack. Her eyes were watering from the stream, and Alice counted, "Three, two..."

Pippa jumped.

FRANCO CREPT DOWN the canyon floor, flip-flops kicking up a little dust, nostrils breathing the acrid air, sweat streaming down his face and body, glistening in his beard, making his hands slippery on the Steyr cannon. He stopped. To his left and right were solid walls of huge rugged machines, towering up and over him, the size of massive buildings. They were wreathed in greased covers, gleaming in the weak sunlight. Franco paused, regulating his breathing, mouth dry, wondering when the shit would ever end. And that was the thing: the shit *never* ended. And this time, as usual, he was in it right up to his neck. *Hot damn.* Up to his cranium tip top!

Franco glanced behind him, and Mrs Strogger eased towards him with a curious sideways shuffling gait. Her hydraulics *hissed* softly, but she was doing well. At least she wasn't making the usual loud whirring and clanging sounds.

Franco moved on. Past rows and rows of dormant

war machines, of tanks and choppers, of mechs and MMAs – Mobile Missile Arms – with flanks of matt green and black DPC. Franco gave a shudder. So much metal. So much potential destruction. In some ways, seeing them dormant like this was worse than seeing them in action; in action, they were imperfect, and often destroyed. Here, there was just a latent *potential* for mutilation. For death.

Getting soft, you old goat, he thought. *Time for a wife and kids, a mortgage and a big fucking TV. Ha. Ha.*

The laughter sounded false in his mind. After all, Franco was here in enemy territory, surrounded by those who wanted to kill him. Pulp him. He was wearing only underpants and a slim sliver of rubber under each foot. He'd lost all military comms, and his only friend was a cyborg. An old cyborg. An old, insane cyborg who *might* flip at any moment and take him out as well. Franco rubbed his eyes, and groaned inwardly.

Why me? he thought.

They stopped at an intersection. A wall of machines met his gaze. They were a kind of cross between mechs – huge, two-legged, vaguely humanistic war robots – and tanks. The two-legged metal monstrosities had tank turrets on their backs, and triple-wheel treads instead of feet. They reared up above Franco, thirty feet tall and utterly terrifying.

"They're TankMeks," said Mrs Strogger.

"Well, I'm glad those bastards are asleep," said

Franco, in a muted half-mutter. "They'd soon turn little Franco into fish paste!"

Suddenly, behind him, Mrs Strogger – who had sidled to a halt – gave the most incredible high-pitched squeal, a reverberating metal moan that sang out like a siren, an alarm, and after reaching the highest reaches of the atmosphere, warbled back down until it was a dull baritone. She twisted, jerked, twitched, seemed to have an epileptic fit, or the cyborg equivalent. Her limbs jerked and twitched spasmodically, and her minigun emerged and fired erratic shots into the ranks of the TankMeks. Bullets whizzed and whined and *pinged,* and Franco hit the ground in a puff of dust and covered his head with his hands, one beady eye fixed on Mrs Strogger, half a mind urging him to take her out with his laser cannon... only, well, only he'd *seen* what she could do, and was pretty damn sure it'd take more than a burst of cannon fire to render her dog meat. It'd take something like, well, something *like* a TankMek.

The bullets stopped. The minigun whirred to a halt.

Silence deafened the canyon.

Slowly, Franco got to his feet and scowled at Mrs Strogger. But her eyes were closed and she was perfectly immobile. She seemed to have passed out, standing where she stood, kept erect by her org mechanicals.

"Dumb bloody machine," muttered Franco. He turned and stared at the huge TankMeks. Nothing had happened: no guards had come rushing, no lights flickered, no guns boomed. "Seems like everybody's got the day off! Things are looking better and better by the very second... *Hot damn...*"

Franco grasped his laser cannon with a rattle. He took a deep breath. Which way to go? And was Strogger dead? But on the up side, maybe Strogger was *dead*? He'd be free of her unpredictability...

Franco had turned, his back to the TankMeks, to stare at the lolling features on the old org. Now, he heard a tiny, tiny *click*.

Oh no, he thought.

Please. No. Not here. Not now. Not like this. Not in my *underpants*...

Slowly, he turned around.

Franco stared at the motionless TankMeks. He looked from left to right, at the wall of formidable metal warriors. There were perhaps two hundred of the machines, each thirty feet high. They were a battalion of steel and guns, stinking of oil.

Franco swallowed.

On *one* TankMek, a small red light blinked.

Franco grasped his laser cannon more tightly.

As...

A rocket fired from the TankMek, sending Franco diving to the left with a grunt, rolling in the dirt and slamming into a tarpaulin-sheathed war machine, and sending a shock through his body that jarred him from teeth to balls. The rocket hissed on a stream of burnt fuel, slammed into Mrs Strogger and exploded, picking her up and sending her spinning over the canyon and the stock-piled machines in a gout of fire and billowing black smoke. Franco aimed his gun and sent a volley of green laser bursts across the small clearing to scar hot metal channels up the TankMek. And it – *roared*. It opened metal jaws and bellowed at Franco and tiny red eyes focused in him, and with a sinking feeling Franco realised... shit. The bastard was an AI. Machine brain. Superior to the humans who created them. Very clever. Very *deadly*.

The TankMek strode forward, hydraulics hissing, and Franco kept firing grimly, face set, eyes locked, mouth dry as a Harmattan. The laser bursts cut runs of liquid metal up the TankMek's hull, scarring it horribly but failing to penetrate the armour. It reared over Franco and he carried on firing, laser blasts scorching his own face with their proximity. A huge fist slammed down towards him, a fist the size of his entire body, and Franco rolled right at the last minute, but a metal tri-wheel track rose over him and stomped down, sending Franco scrabbling away. He ran, arms pumping, and heard the *whine* of a minigun charging. Bullets screamed, as Franco, also screaming, reached the wall of TankMeks and dived between a machine's legs. Bullets spat and clanged behind him and he cowered like a little girl in a forest at night.

But if he'd thought hiding behind a fellow TankMek would stop the machine, he'd been sorely mistaken. Bullets screamed after him, pinging from the legs of the surrounding TankMeks. Franco hunkered down, and the gunfire stopped, followed by a heavy clanking and *whirring*. The TankMek grabbed the TankMek behind which Franco cowered and twisted, launching its fellow war machine down the canyon floor and scoring grooves in the stone. Franco was left, cowering in his underpants, staring up at the evil enemy TankMek. It closed, slowly, as if savouring cornering the weak human shell. Its metal jaws looked, to Franco, like it was grinning.

"Got you," it said, voice gravelly and metallic.

"Well, you got this," said Franco, an instant before the TankMek realised he'd been holding the trigger and building an Impact Charge in the Steyr laser cannon. Franco released the blast straight at the TankMek's groin, and the blast slammed it backwards to land on its metal arse. Franco uncurled, then cursed as, with a growl, the TankMek climbed to its feet. That was all he had. And now... well, *now* the laser cannon would take several more minutes to recharge.

He was weaponless.

Franco ran, dodging behind the line of TankMeks, and heard a pounding sound behind him. Franco veered right, doubled back, then stopped with a skid, kicking up dirt, and grabbed hold of a dormant machine to steady himself. Like a monkey up a tree, Franco scaled the machine, nine and a half fingers and thumbs finding handholds in the grooves and ridges of steel. He climbed over the vertical tank turret and up again, to stand beside the upright gun. *I'll be safe up here. The mongrel won't be able to spot me amongst all the iron work! Look, charging away like a dumb dog after a rancid bone, he's going the wrong bloody way, I tell ye...*

But even as Franco watched, the TankMek whirled with a skid of splintered rock fragments, and he realised with horror it was simply getting enough distance for a decent *run up*... It pounded towards him and leapt, and the whole TankMek on which Franco cowered tipped backwards. With a scream, like a pirate riding the mast of a sinking galleon, he rode the TankMek to the ground, a thundering noise in his ears, a roaring of steel grinding against steel all around and through him. Franco was encompassed, *buried* by the two TankMeks and it was a damn miracle he wasn't crushed to a pulp. When the roaring finished, Franco realised he had lost his laser cannon and had covered his head with his hands. *Shit. Damn. Shit damn and rancid bloody bollocks! I nearly got pancaked!* He opened his eyes, and was confused by what he saw. And then he realised. It was the enemy TankMek's *face*, inches from his own. Its eyes opened and glowed red. Its mouth opened, iron jaws squealing. And, with a fetid breath of old engine oil, of crushed bearings, of sour grease, it said, "I'm going to fuck you up, sonny," before a fist the size of a small car whirred past his head... but Franco had rolled, and was scrambling away from the entangled machines.

The TankMek stood, with grindings of steel, and glared at Franco, who was wondering what the hell he could do now. With only underpants and flip-flops to his name, he was stuffed.

The TankMek charged, then abruptly jerked back, as if on elastic. The second TankMek, which had been knocked to the ground, reared up and pounded the first with a two-fisted hammer punch and a sound like a cubescraper collapsing. Franco ambled to a halt, sweating and panting, bent, his hands on his knees. He watched the two TankMeks knock ten tons of crap out of each other, literally. Fists flew. Shotguns boomed. Chunks of steel rattled off across the dusty canyon floor. Lengths of H-section were wrenched free and tossed away. The fight became a blur, and as Franco regained his breath, he watched the two awesome war machines pounding, kicking, shooting, gouging, then rolling around on the dusty floor like school boys having a scrap. Franco took a deep breath and scratched his chin.

"Well, I never!"

And all the time, he could hear their bickering, gravelly metal voices:

"Attack me, would you?"

"I was after the human meat!"

"You threw me!"

"I'll bloody kick you!"

"Go on then!"

"What do you think this is?"

"A party, dickhead!"

"You shouldn't have thrown me! You've got steel-rot!"

"Oh, steel-rot, is it?"

"Yes, and melt-brain."

"Ha! You're the one who looks like his face has been eaten by an attack of acid SPAWS!"

"You cheeky fuck! That's only because you took a liberty!"

"Oh, liberties now, is it?"

And so on.

Franco's eyes scouted for his laser cannon, his only chance of getting out of this whole place, this whole continent, this whole bloody *world* alive. He saw it on the ground. Near the scrapping *scrap*.

"Aha!"

Tentatively, Franco edged towards the pugilising robots. Metal screamed against metal. The TankMeks were equally matched, and rending and tearing each other with a ferocity Franco had only seen before in smaller, nastier AIs, including the infamous GG models. Bad news. Bad shit.

Franco was close now. His eyes flickered between the cannon and the fight. Another footstep. And another.

With a shriek of tearing steel, suddenly one TankMek wrenched the head off the other and stood swaying, staring at the head's dangling cables as if surprised by its own strength.

Franco swallowed. *Hell! Which one was it? The one which had saved him, or –*

"There you are, you little shit!" snarled the Mek. Oil like blood dribbled from its jaws. One arm was twisted and bent, trailing a battered ammo belt.

"Aaah!" said Franco.

The TankMek launched itself at Franco, who twisted and dived between its legs, grabbing the laser cannon and rolling over – to have the weapon smashed from his hands. The TankMek loomed over him. Franco swallowed.

"Truce?" he whimpered.

"You're gonna die, meatfuck," growled the TankMek, and a claw shot out from its chassis, enclosing Franco's throat and pinning him to the ground. Franco wriggled, legs kicking, like a fish on a hook. His hands scrabbled at the claw, his fists punching the twisted alloy. But the Mek was strong. Real strong.

There was a buzz, and a click, and a gun emerged from the machine's torso. The dark eye of a barrel levelled at Franco's face. Franco stared into that dark eye, into its spiralled barrel...

"Oh feck," he said.

CHAPTER FOUR
MEATPUKE

THE MISTRESS STRODE down the alloy corridor, a hundred gangers parting before her, hands on weapons, eyes turned down in reverence to her Magnificence, her Superiority, her Natural Wonderfulness, for she was The Prime, she was The God, she was... The Mistress. She stopped. For a moment, it looked like her face was a mass of seething pink snakes in a bucket of oil, but then she calmed herself and breathed deeply, and her flesh melded into an approximation of humanity. Any gangers who saw the effect blinked and rubbed at their tired eyes, eyes filled with smoke and gun oil, minds filled with detonation and napalm – and put it down to bad dreams.

"Teddy?" she snapped. She gazed down at the

twisted figure of her faithful assistant. Teddy Sourballs was a pulped bag of pulverised bones. Teddy Sourballs was a bruised and battered shit steak. Teddy Sourballs was a cellophane wrapper of minced human. She was fucked. She was more than fucked. She was worse than fucked. She was *dead*.

"You stupid, stupid *bitch,*" snapped the Mistress, and kicked the corpse. Then she kicked Teddy again. She kicked her a third time, watching the dead body flop about as if every joint was a machine part on fluid bearings in a grotesque parody of the orgs... the orgs whom the Mistress hated with *such* venom.

The Mistress turned back to Ziggurat, who had hobbled along in a sideways shuffle after her. His odd coloured eyes observed her without criticism, then glanced down at the tangled barbed-wire mop above Teddy's dead head. "She died in the line of duty, Mistress," he said softly. His fingers flexed, like a gunfighter ready to draw.

"She was a fucking dim-witted abomination!" snapped the Mistress, eyes glowing as if lit by black nuclear fire on the inside of her skull. "Her failure to follow policy and procedure is *not* what I expect of my Ministers! From my Ministers I expect unfaltering *obedience*. From my Ministers I expect clarity of thought when aligned to my specific gameplan *instructions*. I do *not* expect my Ministers to think for themselves. They are not *experienced* enough to *think* for themselves. They have a rollicking good CV, I'd be the first to admit it, crafted and honed over a thousand different incidents and built on the back of other gangers' hard work – a certain guidance and direction of misappropriated congratulation, a certain *shifting* of reward from others to their own paperwork, and all this I congratulate." She looked down. Kicked Teddy's corpse again. "What I *don't fucking expect is for them to take matters into their own hands!*"

Ziggurat stood, face impassive. The ganger guards around them, mostly RGPF but with a few newly arrived emissaries from The Bad Army, lowered their eyes and avoided the Mistress's fiery gaze. She seemed less than human. Indeed, she seemed less than *ganger*. Which she was.

Ziggurat coughed. "Ma'am? Franco Haggis and the rogue org have been spotted in the Symmetrical Canyon. I believe they are about to activate some of our war machines."

"Good! Get over there, make sure there's nothing left but an oily pulp. Take some Bad Army infantry with you – kick up the shit. And make sure you have some experienced cameramen along for the ride; get it all on vid. We can do a week of shows about what happens when you cross somebody like Opera. And me. Yes?"

"Yes," said Ziggurat, ever-soft. His green eye and his yellow eye gleamed.

"Did you Re-Slush Teddy?"

"She's coming."

Even as the words whispered softly over Ziggurat's

warm, wet lips, the hunchback shifted to one side, and along the alloy corridor came Teddy Sourballs. She wore the same clothing, and had been prepped – a memory update from her mobile memcard. She stopped, and looked down at her own corpse, her original, her template. Teddy Sourballs had been cloned. Copied. *Gangered.*

"You going to follow orders this time, arsehole?" snapped the Mistress.

"Yes, Mistress." She was still staring at her body, a strange, twisted look on her face. She recognised she had made mistakes; ended up dead. And she knew she was still only walking, talking, *breathing* on the whim of her moderately insane employer.

"Good." The Mistress grabbed her shirt, pulled her close. Her breath was sweet and dangerous, like sugared snake venom. "Don't fuck up again," she whispered, then kissed her on the lips and released her. "And – make me a cup of tea! You know I like a cup of tea!"

"Yes... Mistress."

The Mistress wandered down the corridor, hips swaying.

Ziggurat glanced at Teddy. "You okay?"

"Hmm? Yeah. Yes. It's just a surreal experience, staring at your own corpse." She shivered. "It's the first time I've been gangered from Slush."

"I'm going after Franco." Ziggurat gave a twisted grimace. It may have been a smile. "Want to come along?"

Teddy focused on Ziggurat for the first time. "I want that schmuck dead," she said, lips compressed, eyes narrowed. "I want some payback. I want some torture."

Ziggurat gave a nod. "Torture." He toyed with the word on his deformed face. "Now there's a thought. I'll make a deal with you."

"Yes?"

"If you play by my rules, when we catch this... *Franco Haggis*... well, I'll teach you how to play with him properly."

"You up to something here, Zig?"

Ziggurat gave a single nod. "I'm always up to something," he said.

PIPPA AND TARLY stood at the edge of the canyon, gazing down at a vast array of gathered war machines. Sunlight gleamed from the greased metal. Echoing silence filled the space, punctuated by the distant *hum* from the nearby vast city of Nechudnazzar. The canyon was on the outskirts, leading away into arid lands; into a wasteland of scrub, sand and small, spiky, harshland trees.

"I'm getting a lot of readings. A lot of activity down there," said Tarly, looking at her PAD.

"I don't see shit." Pippa, twin yukana swords sheathed on her back beneath her pack, clasping an MPK machine gun in her gloved hands, cut an impressive figure. She smoothed back her bobbed brown hair and glared down into the canyon, as if challenging the whole world to a fight. "The PAD must be throwing a glitch."

"No. No. It's not *physical* activity; its digital."

"Machines?"

"Yeah. Lots of them."

"AIs?"

"Yeah."

"I hate those motherfuckers."

"They have the same rights as humans."

Pippa shrugged. "Yeah, well, when a bucket of steel, alloy and bolts shows me a distinct lack of empathy, a lack of *humanity,* I find it hard to restrain myself from putting a yukana through its spindly neck. I'd like to see them behave like *life.* Truly I would. But until that moment," she withdrew a black sword, formed from a single molecule, with a tiny *shring,* "well, I'll just have to give them extreme violence."

"There!"

Tarly pointed. Pippa squinted. She could make out some distant activity amongst the machines. A fight? It was hard to tell. "Is the ID Franco?"

"Not sure. The PAD is blank."

"If that's Franco, we'll never reach him in time," snapped Pippa. "Let's move."

"We base jumping?"

Pippa nodded, took three steps back, and launched herself from the three-thousand-foot cliffs without hesitation. She fell like a rock, hair whipping, eyes streaming tears. She pulled her micro-chute at the last moment, glided down onto rock, boots landing with a thud. She cut the cords, watched Tarly land close by, and jumped down a series of jagged rock outcrops until her boots hit the dusty floor on the canyon bottom.

"I'm getting AI readings from *all* these machines," said Tarly, softly. She gazed around in awe.

"You mean they're all..."

"Waiting. Awake, and waiting."

Pippa stared around. She estimated there must have been... three, four thousand units of varying types? And all of them were awake, watching, listening, choosing to do *nothing*.

"If it kicks off," said Pippa, "there's going to be a world of shit."

Tarly grinned. "You're Combat K, chick. Deal with it."

"AAAAAAAAARRRGH!" SCREAMED FRANCO as he waited for death, and watched the eye of the gun, and thought in a split of a split-second *oh my God this is it, this is the moment and of all the dirty, stinking, rotten, shitty luck, to think of all the beer not drunk, all the women not interfered with, all the kebabs not suckled, all the horseradish not drooled down my haggard and badly-cropped beard, it's just not fucking fair and it should be fair, I should be allowed to fight my way out of this shit but this metal bastard isn't playing by the rules... but hey, what rules? This is war, maggot...*

He was curled, foetal, hands over his head, eyes watering, lips gibbering. And then there was a hefty *clang* and daylight seemed to flood Franco's senses, as if a great weight had been lifted, a trapdoor opened in the clouds, allowing sunlight to flood in. He opened one eye experimentally, to see Mrs Strogger, face grim, mouth grim, eyes grim, in the pose of one who has delivered a mighty meaty right hook. Ten feet away, the TankMek was on its arse, legs kicking, shaking its head as if it had just received a mighty, meaty thump with a hammer.

"Rockabilly!" grinned Franco, leaping to his feet. He ran to the other, recently mashed TankMek, and grabbed a section of its severed leg with a grinding crash of wrenching steel. He turned on Mrs Strogger. "Come on! Let's finish it off!"

Franco ran at the TankMek, which was only just regaining its senses. Franco delivered a mighty blow to its skull with the leg-part, as Mrs Strogger came up behind it and, dropping to one knee, put it in a head-lock. Franco danced about the TankMek, whacking and braining the AI, cackling all along. "Thought you had me, eh? Thought you'd kill me, eh? Call *me* a meatfuck, eh? Well the shoe's on the other foot, laddie, the sandal's on the other twisted spam appendage..." And as he whacked and clanged with his primeval clubbing weapon, Mrs Strogger squeezed and grunted and was, effectively, locked in combat with the struggling TankMek. It was quite a feat, for the enemy machine was much bigger than Strogger. Her size was no indication of her vast *strength!*

Later, Franco would admit he was probably little more effective than a bee buzzing around the TankMek's face, and that the mighty org upgrades of Mrs Strogger did a fair old job in the events that followed. But he'd only admit it after ten pints of Guinness. Maybe twenty. And only then as pillow talk.

A squeal rang across the canyon as, finally, the TankMek yielded. Mrs Strogger twisted its huge head neatly off, showering cables and sparks, and lifted the huge alloy unit up in both hands with a grin, trailing wires and glowing connectors.

"We are victorious!" she cried.

"We're the Smart Party!" yelled Franco triumphantly, and only sheer bloody decency stopped him pounding his chest in an impersonation of Tarzan, such was his euphoria.

They stood, panting, as silence flooded the canyon. All around, dormant war machines stood a silent, useless watch. Franco dropped his improvised club. He was battered and bruised, and blood trickled from a dozen different cuts. He grinned up at Mrs Strogger. "Shit. We won. And all this against *one* of them!"

Mrs Strogger shrugged, sat with a heavy clank, and wheezed like a failing starting motor. She exuded old engine oil pheromones. She looked, to Franco, suddenly older, more weary, a burned-out hopeless fucking case. But she'd saved him. She'd come back and damn well saved him!

Franco moved over to her, and reaching over, gave her a hug.

Mrs Strogger looked up. "What's that for, bastad?"

"For saving my life."

"You're too good-looking to have your head shot off."

"And you're..." he searched his small repertoire of compliments frantically for a suitable equivalent, "too much of a well-greased engine to give up now. Come on cybe-org, on your feet. I don't know about you, but these damn gangers and their war machine army are starting to *get on my tits.*"

Mrs Strogger stood. She looked at Franco. She smiled. Then her gaze drifted, and her look *shifted* to something less than normal, to something filled with a mixture of angst and certainty of death.

"Er," she said.

"We sure saw that metal meathead off, eh, girl?" Franco picked up the TankMek leg part and waved it around his head like a monkey. "Let's hope no more bother to show up, or we'll take them apart as well, grind them down into buckets of bolts, eh lass?"

"Er."

"Some pussy got your tongue?"

Mrs Strogger pointed. Franco turned. In almost perfect, well-greased silence, the silence of the perfectly balanced, perfectly oiled machine, the silence of clockwork perfection, the silence of machine equilibrium, three thousand war machines had slowly dragged free their tarpaulins and formed a semi-circle around the two escapees.

Franco looked up into the twisted, anger-filled, psychopathic faces of at least twenty TankMeks, and the smile fell from his chops faster than drool from a SPAW's ill-fitting space jaws.

"Truce?" suggested Franco.

"Kill it," snarled a TankMek.

And then all Hell *really did* break loose...

PIPPA STOPPED, HAND on MPK, and stared. Suddenly, missiles roared and fire blossomed. Machine gun fire slammed. Bullets spat. Lasers cut red, green and blue swathes through fire and dust and exploding metal. Roars rocked the rock. Lights flickered like dying stars. A TankMek shot a hundred feet into the air, trailing fire and a thick plume of oily black smoke, then, describing an arc, was lost in a wall of green billowing flames.

"What is it?"

"Franco," snapped Pippa. She hit her PAD. "Alice. We need you. *Fast.*"

"What's the plan?" snapped Tarly.

Pippa grinned. "Get in and out and the motherfuck away..."

*　　*　　*

FRANCO HAGGIS RAN in slow-motion, as if modelling some dodgy rotten hair conditioner. Explosions exploded around him, blossoms of purple, green and red fire encouraging him to run with both hands over his head. Occasionally, his stolen heavy-duty minigun, ammunition belts tossed carelessly across both shoulders, requisitioned from a TankMek Mrs Strogger had thoughtfully cut in two, howled and jabbered like a wild jabberwocky, spitting and snarling, fire erupting, bullets cutting lines of hot metal death into the ranged ranks of the war machines. All around lay death and metal destruction, mayhem and insanity. Franco Haggis tiptoed and scampered through a raging forest of war, dodging one way, ballerina-skipping another, his face and body bathed in fire and bruises and wondering, just wondering how the fucking fuck he was still alive.

Mrs Strogger pounded behind him, hydraulics hissing, face contorted in rage at these *machines* of the gangers which she saw as a direct mockery of her own race. *Those gangers!* she raged, slicing through another torso with her arm-knife, flinching at the explosion from its battery pack. *They think to mock me! To mock us! To mock my entire race! They have devised a group of inferior machines whose very existence cackles at our regal lineage! Well, I will show them, I will tear apart their inferior machinery and show that only a true org, a true blend of human and machine, can reach the pinnacle arc of an evolutionary machine age!*

Mrs Strogger blasted several more TankMeks from existence using their own advanced weaponry which she had, within a few short seconds, bone-welded to her org chassis. Mrs Strogger was not just a war machine, she was a war machine with the ability to *fast-upgrade* during battle.

Franco ran a merry dance, sometimes behind the psychopathic aged org, sometimes before her, and sometimes cowering beneath her legs as all hell raged above him. The Symmetrical Canyon was being gradually blasted into a mad smush of powdered rock, rock globules and liquid magma. Lava flowed from every direction, as the ganger AI war machines endeavoured to liquefy Mrs Strogger and pulp Franco Haggis into pastrami, as per instructions. However, it would seem the ganger war machines were having a bad day.

"Infantry," growled Mrs Strogger.

"Oh, yeah?" snarled Franco, popping up from between her legs like some rabid, bruise-covered, blood- and saliva-smeared last-minute self-ejected caesarean. He turned his head left and right, and lifted his battle-scarred minigun. "Where are they? Let me at 'em! At last, an enemy on my own level..."

And from out of the smoke emerged Pippa, uniform neat, gloved hands clasping her MPK without a tremble, eyes cold. "I see you, Franco Haggis," she said, voice level, eyes looking past him. She squeezed off a burst, removing the head from an attacking AI. "You little maggot."

"Pippa! Lass! Glad you could, ahem, *finally* join the party!"

And explosion rocked the ground, making all of them stumble, and from high above came the whine of engines. Smoke billowed and fire roared. Tarly appeared at Pippa's shoulder.

"Is this him?"

"Aye. This is him."

"I thought he'd be... taller."

Franco strode close, one flip-flop missing. "Hey! Lay off the wisecracks. Have you any air transport?"

"Ten seconds," said Pippa, and sighed. She gestured to Strogger, who was wrestling with a smaller Mek. Grabbing it by metal groin and throat, she ripped it in two with a mighty squeal and a small explosion, engulfing herself in a raging inferno from which she emerged unscathed. "She with you?"

"We have... an arrangement."

"Oh aye?" Pippa raised her eyebrows.

"Not like that, dickhead."

"Dickhead? Moi? You were the one who emerged from beneath her legs with your lips all oil-smeared."

"Hey, hey, that's a bloody misrepresentation of the truth, that is..." But the Hornet arrived at that moment, skimming in low and showing several new battle scars along its flanks from Alice's frantic manoeuvres evading the GASGAM gunbots' attacks. The ship's guns started to pound the brawling war machines, Alice's eye for a target unerring, bordering on perfection. *Metallika* touched down with whines and sighs from the landing gear, and Franco, Pippa and Tarly strode through the smoke to the ramp, followed by a limping, clanking Mrs Strogger. Pippa and Tarly ducked heads, entering the cool, safe interior of the ship. Mrs Strogger, after Franco gave her a nod, shrank from her fighting-war-machine org exterior, reducing into, into, *into* herself until she was the original human size she'd been when Franco first encountered her in the cells. They trooped inside, leaving Franco standing on the ramp. He scratched his beard, scratched his head, scratched his arse, then lit a cigar and blew smoke at a battered, wounded battlefield.

"Shit," he said. "And all because of one pointless little TV presenter."

Then Alice leapt the Hornet into the air, and they banked, and rose on a fast-whine of engines towards the stars...

It lay in the mud, in a slurry of pulped rock. Molten rock had burnt away its legs, but its mind was fine, its AI mind functioning on full throttle and filled with heat for the sacks of meatpuke who had bettered it. But it had one final weapon. One final swan song. For this was a WormMek. It had been built with a very special function in mind...

It's sleek, pointed, alloy head lifted from the mud and it relayed commands to Nechudnazzar HQ. Confirmation was granted – from right at the top. The AI smiled and considered this act of... *suicide*.

But then, was suicide for a machine the same as suicide for a human? Was there Heaven and Hell? In the great scheme of things, were AIs – created machine life – granted the same concessions after death as their natural, organic counterparts?

Whatever. No matter.

The point was, here and now, he, *it*, could do something. Make a difference. Make it matter. Make the waste of AI life surrounding its battered, decimated carcass *mean something*.

The WormMek looked deep into its core and initiated various commands. It agreed various protective subroutines, then watched as code flickered through its processors and the remainder of its body began to meld and blend, panels sliding into panels, ruined legs twisting together into a corkscrew formation with sizeable exhaust ports. It lowered its head, which merged with its shoulders and chest, and all became a dull slick *whole* as the WormMek changed itself into a Rapid Offensive Intelligent *Missile...*

Under the mud, jets fired. Powerful jets. Two-thirds of the body was fuel.

The other third?

HighQ explosive. Able to take down something *big...*

FRANCO SWAGGERED INTO the cockpit, smoking his cigar; the ceiling extractors clicked into life. Pippa and Tarly, in the pilot seats, turned slowly to meet his gaze. Franco looked around, but Mrs Strogger wasn't present.

"She powdering her nose?"

"She's having an oil bath. Alice is prepared for all eventualities. Unlike you." Pippa's voice was curt to the point of rudeness, which was no great shock.

Franco slumped in a chair, and lifting his head, said, "Alice, a bowl of CubeSausage and horseradish, if you don't mind. Gods, that was a painful mission. I thought I was only getting data! And then the data became painful data and the data was just *too* much data."

"What you talking about, Squid Brain?" snapped Pippa.

"Squid? Brain? Me?" Franco grinned, and took the bowl – of what appeared to be lumps of gristle in a mucus sauce – from the slot. He tucked in. With gusto. Through mouthfuls of garbage, he said, "And a pint of whiskey."

"Yes, you, you fuckwit. You fucked up bad, Franco. You were sent in on a simple mission to find out where the Soul of the Junks was. And you couldn't even do that. What a gimp."

Franco ate for a while, his face and body a camouflage pattern of bruises, cuts, smoke-stains and general dirt. His pint of whiskey was dutifully delivered by Alice, and with a sigh Franco drained half the glass in one. His eyes crossed for a moment, then an *even more* contented look crossed his battered face. "That's good," he said. "That's real good."

Pippa snorted, and turned away in disgust.

Tarly, however, stared at Franco, brushing her long red curls aside. "Something happened, didn't it?"

"Ach, leave the pointless little worm to it," snarled Pippa. "He's always doing this. You send him on a simple fucking mission and he gets hopelessly pissed, shags a few robowhores, then comes crawling back without whatever it was you sent him to find in the first place. Franco Haggis put the *I* into *idiot*; he put the *less* into *pointlessness*. And he put the *cunt* into *cunt*."

Franco raised his eyebrows. "That doesn't work," he said, smiling, all amiable-like.

"It does if I say it does," snarled Pippa. Then she focused her fury on Franco, direct. "You!" She pointed. "You had a simple job. You knew what it was. But you had to get drunk, you had to try and play *hide the sausage* with every fucking female alien you met. And then, when you're in the shit, we have to haul ourselves down here to rescue your sorry arse. We put our lives on the line for you, Franco, and you know what, mate? Sometimes, you just ain't worth it."

Franco coughed. He held up a fork, bearing a quivering cube of what looked like raw human flesh. "Pippa. Please. Allow me to correct you."

"Correct me?" she snorted. "Which bit? You going to say your sausage isn't the tiny maggot I can attest to? Because, believe me, I've seen it a hundred times and it's nothing special."

"No. No," said Franco, and the smile was still on his face, and it was a smug smile, and Pippa didn't like that smile, she didn't like that smug smile at all, because it was the sort of smug smile that said Franco had been *up to something* and he knew something important that you *didn't*. It was always that sort of shit that burned Pippa bad.

"Go on, then."

"Okay, poppet. I was SLAM-dropped. A high dive from a high dive, har-har-har. Well, you know little old me, I like a few beers, and yes, I partook of a fair few beers, but then I says to myself, what better place for the garnering of information than a place where a) people are drunk, and b) important people are drunk? So I hits a few bars, and hits a few drinking dens, and it doesn't take long for wily old Franco to sniff out the important civil servants of Nechudnazzar. I mean, that's where all these doobies go – to the drinking pits."

"Civil servants?" Pippa gave a sniff. "Why civil servants?"

Franco grinned. "Because civil servants are the kind of pen-pushing money-grabbing work-shy council-scrubbing social-fucking fuckwits who have lots of insider knowledge, a pointless self-righteousness, they always claim they're stressed on the stress vibe, and after a few beers have very wide-open wide-flapping flapping-open mouths! It's just the way it is." He smiled. Smugly.

"Go on."

"Well, I came across this guy. Proper burned-out useless hopeless fucking case. Knows a friend of a friend who works at the Nechudnazzar Museum, here in Nechudnazzar, funnily enough. I plies him with a few drinks, loosens his tongue, gets him talking about artefacts and suchforth. Told him I was an out-of-town journo doing a story on artefacts with links to the junks. This dude tells me they have a few items knocking about, old swords and shields, the usual junk-history junk littering the place. Anyway, I'm interested, right, and he warbles on, and drinks more and more, and I drink along with him because, like, that's what you have to do in these situations, when reeling out information like bowel-spaghetti. Then he tells me about the Pod Vaults."

"What's a Pod Vault?" said Pippa.

Franco took another swig of whiskey, and slapped his chops. "Ach, that's a fine Mush Blend. Well. As I was saying. Cloneworld, or Clone Terra to be precise, has a series of *Pod Vaults* scattered about the land. They're places for either rarities, such as rare paintings by old winos, or fancy bloody sculptures by artists with one ear, that sorta cultural higgledy-piggledy. Stuff that might get nicked, you understand? You still with me, chicken?"

"I think I can keep up," scowled Pippa, glancing at the screens. They'd left the Symmetrical Canyon, and were cruising west across the vast stretch of Pinetop Forest in one of Alice's attempts to avoid the many AI gunbots that roamed the land. "It's not like you're racing ahead like a rocket scientist now, is it?"

"Hey!" Franco winked. "You never know. This whiskey is like bloody rocket fuel! Anyway, another use for these Pod Vaults is for stuff that's dangerous. He said there was a chip, a computer chip – the 3Core."

"What's that got to do with us?"

"It used to run the junks' global mainframe. They used to say it was the heart, mind and soul of their civilisation. Ergo, it must be the Junkala Soul." Franco glanced up at Pippa. "You buying this?"

"Go on. Let's say you have piqued my interest."

"Anyways, so I gets on with my investigation, if you'd like to call it an investigation, but I was following up leads, reet? And this dude couldn't tell me any more gumf but said there was this woman, called Rebecca, a ganger barmaid who could tell me some more info about which Pod Vault this 3Core was being kept in, 'cos it was reet dangerous to us human types and *even more dangerous* to those junk types. So I wandered down and had a few more drinks, and yes I admit I had a few glasses of SCROTUM'S OLD TODGE CLOGGER – FINEST SINGLE MALT and that to outside and prying eyes I may have *looked like* I was a drunken heap of shit, but I was *actually* doing my mission, and getting somewhere, and getting some results, *whilst being a drunken heap of shit!* Y'see?"

"I see," said Pippa, woodenly.

Tarly leant forward. "You found her?"

"Oh yes," said Franco, with a grin. "I found this Rebecca amidst a hundred other *Rebeccas,* bloody damn Rebecca-clones all looked the same to me, but I finds her using my intuition, yeah, and I asked my questions like a proper useless drunk, then got shuffled on to this shithole called Van Gok's. There, I met a burned-out GG, really nasty case she was, Gill Pilchards, thought she was God and hated the junks with a vengeance. Resigned herself to being a simple shagbot working the cellars of Van Gok's, and after all she'd done for Quad-Gal Military as well! Proper pissed, she was."

"So you did her?" snapped Pippa, eyes glowing. "You stooped to shagging a burned out GG AI in the name of pursuing your investigation? Ha! You're a whore, Franco Haggis, a cheap slut who lets any hairy hand slide up your skirt."

"Hey! No!" Franco puffed out his chest. "I ref – I const – I den – I just don't bloody like that implication! How dare you! I feel quite" – he shivered – "violated. I am a reformed character. I have fresh *moral fibre!*"

Pippa sighed. She handed Franco another pint of whiskey. "Go on."

"Well," he chuckled, "after a bit of cajoling, I gets the info out of her. The 3Core is to be found in a secret Pod Vault deep in the Slush Pits; kept there for safety reasons, 'cos its proper reet protected, like." He sat back and folded his arms. "See! I did it! I did my mission! I found out all the information, and yes, it may have looked like I was on a drunken rampage, but I just has to do stuff the way I think it should be best done best."

Pippa considered this.

"You did well," grinned Tarly, from behind Pippa. "Well done, Francis."

Franco gestured with his thumb. "Who is you, anyways?" He waggled his eyebrows. "I caught a name. Tarly something. Do I know you? Should you be here on this ship? This is a Combat K ship, you know, and you can only come on here if you have special clearance..."

"This is *General* Tarly Winters," said Pippa, smiling grimly. "General, as in from Quad-Gal Military. Come down here to make sure we don't fuck up the mission. Ain't that right, Mrs General?"

Without breaking stride, or indeed stopping stuffing himself with CubeSausage, Franco got down on one knee and took her hand. He kissed it, and grinned up through a whiskey beard. "Nice to meet you, I'm sure," he said. "And as you can see, I have carried out my instructions."

"You have indeed," said Tarly, gazing at her hand where Franco had planted a sausage-greased kiss. She watched him get to his feet and swagger across the cockpit. He was reminiscent of something that had just risen from the dead. Or at least, the pit.

He stopped by the doorway, and turned. "Pippa?"

"Yeah, fucker?"

"Did I do good?"

"Amazingly, and loath though I am to bestow you with praise, you did good, Franco. Real good."

"Hey!" He winked. "They don't call me Franco 'Spy-High Get the Info and Get Pissed Into the Bargain' Haggis for nothing, you know, chick." He winked again. And coughed. "I'm, er, going for a long soak in a bath. Now, I don't want any answers right now, you understand, but if either of you two foxy sexy wayward young strumpets would like to join me..." He winked again. "Well. You know where I am."

FRANCO HAD JUST settled into the hot bath water full of bubbles and lavender, giving a long, languorous sigh, when a tremble made him grasp the sides, brow furrowed, eyes narrowed. "What the..."

Alice shrieked through the intercom –

"ATTACK! ATTACK! WE'RE UNDER ATTACK! IMMINENT ATTACK IN FIVE SECONDS BY SOME SNEAKY, STEALTHY, UNDERHAND, BASTARD, MISSILE-TYPE BASTARD..." There came a BANG and a SMASH and a CRASH and the whole world seemed to turn upside down – indeed, *did* turn upside down – as noise screamed through the Fast Attack Hornet. Franco was picked up from his bath, along with the entire tub of water, and thrown at the roof, where something hard slammed into his head, and the world collapsed into a detonation of explosions and shuddering, bright white light.

CHAPTER FIVE
DAMAGE TIME

FRANCO BLINKED FAST, coughed, spat, and turned over, amidst sloshing, bubbling froth and small pieces of metal and emergency foam. He spluttered and gasped, apparently inhaling most of the bathwater. Then the ship spun again, the alarms shrieked and Franco felt the heat of a distant, blossoming fire cloud, an instant before the internal extinguishers hammered into action. Franco crawled along the ceiling amongst the light fittings and stripped-out mechanicals – the Hornet was a war machine, after all – and the screeching alarms which left his ears ringing, until the ship abruptly flipped again and Franco was flung across the bathroom interior like a stranded, flopping fish, hit the wall mirror with a *crack* that sent spider-web ripples across the glass and cut his back to ribbons, then hit the ground hard. Alice managed to gain control of *Metallika,* and stabilised the ship as Franco crawled along a corridor and into the cockpit.

Pippa was seated at the controls, face grim, a long gash over one eye trailing blood down her cheek. Tarly was in a black nightdress, and seemed unharmed. They both glanced at Franco as he crawled in, stark bollock naked, and heaved himself to his feet.

"What the hell happened?" he boomed.

"And more importantly," said Pippa, snapping her gaze back to the screens, "where the hell are your pants?"

"Who needs pants at a time like this?"

"You do," said Pippa. She glanced at him again. "We were hit. Looks like a WormMek Missile."

"They're evil little bastards," said Franco, striding forward. Franco was an expert in all things detonation: explosives, grenades, missiles, HighJ, HighQ, HighX, guns and bombs and things that go *bang* in the night. "*And* they're illegal. Sneaky. Holy missile bollocks! This is bad bad news. Damage?"

"The fucker's taken out the main engines. I'm bringing us in... over there." She pointed through the evening twilight. They'd reached the edge of the vast Pinetop Forest and were now near the vast, rearing mountain peaks known as The Gangers. Franco watched them hove into view, vast and black, each of the hundred or so mountain peaks a direct imitation of its fellow – as if some freak of nature had created a cloned mountain range a billion years previous in readiness for the weird and wacky race that would one day inhabit the lands. He said so.

"They were built," said Tarly, by way of explanation. "This planet was terraformed."

"How big are they?" said Franco, staring at the peaks in awe. He had a thing about mountains. He hated them, and they hated him. It was a wholly mutual arrangement in loathing and disgust (and effort and sweat).

"What's bothering me at the moment," said Pippa through gritted teeth, as she guided the wounded *Metallika* across the mountain threshold and into a cool, silent enclosure of mountain peaks, losing height all the time, "is the proximity of your *cock* to my *face.*"

"Hey," swaggered Franco, "it wouldn't be the first time."

"Only in your dreams."

"Exactly!"

"Get it *away* before I *chop it off.*"

"No need to be like that," mumbled Franco, shifting his stance so that his nakedness was now closer to Tarly than Pippa. Tarly looked him up and down, face impassive, thoughts unreadable at this robust, stocky, overweight and overinsane naked Combat K squaddie just inches from her personage. "S'not my damn fault I was in the middle of a luxurious bath *after finding out all the information*

I'd been sent to find out and thus progressing our mission, and possibly helping to save the entire damn and bloody Quad-Gal from the invasion of the terrible scourge of the junks!" He grinned.

"Report?" said Pippa, inclining her face.

"It's not good," said Alice. "That was a *very* specialised stealth model. AI. Knew how to side-step many of our built-in protection scanners. It crawled up on us at a leisurely pace – so slow, I didn't even see it coming."

"Are we still spaceworthy?"

"Negative. Main engines are totally destroyed, bar a few stranded tatters of matrix coil. We've also completely lost cockpit integrity; we couldn't maintain pressure in the vacuum of space. You'd all be sucked inside out."

"Shit." Pippa rubbed her eyes. "Give me some good news."

"The majority of our weapons are intact. We are still airborne. The bastard didn't hit the fuel stock. If he had, and I'm sure that was his target, then we would have gone *boom* skyhigh, my friend. And just because I'm an AI, doesn't mean I want to die. The gangers are using illegal AIs – the old kamikaze school. Very old minds. Very *strange* minds."

"You think they're readying for war?"

"A major one, yes. I'd say they propose to wipe out the orgs."

A silence flooded the cockpit. Below, mountains, snow and mist rolled by. Mrs Strogger eased into the cockpit, her mechanicals grinding, and sat down. Her old, lined face was sombre. "I heard all of that," she said, and turned to Pippa, then Tarly, then finally Franco. "I must warn my people. I must stave off this attack. I must..."

"First, I must initiate emergency repairs," said Alice. "Then, I will attempt to get messages to your command. Despite being built as a war machine, a terrible destructor, I do not agree with war in principle. And yours is a war that should have ended a million years ago."

"There is too much hate," said Mrs Strogger, softly. "Too many crimes in the past. We cannot forgive. We cannot forget."

Pippa nodded. "I've heard that one before."

Franco coughed, and suddenly feeling self-conscious in front of the old org, said, "Hey, listen, I'm just going to find some, you know, pants." He looked away from Mrs Strogger, whose eyes were fixed on his flaccid genitalia.

"Don't go on my account," said Tarly, suddenly. Franco looked at her and she met his gaze.

"Er," he said.

"Go on!" snapped Pippa. "Get your deviant tackle out of here! I'm sick of seeing your hairy fucking arse."

"Less of the damn hairy, reet?" muttered Franco, and feeling suddenly oppressed by the sheer amount of oestrogen in the room, he sidled sheepishly out of the cockpit.

"You shouldn't be so hard on him," said Tarly, rubbing at her eyes and moistening lips with tongue.

"*What?*" snapped Pippa.

"I agree," said Mrs Strogger. "He might look a bit queer, but he's a good man to have by your side in a firefight. He was fair aggressive against those TankMeks, the little bastad. I was suitably impressed. For a human, you understand. For we all know that in Org Law, when '*the path of the human meatpie is crossed, one should taketh a bite, and yea, sever a limb, for all human meatpies are a dilution of the Machine Principal, and lo! Machine Principal is Law.*'"

Pippa and Tarly stared at Mrs Strogger.

"Tell me again why you're here?" said Pippa.

"I helped rescue Franco. And he's your friend. So you owe me – a ride, at least. Back to my own world."

"The Org States?" said Tarly. "I'm interested. Why do you and the gangers never cease your endless bloody war?"

Mrs Strogger considered this. "It goes back a long way. A long, long way. Once, there was the Holy Machine Heart, which was stolen by the gangers in an attempt to push us from our home planet, Orgworld. This world. A world terraformed by humans when Earth Oppression made the cyborgs illegal. As if we were," she gave a little laugh, "*dangerous* or something."

"I'm a bit hazy," said Pippa, staring out at the mountains beneath. The Hornet, around her, was clunking and hissing, but Alice was doing a good job of keeping her in the air. Pippa didn't feel nervous; she trusted Alice with her life. "What happened on Earth? That was, what, a few hundred thousand years ago?"

"Yes. We were a religion, back then. We believed in a Rise to Heaven by upgrading our bodies using machine parts. This, we believed, was our Evolution. Our Salvation. The only way to reach God was to *become* God. A Machine God. The Earth Authorities saw it different; the varying religions of Earth collectively agreed to see our new upstart religion banished to an offworld colony. So Orgworld was created. Built *for us* in order to get *rid of us*."

"We need to land," said Alice, voice a gentle hum. "I suggest you all strap yourselves in."

"Rough ride?" said Pippa.

"Possibly. And I don't like to take chances."

The Fast Attack Hornet *Metallika* cruised over The Gangers, engines grumbling, and Alice found a high, snowbound plateau. Kicking out the Hornet's landing gear, she settled in a cloud of steam and streaks of molten rock. The engines cooled and clicked, and the titaniumIII ramp unfolded and touched down on rock.

Pippa strode out, followed by Tarly. The two women stood, surveying the vast mountain range as a bloated red moon coloured the sky crimson, and red light cascaded into every hollow, into every crevasse, scattering rubies of crystalline ice across scree slopes and icy, jagged pinnacles.

"What a beautiful place," said Tarly, taking a deep breath. "Can you smell that ice?"

"Yeah. Drink it in, lap it up, *General*. This is a place to fucking *die*. Don't be conned by the pretty colours and lavish pastel shades. This mountain range is as savage as they come; it'll drink you in and puke you out."

Tarly stared hard at Pippa, as an ice breeze rustled her curls. "Has anybody ever told you that you're a maudlin, stroppy and aggressive bitch?"

"All the time," smiled Pippa. "But they usually end up with a sword in the spine."

"I'll make sure I don't turn my back on you," said Tarly, curtly.

"That'd be for the best," said Pippa, turning back into the warmth and security of the Hornet's battered interior.

FRANCO LAY IN all his glorious nakedness on his bunk, staring up at the ceiling and replaying events in his mind. Cloneworld. Clone Terra. Orgs. Gangers. Nechudnazzar. Pubs and Guinness and drunken AI women. Information. 3Core. The Junk Soul. Over by the Slush Pits. An easy gig. An easy steal. Bugger.

Franco coughed, and sat up, and rubbed at his weary eyes. It had been a long mission. But then, they always seemed to be long missions nowadays. Nothing was ever simple anymore. And people – aliens, people, monsters, robots, just *enemies in general* – just didn't seem to give him a break. It was like the entirety of all fucking creation was out to get him. Yes, maybe he was paranoid. After all, being mad (sometimes), and having been incarcerated at The Mount Pleasant Hilltop Institution, the "nice and caring and friendly home for the mentally challenged" for what felt like *decades* and forced to imbibe as many legal, illegal and *immoral* intoxicants as his body could no-doubt endure, all of it *had* to have coloured his perception on reality. But it did feel, sometimes, just occasionally, like Franco Haggis was just a comedy pawn in some omniscient bastard's insane Game of the Galaxy.

Franco sat up. Poured himself a drink. This was wind-down time, post-mission time, although he knew – painfully, clearly, obnoxiously – that pretty soon he'd be out and down in the shit again. And next time, maybe he wouldn't return. Maybe next time he'd end up dead and squished. And what then? What the fuck would happen then? He'd be a footnote on a single page of a pointless history. A squib who never made his mark. A grease stain who'd barely had the grease to leave a grease stain.

Shit. I'm drunk. But then, I earned it, right? I spend my entire life with people telling me I shouldn't get drunk, and then when I bloody do something of worth, of candour, of vigour, of importance, then they bloody stick their oar in once again and moan about how I shouldn't get drunk. Well – why the fuck not? It's not like I've got a wife and kids to look after! Is it?

Wife.

Kids.

Franco thought about Mel. Melanie! She'd been his true love. Love at first sight! Okay, technically she'd been investigating him for non-payment of taxes, but they'd hit it off pretty fast after a humorous incident concerning the chopping of raw chillies and a rather vague fumbling in the vaginal area. But they'd gone from strength to strength, making love, not war, and then... then...

Franco's eyes filled with tears.

Mel, after foolishly dipping of her toe into the realm of illegal biomods at the hands of the Nanotek Corporation, had been turned – along with pretty much the entire population of the planet known as *The City*, or at least, those who had experimented with personal augmentation – *turned into* an eight-foot-tall deviant super-soldier. One who was a mass of pus and drooling saliva. One who was a little bit necrotic. One who was, to all intents and purposes, a *zombie*. Shit followed shit, and after the mission, and the rescue of The City by the dutiful Combat K squad, it emerged that Mel's affliction was a *special case*. She was a one-way transmogrification. There was no backtracking on her zombification. She was undead. Undead as an undodo. And proud of it.

More shit followed more shit, and after a bizarre sequence of arguments, Mel had filed for divorce. Franco had been *divorced* by an eight foot mutated super-soldier! This still rankled pretty deep with him. He was filled with bitterness. Annoyance. Disbelief! After all, he'd been the one brave enough to go down on a jellied pussy!

Now, however, it brought a tear to Franco's eye. In those long and lovely moments after making love (before she became a zombie), when he and Mel had been curled together, a tangle of pale limbs, their hearts beating as one, they had planned out their future. And their future had contained children. Franco, goddammit, wanted children! He lusted after having his own family! Not just something to secure his genetic longevity, but something to drag him away from the demands of... War.

Franco was getting old.

Franco was getting tired.

Franco wanted babies!

A bit drunk now, he stood, and swayed, and at least had the foresight to pull on his knife-cut combat shorts. He staggered out into the corridor. All was quiet. He staggered down the corridor. He staggered out into the cockpit area. He leered around myopically.

"Hello?" he said, slurring his words a little. *Damn, that whiskey was strong. Or maybe it was just the three pints he'd drunk? Drank? Dunk? But then, with a fine Japachinese Single Malt, it'd be rude not too, right?*

"Hello."

The pilot's chair swivelled, revealing General Tarly Winters, *sans* uniform. She wore a long black nightdress and her red curls were scraped back. Her china skin glowed under the ship's ambient lighting.

Franco blinked, and licked his lips, and thought, *play it cool, remember, you want some babies. Kids! A family! A family unit with which to play on the beaches, using buckets and spades. Hot damn, I WANT to change shitty nappies! I WANT to be squawked at through the night, precluding any sort of sleep for at least four years! I WANT to be puked upon just after putting on my finest black suit! Hell, I WANT aggravation for every waking moment, because, because, BECAUSE, with all the hard shit, all the tough shit, all the impossible shit, there'll be a million tiny perfect moments which is what life is all about.*

In a glimmer of perfect clarity, Franco realised he no longer wanted to be alone.

"Come and sit down," said Tarly, and patted the pilot's chair next to her. "Come on. I want a good ol' chat with you, Franco Haggis. Because – you are a conundrum to me. I come here ready to fire your ass from a fucking rocket, bust you down from Combat K on a list of severe competency issues so long you could have used it as a toilet roll. But you got the job done, didn't you?"

"I always get the job done," said Franco, and took a seat next to Tarly. He eyed her up and down, crafty-like, a technique most men employed. Only Franco wasn't that crafty. The whiskey made an idiot of his brain; made him grin like a Cheshire Cat.

"I've looked at your QGM sheet."

"Yeah, and full of shit that's likely to be. As full of shit as a pint of SCROTUM'S OLD TODGE CLOGGER – FINEST SINGLE MALT."

"Not so." Tarly tilted her head to one side. "It made for some... *interesting* reading. Made for some hilarious damn reading, if I'm brutally honest. I mean, Melanie *divorced you*? How the hell did that happen?"

"Hey, laugh it up. The rest of the fucking army have."

"I'm not laughing, Franco. I think she just didn't understand and appreciate your masculine side. I mean, any more macho and you'd be joining The Village People, right?"

Franco eyed Tarly warily. "Okay. Come on. What's the game?"

"No game." Tarly smiled. "I'm just... intrigued. You intrigue me. Believe me, I've waded through the paperwork of entire *battalions*. You, however, stand out as a true conundrum. As you say, you're wild and weird, but strangely, you always seem to get the job done."

"I just am what I am. There's no secrets here. What you see is what you get. I'm exactly what it says on the tin."

"And what's that?"

Franco shrugged, and hit the InfinityChef™, which obediently delivered him a pint of frothing Guinness, complete with sculpted shamrock atop the creamy head. Franco sipped it, giving him a moustache atop his goatee beard. He stroked his beard thoughtfully. "You're the one with the qualifications, General. You tell me. After all, I'm just a grunt."

"No. You're Combat K," she said, and untied her long curls, allowing them to tumble across her shoulders. "But anyway. Let's talk about something else."

"Such as?"

"Keenan. Tell me about Keenan."

"Aah, so that's the game you're playing," said Pippa, leaning against the doorway. In her hand was a battered Techrim 11mm, which had once belonged to Zak Keenan – Pippa's lover, and Pippa's nemesis. "Here to sniff out what happened down on Sick World, are you?"

"I read the reports," said Tarly, softly.

"But you don't believe them," smiled Pippa. She played distractedly with the gun. "Well, General. What I'd say to you is, what we wrote in the QGM Post-Mission reports is exactly what actually happened. Take it or leave it. There are no other answers to give."

"And that's your reply?" said Tarly, shifting her gaze to Franco. He gazed into her beautiful eyes. He licked his lips nervously. Here was a dangerous woman. Here was the most dangerous woman of all: one he desperately wanted... which pretty much summed up anything that walked or crawled.

"Err..."

"Yes, it is," snapped Pippa. "Now I'd ask you for

a bit of privacy. Me and Franco need to talk."

"No problem," smiled Tarly, standing, and for a moment showing a tantalising amount of pale thigh. Then her black nightdress fell into place, and Franco swallowed, and somehow the fact she was fully covered was a million times worse. She moved to the doorway.

Franco coughed, an over-deep, masculine, macho cough. "Er, yes, well, thanks for the chat Tarly, we'll be seeing you around."

"Yes, Franco," she smiled. "I'll be seeing you around."

She disappeared and Franco gawped, and then went cross-eyed as the barrel of the Techrim 11mm touched the end of his nose. "I ain't even fucking with you," snarled Pippa, "when I say that if you speak about Keenan, even one fucking word, I'll shove this gun so far up your arse you'll be coughing bullets."

"Yeah, and I'm sure Keenan would like you to arse-render me with his favourite 11mm, for sure."

"It's just a warning, Franco. Just a warning."

"I don't *need* your warnings. I have my own in-built warning systems. Like, er, whiskey. And sausage. And, er, using my brain. I *can* use my brain you know! I know you think I can't use my brain, and it's something that's overrated, but I can use my brain when I need to use my brain!"

"Quite," said Pippa, removing the gun and gazing down at it, lovingly.

Franco drank his pint. In one. And smacked his lips. "You miss him. Don't you?"

"I miss him," nodded Pippa, and there were tears on her cheeks. "When he stepped into... when he was *absorbed* into VOLOS, in return for the information leading us to the Junkala Soul – well, I know what he was thinking, I know he felt guilt, like the weight of a planet resting across his shoulders. He wanted to see his dead girls again, travel beyond the realms of *life* and seek them out. See if there was something beyond."

"He didn't die," said Franco, softly, reaching out and placing his hand over Pippa's.

"Yes, but he isn't fucking *here!*" she snapped. "It was a one-way journey. He gave away his body, his flesh, his soul – to that *thing*. That eternal creature! Well, I'm telling you, Franco, one day I'm going back for him – when all this, all this *shit* is over and done with. One day I'm going back to VOLOS and he'll given me Keenan back, or I'll destroy the whole fucking planet trying."

Franco thought about this. Pippa's hand was warm under his. Comforting. It felt good to have human contact again. Felt good to have a *connection* with a woman.

"He did what he did for the greater good. And I also think he'd had enough, you know? Enough of the struggle. Enough of the fight. These are hard times we're living through, Pippa. Savage times."

"I know that, Franco." She softened. Then she

hardened again. "But I swear, if you tell that Tarly bitch *anything...*"

"Hey! Trust me!" Franco grinned. "They don't call me Franco 'Perfect Trust' Haggis for nothing, you know!"

"They don't call you that at all." She grinned at him. "We've been through some shit together, haven't we?"

"Sure, sweetie." He squeezed her hand.

"Fancy a walk outside?"

"In the mountain air? Don't mind if I do."

"I'd put some clothes on first, though. Might be a bit chilly."

"Ha! Yes!"

Five minutes later, they trotted down the ramp. Night had fallen, and three moons sat at varying degrees on the horizon, two white and one blue. Blue light sparkled on snow, and a cold wind whipped down from the peaks as Franco and Pippa walked across the barren rocks, and stood staring down from the edge of the plateau.

"It's beautiful," said Pippa.

"Bloody freezing, is what it is," said Franco, ice riming his beard.

"Come here." Pippa put her arms around his waist, and they stood for a while, hugging, sharing their body-heat. Moonlight spread in mercury pools across the vast landscapes beyond, and below, stretching for mile after mile, reared mountains and rocky slopes, towering crags and sheer chimneys.

Pippa and Franco watched The Gangers under pastel moonlight, and it was rarely that either had seen anything quite so beautiful.

"Much as I love you pressing against me," said Franco after a while, "I think I'm in serious jeopardy of my nuts retreating so far into my body they'll be Missing in Action. Or No Action, as the case may be."

Pippa turned. "Gods, look at the ship! That WormMek Missile sure made a mess of it."

They stared for a while at the damaged rear end of the Fast Attack Hornet. Huge struts emerged from the ship's arse, and the whole rearward bulk was a jagged, shattered mess filled with molten scars and scorch marks. As Pippa and Franco watched, the tiny PopBot repair modules buzzed and skimmed about, welding and sparking, disappearing into the long dark spaces and reappearing in bright flashes, and carrying out other essential repairs. It was like watching a hive of buzzbees, or a nest of mutt ants.

"Busy busy busy," said Pippa, lips compressed.

"I'm going in for a whiskey. You joining me?"

Pippa looked up at him. She smiled, a genuine smile of warmth and friendship. "Yeah, Franco. Don't mind if I do."

Pippa followed Franco up the ramp, and as he disappeared into the gloom of the hold she stopped, and turned, and gazed out over Clone Terra, over Cloneworld. In the distance, artillery boomed. Tiny flickers, like fireworks, but she knew from experience they were tracer and explosions. People fighting. People dying. Dying, massacred in the mud. She shook her head, lips compressed, and followed Franco into the darkness.

IT WAS LATER. Much later.

Both Franco and Pippa were draped over SlumCouches, which moulded to your shape to mimic every whim and desire. Drinks were in hand, lips were wet, eyes were glazed. Mrs Strogger had popped in for a chat after her oil bath, and was looking... *younger*. Still a cyborg, metal machine parts gleaming and making both Pippa and Franco feel just that *little bit uneasy* – conscious that with machine elegance, she could reach out and rip off their heads – but they tried not to let that worry them. After all, she had helped rescue Franco. And they still had the resources to fulfil their half of the bargain of returning her to The Org States.

Provided Alice managed to fix the Hornet. It didn't bear thinking about what would happen if she couldn't...

"You know what?" laughed Pippa, swirling her glass around, "I still can't believe you did it."

"Did what?"

"That mission. I thought you'd, y'know," she hiccupped, "screw it up."

"Hey! I might have an odd way of going about things, but they don't call me Franco 'Gets The Job Done' Haggis for nothing, reet? I said, reet?"

"Ha! I suppose they don't."

They sat in the gloom, with only purple Eezeelights flickering through the air, supposedly calming their collective mood. Franco watched Pippa fill her glass for a fifth time, then looked at his own. It was still full. For once in her life, Pippa was out-drinking him. He growled something, and decked the whiskey in one. "Can't be having that," he muttered, and held out his glass for a refill. Pippa filled it, then spilled some over the edge and across his combat shorts.

"Ach, Pippa, you sloppy lass."

"Your groin was in the way." She giggled.

"You're drunk."

"Wish I was," she said, and waved her glass around, catching the purple lighting. "Have you ever been in love?"

"Lots of times," grinned Franco. "With all sorts of laydees."

"No, no, properly, you dickhead, have you properly been in love? You know, where somebody expands to fill your life, fill your world, and you become a lost, whimpering puppy, willing to do anything for them. You lose your edge, er, you lose your fire. You lose all ability to think straight, or to follow your own senses; it's like drowning in honey and time no longer has any real meaning. Do you know what I'm talking about?"

"Yeah, Pippa. I know exactly what you mean."

"I miss Keenan, Franco."

"I miss him as well, sweetie."

"Do you know what today is?"

"Go on?"

"You mean you don't know?"

"Surprise me."

"It's the anniversary of the deaths of Keenan's wife and girls, Rachel and Ally."

Franco chewed his lower lip, and wondered how best to progress. This was not easy territory. This was territory likely to get him shot. Or skewered. Or both. Best proceed with caution. Best keep big flapping mouth shut.

"I didn't know that," said Franco, and rubbed at his eyes. He watched Pippa refill her glass. Again.

"I killed them! Apparently. Did you know *that?*" She gestured hard with her glass, and whiskey slopped down her black shirt and combats.

"I know you were implicated," said Franco, carefully. "You said you'd been wrongly accused. You had no recollection of that night."

"But Keenan fucking *believed it!*" she hissed. Then laughed. "He almost killed me over that one. Several times. Tried his damned best. He hunted me for a while, did you know that? Of course you know that. You probably helped the motherfucker..."

"Pippa, I never hunted you," said Franco, softly. He sat up. Reached forward. Touched her hand.

"Get off!" she hissed, her hand snapping back, a blur. "What, you after another cheap fuck?"

"No," said Franco, meeting her gaze. "I'm here to listen. And to understand."

Pippa brooded for a while, head hung low, then looked up, face lost in shadows, eyes hooded and dark, probably one of the most menacing and dangerous creatures Franco had ever seen.

"It was a clone. Apparently." She laughed. It was a bitter laugh.

Franco nodded. Said nothing. He watched for a while as Pippa finished her drink, a range of emotions crossing her face like clouds across a stormy sky. Then, she slipped eerily into the ooze of unconsciousness.

Franco sipped his drink, but no amount of alcohol could touch him.

He thought about Keenan.

He thought about Pippa.

He thought about the junks, and their spreading evil and violence and how they, *he*, might have a chance at stopping them. By reverting them into something other than a race of psychopathic, warmongering aliens.

Franco finished his drink, and stood, and stretched. He placed his glass down with a *clack*. "Come on, little lady," he said, and stooping, picked Pippa up in his arms. She was surprisingly light, considering her strength and iron, and Franco carried her down the corridor. Her hair was in his face, and it smelt good. He shifted to the right, and her skin glowed, and this, too smelt good.

"*No*," he growled, and lifted his head, and carried Pippa's lithe form through to her sleeping quarters.

The door closed behind him with a tiny *click*. He laid her out on the bed. There. Beautiful. A goddess.

Franco sat down next to her, and gazed at her face.

In sleep, she was younger. Carefree. The lines of stress and iron were gone. She looked like... looked like any ordinary beautiful young woman. Franco traced a line down her face with his finger, and sighed, recognising how truly complex she was – inside her skull. An emotional wreckage. A social misfit. A psychological conundrum.

"Mmm?" she said, and her eyes fluttered open. "Franco?"

"I put you to bed."

"Thank you."

"My pleasure."

"Come here."

"Now wait a minute..."

She grabbed him, stronger than him, and pulled him down into a kiss. A long, lingering, gentle kiss. Then she rolled over, and started to snore gently, fingers twisting through the thin silk sheets.

Franco got up, stepped out into the corridor, and closed the door behind him – with an act of iron will.

"Hot damn and bloody bollocks," he muttered, shaking his head. "I need another drink!"

FRANCO AWOKE, GROGGY in his airblankets, and yawned a long, long yawn. *Gods, that feels good.*

Good to sleep so deep. Good to have good dreams. Good to feel so... fresh! He thought back to the previous night. To Pippa. And whereas one side of him, an old side of him, would have said *shit that's an opportunity for love wasted, and a* REAL *chance to piss Pippa right the hell off,* another side of him, a new, mature side of him, thought, *it was the right thing to do, a good thing to do. She's damaged goods. She needs some loving. Not Franco Big Boy loving, but* REAL *loving...*

Franco sat up, and stretched, and froze.

Pippa sat cross-legged on the end of his bed, one of her yukana swords across her lap. Her face was down, eyes hidden, body tense. Franco was instantly fired with warning screams. This was not a good situation. This screamed *murder...*

"Er..." he said.

"What happened?"

"Nothing."

"Liar."

"I most certainly *am not,*" snapped Franco.

"You could have done anything."

"I could have done anything, yes, and chose to do *nothing,* ya idiot. You got drunk. You talked about Keenan. I put you to bed. End of. And if you don't believe me, go ahead, cut my fucking head off. I'm sick of being the underdog. Sick of being labelled unfairly. I am" – he puffed out his chest, quite a feat from a sitting position in bed – "a newly baptised *honourable man!*"

"So *nothing* happened?"

"Well, you kissed me."

There was a *hiss* as yukana cleared scabbard. Pippa's head came up. Her eyes were glowing.

"And that was it. I love you, Pippa. And yeah, giving you a good old Franco-time is very high at the top of my sexual fantasy wish-list, but believe me, taking it like that – no, not even an option, love."

"Bullshit."

"Why?"

"Because... because I fucking *know* you, Franco! I know what a sexual deviant you are! I know the places you've been, the things you've done, the *aliens* you've done..."

Franco met Pippa's gaze. He smiled. A warm, friendly smile. "Trust me," he said, simply.

Pippa suddenly frowned and leapt from the bed, holding up her hand. "Something's wrong."

"Wrong?"

"Outside."

Pippa padded through the ship, Franco following in his underpants. Pippa moved down the ramp, out into a fresh, crisp, wild morning breeze blowing through the mountains and carrying the smell of snow.

Franco stood at the top of the ramp, bemused, as Pippa moved onto the rock plateau and stood, sword at the ready, second yukana sheathed on her back. She was rigid, poised, readying for combat.

"Is she feeling alright?" he muttered.

"My analysis is that she has a bad hangover," said Alice, voice soothing.

Tarly appeared behind Franco, yawning, red curls tousled, skin sleep-warmed. She looked at Pippa, then to Franco. "Something I need to know about, soldier?"

"Er, Pippa going slightly mad? Stuff this, you fancy joining me for a coffee?" But even as he spoke, there came a tiny noise, a scattering of loose stones over icy rock, and a figure climbed into view. It was tall, lithe, clad completely in black. He, or she, wore a mask covering the entire face, and like Pippa, carried two yukana swords.

"Alice?" said Tarly. "Early warning signals are important, yes?"

"This creature is not registering on any scanners."

"Impossible," snapped Tarly.

"Fact," said Alice.

Franco sighed and cracked his knuckles. "I'll go and get my guns, shall I?" he said. "It's always the bloody same. You're just about to have breakfast and sexy chit-chat with a beautiful, scantily clad *General of Quad-Gal Military,* when some baddie comes along to ruins your morning's free juicy entertainment."

Pippa turned. "No! This is my fight."

"How'd you reckon that one, love?" frowned Franco.

"I knew she was coming."

"What? By telekinesis?"

"Just call it womanly intuition," she smiled, as the black-clad figure, breath streaming like dragon smoke, leapt forward with sword raised, bringing it slamming down – to be met by Pippa's yukana blade. A cold brittle *shring* rang out across the plateau. It sounded like shattering ice.

Both figures took a step back, studying one another, then stepped in fast to deliver a blur of sword strokes, one-two-three; both figures twirled, swords flashing in the early morning sunlight, then connected again in a grinding shower of sparks.

They stepped back. They moved slowly, in a circle, pacing like wild cats.

"They're weighing each other up," said Tarly, softly.

"I'll go and get my guns," repeated Franco.

"Pippa will be pissed."

"She'll have to be pissed, then. I'll not stand here and watch her massacred." He disappeared.

Pippa attacked, but the silent, black-clad stranger defended fast. Swords flickered out, ringing cold and sharp, and more strikes echoed as Pippa defended the stranger's counterattack, and both pulled back. They paced again, in a circle, engaged again, withdrew. Sunlight gleamed on blackened steel.

"Who are you?" said Pippa.

No answer.

They paced. The stranger attacked, and their swords clashed. Pippa's blade glittered like a striking snake. The stranger parried and counter-attacked in perfect balance.

Pippa was matched.

Franco reappeared. He now wore shorts, and carried two Kekra quad-barrelled machine pistols.

"Stand back, Pippa! I'll fill this fucker full of lead!"

"No!" said Pippa, without turning. "She's mine."

"She?"

Pippa was gleaming with sweat. She charged, their swords clashed, and the two warriors pushed in close, face to face. "Take off your mask, bitch," Pippa snarled.

"Fuck you," growled a harsh female voice, muffled by the mask.

They broke apart, kicking away from one another and performing somersaults. They landed neatly, twirling swords, and Pippa withdrew her second blade, hissing, from its scabbard. As if in mirror image, the female assailant also drew a second blade.

Franco aimed down his Kekra, and fired off a shot. There was a *ping* as it skimmed past the black-clad attacker's ear and ricocheted from a rock. The attacker did not flinch. Pippa turned and scowled at Franco.

"Do that again, and *you'll* be tasting my blade."

Franco shrugged, and grinned over at Tarly. "Bit feisty, is our little Pippa, hey?"

"So I see."

"Go on."

"What?"

"You're supposed to say, *it'll be going in my report*. Or something equally anal. That's what all you senior management types are like. I've seen it all before, so I have. You're the kind of bureaucratic motherfucker who put the *urea* into bureaucracy. As in, you're a product of piss, mate."

"Harsh, Franco."

"You boss-types bring it out in me."

The four yukanas clashed across the plateau, as Pippa and the attacker moved backwards and forwards, swordblades a blur of perpetual movement. They glittered, like lightning from storm-dark clouds. They spun and wove patterns of black and silver. The skill on show was incredible. It couldn't be long before somebody grew tired, and made a...

Mistake.

Both women stopped, Pippa pouring with sweat. She had slowed, weariness showing with every movement. But hatred burned in her face; hatred and frustration. She could find no way through her enemy's guard. It was too good. Too neat. Too *perfect.*

"Show yourself, coward!"

"Why?"

"I need a name, for when I skewer your arse with my blade!"

The attacker reached up and whipped off her mask. Her brown bobbed hair tumbled free. Her green eyes glared at Pippa – from a face that was her exact clone.

Pippa stared, mouth open...

As her ganger attacked.

Franco leapt down the ramp, Kekras in his tattooed fists. He was scowling, blinking, looking from one Pippa to the other. They were the same, perfectly matched, and their sword strikes rang through the early morning chill as Pippa fought *herself*. Every strike she made was anticipated, every block a narrow escape. But, despite appearances, they weren't evenly matched; her clone had the upper hand – because she *knew*.

"Let me kill it," shouted Franco.

"No!" hissed Pippa through gritted teeth. Nearly frenzied, both blades a dazzling blur, sweat pouring down her face and through lank hair, Pippa forced her clone backwards. The squeals of their clashing swords echoed through the stillness. They were near the cliff edge, now, still battling, blades glowing in the early morning sunlight. Pippa blocked, sent a low, horizontal cut slashing through thin air, then launched herself, both boots hitting her own mirrored face. Her ganger grabbed Pippa's legs and staggered back, and both women flipped from the ledge and disappeared...

The plateau was left in a sudden, icy silence.

"No!" yelled Franco, and leapt forward – as behind him a huge, droning gunship rose from a ravine, rotors slamming, engines pounding. Its miniguns roared, and heavy-duty bullets slammed into the Hornet, kicking up sparks and violence and chaos. In Franco's earlobe comms, Alice spoke calmly:

"We need to leave. Now."

Franco skidded to a halt, gazing at where Pippa had fallen, then back to the gunship, guns roaring, lines of bullets kicking up towards him. He could see a pilot, clad all in black. Franco growled something incomprehensible, face stubborn, eyes hooded, and watched impassively as twin lines of churning rock sped past him to either side – missing him by a miracle – and lifted both his Kekra quad-barrel machine pistols to send a volley of bullets slam into the gunship's cockpit glass, cracking it...

"Come on!" screamed Tarly from the ramp. The Hornet's engines were whining, and only Franco was stopping Alice kicking them into the air and turning missiles on the ganger's gunship...

"What about Pippa?"

"We'll find her! COME ON!"

Franco sprinted for the Hornet, and even as he scrambled up the landing ramp it was folding inwards, and Alice leapt the Hornet into the sky, turned its missiles on the ganger's gunship – and paused in horror, as her computer scanners screamed at her in frantic disarray. In raw digital *panic*...

The gangers hadn't just brought their own gunship, something Alice had thought not only illegal under QGM Law, but *impossible* thanks to the countless anti-aircraft GASGAM gunbots that patrolled Cloneworld on a mission of aerial destruction... no, they'd also brought their own *gunbots*, two of them, huge sleek machines manufactured by QGM and deadly to anything which took their fancy. In an instant, Alice saw their danger – the gunbots were rogues, they'd been *hacked* by the gangers. Cracked and hacked and corrupted. Now, the gangers held all the aces...

In a flicker of binary she made a decision, and hurled the Fast Attack Hornet skywards in a glittering beam of insane acceleration, as below, the gunbots launched directional missiles which screamed after them, snapping at the Hornet's heels like a pack of hungry metal wolves...

Franco, tossed about the cabin like a pea in a bucket, watched in horror as Cloneworld disappeared, faded, in a flicker of dissolving colour.

CHAPTER SIX

THE GANGERS

PIPPA FELL, HIT rock and ice with a grunt that knocked both yukana swords from her grasp, then slid on the near-vertical rocky face, which tore at her clothing, tore her flesh and gave a her a vast view leading five thousand feet straight *down...*

The sight welled up and punched her in the face, the mouth, the throat, the heart – it filled her like a detonation, and a scream bubbled in her throat as her gloved hands and boots scrabbled to find purchase, and she slid with acceleration towards a vast, yawning abyss of black rock and deep, panoramic ravines of snow and welcoming death...

Pippa hit the rim and sailed out over the edge, and something hard clamped around her wrist and slammed her against the vertical rock wall. Pippa hung over the sheer drop, panting, blood and sweat in her hair, in her eyes. Slowly, she groaned, and looked up – into her own face.

Pippa had been saved by her own ganger. The clone stared down at her, a wicked, mocking smile on her features, her iron grip holding Pippa's wrist, fingers leaving deep imprints.

"Got you," she said.

"Why save me, *bitch,* when you were sent to kill me?"

"Who said I was sent to kill you?"

Pippa considered this for a while. The ganger hauled her up and sat her on the rim of the ledge – of the *world,* which opened up beneath and before them. They stared out over a circle valley, below and beneath and *beyond*; a vast, circular pit lined with towering monoliths. The Gangers, huge black teeth, vast and brutal and pointing, mocking, to the gods.

A cold brittle wind whipped Pippa's hair in her face. "Shit," she said, and spat, looking at her ripped gloves. Pain battered her, beating at her arms and legs, hips and back, chest and neck and head. It felt as though somebody was dancing on her. It felt as though the whole fucking world had given her a right hook.

"Good to be alive, yes?" said the clone, and Pippa saw her cradling her yukana swords. *Better than me,* she thought bitterly. *The bitch is better than me.*

"Pass me a sword, I'll show you how good it is."

The clone laughed with genuine humour, and

nodded out at the vast savage world beyond. "That's the way you want."

"What do you mean?"

"The Slush Pits. That's where you're going, right? To the Pod Vault. After the 3Core."

Pippa said nothing, face remaining blank. But her eyes gleamed. How could she know? How could *it* know? Where was the fucking chink in their armour? How had their plans possibly been leaked? Tarly? The old ragged org, Mrs Strogger? Franco's flapping mouth after a pint of whiskey?

"Come on, up you get."

"Oh yeah? Like I cooperate that easy."

The yukana tip touched Pippa's throat. "It was a demand, not a request."

"That's more like it, bitch."

Pippa stood, and stretched, and her body screamed at her, but as the cold wind whipped down from vast mountain peaks, and her eyes watered, and she breathed deep the crisp snow and fresh air from vast lonely places, by all the gods it *did* feel good to be alive. Pippa looked up, and back, but there was no sign of the ganger gunship.

As if reading her mind, her clone said, "It's too wild. We'll rendezvous down in the valley. I hope you're good at climbing."

"I'm good at killing," snarled Pippa, some of the fire coming back into her belly and destroying the mountain euphoria. "Want to see me try?"

The clone seemed to sigh. "I don't want to kill you,

Pippa. Truly I don't. But you will come with me, or I'll chop off a limb at a time. Ever seen somebody climb with only one arm? Me neither, but I think I'm interested enough to experiment."

Pippa gave a small nod. "Down?"

"That way. The narrow path."

Pippa led the way, shivering now despite her WarSuit. It intrigued her to see her clone wore similar attire – but with subtle differences. As if the gangers had copied the WarSuit, as well as Pippa's genetic substance. Pippa gave a grimace. The bastards. The cheating, cheating bastards.

She picked her way carefully down the narrow, icy trail. It was mostly bare rock, and sometimes short heather, or harsh winter grass, clung to the steep slopes. Boulders rested treacherously on either side. The wind snapped at her like an angry little dog. A yakker snakker.

Pippa's clone followed close behind, one yukana drawn, one sheathed against her back. She did not speak. Pippa heard her breathing occasionally – it matched her own. The same beat, same rhythm, same heart, same lungs, same veins and blood. Damn. Shit. And if she, Pippa, had been given a mission to hunt down her clone and bring her in, would she?

Damn right she would.

Would she have compassion?

No.

Would she be willing to skewer the bitch like a fish on a spear?

Oh, yes.

"What made the path?"

"What do you mean?"

Pippa shrugged, and glanced back. For a moment, vertigo took her in its fist and threatened to toss her down the mountain. She swallowed and breathed cold air deeply. "It's a simple enough question. The path. The trail. I don't see any happy ramblers in the vicinity; can't imagine the gangers going in for a whole lot of active mountain pursuits."

"You're right. Keep moving, bitch, we have a lot of ground to cover."

"I'm right?"

"Gangers don't come here. It's forbidden by the Mistress."

"Why forbidden?"

"You have a lot of questions."

"Just trying to soak up my environment."

"All the better to escape with, eh?" But she was smiling. "That's what I like to see. Never lose that fighting spirit. Never lose the will to escape. You're certainly a girl after my own... genetics."

"So answer the question."

The clone shrugged. "I know on paper, Cloneworld – or at least, Clone Terra – may look like a pretty contained and understandable world, society, infrastructure, whatever. But it's had a turbulent history. There's been a lot of *experimentation*. A lot of genetic manipulation. And sometimes, things can go wrong."

"How wrong?"

"Pretty bad wrong. It's like the Slush Pits, the place you'd so painfully like to visit. That's a bad place, Pippa, old girl. And if you ever did escape my nasty evil clutches, then I'd advise against seeing it. Some things are best left to the imagination. Or at least, best left *dead.*"

"What's that got to do with the mountains? And this trail?"

"Over the years, the decades, *the centuries,* certain *things,* creatures, were bred, and grown, and manipulated. You can do a lot of shit with genetic malfunction if you try. And believe me, in this endless fucking war between orgs and gangers, the gangers have been trying their best to gain the upper hand. They bred soldiers. *Monsters.* Only some escaped from the Slush Pits. Some escaped into the mountains. And over the years, they interbred. They changed and warped and deviated."

Pippa looked about sharply as, distantly, over some lonely dark peak, a howl went up, a high piercing note which held for what seemed an eternity, then slowly dropped in volume and pitch, trailing off into a bestial, gurgling growl.

"We call them Pit Creatures, or just *critters.*"

The clone had stopped, catching her breath, and Pippa turned to her. The trail was so narrow she felt herself lean unconsciously *forward,* towards the side of the mountain, as if willing herself to cling to the rock, allowing the mountain to wrap her in an embrace to ward off falling. She reached out and touched a boulder to steady herself. Damn that vertigo.

"These critters friendly, are they?"

"What do you reckon?"

Pippa laughed, a brittle crack of ice. "Give me a sword."

"No."

"You'd leave me defenceless?"

"A woman like you is never defenceless, *sweetie.*"

"Give me a *sword*, dammit!"

"The only sword you'll take from me is one you pry from my twitching, dead fingers. And if you look inside yourself, look into your heart, you'll see that's the same answer you would give me if this were reversed. We're the same, Pippa. The same person. The same code. And you can't fucking argue with genetics."

Pippa stared at her. "Who *are* you?"

"I am you, and you are me."

"When were you cloned?"

The cloned Pippa grinned, and her eyes sparkled with humour, with mischievousness, and with a bright, deadly intelligence. "That sort of thing is classified. Not available for open public consumption."

"Tell me, damn you!"

"Not today. Now let's get moving. If I'm not mistaken, that was a call to hunt."

"So they're on our trail?"

"Hmm," said the clone, and looked across the mountains, then down, where a huge sections of scree slopes and chimneys greeted her wary gaze. "I really wish you hadn't kicked us over that ledge. We would be having so much more fun right now."

"I really wish you hadn't been born," muttered Pippa.

"I could say the same to you. This world isn't big enough for two Pippas."

"I can soon sort that problem out," smiled Pippa. "Now, are we going to chatter all day like a couple of inbred footballers' wives, and get eaten by these genetic mutations? Or shall we keep moving?"

"That way."

Pippa gave a nod, and between the icy rocks of The Gangers they continued to climb.

IT WAS HOURS later. Pippa was bone weary. A cold sun hung in the sky, filtered by the heavy iron storm clouds. The wind howled mournfully through rocks, and it seemed to Pippa they were no closer to their destination in the vast bowl valley below than when they had started. She looked at the sky, trying to gauge the weather and time of day, but for too long had she been reliant on tech kit. Her PAD was back in the Hornet, along with nearly everything else useful she owned, including most of her weapon stash. Now, without even her yukana swords, she felt naked. Naked and vulnerable.

She reached a rocky lip, and crouched cautiously, fingers gripping the edge. She peered over. Black rocks tumbled away into a narrow chimney, down which maybe two people could climb side by side. It looked treacherous and slippery. And even as she watched, a mist had curled in from nowhere, obscuring the valley below and filling the world from the bottom up.

"I hope you're good at navigating," she said, glancing up to her clone.

The ganger shrugged. "We're going straight down. One way or another."

"How long will it take?"

"Too long."

"Will we reach the bottom before dark?"

The clone hesitated. Pippa saw the flicker of fear cross her eyes, then it was gone, replaced by her own stubborn steel. "No. We'll have to spend a night in the mountains."

"With those *critter* things?"

"If we're lucky, they won't pick up our trail. The mist helps. Damps everything down. Disguises our scents."

"So they hunt us by *scent?*"

The clone nodded. "There's a lot gone into the genetic melting-pot. I think, somewhere, one of them has some dog in it."

"Great," muttered Pippa, and leant forward, easing herself over the rim. It was tempting to try the climb backwards, but she knew from experience you went nowhere fast. You had to swallow down your fear, look the world in the eye, lean back into the rocks and climb down facing *out*. Only then could you see what the hell you were doing. Only then could you make some *time*.

It was steep. No, thought Pippa. It was *steep*.

She edged forward with care, the rocks seeming to envelop her. It went darker as she shifted down the narrow channel in the mountainside. The mist didn't help. It crept up further, thicker now, and disguised the ground far below; disguised the *fall*.

"Nice and easy," muttered her clone. "There's no rush, girl."

Pippa grinned. Good. Her clone was feeling the same icy, creeping dread. Not just fear of the grave, but fear of falling in this vast, lonely, endless space, and never being found. Nobody to bury you. Nobody to mourn over you. Just an eternity trapped, wedged, rotting between icy rocks – entombed by the merciless mountains.

They climbed on. It grew yet darker. Shadows crept forward, mocking them. The rocks were cold, even through gloves, and occasionally Pippa's boots slipped, making her heart climb up her throat and sit in her mouth, pumping her with raw fear. She moved on down, carefully finding footholds, inching her fingers into spaces, contorting herself into peculiar shapes she just knew, *knew* Franco would make some wisecrack about if he'd been there. The dirty but lovable little pervert. Franco. The Hornet. Shit!

If she could get to the valley below, that would be the most likely place for a pickup, a rescue attempt...

She'd have to be ready to fight.

She glanced up, at where her clone was carefully picking her way down the rocky chimney. Then she blinked, as from a narrow dark cave to one side she saw... *something*. Something she herself had missed until now that she was beneath it. From the cave emerged a long, blood-red snout, like a dog's snout, only without fur and without skin, and her mouth went narrow and dry, and her tongue limp, and she wanted to cry out a warning, but the words stuck in her throat, and something long and thin crept out behind the snout, as the body emerged, and it was like an octopus, big and fat and white and bloated, only with four thick tentacles instead of eight, and from its muscular body emerged the dog's neck and bloody snout and it turned, and its dark black orbs fastened on her, and she felt a thrill of terror course through her body like liquid nitrogen injected straight through her veins. It growled, tentacles whipping, and leapt even as her clone heard the sounds and reached fast for her yukana... but the critter, the creature, the genetic *mutation* hit the clone fast, tentacles wrapping tight around her and making her scream as she lost her footing, and the two entwined creatures slipped, cannoning down the narrow rocky chute and *into* a shocked Pippa, who got a bloated white tentacle slapped in her face, leaving a thick smear of clear jelly. Pippa felt, *heard*, jaws snapping at her face and realised her eyes were shut. She'd slipped down, banged her back on rocks and was stunned. Her eyes clicked open. The dog-face was snapping at her, inches away, whilst the cloned Pippa wrestled with three of the thick tentacles and the bloated body pulsed with the heavy rhythm of its thick, squirming muscles.

What is it? screamed her mind. *What the fuck is it?* but the professional part of her took over, took stock of the situation, and her Combat K training weighed up her predicament and made a snap judgement. She pulled back her fist and rammed her index and middle fingers into the snapping dog's eyes as hard as she could. Pitiful dog yelps cried out, reverberating up the stone walls of the chimney as the creature now tried to scrabble backwards, away from her. Pippa lunged at the beast, but slipped, sliding down yet more diagonal rocks, which battered her as she bounced from wall to wall. She had a vague impression of the dogopus, critter, or whatever the fuck the gangers wanted to call it, slithering away, using its tentacles to find instant purchase on the rocky slopes; then her clone crashed into the creature, and the yukana sliced through a thickly-muscled tentacle. A high keening rent the air, along with a wash of blood, soaking Pippa. The dog snout lunged forward and grasped the clone's throat, and she shrieked as it lifted her up. The yukana clattered, tinkling like ice, and fell through the rocks to land on a flat ledge twenty feet below.

The dogopus threw the cloned Pippa against a rocky wall and she tumbled past Pippa. Her fingers snapped out, grabbing the woman instinctively, and she was jerked from her little ledge by the weight. Like marionettes they toppled together, lodging in another V of rock.

Pippa groaned, and opened her eyes. Her clone was breathing, but there were puncture wounds in her throat, leaking rich blood. *It bleeds! It is real!* cackled an insane part of Pippa's mind, as she gradually became aware of a slithering, yapping sound, and was brought clattering back into painful reality. She glanced up. The dogopus, head swaying, eyes squinting through their weeping sockets, was shifting from rock to rock in a three-limbed descent. Pippa cast about, saw the yukana only feet away, and, hoisting her groaning clone's dead weight off her own torso, leapt for the sword. She took a tight hold on the hilt and turned to gaze up at the monstrosity weaving towards her, swaying, cackling, growling, yakking and snakking like some poisonous little bastard terrier with an insane love of its own yakking voice.

"Come on!" snarled Pippa, "come *on*, you bastard!"

At the sound of her voice, the dogopus critter slowed and its head lifted, ears pricking. It gave a little whimper and finally stopped, perched on a big rock just above Pippa's head. Blood pattered down. Pippa saw it had shiny, curved claws on the undersides of its three remaining tentacles.

"What in the name of *fuck* are you?"

The creature whined, its ears flat against its canine skull. A long tongue lolled out and the creature started panting.

"*What?*"

Pippa stared in disbelief. *No, it couldn't be, how could they engineer something so insane? Was it really a hybrid of what she thought it was? And did it really inherit those same traits? Surely, that was impossible. Surely, that was just God having a laugh...*

"Good boy," she said.

The ears rose. The panting became more pronounced.

"Er. Lie down!" She ordered, emphatically.

Squelching, the dogopus lay down, canine muzzle resting on one tentacle. It stared at Pippa with blood-rimed eyes. It seemed to be grinning a doggy grin and Pippa felt her stomach flip and lurch. She came close to losing her breakfast. Or would have, if she'd eaten any.

"Bad dog!" she tried.

The dogopus whined.

"Good boy!"

The dogopus put its head on one side, and panted at her, almost grinning. *Almost.*

Pippa stood, wedged between two rocks, one boot on either side of a drop that could kill her, crush her, maim her in an instant – and traded dog-friendly instructions with a mutated mutant.

Pippa licked her lips. *Go on. It's worth a try. And the bastard is too pitiful to kill, even though I know I can. After all, a yukana can easily cut through hull steel...*

She pointed, back off up the rocks. "To your bed! Go on, get to your bed!"

The dogopus stared at her with those evil black eyes, licked its incisors, then slowly stood and turned and, with a little whine, squelched back off up the mountain chimney, making short work of the tricky, dangerous ascent. It picked up its severed tentacle and then retreated into its cave, far off up the chimney. And then, as quickly as it had come, the dogopus had gone.

Pippa swallowed, and ran a hand over the smears of blood on her WarSuit. She grimaced, looked down at her clone, and cursed, and for a long minute thought evil thoughts. Then, almost reluctantly, she moved to the clone, who was breathing heavily, and drew the second yukana from its sheath, examining the blade with a faint air of curiosity. It was exactly the same as her own. Then she sheathed the blade neatly, and with a tiny *snick*, against her own back.

"Come on, wake up," said Pippa, without much compassion.

Groaning, the clone opened her eyes. Her hand went to her throat, and the new puncture wounds there, two of them deep. She croaked, and spat out a lump of phlegm and blood, then slowly sat up. She was wincing, and coughing, and Pippa pulled a medkit from her own pack, complete with skinglue. She tossed the kit to the clone, who caught it deftly.

"You got two minutes to patch yourself up. Then we move."

"Your compassion overwhelms me."

"Look into your own heart, bitch, and see what you'd do if the situation was reversed."

The clone of Pippa nodded, and cleaned her wounds as Pippa kept watch, yukana in one fist, eyes wary on the cave above. She could hear occasional panting, and a grotesque tearing sound. *What do you bet the genetic freak is reattaching the fucking limb? I guarantee it. I just bloody guarantee it!*

The clone glued her own throat back together, and lay for a few moments, head back on a rock, damp hair spread out around her pale face as she waited for the glue to fix. When she tentatively removed her hand, she sat up and glared at Pippa.

"You *bitch*."

Pippa grinned. "Hey. I'm just the way the world made me. Now get on your fucking feet and get moving; you're lucky I didn't leave you for the dog-pussy thing. Lucky I didn't leave you as chopped up dog liver!"

The clone tilted her head to one side – as, Pippa realised, *she* must have done a million times in her own lifetime. "How did you pacify it?" she said. "How did you stop it attacking? They are renowned for being fearsome indeed..."

Pippa shrugged. "Let's just say, as an educated

woman of the world, and having spent many an evening in a drunk-filled nightclub, that I've got a particular knack at fending off dogs. Now, on your feet and start climbing."

DARKNESS WAS DESCENDING like a veil over the mountains. Pippa crouched on the narrow ledge, perched like a hunter, surveying the landscape before her. The mist had cleared, at least partially, and the sky was a pastel backdrop of smeared ochre and magenta. The surrounding mountains, The *Gangers*, were alien teeth smashed up from the HeartStone of the world. Pippa grimaced, and glanced behind to the cave they'd discovered. It seemed as good a place as any to spend the night. To... *defend,* if the necessity arose.

Pippa's clone had lit a fire at the back of the cave, and was cooking some kind of emergency ration stew over meagre flames. It stank like a dead cat, but Pippa had to admit her stomach was a bunched fist, her body deprived of nutrients. Damn, but she could have eaten Franco's arse if it was served to her on a plate with salad garnish and sour cream!

Pippa retreated into the cave and hunkered down before the flames. They'd found a little dead wood, but not enough to keep the fire burning all night. It was more of a morale boost than anything else.

"Any sign?" asked the clone.

Pippa shrugged. "What, of the ganger mutants

or your soldier friends? Or maybe the two aren't mutually exclusive?"

The clone smiled. "I work for the Mistress. My contact is Ziggurat. And yes, they will be searching for me. The Gangers do... *strange* things to communication devices. And engines. They'll wait for morning, knowing I'll head for the valley below. Nice easy pickup. If I survive."

"What, so they'll be willing to let you die in the mountains? Some friends!"

"Who said they were my friends?" The clone stirred the stew, and met her own gaze. It was like looking into a mirror. The two women were *identical*. Clones. Freaks.

Pippa shivered.

"I'm a mercenary," continued the clone. "I work for money."

"And you copied me?"

"Yes." She gave a tight little smile. "A long time ago. And I've kept the... *structure*. It suits my profession."

"You killed Keenan's wife and children," said Pippa, not looking up, but staring into the flames. They danced like tiny orange demons, obscene and erotic. She watched the fire and felt her anger rising, felt her hatred seeping into every molecule of her being. She had carried the false guilt for too long, her brain twisted and confused like broken shards of mirror. Now here was this creature, this diluted echo of herself, this very mockery of her own life and being and existence. This was the tool QGM had used, to control Combat K, to control Keenan and Pippa. For, with Keenan's family dead, he had become the ultimate QGM machine. Lost his humanity. Became the perfect killer...

And Pippa?

Pippa was the fucking scapegoat.

She thought back to Hardcore, the Sick World... thought back, and dreamed her dreams in the twisting leaping fire, remembered Keenan, and tears rolled down her face. She remembered Keenan's gentle touch, the touch of a killer...

Pippa gave a little shake of her head, caught Keenan watching her, and returned his smile. She started, wondering how she looked, and stood, locating a polished plate of chrome by the door. She stared into the face of a stranger, a battered, bruised, bloodied, tattered hooligan, a street-tramp with crap in her matted hair, grease and dirt-streaks on her swollen face. 'Shit,' she muttered.

Something touched her hand, and she looked down at Keenan's questing fingers. She took his hand, and he squeezed her fingers, and in that simple single moment, in that spark of connection, of brushed skin, of honest intimacy, she suddenly realised everything was all right between them.

Well, not all right, but the kill had gone. Keenan no longer wanted her dead. And that, in itself, was a massive leap forward; a milestone achievement of incredible understanding. Possibly... even forgiveness.

I didn't do it, she said to herself.

And she almost believed it.

I didn't kill his family.

It was a set-up. I was framed.

But how? Why? And by whom?

And a word leapt to her mind, and she felt a tickling sensation that swept through her veins, and this connection with Keenan, this reawakening of trust, sent sparks running up and down her spine, and seemed to ignite the alien essence left in her by the Kahirrim, Emerald. Ganger, came the word. Search the ganger. *And Pippa knew. Knew it was her employer, Quad-Gal Military, who had turned her into what she had become; but more than that, they had betrayed her, made Keenan hate her. In a flash of understanding, she realised QGM had murdered Keenan's family. But why? Why would they do such a thing? And how had they used her as the puppet?*

Did she really use scissors?

Pippa realised she was crying. Keenan stood, his body close to hers, rocking gently with the lull of the charging train. The motion pushed them together, and for a brief instant the lengths of their bodies touched. They shifted away, and Pippa looked up into his eyes.

"It wasn't me," *she said.*

"Shh," *said Keenan, and touched her lips.*

"I wouldn't do that to you."

Keenan grinned, like a skull on speed. He wanted to say, of course you wouldn't, I believe you, I love you, I know you would never do anything to harm my family. But he didn't believe it. He knew; knew Pippa was a killer, a psychotic assassin of the lowest order. He knew it. She knew it. And she knew he understood her soul. The dark corners. The dark places only she, alone, could explore in the lost hours of the night.

Instead, she rested her head against his chest. And was happy with that.

Except now, now he was fucking *dead*, twisted into the heart of the machine god known as VOLOS. Or at least as good as dead; no longer an individual entity, but a strand within a strand within a million strands. Keenan was good and gone, part of a chemical soup.

Her head came up and she gazed long and hard at her clone. "You have caused me great pain."

"I did a job. Was *paid* to do a job. The same as you."

"I would never have slaughtered Keenan's family like that. It was brutal. Unnecessary. You're a fucking disease, and I'm going to give you a cure," she rose, yukana out, eyes reflecting the fire, which turned her, Pippa, the *real* Pippa, into a demon.

"Wait," said the clone, and held out a hand.

"You're going to die, bitch. I'm going to carve you up like you carved up Keenan's kids."

"Wait! I have something to say. Something important."

"Oh, yeah? There's nothing you could say to stop me carving out your heart..."

"I'm not the clone," she said.

Pippa halted, head twisted, lips in a snarl. She gave a laugh more like a bark.

"*What?*"

"I'm not the clone," repeated Pippa's clone. "You are."

"*Get to fuck*. Like I'd buy that crock of shit..."

"Tell me about your childhood."

Pippa laughed, and placed one hand on her hip, the other holding the yukana loosely. "What's this going to be? Your basic, back-street abortion-butcher psycho-analysis? You got a form with tick boxes on it, love? Maybe you want me to take a Voight-Kampff test?"

"How could I know about the fire? About Emelda? About the *pig roasting...*"

"*Where's daddy?*" *she asked, wondering why her daddy hadn't rescued her.*

"*He's been burned. In the fire.*"

Then the paramedics were there, checking her over and rushing her into the ambulance and away, to the burns unit at the local hospital. Most of her hair was scorched away, and the back of her neck and entire back seared by flame to a black, charcoal cinder. When the fire wall had leapt at her, she turned to run...

Pippa blinked, now, remembering the following months of pain, the skin-grafts, the agony. Tears formed at the corners of her eyes, for here and now the smell of frying flesh reminded her of her own, all those years ago, when she'd been nothing but an innocent little girl. She discovered, much later, her father had fallen asleep, in bed, with a cigarette. The happy glowing little cig had burned down to its filter, a long and delicately balanced cylinder of ash, a mocking middle finger of grey which gradually crumbled, and ignited the duvet. In seconds her father's legs were consumed, and he ran from the house, screaming, setting fire to the stairs and landing in his fast, self-preserving exit – thus condemning Pippa to a fire-ensnared tomb. If it hadn't been for the bravery of the firemen, she'd be dead...

"Bastard."

She spat the word with a snarl, and even now Pippa felt the old scars on her back itching, and she thought of her father, and she hated her father. She remembered the thick yellow cream, remembered vividly the many skin-graft operations, six years of them, simply to return her to a semblance of normality. She remembered school, and the way she was tortured: kids were evil little bastards at the best of times, she knew, and even now she shivered, remembering the other kids chasing her with matches and lighters, making dolls of her and burning them in the classroom and playground. She'd wept, oh how she had wept and begged to be left alone. But the bullying continued, merciless, endless. Her parents couldn't stop it, her teachers couldn't stop it, because bullies were clever, cunning, they knew when to strike in those tiny moments when nobody else was around, nobody else there to witness the pain.

The worst, Emelda, a big butch lass with legs like

girders and a spotted face like a burst melon, with facial lumps and frizzy hair like bad candyfloss, Emelda, yeah, Emelda had taken particular delight in torturing Pippa, chasing her on long winter mornings across frosted fields, throwing lit matches at her in class, singing, "Burn the witch, burn the witch, burn the witch!" This went on for years. For long, agonizing years. Years of subtle fear, of checking the coast was clear before leaving school and before joining the dinner queue; always the last to enter the classroom, just after the teacher, much to the amusement and general hilarity of Emelda and her group of mocking cronies. Pippa the Prick, they called her. Pippa takes Prick. Pippa the Witch. Pippa the Bitch, Pippa the Walking Corpse, fucking burnt bitch, you should have died in that fire with your mum and dad, you should be a blackened stick-corpse, stinking like fried pigmeat, lying in a mass grave for the burned, all curled up together like burnt bacon and your fingers like black twisted twigs.

They caught her by the local shops. Ironically, her dad had sent her to buy cigarettes and matches, and she stood, arms limp, matches in one hand, as the girls formed a semi-circle, cutting off her escape, and Emelda, with her frizzy mass of back-combed curly hair, snarled words filled with poison and hatred and Pippa did not understand, did not understand this hate. What had she done? She said it, finally plucked up the courage to say the words which burned in her breast.

"Why, Emelda? What did I do to you? Why do you hate me?"

"You fucking burnt witch, we want you to die, we hate you, hate your stupid little bitch face and stupid little burnt-stick arms and legs."

There was no reason. Something snapped inside Pippa.

She smiled, even as Emelda slapped her a stinging blow across the face, making her skin smart with an imprint of fat, red, crooked fingers, making blood trickle from her split lip, and Pippa's eyes turned triumphant in a cold, analytical, grey glow.

"Burn the witch?" she whispered, understanding flooding her, and she struck the match and threw it into Emelda's frizzy hair in one swift movement. Emelda's hair was a monstrosity of curled hair filled with hairspray. Flammable. Her head went up like an inferno, curls crisping and Emelda screaming like... like a live pig on a spit.

Pippa smiled as Emelda rolled around on the floor, screaming, trying desperately to put out her blazing hair. None of her friends helped. They backed away, like the cowards they were, and faded into the shadows for eternity.

Pippa stood, watching Emelda squirm, head tilted to one side, eyes bright, screams now gone as her lips melted, her skin melted, but the eyes were there, would always be there, watching her, haunting her...

"Check your back," said the clone, her words gentle, her words gentle. "Go on. There are no scars.

You were never burned in the fire. It's a memory implant, Pippa. When my genetic code was copied, cloned, *gangered*, it contained the information for your basic construct; not wounds and scars attained after birth, modifications to your shell that are not part of the basic construct. Those burns happened to the *real* Pippa. Those scars are mine to carry, not yours to bear."

"Bullshit," snarled Pippa, swirling the yukana. "I'm going to cut you up."

"Check."

"What?"

"Reach behind yourself. Check."

Pippa stood, undecided, her mind fractured. The world tumbled down the years. How could this be happening? How could she doubt herself so? How could this be real? *What was real?* She reached behind herself, twisting, watching her clone from the corner of her eye for any tricks; and even before her fingers wormed beneath her WarSuit she knew with terrible certainty what she would find, knew what lay beneath her second skin. Her fingers touched her own cool, regular flesh. It was smooth as a baby, unblemished by fire, no scars, no terrible grafts. *No*, she thought. *This cannot be. It is impossible. It is unreal. This cannot be happening... but she had operations, operations to repair the scars, to remove the scars, to take all the bad memories away...*

The clone was messing with her mind...

Destroying her memories...

And the mind can only take so much.

And so... your world folds in.

And your momma hated you.

And your father hated you.

And your friends hate you.

Friends? What fucking friends? What is friendship except a convenient word for people to get one over on each other, stab each other in the back? Hell, yes. There's too much jealousy. Too much hate. Too much pettiness. And is that it? Is that what the human machine has become? A petty, sniping, back-stabbing pile of bullshit? What happened to honour? What happened to duty? What happened to love? Washed away, pissed away in a mudslide of a million years of pettiness.

I am not human, thought Pippa.

I am not human anymore.

"DRINK."

The world was a hybrid gestalt. Nothing was real. Not guns, not ammo, not soldiers, not sex, not family, not friends, not alcohol – *aah, pleasant alcohol, let me drink you down and sink in your velvet pink vulva. I don't want this anymore. I don't want this world. I don't want this existence. How could this happen to me? How could it all become so confusing? How could it all become so twisted? So fucked up? It's like a man in a bad shirt forcing his fist down your throat. Like a best friend stabbing you in the back with a rusty dagger,* et tu brute *and all that. Wink, wink. Like a mother pissing on your grave. Like a father giving a blow job. Like a lover drowning you in acid. Like a brother ignoring your pleas for help.*

"Drink..."

She spluttered. It was acid on her tongue and in her throat and it burned, it burned bad, baby, and she screamed and lashed out, knocking the canteen away. Soothing noises came and she rested her head on cold butter which gave way, and she sank into the soft fat belly of the (under)world and wondered why all the lights had gone out.

"IT WASN'T SUPPOSED to be this way."

Pippa opened her eyes. She felt whole again. She felt clean again. Then she remembered she wasn't real, she was a genetic construct, a clone of a clone of a clone, a collection of genetic matter which mimicked another. And she'd done bad things. Terrible things. And what right did she have? She wasn't life. She wasn't *real* life. Just an imitation of a copy. But weren't we all? Aren't we all? Isn't that the way human genetics work? Longevity, earned the hard way. Codes passed down through the centuries. Fuck a long life, fuck immortality, you get immortality through your children and grandchildren and great grandchildren. But that doesn't do you any good. Because you're dead. Dead and *fucked*.

"Sit up. We need to get moving."

Pippa's eyes snapped open, and she hissed between clenched teeth. She smashed a blow left, but her clone ducked and she laughed, laughed out loud, for none of it was real and *she was the fucking clone*, so the real Pippa ducked, and she was faster than her clone, better than her clone, more real, more lifelike, more human, more human, Dear God is there a heaven for the copies? If the copies believe in God, does He accept them in past the Gates of Heaven? Or is there a fast-track McChute all the way down to Hell?

After all. How can you have a soul if you were *made*?

How can you find peace, or love, if you're a pressing from a template?

How can you find redemption when you don't even exist?

The world spins round and round and round, and we want to get off, but we can't get off 'til we *die*. And that was the point. Pippa realised she wanted to die. She was tired of it all. Tired of the fight. Tired of the loss. These things never came easy. Victory never came easy. Nor redemption or love or life. And to find she wasn't really real, to find she was just a... just a fucking *clone*, made a mockery of her entire existence.

Implanted memories.

A rewritten history.

I don't believe in a God that I need to worship.

I don't believe in a need to get down on my knees.

Lies, lies. All lies.

But wouldn't God help? Help you how?

You need help, Pippa. You need something.

You need the Light.

You need the Path.

Pippa sighed, and drank, and sat up, and looked around at a bleak world through bleak eyes. It didn't matter that she hadn't killed Keenan's family, his wife, his children, and lost him to VOLOS. She wasn't real. She was the clone. Which meant... the *real* Pippa did those things. Committed those crimes. Atrocities. Betrayals.

It was all true, wasn't it? All fucking true.

Pippa was an evil, helpless, hopeless creature.

But then... aren't we all?

Pippa, the clone, looked at her real self, whom she had once believed unreal. And she pitied the reality.

"We've got to get moving," said Pippa.

"I know," said Pippa.

"The monsters are coming in the night."

"I know."

"We must fight."

"Yes."

"Together."

"As one."

Nothing mattered any more. Not identity, not individuality, not the unique; the chances were that they were both going to die. And that suited Pippa, and Pippa, just fucking fine.

The screams started. Distant wails. Claws scrabbling on stone, feet pounding scree. The hunters had tracked them. The mutations of mutations had hunted them down and Pippa and Pippa took hold of a yukana sword each and moved to the doorway, past the small fire, and stepped out into the cold wilderness of The Gangers.

From high up the dark slopes came an army of creatures. Ten, twenty, thirty, a hundred. The shapes were dark blurs under the light of a velvet moon. They moved fast, on two legs, four, six, some skidding on single ski-like appendages. Some looked like tigers and bears and wolves. But blended. Mutated. They had long claws, like scythes. Some had fangs, curving over massive jaws and glistening with snake venom. Some slithered on bellies but had the faces of women, which screamed and screamed as bulging bodies pulsed with strings of unborn children. Some were blended with insects, human faces above giant scorpion claws, or crab bodies with pincers and strings of salami intestine trailing like over-fat over-ripe sausages from punctured, bulging anus-sacks. Some were fish, clacking and snapping, dead eyes staring ahead as they slithered and ran and crawled and flopped down the scree slopes towards the two women, standing side-by-side now, standing shoulder to shoulder, together, facing a common enemy, facing death, and not just death but an eternity of suffering and agony at their hands and claws and pincers.

"We must fight together," growled Pippa.

"Yes," said Pippa.

"We will die here," said Pippa.

"Tonight," agreed Pippa.

"We will make them suffer," said Pippa.

"As we have both suffered," said Pippa.

They lifted their swords, and under a yellow moon watched calmly as the charging hordes approached.

CHAPTER SEVEN
CRASH AND BURN

FRANCO SAT IN the UChair, scowling up at General Tarly Winters and Mrs Strogger, who stood, side by side, arms folded, watching him with the baleful glares of the terminally wary. He might look like a comedy munchkin, but Tarly had read the reports and Strogger had seen him fight first hand. He was a right bloody handful when he kicked off, and no mistaking.

"We have to go back for her."

"I agree," said Tarly, and ran a hand through her red curls, "under normal circumstances. But these are *not* normal circumstances. These are *exceptional* circumstances, and there's a damn sight more at stake here than one little lady; we have a planet about to go supernova with an internal war *you helped to start,* and we have ten million rogue alien junks scouring the Four Galaxies intent on our fucking annihilation. So call me old fashioned, Franco Haggis, but in my book there's a bigger game being played. That's why I'm a QGM General and you're a dog-soldier soldier-grunt. And that's why I'm pulling rank on you."

Franco regarded Tarly for a few moments. Her anger was up, and she was flushed red. Franco narrowed his eyes a little.

"You ain't been laid in a while, have you, love?"

"*What?*"

"You heard."

"I'll fucking bust your balls to the brig, you whiny little bastard. What the fuck has *that* got to do with our current predicament? What has that got to do with saving the planet? Halting the war?"

Franco gave a little shrug. "Jealous of her, are you?"

"Clever tactic, but it won't work on me. This is not personal. And anyway, I don't have to answer to a moron."

"You do it every day when you look in the mirror."

"Franco, you're a minute away from being locked up. And Mrs Strogger here has kindly agreed to help enforce any decision I make. Not," she hissed, moving closer to stare Franco in the eyes, "that I need any help doing that."

The Kekra touched her temple, and Franco grinned, showing his missing tuff, one of the many victims from his bar-brawling days. "Not with a bullet in your skull, you can't," he said, voice now very quiet, very dangerous, because the fuckers had cooperated back on the Hornet under the pretext that they'd go back after Pippa, only now, *now*, just like every bastard in command Franco had ever met, back through the years, past drill instructors and sergeants, even to his old power-hungry, ego-infused, spunk-stained old Headmaster at *Botton School for Boys*, Killian Britchards, they were pulling rank, changing the rules, changing the game, and as usual Franco was stuck in the middle with his head up his arse. It was always the same; the people with the power did what the fuck they liked, and to hell with the Little Guy. Well, this Little Guy had given many nasty people many nasty shocks in his lifetime; he was a distillation of surprise, and the Master of Mayhem to those who tried to take advantage. Which was most people.

"Are you threatening a superior QGM Officer?" came Tarly's soft, dangerous voice.

"Ha-ha-ha, of course not," mumbled Franco, and the gun went *click*. "See, no mag. I was only fucking witcha. But the point is, *you fucking promised* we'd go after Pippa. And now you're reneging on our deal. The deal that got me back here. Hell, I was happy to go over that cliff after her. But oh, no, you had to make your false fucking General-promises, like all you snivelling Top Brass do, then pull the plug and flick the switch and turn Franco off when

Franco's ready to go! Well, Franco is here to tell you he won't take no shit, and he won't let Pippa die because you didn't have the balls – quite literally – to go after her and help."

Tarly moved away, poured herself a drink, and sipped it, looking at Franco over the swirling amber liquid. "Hmm," she said.

Outside, engines hummed. Space was black. Cloneworld was distant, a swirling blue-grey mass peppered with clouds, a planetary *clone* of Old Earth, Bad Earth, Shit Earth. The irony was not lost on Franco. He was a lot more sophisticated than he looked. A *lot more*. Although you wouldn't believe it.

Franco uncurled from the UCouch and stretched, looking to his right, out of the porthole. Stars flickered. Franco cracked his knuckles. He stared back at Tarly, challenge in his eyes and in his face. He looked calm, but a beast raged within him and Tarly could see it; had seen such things, a million times before. She hadn't got to the position of *general* by being a dumb ass. Just by being brutal.

"So what's it to be, eh?" said Franco.

"New things have come to light."

"Oh, yeah?"

"Yes."

"Such as?"

"Mrs Strogger, and your quite masterful exfil of such an important personage."

"Eh? The old crone?"

"Hah! Bastad!"

Franco stared at Strogger. Stared at Mrs Strogger. Stared at – *what had she said? Strogger 7576889?* And Franco had to remember that Mrs Strogger had five hundred and thirty-three children. That was a lot of children. That took stamina. That took resourcefulness. It showed a certain... *masochistic* tendency.

Franco stared at Mrs Strogger. Stared hard. He'd kind of got used to having her around during recent exploits. She had become, he shuddered to admit, like part of the furniture. Now, he reappraised her. Her old and wrinkled skin. The malevolent green glow, deep in her eyes. The spikes along her arms. The mechanical legs and armoured feet, ready to leave an imprint in steel, baby, steel! He watched her chromed teeth clacking manically. Looked at the bad join where her greased midriff-piston could elevate her to the rank of, well, to the rank of *very tall org.* He listened to the clanking and whirring, and breathed in the stench of aged engines and manky old oil. She stank like a backstreet mechanic's workshop. She oozed exhaust ports. She ejaculated *decay.*

"What about her?"

"She's special," said Tarly.

"You're damn right she is," said Franco. "Special needs."

Tarly sighed. Glanced up, as if expecting Alice, the ship's computer, to help – but Alice kind of *liked* Franco, and was capricious for a ship's computer, so she kept quiet and let Tarly sweat, and enjoyed the scene for what it was: entertainment for a thousand-year old mind.

"Explain," said Franco, as he moved to the InfinityChef. He punched in several digits and the device buzzed, like a fart, as if the billion-dollar top-of-the-range perfect culinary machine was quite literally *offended* by the choice Franco had forced it to create. There came a pause. From the slot emerged a long, quivering, grease-smeared sausage like nothing Tarly Winters, nor indeed Mrs Strogger, had ever seen in their lives. To call it phallic was an insult to the phallus, all the more painful an association by the way Franco tore the end savagely from the wiener and chewed, cubes of gristle gleaming between his teeth. He waved the long, quivering sausage at Tarly. "Go on then. Spill the beans, Bagpuss."

"Bag –" she frowned. "Okay, sausage-brain, it goes like this. Mrs Strogger, here, this lovely old, er, lady, is a very important person in the Realms of the Org. She is revered and considered Holy across the entirety of The Org States."

Franco stared at them both, chewing. He considered Mrs Strogger's anger, hatred and violence. What had she said to those two helpless clone guards? *Your families are from the clone vats, picked out to look like whatever deviant sexual fantasy you had on the day! Your children are slush grown puppies designed to give you a hard time! So stop your whining, you sado-masochistic maggots!*

Very Holy! Har har!

"Pull the other one, General, it has bells on it."

"Really?" said Tarly, her face perfectly straight. "Mrs Strogger, *this* Mrs Strogger, is in fact Queen of The Org States, Ruling Monarch from Tak to Kakfuk, Seventh Deity of the Heap7 Mountains, Ruling Matriarch from the Heights of Zeg Top to the lowliest Spindlebot on the island of The Pig. Queen Strogger XXIV, stamped STROGGER 7576889 from the Factory, has ruled for nearly three hundred years, and *you*, Franco Haggis, rescued her, *you* aided in her escape from Clone Terra captivity. You are a hero. No. A *Hero*. Your reward will be magnificent. They'll probably make you a... oh, a general!"

Franco spat a lump of sausage across the Hornet's interior. It bounced from Tarly's chest, and a FloorSuk cleaned it up with a *fizz*.

"That's a lot to take in," said Franco, eyes gleaming now. He'd rescued a Princess! Well, an old oil-stinking org, who wasn't *strictly* a *Princess* as such, but an old Queen, but hey-*hey*, he'd done something *right* for a damn and bloody change, and now he was up for a big reward which would no-doubt entail lots of money and drinking and sex. He frowned. "Er," he said. "This ain't no kind of trick, is it?"

"Not at all," said Tarly. "This is the Queen of The Org States. You rescued her. Okay, you didn't realise she was Royalty when you did so, but don't you see what you've done? On the one hand, you slaughtered

Opera, which was a pretty dumb-ass thing to do, escalating near-peace to yet another emergency state of war. But if the gangers had executed Queen Strogger – which they probably would have done once they discovered her true identity, and certainly in a most horrific and terribly gruesome manner – there would have been all out war. Unstoppable. Non-returnable. The sort that wastes planets. You understand?"

"And I stopped it." Franco beamed. "Hmm. Yeah. But what about Pippa?" he snapped.

"I can help even the odds there," said Alice, voice soothing. "If we are to go on a mission to return Mrs Strogger to The Org States intact, and without further ganger molestation, I agree with General Winters that it must be done *now*. Pippa knows her mission, to reach the Slush Pits and retrieve the 3Core. We, on the other hand, have a new task – to see Queen Strogger returned to her Throne at the Strogger Palace in the capital city of Org."

"Where is Pippa?" said Franco.

"She has teamed up with her ganger, and they are crossing The Ganger mountain range. However, that gunship you saw earlier is about to make an appearance. I can help out with that situation, Franco, if you'll agree to accompany us to Org. If you agree to help us take Queen Strogger *home*. We need your skills. We need your... Old Magic."

Franco looked around suspiciously. "This is starting to feel like a bloody set-up," he muttered. "All three of you, in this together, are ye? Well, listen, I know Pippa can look after herself; I know she's a lot more efficient than me. But if she ends up dead out of all of this, there's no Betezh, or fucking Rainbow Pills, that'll stop me seeking out some payback. Pippa don't need me to hold her hand, but we're Combat K, we're a team, and that's what counts. Once Strogger is back on her throne, then we head straight back to pick up Pippa. Reet?"

"Agreed," said Alice, instantly.

"How long will it take to reach Org?" said Franco.

"We have to circumnavigate the band of five-kilometre-high mountains known as The Teeth; taking into consideration high-level low-speed flying to try and avoid unwanted gunbot intervention, I'd say, ooh, twenty-four hours. Until we get back to Pippa. She might even have acquired the 3Core by then."

"Yeah," grinned Tarly, "after all, she won't have you underfoot, tripping her up at every obstacle."

"What you gonna do to the gunship?" said Franco. "I've seen what their bastard miniguns can do! And it ain't nice."

Alice's voice sounded smug. "Well, you know those GASGAMs the gangers hijacked? I think I might just be able to help out there..."

FRANCO STILL WASN'T happy about it. It sat badly with him. Like he was abandoning Pippa. Leaving her to die. However, they had an agreement, and the bottom line was, he'd been given new QGM orders.

And orders was orders, right? Wrong! He wrestled with this internal dilemma as he thumped about his sleeping quarters, getting his kit together in a pack, tweaking the code on his PAD, checking his weapons, oiling his guns, loading his belts and jacket with ammo. He was sat on his bunk in his underpants, a screwdriver poked into the buzzing innards of his WarSuit control pack when there came a knock on the door, which slid open to reveal Mrs Strogger. Or *Queen Strogger,* as she was now to be known.

Franco glanced up. "What do you want, eh?"

"Listen," said the old org, shuffling in. She had reduced in size again, so that she was a wrinkled, little old lady, albeit it with mechanical legs and forearm spikes that could rip out a man's lungs. Franco appreciated that she was trying to make herself look less intimidating – which was a nice touch – but Franco had seen her fight. Even now, reduced and wrinkled, she filled him with a primeval terror.

"The thing is," said Mrs Strogger, and her voice had changed, had lost its brutality, and Franco realised it had all been part of an act, a disguise, to stop the damn gangers from discovering who she really was. Now she felt safe, she had dropped the mask. Now she was once more Queen Strogger, Ruler of The Org States. "I wanted to thank you. I wanted to give you my Royal Blessing for your aid in escaping from Clone Terra."

Franco gave a shrug, and went back to his screwdriver. In some ways, this new voice, this new *persona*, gave him the creeps. He'd preferred it when she kept swearing at him. "Cheers. I think it was a situation of mutual benefit, no? I wasn't working on an act of charity; it wasn't from the depths of my heart, you understand?"

"Yes," smiled the old org, "but then, they don't call you Franco 'Honest Injun' Haggis for nothing, do they?"

Franco gave her a cold grin. "Clever. Very clever."

"Merely an observation. Still, I want you to rest assured that once I reach Org and the Strogger Palace, anything you desire that I can provide will be yours. You want untold wealth? You shall have it. A palace of rubies? Yours. Concubines to make your thighs ache? For the rest of your life..."

Franco gave a lazy blink. "Hmm," he said. He'd heard promises like this before. And in Franco's experience, nice things tended to happen to *other people*. "Like I said. Thanks. I'll kinda believe it when I see it. And the conkybines will have to wait. Until Pippa is safe, at least. Until we have the 3Core. I have my principles, you know."

"As you wish."

Franco prodded something, which went *buzz-clack* and gave him a shock. "Aiee!" he squealed, as actinic sparks flickered over his hand, and he sucked at his index finger. "Little *son of a bitch*!"

Queen Strogger was staring at him. "I see your finger is healing. A little shorter than it was, but healing well."

"Yes. You cauterised it. That was quick thinking." Franco looked at the stump of his little finger, and wiggled it forlornly. "I'll miss that little finger. Me and that little finger, we were quite attached. I loved that little finger. It was a part of me. Like... a little finger. And now it's not. Now it's gone. I'm little-fingerless."

"Very poetic," said Queen Strogger. "I can help."

"No, no, it's okay," sighed Franco, placing his screwdriver to one side. "I mean, it looks a mess, right, all burnt and *missing* like that, but it's okay, I'll survive, I'll get over it. If we were at QGM HQ Central they could have grown me a new one and grafted it on; but I fear, in times of war, one squaddie's lost little finger is hardly high on their emergency operation list." He wiggled his stump. He looked very sorry for himself. It was a quite pathetic sight.

"Come here," said Queen Strogger, and she shuffled closer and grabbed Franco's hand.

"Aah, no, no, thanks, that's all right, I'll be all right, indeed, all right I'll be," he said.

"I can help."

"Aah, er, don't be thinking, old crone, just 'cos you're a Queen and everything, that you can take any form of sexual liberties with me, I know what it says in my file, but I'm actually a man of honour and integrity..."

An opening had opened in Queen Strogger's torso. Franco caught a glimpse of complicated machinery. A stench of hot oil flooded out, with an accompanying sound of clacking and gears and heavy chains and weights that went *thump*. Inexorably, Queen Strogger dragged Franco's hand towards the glowing green chasm in her own wrinkled flesh.

"Ahh, no, argh, really," said Franco.

His hand plunged into the hole, which puckered and closed around his wrist, holding him tight. Suddenly, panic welled in Franco's heart and mind and he started to struggle. Metallic limbs shot from Strogger's body and pinned him down. "Be still, be calm, this won't hurt a bit. Well, not much, anyway."

"Geddoff!" wailed Franco, struggling like a hooked maggot.

From deep within Queen Strogger's body could be heard several deep *clangs*. Then a ratchet sound. There were thuds, and a chugging noise like an old steam engine. Franco's eyes went wide.

"What're you doing to me? Stop it! I don't want it! Whatever you're doing, stop it now! I never asked for it! I don't want it!"

CLANG. CHUNK. THUNK. WHACK.

"Argh no! Stobbit! Geddoff!"

WHUMP. RATTLE. RATTLE. *SHRING*. CHUMP.

Steam hissed from Queen Strogger's ears, and Franco felt his little finger grasped tight and then it was hot, and it hurt, and pain raced up his hand and arm, and he squealed like a pig on a stick in a fire, but he could not move, for the mechanised org had him pinned down and held tight.

And then it was done. And gone. And over.

The orifice released Franco's hand, and in horror he dragged his shaking limb before his eyes, to see –

"Oh," he said, and frowned.

"The finest I can make," said Queen Strogger, smiling proudly.

"You, er, you gave me a metal finger," said Franco, and flexed his hand, turning it this way and that, analysing the shiny metal little finger where once had been only a forlorn stump.

"A cyborg finger," said Queen Strogger, with a bigger smile.

"Er, a *what?*"

"An org finger," said Queen Strogger. She patted Franco on the back, as he stared with open mouth at the cybernetic addendum to his physical shell. "It works just like your real finger did. See it as a present. For helping me escape certain death."

"Er. Yeah. Right."

"No need to thank me," she said, and started to shuffle from Franco's sleeping quarters. "Let's hope nothing else gets amputated, eh?" She laughed. "A-ha-ha-ha." Like that. As she reached the doorway. And disappeared into the Hornet's interior.

Franco looked up then. His face shone with sweat as he thought about losing another limb, some extremity, maybe something dangling, and he paled even more. "No, let's hope," he said quietly, and swallowed. Hard.

Queen Strogger's face reappeared.

"Welcome to the team," she said, smiling with her chromed teeth.

"*What?*"

"Well. You're one of us now. You're an *org*. Part man. Part machine."

All idiot, the ghost of Pippa muttered in the back of his mind. Shit. Franco was starting to miss the old girl.

And then Queen Strogger was gone.

Franco stared at the metal finger. He scowled. He grimaced. He mumbled something incoherent, then coughed a cough heavy with phlegm and the need for a strong triple-pint of whiskey.

"Fucking great," he muttered.

ALICE CRUISED THE Hornet at super-slow speeds to throw the AI gunbots off-scent. Night fell over the edge of the world. Green sunlight sparkled through the higher reaches of the atmosphere, and silence rolled over them like galactic foam.

Franco sat in one of the pilot's chairs, swinging from side to side. A bowl of PreMeat Meatballs lay untouched next to him, with some foodstuff which had been recommended by the InfinityChef™, but of which Franco was deeply suspicious. Was it an AI's act of retribution for all his horrible sausage orders? The InfinityChef™ said it was called *spaghetti*, in its soothing, asexual voice. Franco thought of it as *stringy shit*.

He poked around with his spork. The *spaghetti* looked like it might poke back.

Franco sighed. He poured himself another dram of SCROTUM'S OLD TODGE CLOGGER – FINEST SINGLE MALT. But it didn't taste good, didn't go down well (with that fiery feeling, like one was drinking undiluted hydrochloric acid), and Franco pushed his glass aside, disappointed in alcohol for once in his life.

Getting old, bro!

Getting boring. Like a fetid old goat.

"Let me show you something," said Alice.

"Amaze me."

The screen before Franco cleared, and showed a high-altitude map of the planet. There were two huge land masses, to the left and right. An ocean divided the two continents, but down the centre was a narrow vertical strip of rock containing nothing but mountains.

"What am I looking at?" said Franco, sounding bored, when no other words were forthcoming.

"This is Cloneworld," said Alice, soothingly.

Franco drank his drink. "So?"

"To the west is Clone Terra, to the east The Org States. They have been physically divided using terraforming equipment; hence the huge mountains, called The Teeth, and a ban on all manner of aeronautics."

"Aerowhatics?"

"Planes."

"Ach. Of course." He poured himself another

whiskey, and started to find Alice's voice sexy. He wondered if she had an avatar. If she did, he hoped it wasn't blue, like that last one. The blue ones smelt funny. Like rotten off-marzipan. Or something.

"You see all the tiny red dots?"

"Aye?"

"Watch what happens when I accelerate."

The dots started to move, fast, homing in on the blue dot.

"Now I'll slow down again to our current cruising speed." Within moments, the dots started to disperse, moving randomly about the map.

Franco frowned. "Ahh," he said, looking wise and placing his goatee-bearded chin on the tip of his index finger. "I see. Fascinating."

"Don't you think? And that explains our current velocity."

"What does?"

"What I just showed you."

"What did you just show me?"

Alice sighed with the patience of tectonic movement. "The blue dot is us. The red dots are the AI gunbots. When we increase velocity, they detect our speed and start to home in on our location. We slow down, to what is effectively a snail's pace, and they no longer track us. So it's not so much aerial targets they detect, but speed greater than that capable on land. Within reason."

"Fascinating," said Franco, face blank. "So. Fucking. What."

"It means we do not have to relinquish our flight; merely our speed."

"Let's hope we don't have an emergency then, eh?" If he could have, he would have slapped her on the back. But she didn't have one. So he didn't.

Franco was just about to ask, *Hey Alice, have you got one of those avatar things? Even a blue one? It's been a while, you see,* when Tarly Winters entered the recreation quarters behind the cockpit. Franco watched her over his glass. She wore a black uniform, with glittering silver insignia, and black boots. Her red hair was tied back tight, accentuating her high, beautiful cheekbones, and her eyes glittered cold, like frozen hydrogen.

"You all right, Killer?" said Franco.

Tarly gave a cold smile, and moved through to the cockpit. "Not so bad, Fat Boy."

"Hey," said Franco, cupping his rotund belly, "it's all muscle."

"Better there than in your head," smiled Tarly, sweetly.

"I might be fat," said Franco, "but I'm happy and I have morals. Not like some of the high-ranking military scum you find kicking around the universe." He glanced sideways at Tarly. "Makes you wonder how some people sleep at night."

Tarly shrugged. "I sleep just fine."

"You are a bitch," said Franco.

"Don't ever forget it," smiled Tarly.

"Must get lonely?" ventured Franco.

"Not really," said Tarly, and seated herself in a pilot's chair. She started punching digits into the console.

"Not even a bit? I mean, we all know what it's like with you general-types and high-fliers, standing on the fingers and toes of all your friends on your way up the shit-slippery pole of the ziggurat. What's that saying? The toes that you step on when you're on your way up, will be the same ones kicking you in the face on the way down. Heh. I like that saying. Reminds me of a few people I know. Ones I kicked, that is."

"It's unlikely," said Tarly, glancing at Franco.

"What? The fact that you might slide down the pole, or the fact that your ex-friends will be kicking you in the chops on your meteoric accelerating descent?"

"Neither. Because I didn't leave any enemies behind."

"What happened to them?"

"They're all dead," said Tarly, softly.

"A lot of, er, unlucky groundcar accidents, I expect? Yachting accidents round the Rings of Pluto? Accidentally *bathing* in tubs of Perushian yoghurt acid, perhaps?"

"Franco Haggis. Do you actually *know* what department I worked in on my toe-stepping rise to the higher ranks of Quad-Gal Military? Have you any concept of who you're dealing with?"

"Let me guess. You spent a few years cleaning out

the industrial bean bins? Wait, wait, don't tell me! You gave a couple of Fleet Admirals an admirable blowjob when their wives were on the latrine? Wait, wait, it's knocking me out, this, what a game! I suspect you might have bent over a few battalions and *fucking give it them violently from behind.*"

"I worked the Suicide Squads," said Tarly, quietly.

Franco paused, which was impressive, because it usually took at least a right hook, and more often than not a pistol-butt to the back of the head to halt Franco in mid-rant. He stared hard at Tarly.

"You're shitting me."

"Nope. Fifteen years. Rising through the ranks. It was said I had exceptional skill and discipline. Then I transferred to the War Fleets. Served under General Kotinevitch, First General of Quad-Gal Military's Prime Fleet. I was her 2IC until that... unfortunate incident."

"Ahh, the one with the planet rings? Jekyll, wasn't it called? Solar rings hit her in the face like a fucking galactic hammer. Yeah. The junks pulled a fast one there. Clever, corrupt little bastards."

"The point is..." said Tarly, and moved so fast she was a blur, landing astride Franco, her face inches from his, a long slender stiletto dagger at his throat, poised over his jugular vein. She pricked it a little, and a trickle of blood ran past Franco's collar line, "I'm deadly."

Unperturbed, Franco locked eyes with Tarly's dark steel gaze. She was so close, he could have kissed her.

Yes, she would have cut out his voice box, but that was not really the point.

"It's been a while since a bird pushed her tits in my face like this. You should be commended on your willingness to mix it with the common dog soldier grunts, my sweet."

"You feel that little prick? I expect you're used to feeling little pricks, yes?" Tarly was smiling, and licked her lips, making them gleam. Her breath was sweet in Franco's face.

"Not little ones, no. But I expect you can feel that big one."

"Oh."

"I'm sorry. It's just, the way you've got your legs clamped round me, er, sorry." And as Tarly was starting to apologise, she felt another blade touch her ribs. "However, *this* little prick," said Franco, smugly, "would drive straight through your ribs and cut your heart in half before you blinked."

Tarly considered this. "How can you be *erect* and still threaten to kill me?"

"It takes practise," admitted Franco.

"I suppose I'd better get off you."

"Don't rush on my account," said Franco, and grinned as Tarly stood, twirled, and sheathed her blade. She glanced down at Franco, wearing nothing more than his pyramid-shaped knife-cut combat shorts.

"You really are a dirty, horrible little man," she said.

Franco winked. "Hey girl, I wasn't the once forcing myself on an unsuspecting party."

"Hmm."

"So then?"

"Go on."

"Fancy a drink and a curry? I hear the InfinityChef™ does a fine line in Space Worm vindaloo."

"What?" Incredulous. "With you?"

"It's either me, or the psychotic half-metal geriatric cyborg queen from Hell."

"Okay then. You've twisted my arm."

"That's what I usually have to do."

Tarly giggled then, her face breaking into sudden good humour, and she slumped down next to Franco. He poured her a dram of SCROTUM'S, which she downed in one. He poured her another.

"Were you really?"

"What? In the Suicide Squads?"

"Yeah. I heard each mission was practically *suicide*. They only took on people with a certifiable deathwish. Used to recruit from the crazies; the burnouts, the psychos, the lunatics."

"That as well," smiled Tarly, lips gleaming with whiskey.

"So you were?"

"Just like I said. I don't think they thought I'd last that long. I had a few... *problems*. But hey, don't let that ruin our evening. After all, we might be dead tomorrow."

"Wait," said Franco, and frowned. "This mission, right here and now. That's why they sent you, right?"

"At last! The penny drops."

"So we're doomed to die?"

"Only as much as the next man. I don't play the odds. I own them."

"So I'm safe with you?"

"I wouldn't go that far," said Tarly, and giggled again. Franco shook his head. *How?* his mind was shrieking. *How can she be so funny, and charming, and sexy – all right she was going to cut your throat, but hey not every girl's perfect, right? – But how can she be all those things, near-perfect in every respect, except for the obviously dodgy past psychotic military career, but not every chick has it all, do they? How can she be so damn good and scrumptious, and yet display such a list of checkboxes pointing straight to the Damaged Goods aisle? Eh? I ask you? Eh?*

As if reading his mind, Tarly smiled. She touched a finger to his lips. "After all, I was the top of the league. And you only get there by stepping into Dead Men's Shoes."

"Vindaloo?" said Franco brightly.

"Doesn't it bother you that I'm an insane killer?"

"Hey," said Franco, holding his hands apart and grinning, "I think even insane killers deserve happiness, right? And they don't call me Franco 'Give Sexy Insane Killers A Chance' Haggis for nothing, reet?"

IT WAS STILL dark outside when Franco awoke. He'd drunk an insane amount. He awoke in his sleeping quarters, naked except for a comedy frog thong. He quickly removed it and tried, in a familiar manner, to piece together the events leading up to his testicular incarceration in a furry frog.

I know, he thought. *I'll make myself a wee drinkie to help pass the evening as I contemplate events, and decide on further events, in order to event an event! Yay!* He pulled on his army shorts and sandals, and staggered out of his sleeping quarters, into the lounge, and stood for a while swaying. Tarly was curled in pink pyjamas on a couch, snoring gently. Franco frowned. *If General Tarly is there, then who – what – why am I in a furry frog thong? Oh my God? Mrs Strogger? Queen Strogger? Back for payment for my cyborg finger replacement? Oh my GOD!*

He flexed his metal finger. He looked around for the old cyborg, but she wasn't there.

Hot damn and bloody bollocks! Now I DEFINITELY need a drink!

He staggered over to the InfinityChef™. The InfinityChef™ could conjure any food or drink in the known universe. It was an industrial model, as befitting a military class Hornet. An InfinityChef™ was designed to operate in any environment. It was designed to withstand a bomb blast. It was tougher than hull steel.

Franco punched in various digits. The lights were low. The InfinityChef™ flickered extra lights at him, and a drink emerged. It was whiskey. Franco took a slug. It was *good* whiskey! Hot damn, it was good and fine whiskey! But Franco was feeling particularly anarchic, and was worried about Pippa, and worried about Mrs Strogger and the frog thong. He punched in new digits. The InfinityChef™ gave a buzzing noise, as if to say No.

Franco frowned. He punched in the digits again.

Once more, the InfinityChef™ gave a long buzzing noise, as if to say, ARE YOU INSANE?

"Listen," growled Franco, "if I wants a drink of extra hot vindaloo chilli whiskey, with a hint of PreSausage, then that's what I'll be bloody having! So DO IT, bozo."

For the third time, the InfinityChef™ gave a long, low buzzing noise, as if to say, GET FUCKED.

Scowling, Franco pulled free his screwdriver and prized off a panel. "Oh yeah?" he muttered, having had this problem once before when trying to order a rare Space Worm kebab. He worked on the InfinityChef™ for a moment, face curiously demonic in the purple glow of the ship's night-lights.

"Okay, baby!" He prodded in the digits, and the machine buzzed, and then a glass of something slightly bubbling was delivered in the output hopper. Franco took a sip. "Wow!" he cried, as he started to choke. Through tear-streaming eyes, as he clung on to the InfinityChef™ for stability, as he wheezed and choked and thoroughly enjoyed the *kick*, he punched in more digits. "Give... me... a... bucketful..." he croaked into the microphone.

The InfinityChef™ started to rock gently from side to side, buzzing and moaning, as a shiny metal bucket was duly delivered and started to fill with frothing fizzing vindaloo chilli whiskey, with a hint of PreSausage.

"Yeah, baby," grinned Franco. He hiccupped, and took another blast. Through gritted teeth he wheezed, "They don't call me Franco 'Chef Ramsey Fiery Balls' Haggis for nothing, you know?" The Infinity Chef duly finished delivering its quota of steaming vindaloo chilli whiskey, with a hint of PreSausage (cubes of which Franco could see floating in the broth) and gave a loud honking noise, which could not be mistaken for anything other than FRANCO HAGGIS – YOU ARE A FUCKING MORON.

Franco staggered away, holding his bucket by the handle, and heading roughly in the direction of Tarly Winters, snoring in her pink pyjamas, with a vague idea of asking her if she wanted to share a nightcap. Of chilli whiskey.

It had to be said, Franco Haggis was grinning like a village idiot.

Franco Haggis was panting like a diseased steam engine.

Franco Haggis had a twinkle in his eye...

Right up to the moment he looked down, wondering why the bucket was growing lighter in his hands, and realised the damn vindaloo chilli whiskey with a hint of PreSausage had *eaten* a large hole in the bottom of the bucket and he'd left a trail across the lounge floor.

"Ah," said Franco, stopping in his tracks. "It eats

through metal? Who would have thought that?"

Franco scratched his beard. And watched the trail of vindaloo chilli whiskey eat a long crevasse into the floor of the Hornet fighter.

"Er," he said.

Steam rose. The floor started to buckle. Metal mesh twisted and dissolved.

"Er, somebody?" said Franco, looking around him. "Er, I think we might have some kind of minor emergency?"

Suddenly, the lights flicked on. Alice's voice snapped at him. "What is it? What's eating the floor?"

"Er." Franco whistled a little tune.

"Idiot! Answer me! Those panels are straight over the engines!"

"Er. It could, maybe, might be a distillation of, possibly, vindaloo chilli whiskey."

"What the *hell* is vindaloo chilli whiskey?" snapped Alice. Then, "It doesn't matter. Shit. SHIT! Haggis, don't move. Don't blink! Don't even *fart!* Your evil little concoction has reached the core matrix cabling, but that stuff is... ah..."

Franco felt Alice's presence... *disappear*. As if the ship's computer was frantically turning all her existing cores to solving a really bad problem. Franco whistled a little tune again. *Don't worry! It'll be reet! 'Tis but a little spillage. Soon be mopped up. Soon be dabbed up. Soon be put back in the bucket and all t'will be forgotten. Yup.*

A siren screamed through the ship on full volume.

Tarly sat up, bleary-eyed, face confused.

Queen Strogger came clanking in from her sleeping quarters, pulling on whatever moth-eaten, ragged clothing she used to cover her wrinkled flesh and metal frame.

Everybody stared at Franco.

"What?" he said, shrugging and frowning, and having to shout to be heard over the alarms. "It's just a drill, right? Don't be bloody panicking!"

The Hornet's interior contained perhaps thirty large black screens. Now, one word in glowing white letters appeared on all of them.

EMERGENCY, it said.

Tarly and Strogger stared at that word. Then they turned and stared at Franco.

"There's no problem!" he insisted, flapping his hands.

"Alice?" shouted Tarly. "ALICE?"

Alice did not respond. It was as if she was too busy. Or maybe even *disabled*.

"Er," said Franco again, and looked forlornly down at his bucket. *There's a hole in my bucket,* he thought miserably. *I think I might just have fucked up. Just a little bit. But fucked up, all the same.*

There came a deep rumbling sound. The Hornet shuddered. Everybody looked at each other.

"What did you do?" screamed Tarly, grabbing the forlorn Combat K squaddie by the shoulders and shaking him. Suddenly an automated ship emergency drone-voice came booming over the speakers:

THIS IS YOUR CRASH COMPUTER SPEAKING. PLEASE DO NO BE ALARMED. YOU ARE ABOUT TO CRASH. THIS HORNET FIGHTER VESSEL, REGISTRATION LA05999ZXSPECCY200, WILL CRASH IN NINETY SECONDS. PLEASE STRAP YOURSELF INTO A CRASH COUCH. CRASH FOAM WILL BE DEPLOYED IN SIXTY SECONDS. IF YOU ARE NOT IN A CRASH COUCH, FULL LIFE SUPPORT SYSTEMS CANNOT BE PROPERLY ADMINISTERED. ALICE HAS BEEN DISABLED. HER BLACK BOX WILL BE AVAILABLE DIRECTLY VIA POST-CRASH SCAVENGE AND WILL CONTAIN ALL DETAILS AND COORDINATES NECESSARY TO COORDINATE A COORDINATED RESCUE OPERATION. PLEASE MAKE YOUR WAY CALMLY TO THE CRASH FACILITY. YOU ARE ABOUT TO CRASH. WE APOLOGISE FOR THIS CRASH. THIS CRASH IS DUE TO UNFORESEEN CIRCUMSTANCES. CRASH FOAM WILL BE DEPLOYED IN THIRTY SECONDS. PLEASE DO NOT PANIC. THERE IS A SEVENTY-FIVE PER CENT PROBABILITY YOU WILL SURVIVE THIS CRASH WITH ALL LIMBS. THIS IS YOUR CRASH COMPUTER SPEAKING. WE APOLOGISE FOR THIS IMPENDING CRASH. THANK YOU, AND GOOD NIGHT.

Rushing slightly, Franco, Tarly and Queen Strogger hurried down narrow alloy corridors and strapped themselves into Crash Couches. All the time, Tarly was saying, "I don't believe it, I just don't fucking believe it, I mean, you train for these eventualities, but you never think it's going to happen to you. What happened, Franco? Where's Alice? Why were you carrying an empty bucket? WHAT THE HELL IS GOING ON?"

"I think we must have been struck be a missile," lied Franco fluently, and Tarly stared at him, teeth bared.

"I thought this Hornet had a wealth of scanners and proximity detectors?"

"Yeah, well," said Franco, face crafty, "it'll be one of those damn clever AI gunbots, won't it?"

But he didn't get to say any more.

Because at that moment the Hornet's nose dipped, the engines stalled, and it tumbled from the sky like a duck with an arse full of red-hot lead shot.

Crash Foam v2.7 was deployed.

And there's nothing better than a face full of Crash Foam v2.7 to really shut you the fuck up.

SIRENS SCREAMED. WAILED. Spluttered. The Hornet was thrashing. There were a thousand *clicks* as crash-injectors flipped down from recesses. "Holy shit," mouthed Franco, but his voice was lost as several thousand crash-injectors hissed and squirted, filling the entirety of the Hornet's interior with Crash Foam v2.7. They were hit by the foam, locked rigid and yet floating, as it surrounded them in an instant. The Crash Foam v2.7 filled open mouths and nostrils; it plugged their ears, and the world was muffled and *killed* as they descended into a cool green suspension, divorced from reality. The Hornet's emergency systems had taken control. Franco breathed the weird rubbery substance, which was infused with oxygen and a sub-prapethylene agent that would sustain him in stasis for around thirty minutes...

This was enough time to crash. In theory.

Then Franco felt like he was in a tumble drier. He felt like he was drunk, in a boxing ring, spinning round. He felt his ears and brain bleeding. He felt his rubber head turn inside out, his brain plop from his ears, his internal organs fry in a pan of butter and garlic, his testicles rise up through his body until they parodied his tonsils so that all he could talk was bollocks... and Franco screamed through the Crash Foam v2.7 and he heard distant, million-mile-muffled screams from Tarly and Queen Strogger and, he imagined in a fantasy world on another planet, even *Alice,* the ship's computer.

Shit, thought Franco.

We're going to die.

THE WORLD FELT like putty, and Franco a pellet of dung thrashing around in slow-motion at the centre. His lungs were fit to explode, filled with a billion old smoke rings, and he coughed and coughed and coughed, and wondered what the hell was wrong with him – was he dying? Was it cancer? And he was crying in pain, a raw, sweet agony, worse than any chilli powder in his eyes, and he rolled around on the soft squidgy floor but that couldn't be right, because the floor shouldn't be soft and squidgy like that – surely? Franco coughed and coughed, coughed till he thought his lungs would come out of his mouth, only instead he disgorged a long drooling stream of melting Crash Foam v2.7, which spewed out of him like some five-course salmonella curry. Pain ran circles in his skull, and his eyes felt they were about to pop. He reached up, pulled barrels of Crash Foam v2.7 from his nostrils, and only then, only when he could *breathe* cool sweet fresh air, did he gasp and suck in great lungfuls and feel even *vaguely* human again.

You crashed the ship, said a mocking, nagging voice in his brain.

Like an ex-wife.

Like an irascible student.

You *crashed* the damn Hornet!

Oh. *Shit*.

Franco opened his eyes. Unnecessarily, he felt, somebody said, "He's awake."

The world spun around like an elastic yo-yo, until it finally settled and he felt hands helping him to sit up. It was Tarly. Her hands were strong. She looked concerned.

"Are you okay?"

"I'd rather be dead."

"You certainly look it."

"Hey, I ain't no fucking zombie," muttered Franco, and continued to cough up phlegm and Crash Foam v2.7, picking it from his nostrils and scraping it from his beard. "Where are we?" he eventually spluttered.

It was dark. Pitch dark. Above, the heavens were a vast, sable blanket glittering with stars like crushed ice. He could smell old matrix fuel. And fire. Definitely fire. A cold wind blew, and Franco suddenly realised they were *moving*.

"Where are we?" he repeated, and got to his knees and gazed about. "We're on a boat! How the hell did we get on a boat? What are we doing on a boat? We shouldn't be on a bloody boat! I mean, one minute a spaceship, next minute a boat! What's the bloody world coming to?"

He looked around again. It was a large, inflatable, QGM emergency-issue vessel. Franco rolled his head, and his neck and shoulder muscles howled in protest. His aching body battered him like a pit-fighter. His balls felt like shrivelled pips.

"We crashed," said Tarly, voice quiet, calm. The wind ruffled her red curls. Starlight glittered in her eyes. "Alice deployed this boat at the last moment and an S-PopBot cut us out of the Crash Foam v2.7 and dumped us here."

Franco looked around. "Where's the Hornet?"

"Sunk."

"Ahh."

Tarly gave a weak laugh, and Franco saw it in her eyes; fear. They were stranded now. Not just on the sea in a little inflatable lifeboat, but *here on the planet*. The only space-going vehicles allowed were QGM. And they were busy fighting a war...

"I can't believe we crashed."

"Must of been a missile," mumbled Franco, miserably.

"I'm sure Alice would have seen it coming." Tarly settled back, next to Queen Strogger. In the middle of the boat were several emergency crates. The boat rose and fell on the swell of the ocean. It was cold, but not uncomfortably so if one hunkered down out of the wind.

"Well," said Franco brightly, "it's unfortunate Alice went swimming down with the ship, hey? Now we'll never know what happened, because if there was a gross incompetence issue then we'd need to know about it, because crashing a Hornet is a *big thing,* right, but hey it's a shame, not that I'm saying it was some kind of incompetency spillage issue or anything, because that would just be insane, and I'm sure Alice in all her wonderful wisdom would have seen any such depravity on its way to the Asylum Dock. Yeah?"

"Are you still drunk?" said Tarly.

"Only on love juice," grinned Franco, and shuffled closer.

"Anyway," said Tarly, frowning at him, "we *will* get to know what happened. I've got Alice's BBR here."

"Her BBR?" said Franco, heart sinking as he looked at the small black cube in Tarly's gloved hands.

"Yes. Black Box Recording. Although in reality it's more complex than that, because it's a BCube. Alice's *Brain Cube.* Just because her shell, her whole *ship* has been destroyed, doesn't mean QGM are going to junk her fucking mind, does it?"

"What, so that there box is her CPU?" snapped Franco, eyes wide.

"More than that," said Tarly. "It's *her*. She's all clammed up at the moment; a preventative measure due to the crash. She'll come round soon enough. Reboot herself. Like a turtle emerging from its shell after being used in a game of volleyball. Then she'll tell us what really happened. Should take her a few hours; or that's what the specsheets claim."

"You read the specsheets?" said Franco, aghast. It was rare he even read his Mission Directive.

"Oh yes," said Tarly, and gave Franco a slow wink. "I like to be prepared for any eventuality."

"Okay, you guys, listen up," said Queen Strogger, and now, despite her wizened old appearance, mixed in with that of a rusting old mekbot, she seemed that little bit more... assertive. She was getting closer to home. She was out of Clone Terra, over The Teeth, and on her way to the good old Org States.

"I suppose you have a plan?" said Franco, feeling suddenly weary. Here he was, in enemy territory – so to speak – in just his combat shorts and sandals. This was a familiar feeling. God had a way of catching Franco Haggis with his pants round his ankles.

"We need to fire the engines," said Strogger. "And head east."

"You're nearly home," said Tarly, and placed a hand on hers.

The org smiled and gave a nod. But her glowing green eyes seemed to grow more intense, and Franco felt he had a premonition; suddenly, the old org didn't feel quite so friendly, and he felt just a little bit like a pawn in somebody else's diseased shitgame.

"I'll soon be back on the throne," she whispered.

DAWN WAS BREAKING. Franco was cold, and he and Tarly had snuggled together for warmth, her in her pink pyjamas, and he with his bushy masculine chest. As he'd pointed out, though, it was all about survival. And he'd failed to pack WarSuits in the crates.

Still huddled together, as a salty sea breeze washed over them, and waves lapped the sides of the boat through an early morning mist, Tarly pulled away a little and stared at Franco.

"You packed the emergency crates?" she said, softly, half-confused by sleep.

"Oh yes," said Franco.

Tarly considered this. "But they're hermetically sealed," she said.

"I hermetically *unsealed* them," Franco said.

"But why?" asked Tarly, slowly.

Franco grinned, showing his missing tooth. "Well, you know, I wouldn't like to trust my life in an emergency situation to some other fucking monkey garbage, would I?"

Tarly felt a groan welling within her. "Franco," she said, "the emergency crates are packed by QGM. They contain *everything* you could possibly need in an emergency situation on *any* of the worlds in the Life Bubble. I mean, food, shelters, oxygen, *everything. Every* eventuality. They're the product of centuries of research! Statistics! *Science!*"

"Yes. But."

"'Yes, but' what?"

"Well, all this research baloney is just donkey bollocks, isn't it? Hey, I have my own Franco lifestyle to think about, alreet? For example, I wouldn't like to be trapped out in the wilderness with no damn and bloody horseradish to speak of."

"Horseradish?"

"Or sausages."

"Sausages."

"So I repacked the emergency crates."

"Franco, that's *illegal.*"

"Ach, fuck off."

"And it's immoral!"

"Get fucked and over to fuck."

"You'll be court-martialled for this!"

"Yeah, yeah, yeah, lock me up. Stop moaning. We have everything we need, right?"

Tarly stood, taking charge. Leaning forward slightly to counter the thrust of the boat as it headed east, its engines on *stealth*, she moved to the first crate. She punched in the release code and the digital locks hummed, releasing the lid. Inside, there were lots of tins.

"Lots of tins?" she said, slowly.

Franco appeared beside her, staring over the rim

of the emergency crate. "Yeah," he said, frowning. "Food rations. And stuff."

"What food?"

"PreCheese."

"Go on."

"Cube Sausage."

"Go on."

"Jars of horseradish. Well, you have to spice up the PreCheese and Cube Sausage, don't you, because it all tastes so fucking *rancid*."

"The thought occurs, Francis, that you could just pack *something that wasn't rancid*?"

"Never thought of that."

"What else?"

"What do you mean, 'what else'?"

"What other foodstuffs?"

"PreCheese."

"You said that."

"Cube Sausage."

"You said that, as well."

"*Weeeell...*"

"If you say 'horseradish,' you're going over the side, buddy. I didn't train to be an elite assassin killer to listen to the ramblings of an idiot on a boat."

"Inflatable."

"Whatever. So go on. What other food have you brought? We could be marooned here for weeks. *Months.*"

"I confess," said Franco, holding up both hands, palms outwards as early morning rays of crimson bounced from the metal of his cyborg little finger, "that *that* pretty much sums up our menu for the duration."

"Just PreCheese, Cube Sausage and horseradish?"

"Yup."

"Are you fucking *insane?*"

Franco considered this. "Yup," he said. "But look on the bright side. You're the guys who keep giving me contracts, yeah? I must be doing *something* right!" He grinned, and it was a Big Grin, and it was The Grin of the Mad.

"So what else have you packed into the Franco-style emergency rations for the terminally suicidal?"

"Stuff."

"Stuff?"

"Yeah, stuff."

"Like what stuff?"

Franco shrugged. His lower lip had come out a little bit.

"Are there medical kits?"

"No."

"Oxygen tanks?"

"No."

"Rebreathers?"

"No."

"Alien-INOC pills?"

"Um... no."

"Antibiots? Nanopills? Warpills?"

"No. No. And, er, no."

"Hydrapills?"

"No."

"Tools?"

"I got my sonic screwdriver!"

"Very funny. *Real* tools?"

"No."

"Body bags?"

"Why would I need body bags?"

"Haven't you worked that one out yet?"

"Ahh. I see."

"Guns?"

"Of course, guns! Yes!"

"At last," muttered Tarly, as Franco removed another lid from another crate and displayed a small arsenal of weaponry. There were Techrims, Kekras, D5, D6 and D7 shotguns, MPKs, and many, many boxes of ammunition, along with knives and TagLasers.

"See," said Franco, puffing out his chest. "I'm not *completely* devoid of my senses. Weapons and food. All that a bad girl wants."

"Hmm," said Tarly, and lifted a D5. She loaded it with ff micro-shells, and pumped the weapon with a satisfying *cla-clack*. "The irony is," she said, half smiling, "we're pretty much on friendly soil now. We're with Queen Strogger and heading for her homeland. It's not like we're going to *need* weapons, is it?"

"I wouldn't say that," said Queen Strogger, quietly.

"How's that, then?" said Franco.

"Yes, I am Queen of the orgs. But our land is, shall we say, a very dangerous place."

"With what?" snapped Franco.

"Rogue orgs," said Strogger, simply. "They're everywhere. They roam the Badlands, the Wildlands, the Heartlands, the Fuklands. There's the DIYers, lashed-up half-machines with a grudge against any org who didn't *do it yourself*. Vast, ugly brutes! They're not very bright."

"Okay," said Tarly, slowly. "And what else?"

"There's the Dorgs, which roam in packs. An experiment that went wrong, hundreds of years ago. Then there's all manner of corrupt systems and AI self-built self-modified freaks of metal and bondage which roam the land and sea."

"Land and sea, you say?" said Franco, looking nervously over the side of the boat. Sorry; inflatable.

Queen Strogger gave a brittle laugh. "Oh, don't be silly. Nothing in the water – the salt rots components faster than you removed Opera's head! No, these are..."

"Go on?"

"Well, like, *pirates.*"

"Pirates?" said Franco, and stared at Tarly, but Tarly was staring across the Teeth Ocean behind him. She gave a short nod.

"You mean, like those?" she said, quietly.

Queen Strogger turned, as did Franco. They stared at the *huge* old galleon, vast and black-timbered, and sitting on the horizon like a cat on a fence. It seemed motionless, its vast sails billowing gently in the dawn light. Franco could have sworn the sails were black. With some kind of white, skeletal motif.

"Er," said Tarly.

"Ha, don't worry," grinned Franco. "Don't ye worry ye not about that old heap of rusting shitty sea wreckage! This is a Quad-Gal Military boat, good for a billion miles on the same hydrogen cell. That fucking heap of junk wouldn't stand a chance catching us."

"Good," said Tarly, voice tight.

"Why good?"

"Because they've just seen us."

Franco grinned, and flapped his hand with a look of scornful dismissal on his face. "Look, don't ye worry ye none. One, they couldn't catch us if their lives depended on it; and two, and this kinda makes me laugh 'til I poop in my pants, but they have *old cannons*. Oh, ho, ho, ho and a bottle of rum, me hearties, those ol' cannon balls wouldn't reach us in a billion, trillion, million..."

There came a distant *boom*, and a flash of actinic fire, accompanied by billows of smoke, a long drawn-out whistling sound, and an explosion of water several metres from their inflatable boat, which sent a small wave washing over them, drenching them instantly and nearly capsizing the little rubber vessel.

"Shee-*at!*" screeched Franco.

"You were saying?" snapped Tarly, infused with anger.

In the distance, the org pirate ship had fully made its turn. Around it, something seemed to glow on the water, which started to thrash. A whine reverberated, like a SLAP across the rolling ocean, crashing from the ship in a wild acoustic rhythm. The pirate ship started to accelerate. It was fast. No. Shit. It was *fast*.

"Er," said Franco.

"It's had upgrades," said Queen Strogger, almost wearily. Her face had a haunted, hunted look. "Just as I thought we were, aha, out of the water. What did that wise old Philosopher The Meechelle Org III say? Out of the fire and into the frying pan?" She covered her face with her armoured hands. "If they discover who I am..."

"Yes?" said Franco, only half interested.

"They'll burn me alive."

"Oh." He considered this. "What kind of upgrades have they got?"

"A hyperdrive."

"Pretty impressive, for an old sea galleon. Does it, er, work?"

"Well, our patrol boats could never catch them," growled Strogger.

"Ah." Franco was watching the huge barnacle-encrusted pirate galleon. Despite his foolhardy mocking, *avast*, the ship was gaining on them at quite a lick. On the upper deck Franco could almost, if he squinted hard enough, imagine a hearty crew of large and fearsome deformed cyborgs wearing, if he wasn't very much mistaken, period costume. "Oh, gods," he said. "How do I get myself into this mad brain-twisting shit, time after time?"

It's your own fucking fault, hissed his subconscious. *You crashed the bloody Hornet, remember?*

"They're catching us," said Tarly, calmly, and started strapping various guns around and about her lithe, powerful body. "If they catch us, I'm not going out without a fucking fight!"

Franco scrambled for the guns, and strapped a goodly number about himself as well, until he bristled like a steel hedgehog.

Then they stood, watching the galleon bear down on them.

There was little else they could do.

Its vast, barnacle-encrusted timbers reared over them, creaking, and Franco had been right. The crew were vast and fearsome looking, a hybrid army of men and women, heavily machine-augmented, totally ugly in their shining, spiky, gear-driven ferocity. The ship's engines whined, and the hyperdrive which made the sea glow suddenly powered down. The galleon towered over the little QGM inflatable, and nudged it gently, with a tiny... *bump.*

"They're The Pirates," said Queen Strogger.

"Eh?" snapped Franco.

"The Pirates of the Orgibbean."

"Ahoy there!" boomed a vast, reverberating, totally machismo-infused voice from above. "This is Cap'n Bluetit, a-HAR! Known as the Rabid Arsehole of the Ocean – and I've been called a lot worse even by the people I love, so I have, a-HAR-HAR-HAR – and let me tell you, weak meat humans, you are about to be boarded! So submit your weapons, drop your trousers, bend over, and... a-HAR-HAR! take it like a man!"

CHAPTER EIGHT
SLUSH PUPPY

PIPPA'S SWORD GLEAMED under the yellow moon. She stared without emotion at the charging wall of deviated gangers. There were men with three heads, no lips, and teeth gnashing like fevered surgery victims. There were women, totally naked, long and spindly limbs thrashing as they ran, squealing with the voices of the babies they'd ingested. There were curious hybrids, of men, women, dogs, cats, rats, men with furry ears and whiskers, women with the wings of birds flapping like bloodied fans from their knobbly shoulder-blades.

"We're going to die," said Pippa, rolling her neck.

"Not if I have anything to do with it," said her clone, twirling the yukana sword.

Then a noise crashed over the surroundings,

echoing and reverberating from towering mountain walls. It was a rhythm of thunder, of hissing and smashing, and Pippa blinked as she realised it was the spinning rotors of a helicopter gunship... the same gunship that had attacked their hornet alongside a backup retinue of AI gunbots!

She set her mouth in a grim line. These were her clone's masters – the enemy. She suddenly laughed out loud at her choices: to die at the hands of the deviant gangers? Or their creators?

The gunship reared over the mountains, huge photofloods cutting through the night and making the charging deviants falter, howling and throwing up their arms, legs and tentacles to cover their eyes. Many turned and fled, aware of what was to follow... and follow it did. The miniguns screamed, as thousands of rounds cut into the mutants' ranks. Then, with a thunderous clanking, two rogue AI gunbots, like tall slender mechs with heavy missiles strapped to their arms, their slick alloy heads shining, came charging down the narrow paths from over the mountains, kicking house-sized boulders aside, their heavy steel claws gouging the rock.

"The cavalry has arrived," said Pippa's clone.

Pippa gave a nod. "Looks like you won." She tilted her head.

Her clone gave her a strange look, and stood up straight, gazing at the hundreds of fleeing deviant gangers. They were making a spirited attempt at escape, but the gunship had other ideas. The ship's rockets left trails of exhaust smoke, as explosions filled the rocky valley. Flames gushed and roared, and the twisted gangers were tossed like broken skittles, some on fire, their screams echoing against the dark vaults of heaven, many torn and shattered into hundreds of pieces.

Pippa turned away, then looked up to the gunship wreaking havoc on the ganger deviants. She could see a face in there, framed by a shock of barbed-wire black hair. The face was a concentrated funnel, a ferret of concentration as she – for it was a woman, Pippa realised – mowed down the ganger mob without remorse.

Fire blossomed from the red-hot gun barrels. Pippa ground her teeth.

"We've got to stop her!"

Her clone glanced at Pippa, and gave a nod.

"So you'll help me?" Incredulous.

"You saved my life."

The two women, genetically the *same* woman, stared at one other. Above them, the gunship lifted a little, and its blazing searchlights swept backwards and forwards, as behind it the AI gunbots came to a halt on the side of the mountain cliffs, perched precariously a thousand feet from the valley floor, like monkeys on the branches of a rocky tree. Their heads swivelled. In the gunship, Teddy Sourballs resumed firing heavy-calibre minigun rounds at the fleeing gangers. Bullets churned through flesh. Limbs were shot off. Bodies merged into the soil...

"What I'd give for a gun," growled Pippa... as the incredible happened. The two AI gunbots leapt, as one, crashing through the rotors of the gunship with high-pitched squeals of compressing, folding, breaking steel and taking hold of the huge gunship. The engines screamed, sparks and fire ejecting from the smashed machine, and the miniguns scored trails into the rocky walls as the helicopter spun around and around, as if fighting the gunbots. Then the whole screaming, flailing, spinning mess of merged metal and folding steel nose-dived, ploughing into the canyon floor. Pillars of fire spat from the fuel tanks as the AIs jumped free and stood, hands on hips, surveying the destruction they had wrought.

"Shit," breathed Pippa, as after-images of the fire danced on her retinas.

"What happened then?" said her clone.

"I thought they'd reprogrammed the gunbots? As slaves? I thought they were immune?"

The clone shrugged. "They did. Maybe they had a change of heart, seeing so many helpless gangers ploughed into the rocks. Come on. Let's go see what happened."

They started down the huge, sloping, rocky descent, moving quicker than they would have liked. Boots squealed on shale and granite, slate and scree, and they spent the last hundred metres half running, half sliding through a sea of loose black stones. Hands out for balance, they were like surfers in the velvet of night, riding the mountain to its final rocky floor.

Pippa's clone moved towards the wreckage of the gunship, broken and bent, like a child's toy after a tantrum with an iron bar. Fires burned, too bright against the blackness, glittering from scarred alloy. The clone glanced nervously at the huge gunbots, which stood, one on either side of the ravaged gunship. They were motionless sentinels.

Pippa's clone halted fifty metres away, and Pippa came up beside her. They surveyed the wreckage, and watched the two gunbots watching them back.

"If they wanted us dead, it'd be a real short fight," growled Pippa. She looked the gunbots up and down – realising how *huge* they were close up. Thirty feet in height, they were skilfully crafted from a black alloy not unlike the yukana swords, or the QGM-created AI GG machines used for so many thankless tasks across the Four Galaxies. Despite being functional, the gunbots were *sculpted*. They looked modern, sleek, and despite occasional scarring on their robotic shells, they were in prime condition. Each one carried a personal arsenal of weaponry and Pippa knew, from reading specsheets years ago during a particularly dull training day in a huge room full of plastic chairs and free cakes and coffee, that the AI gunbots could scavenge, self-repair, and self-improve, and held detailed files on all manner of engineering and weaponry. They were awesome machines, not just useful as mobile self-propelled intelligent anti-aircraft measures – as they were being used here – but also on any field of battle. Especially against infantry and tanks. *Especially* against the infantry and tanks of races with inferior technology. After all, QGM always liked to have the upper hand.

"What happened here?" said Pippa, stepping forward. She decided that if she was going to die, then fuck it, she wouldn't do it with her head in the sand. She'd go out with some fucking *conviction*.

The two gunbots turned to survey her. *Uh-oh*, she thought. *This is where I get a Kickass Stinger missile in the face!*

She tensed, then frowned. "You two! State your model and mission directive," she snapped, voice harsh with a military abruptness she'd picked up from a hundred drill sergeants across a handful of star clusters.

One machine took a step forward, feet like clawed metal hands grasping the rocky floor. "We are Quad-Gal Military General Active System Gunbot AI Mechanisms, otherwise known as GASGAMs. Our mission directives are to protect and serve the Combat K operatives known as Pippa, Franco, Keenan. Scanning now. Your samples have been accepted. You are Pippa. We hereby serve."

The two GASGAMs stood a little bit straighter, with sleek hisses of digital hydraulics. They both orientated on Pippa, whose mouth had opened a little bit.

"You're sure about that?"

"Yes, O Commander."

"Can you be a bit less formal?"

"Sure thing, boss."

"Have you got names? Or do I have to keep referring to you as Quad-Gal Military General Active System Gunbot AI Mechanisms?"

"That's Frank. I'm Bert," said the huge machine, looking down at Pippa with emotionless silver eyes.

"Thirty foot, heavily armoured killing machines called Frank and Bert?"

"You said to be less formal."

"That I did. That I did." Pippa stared even harder. *Hmm*, she thought. "Who initiated your mission directives?"

"The QGM ship's computer known as Alice, registration LA05999ZXSPECCY200."

"That would explain a lot," said Pippa's clone, moving close to her. Words tickled Pippa's ear. She gave a curt nod.

"Yeah. These machines were hacked by the gangers. That needs hardware; pretty fucking sophisticated hardware – greater than these idiots possess. All Alice did was follow the same path in, and freshly corrupt the already corrupted data. She's put my DNA and codes in there. Now they're my tools. To help me get the job done. Clever, Alice. Real neat."

Pippa stared up at the thirty-foot high machines. Distantly, the sky brightened with a promise of a cold, bleak dawn. Light glinted from the GASGAM's alloy shells.

"So you're my boys, hey? You ready to work for your stripes?"

"Sure thing, boss," said Bert. Frank nodded. He seemed to be the strong, silent type.

The destroyed gunship, a destroyed crumpled husk, like something which had been crushed in a giant's fist, ticked and crackled softly on the rocky floor. Fires burned low. Oil dripped from somewhere inside it, forming a large black pool.

From inside, there came a curse. Then a scrabbling sound. A head appeared, a tangled mass of black frizzy hair above a narrow, nasty face. Teddy Sourballs looked up at the two gunbots.

"What the fuck did you do that for, *idiots?* I thought Ziggurat had you reprogrammed? I thought we were all... in this..." She stopped. She stared at Pippa, and Pippa's clone. "Oh. It's you." Her gaze narrowed. "And you. Why are you both alive?"

Pippa took a step forward. "I'm assuming you're the pretty lady I saw behind the controls of the minigun. And also an integral part in the scheme to have me *gangered* – and murdered." She took another step forward, and her boot connected with Teddy's face, snapping her head back with a spray of blood from lacerated lips. "Nice to meet you, cunt."

Teddy clutched her mouth and scowled, as Pippa's clone moved forward and hauled her to her feet. "We need to be careful. This bitch is a wild one." She ripped some optic cabling from a twisted housing on the gunship's battered flanks, and with her knee in the small of Teddy's back, bound her hands tightly behind her.

Teddy looked back, blood on her teeth. "You'll be exterminated for this, *ganger*," she said, quite calmly. And there it was. It settled into Pippa's mind... another puzzle. Who was real? Who was the copy? Maybe they were *both copies* and the real Pippa was on a different mission?

Pippa's clone grinned. "Let's just say I've had a change of heart."

"You'll have a fucking change of heart when Ziggurat gets hold of you. He's an expert with sharp implements. He'll be spending *months* with you in his cellars. And that's *before* the Mistress gets involved."

"So that's the hierarchy, is it?" said Pippa softly. "This muppet, then Ziggurat, then the Mistress right at the top, overseeing mindless exterminations and warmongering like a shitlist bitch, lusting after another fucking wargasm."

"Yeah, the Mistress is Prime Core, General of the Royal Ganger Police Force and Commissioner for the entire CLONE TV network. She's the one who, basically, controls the entire planet's TV, filmy and computer networks. She's the one in charge of media, the government, you name it. She's the bitch at the top."

"The bitch who needs stopping."

"I thought your mission was to find the 3Core? You know I know it. And you know I know you were heading for the Slush Pits; that's where the Pod Vault is, of course." She winked.

"And the Mistress knows I'm coming?"

"Of course. She knows everything that's going on, down here on Cloneworld. After all, she wouldn't be the unofficial Ganger Queen, if not."

"Queen of the Gangers, eh? I never did like royal blood."

"Unless it's on the tip of your sword."

Pippa chuckled. "You're so good, you remind me of me. I wonder, sometimes, who really is the clone. Maybe both of us, eh, girl?"

The clone nodded. "That would be a good fucking mind-job, wouldn't it?"

"To clone the clone. A copy of an imitation. Beautiful."

"But then, who's to say what's real? Who's to say who's the copy? To be honest, Pippa, I no longer care. My drives are your drives, and if I *am* a clone, as these bastards believe, they made a big mistake trying to replicate the real Pippa's DNA."

Teddy Sourballs started to laugh, and both Pippas turned to look at her.

"You think you're so clever, a couple of bitches fresh out of the Slush Pits. Go on, head for the Pod Vault; see what's waiting for you there. We know what you want, and you'll die trying."

Pippa took hold of Teddy's hair, and dragged her head down to the ground. She put her boot on Teddy's face, and pressed down hard. Teddy squealed like rat in a fire.

"Well, looks like I'm going to need a bartering tool, eh, love?"

"The Mistress will never give you what you want!" panted Teddy, face chewing dirt.

Pippa bowed low, and stared in Teddy's eyes. The yukana sword shifted, tip wavering before Teddy Sourballs's eyeballs. The steel glinted, a reflection of promised death. "Well, she can say goodbye to her little monkey, then, you mass-murdering piece of shit."

THE GASGAMS THUNDERED across the landscape, hydraulics working smoothly, fluid machines rolling with ease. One had opened its chest into a kind of wired cage, and into this metal kangaroo pouch Teddy Sourballs had been flung without dignity. Steel cables had pulled her tight, compressing her face into a parody of the human.

"It hurts!" she said, muffled by the mesh, her features contorted into squares.

"Good," said Pippa, without even turning.

Pippa and her clone rode on the backs of the GASGAMs, secured by safety harnesses and heady with the rush of height and speed. The final descent from the Ganger Mountains had been a mad panic of flight, of falling rocks and scraping scree, of gasps and violent feelings of spinning vertigo as the two women rode the mechs like upright metal steeds. But The Gangers had dropped, then risen again into rocky foothills devoid of life and, thankfully, devoid of ganger deviants.

Pippa, the real Pippa, the old Pippa, the *true* Pippa
– in her mind, at least – rode in silence, but her skull
was a maelstrom of confusion. She doubted herself.
She doubted reality. She doubted sanity. *Is this it? Is
this what happens when your mind fractures? When
you go insane? When reality cracks like a broken bad
egg? Am I real? Am I really real? Am I Pippa, or a
simple carbon copy? An imitation? A doppelgänger? I
feel real. I think thoughts and feel feelings, emotions,
ideas, I have memories as real as anything else in my
head. Surely I'd just fucking know I was the real me.
Instinctive. Like a lion knows to hunt meat. Like a
spider knows to spin a web. In-built, a part of you.
Surely I'd just know, right? Because... well, if I don't,
if I can't feel something so basic, something at a
molecular level, if I can't differentiate between being
human, a first breed, and being a copy – well, surely I
don't deserve to live?*

They moved through a wasteland of rolling,
desolate hills. A cold wind blew down from the
mountains, and the sky was filled with towering
clouds promising a fight. Pippa glanced left, to the
smoothly-pounding GASGAM with its piggy-back
human rider.

*She said I was the clone. That she was real. But
now it turns out she might be a clone. Both of us
could be clones! What a joke. And if that's the case,
where the hell is the real Pippa?*

*None of us want to feel like copies; we all want to
be the original, the master, the template. None of us*

want to feel second-hand. Used. Abused. Cast aside. Another's useless fucking toy.

Am I real?

Am I Pippa?

And it went back, further and further, spearing into her memories, all the way back to that moment, that moment she hated, that she always revisited in her dreams and in her fucking nightmares... the murders. Keenan's family. It had all been so perfect – ha, yeah, right. She'd fallen in love with a married man, a man with two children, bright-eyed young things called Rachel and Ally. And then somehow they'd all ended up dead, and Pippa thought, *knew, fucking believed* that she'd done it...

Murdered them. Murdered them all.

IT WAS UNFAIR, so incredibly unfair; but then I find these things always are. The cool breeze ruffled my hair; filled my senses with life, and with a calmness which should have been impossible. The wall was rough under my gloves, and I smiled to myself, staring out across a dark street. Rain fell, cleansing the world with gentle acid. I revelled in the rain; it provided me with extra cover.

I stepped out, boots silent on wet alloyconcrete. The hour was late, the moon peeping from behind fists of cloud. I moved cautiously, still not sure what I would do or what the outcome would be; but I knew, knew there had to be confrontation, some form of retribution. These things could not go unpunished. There had to be justice in the world; not the insane ramblings of some aged incontinent judge, sat in his skewed wig, his only desire a lust for port and brandy and bent-over young boys later that evening. Where was the justice in that? No: this was justice, real justice, the law of the land and nature and blood.

I crossed the road, skipping onto the pavement, looked about. The world was dead. My eyes hardened. *It has to come*, I kept telling myself; this moment has to come. Like night follows day, smoke follows fire, death follows life.

The path was heavily crowded by trees: conifers, their pine scent filling my nostrils and making me yearn for a childhood in the woodland behind my home. Those days, however, were gone. Buried. I walked slowly, almost reluctantly, until I reached the door. The pretty house – all white and terracotta – was in darkness. Distantly, I could hear the sea.

I reached out to knock, but something stopped me. Instead, I stepped from the path and moved around the perimeter. I halted by a set of patio doors, peered in at discreet alarm sensors. I opened a small case at my hip, slid out several identity-card sized items, and eased them under the door. Remotely controlled, the two slivers of metal glided across black marble tiles and stopped. With a *click* I killed the alarms. Then I prized open the door, stepped inside, closed it behind me.

The room was still. It smelled good; home cooking

mixed with lavender and the recent aroma of extinguished candles. I moved across the carpet, all senses firing, stealth a priority; I orientated myself, moved through the hall and to the foot of the stairs. The house was silent around me. It was welcoming, and yet I shivered. Something bad had to happen here tonight. I did not know what, but the conflict was *there*. Suppressed. And like a caged serpent, it could not rest.

I moved up the stairs, a ghost.

I drifted across the landing, paused, heard breathing, and a mumble in sleep. Passed the door, slightly ajar, nightlight casting a blue glow, and came to the master bedroom. Pushed the door, which opened noiselessly. Again, a blue nightlight in the corner of the room highlighted an eerie, haunting scene. Long hair lying across a pillow. A face, serene in sleep. Eyes fluttering in a dream. One pale, smooth arm thrown wide.

Jealously forced a fist down my throat, gripped my heart and wrenched it from my chest. I choked on anger, and a sudden welling hatred, and it wasn't supposed to be like this, I wasn't supposed to *feel* like this, but fury swamped me and the words I wanted to say to her, *the bitch, the cunt,* Freya, Keenan's wife, dissipated like smoke, and my eyes narrowed, and I staggered, physically *stumbled,* as my head spun, whirling with colours and darkness and images of blood, and I fell against the dresser, my hand lashing out to steady myself, my fingers curling around a gleam of long, sleek metal –

A pair of scissors.

Freya's eyes opened, fixed on me, confusion taking her mind. But then sleep fled, I saw recognition develop on her face (of course, she'd seen my pictures in the news after the incompetence that was the *Terminus5* reactor incident) and she *knew*, she *understood*, she saw I was Keenan's lover and come here to –

To what?

To sort out the problem? To talk about his *betrayal* – of us both? To attempt to *understand* the situation, and the reasons, and yet all this fled me, and a terrible demon squatted in my mind, and I lifted the scissors and saw Freya's mouth open to scream and I leapt, meaning only to silence her, to quieten her, then I was atop her struggling, powerful body and the covers fell away, exposing milk-white breasts and my hand covered her mouth, covered the scream, and she struggled, *struggled hard*, but I lifted the scissors – glanced up then, at their gleaming mated blades, then down into eyes now frightened and *understanding*, and I smiled. Smiled a thin cruel smile. I hammered the scissor blades into Freya's heart, and she went rigid at the impact. Blood fountained, pumping over me, drenching the duvet in seconds. She spasmed, started to struggle again, but I held her there, in her death throes, abusing my strength, my power, my training, my trust, my honour, and I held her there, the twin blades embedded in her chest, in her *heart*, and I watched with blank eyes as the struggling grew swiftly weak, and she slumped back, and I removed my hand from her mouth. She stared at me, and I watched the life bleeding from her eyes. Her lips trembled.

'Why?' she croaked.

And then she was dead.

I stood, reversing neatly from the bed, using the covers to wipe my gloved hands and the scissors. I stared at Freya; she seemed broken at impossible angles. I did not feel proud. But I understood. This was something: a necessity. I had not travelled to Keenan's house to kill, but the murder released a great weight from my heart. From my soul.

I turned, moved out of the bedroom.

Stopped.

Around me, the world turned.

I heard muted sobbing from the children's bedroom. They had heard. Heard the struggle. Maybe even come in, all sleepy-eyed and tousle-haired, as I pinned Freya down in her frantic last moments of precious, squirming life. In which case... they probably saw my face, my features, my joy, caught rigid in the act of murder.

I stepped towards the door and pushed it open.

I saw the young girls, silhouetted in the gloom.

They were staring at me, tears wet on their cheeks.

I put my finger to my lips.

'Shh,' I said. 'It's going to be all right.'

I walked forward, still carrying the scissors.

* * *

THE FIRE BURNED brightly, demons crackling, wood popping. Pippa's clone had built it, and both women sat dejectedly, staring into the flames. Night had come, and Pippa called for a rest. She said she was tired; exhausted. What she really meant to say was, *I am haunted by the past, by bad dreams, by nightmares that stick in my brain like needles and WON'T FUCKING LET ME GO!*

The two huge GASGAM's stood, motionless, silent, flames reflecting from their dull alloy shells. Perfect killers, right? Wrong, thought Pippa as she stared into the fire. *I am the perfect killer. I am the ultimate fucking prize.* That's why QGM gave me a job. That's why they had me cloned. That's why I killed Keenan's family. Because I must have killed them. I barely remember it – or maybe the memories, the echoes, are implanted? Whatever. Every crime has its price. Every killer must face the consequences, somewhere down the line... and if not in this life, then the next or the next or the fucking next.

I feel my mind unravel.

I feel it spin out, drawn out unto infinity by the claws of the solar spider.

Pippa's clone, or her template, her reality, was asleep. Snoring gently. The flames cast gentle orange shadows on her features, softening them in sleep. Pippa found herself caught in the bizarre situation where she could study herself. Study her own face in sleep. And she shuddered. *I'd be better off dead,* she realised.

Better off exterminated, my ash ploughed under the soil.

ANOTHER DAY HAD passed in uncomfortable travel. Whilst the GASGAMs were unparalleled for bringing down a wide range of aerial warcraft with minimum fuss and maximum violence, they were *not* the comfiest of donkeys. As a long day of biting wind and diagonal drizzle across vast, open plains filled with hidden rocks and unexpected peat bogs finally dragged to a painful, back-breaking end, so they dismounted in the lee of a group of lode-streaked boulders beside a small stand of black conifers.

Stretching, and feeling in need of exercise, Pippa climbed up the rocky outcrop, enjoying the sudden exercise after miles and miles of cramped, thumping travel.

Fingers burning, she stood on the top and surveyed the landscape. The sun was sinking in horizontal slashes of magenta and pink. Shading her eyes, Pippa tried to make out the distant Slush Pits, but saw nothing. She turned, and behind towered The Gangers, a violent, serrated knife in the belly of the land. They looked ominous, even from this distance, and Pippa shivered. She never wanted to go back to their deviant, freak-infested peaks...

"Fresh air?"

Pippa glanced at her ganger cousin. She'd decided it best to think of this *other Pippa* in that way, in the hope of dispelling the random murder images and *lusts* which kept slashing through her mind. Whilst the sane part of Pippa thought to herself – *she's you,* the same blood, the same mind, the same person – another part of her replayed the attack back in the mountains, and even worse, the murder of Freya and the girls... and Keenan's willingness to join them in the Chaos Halls.

Pippa shuddered, and took a deep breath.

"You still want to kill me, right?"

"It's the nature of the beast."

"You're undecided. Unsure. Confused. Broken."

"I've been broken for a very, very long time."

"You can be fixed, Pippa."

Pippa stared at her clone, and shrugged. "I think, sometimes, in this world, in this life, some things cannot be repaired." She turned and leapt onto a parapet of rocks, then scrambled down the incline.

Her ganger turned and faced the sinking sun.

We all die, she thought.

Some, sooner than others.

Then she followed Pippa into the shadow-lengthening camp.

TEDDY SOURBALLS STARTED to laugh.

"Something funny?" said Pippa. She was reclining, eating some kind of thin gruel supplied by the GASGAM's emergency life-support stores. They could keep a human alive indefinitely by reconstituting any kind of organic materials into a thin but *very* nutritious grey gruel. But, as Pippa had pointed out, it didn't do one's appetite any good to think they were eating pulped rodents and genetically reorganised horse-shit.

"You're going to the Slush Pits. Ziggurat will be waiting for you."

"Yeah, but we have *you* as a hostage, right?"

Teddy shrugged. "I can always be rebuilt."

Pippa frowned. "What does that mean?"

"She means when she dies, they just clone her. In a Vat. In a place very similar to the Slush Pits, only this one is a bit more refined and reserved for *TV Royalty* and *Important People*. Usually ganger politicians and filmy stars. It makes you sick to see such an abuse of money and power. Ordinary people have to go to the Slushers, and even that costs them an arm and a leg. Quite literally, sometimes. They're the equivalent of back-street, rusty-knife abortions carried out by sick doctors struck off the medical register for unsafe practice."

"So when a ganger dies, they can be brought back?"

"Yeah. A ganger is – how can I put this? – *allotted* a certain amount of changes in their lifetime. Some famous people, like the TV and filmy star *Rebecca Rebecca*, sell templates of their DNA so that gangers can copy them, with a few minor twists of course; somebody as famous as Rebecca Rebecca wouldn't want to be refused entry to The Ganger Awards or anything like that, would she? So sometimes they build in genetic *Clauses*."

"So this is a society surrounding TV? That's how it looks. Especially going off the reaction when Franco – the idiot – slotted Opera."

"Yeah, media is everything to a ganger. Vanity is everything. I mean, would you want to copy somebody else's DNA, absorb it into your own system, make it the dominant life force? It takes a certain type of ego, of narcissism, to do that."

"Surely if you absorb an alien DNA, then you take on other things? Their thought patterns, for example. Characteristics. Social views and habits. That sort of thing."

"In the Slush Pits you can have Options. Whereas Clauses are *enforced,* Options are your chosen preferences – they buy you different grades of cloning. If it's a Straight Cheap Transfer, you're fucked. But if you have a bit of money, or want to remortgage your five bedroom ApartBubble, you can have more control. Gradients of cloning, if you will."

Pippa scratched her head. "I'm sorry. I'm a bit lost. I thought gangers had a natural, innate ability to clone others? I thought any ganger could take a sample from me, be it hair, or saliva, and copy me. That's why they were so feared. That's why they – you – were effectively imprisoned here by QGM. No off-world travel for the gangers; or next thing you know, one's impersonated General Steinhauer and is running Quad-Gal Military behind everyone's backs." She laughed, coldly.

Pippa's clone smiled. "Yes. Quite. We are massively different, organically, from the base human species.

I think gangers always thought themselves superior; after all, they could mimic and imitate without problem, without remorse or empathic regret – and that could and *would* make us naturally superior. A ganger could take the strength of one creature, the agility of another, the ferocity of a third, and blend them all into one psychopathic killing-shell that would piss all over human armies. That's why we were banished here. Imprisoned. That's why everybody is so scared of us. We have the potential for massive... upset. *Domination.* Now, the elite are simply used by QGM for missions. With certain caveats, of course."

"Caveats?"

"Spinal Logic Cubes. Control implants. A little bit like what they used on you and your Combat K buddies. AI control. Behaviour devices. If I go walk-about from Cloneworld – bam! I'm a jelly donut in a skin sack."

"Is that why the orgs were put here?"

"Yeah." Pippa's clone gave a cold smile. "Yet another control mechanism, although the orgs claim they were here first – I think it helps pacify their religious warlike tendencies. Gives them credence. It was QGM playing Mother Nature again. A balance, you see? I came to understand after decades of study. The orgs were introduced as creatures of hatred – and vice versa. We are at war continually; and when a race is at war, it helps keep the numbers down, right? We're fighting ourselves into an extinction pit, and nobody seems to see the irony."

"The irony?"

"We're all pawns. All game pieces on a planetary gameboard. It makes me wonder sometimes if the whole fucking show isn't being televised for God's benefit." She gave a cold, bitter laugh, and Pippa realised with a shock that the ganger still had layers of her own personality. Which meant...

She wasn't a direct copy of Pippa.

She *did* kill Keenan's wife and children; must have! For Pippa knew, felt deep down inside, that this was something *she* could never knowingly do. But the ganger, the half-clone – it looked like Pippa, walked like Pippa, even killed like Pippa. But there were essential differences.

The clone didn't love Keenan.

Pippa did. And because of that, she knew she was the *real* Pippa, the real woman, the template; and the ganger, the clone, it was fucking with her skull, playing games with her mind and soul.

Slowly, Pippa closed her mouth. Her eyes went hard. Her heart went hard.

Soon, she would kill her.

After they reached the Slush Pits.

After they found the 3Core.

After she had served her purpose...

IT WAS DAWN. The sun crept over a blank horizon and threatened winter sunlight, slung low like a sharpshooter's sagging gun-belt. Pippa peered over the rocky ground using binos supplied by the GASGAMs.

The Slush Pits, from the outside, looked like one huge warehouse. A warehouse five *kilometres* wide. It was a characterless black building, which looked like it had been constructed from corrugated black alloy. It rose perhaps five stories in height, but without windows. The only markings on the surface, mid-point down the five-klick stretch, were the giant words: GANGERS INC. Sunlight gleamed from alloy walls, highlighting morning dew and hints of frost.

Pippa sat back, and bit her lower lip.

"Heavy fortifications?"

Pippa shook her head. "On the contrary. Wire perimeter fence, one road in and out, security hut with a guard picking his nose and reading filmy slips. But then, that's what makes me suspicious, yeah?"

"There's an underground train for gangers coming here for modifications or with cloning jars," said Pippa's clone. "That's all I know. I've never been in. Never *wanted* to go in."

"There's a big surprise waiting in there for you, fuckers," snarled Teddy Sourballs, face a curious mixture of sneering superiority, and fear, and hate – all blended into a face like a punchbag. A used one.

Pippa barked a laugh. "Not much of a surprise now, is it? You've told us about it. And if we know about it, we're *prepared* for it. Understand, idiot?"

Teddy frowned. "Er..."

"You're a dumb clone, that's for sure. What does the Mistress pay you for, anyway? Stupidity?"

"It's not my fault," scowled Sourballs. "This," she waved her bound hands, "wasn't part of my original job description! I was a teacher, all right? My job was to win over the rich parents, get the little bastards into the building, and make sure we filled up their books with as much stuff as possible to justify our huge fees. Didn't matter what we put in their books, any old shite would do. We used to bribe exam markers. Got the top results! One of the top schools on Clone Terra! Bloody gangers thought we were supreme!"

She looked up. Pippa was staring at her.

"You were a fucking *teacher?*" snarled Pippa. "A teacher, piloting a gunship? Call me old fashioned, but there's a conflict of images here. What do you do during break? Torture? Rape? Sodomy? What about your spare time? Do you pilot submarines? Fix leaking Deep Space Marine Vessels? Machine gun combat fucking GKs?"

"No." Teddy had retreated into her shell like a snail under the shadow of a boot. "I never asked for this. But I got dragged along, all right? My job description specified that I was to take useless little fuckers, fill their books with irrelevant crap, then punt out top-level gangers who looked good on *paper*. We didn't care about their *education*. Oh no. We cared about their *monies*, because it was on the back of that cash the Mistress built the TV networks. She'd funnel the money from excessively wealthy parents into expanding her TV Empire. It was all for the greater good. You see?"

"What did you teach?" said Pippa, softly.

"English." Teddy sniffed. "Actually, I was the *Head* of English."

"How can you be the Head of something when you freely admit you weren't actually interested in teaching? Simply justifying your excessive fees? Gods, what kind of school was it?"

"We provided a service," growled Teddy, barbed-wire hair bobbing like a particularly badly fitting wig. "And we did it to the best of our ability!"

"Oh yeah? A service to your own back pockets to make a fucking big pot of cash."

"There is no crime in making money!"

"There is when it's at the expense of somebody's education! Go on, what was your prime objective? The school's mission statement?"

Teddy thought for a moment. "Okay, yes, I agree to some extent, we *were* a business. We had to make money to survive, to prosper, to expand! We were oppressed by QGM, the gangers were downtrodden and forced into a position of weakness. But one day," her eyes gleamed, "one day we will overthrow you! You've already seen, we have learned how to crack your GASGAMs. We have built a secret..." Her voice trailed off. "No. I have said too much."

Pippa stepped forward and snapped out a right straight that dropped Teddy in an instant. The frizzy ganger glared up at her through tear-filled eyes, blood dripping from her nose. "That's for all the kids you fucked over," Pippa snarled through a mouthful of saliva and hate. She kicked Teddy in the face, slamming her back and rendering her unconscious. "And that's for being a bitch. I hate bitches."

Pippa's clone stepped forward. "But *you're* a bitch!"

"Yeah, well, I hate myself," snapped Pippa.

"That's my boss you just laid out cold."

"Well, I don't want her screwing up my plan. Because it's a good plan. And it needs her unconscious so her big, flapping mouth can't flap like a bitch-landed fish on a schooner's deck."

"You've thought of a way to get in?"

"Oh yeah," said Pippa, her green eyes gleaming.

THE GUARD'S NAME was Squib, and he was a squib. All squibs were little fellas, about two feet in height, and bred in a FatVat with identical DNA. They were all called "Squib" which, in terms of individual identification, made life a nightmare, but because nobody working for GANGERS INC. gave a flying bollock about any forms of personal identification or the rights of the squib individual, it was a moot point.

Squib sat in his guard box, scowling, and he scowled a lot because the squibs, as genetically-engineered servile species go, were a pretty bad tempered bunch. Not to their Lords and Masters and Betters, of course, oh, no; that had been genetically dredged out of them with a fine clawed hammer. But to one another. There wasn't a single one of the six thousand squibs who worked in the Slush Pits who wasn't filled with absolute hate and loathing for his fellow squib, despite their identical nature.

And so Squib sat, his metal guard box gleaming with the crimson rays of the sinking sun, and he watched the road, and the fence, and searched earnestly for signs of intruders. *Oh* how he'd like to find an intruder. "I'd love to find an intruder," he often said to himself, "just to see what it was like to find an intruder!" This would obviously necessitate acts of hideous violence, for what Squib lacked in verticality he made up for in raw aggression and a willingness to torture even small animals to within an inch of their death.

Squib sat.

Squib fumed.

Squib contemplated.

Squib hated.

Squib had managed to build up quite a *well* of hatred, frustration, anger, apathy, disgust, loathing and downright *detestation* for everything, because he'd been sat in his hut for nearly ten years now. Ten years without an intruder! Ten years waiting to vent his glowing ball of intensity on some unlucky traveller stumbling stupidly into his nasty web.

"I'll show them," he'd often muttered over the past ten years, ragged eyebrows frowning so hard they'd touch in the middle of his round, pudgy face. "I'll kill them! Wipe them from the planet! Torture them! Cause them raw agony! I'll peel them! I'll, I'll,

I will..." And he'd realise, with sinking dejection, what he really *would* do. What he really *would* do is *ask for their pass*. Shit. Ha! But if they didn't have a pass? *Hey! Then* killing, torture and raw agony were on the menu, that's for sure!

Squib sat, as he had for countless thousands of days, contemplating the bleak rocky horizon. Occasionally, he would turn and examine the huge black fortress building behind him, worried that somebody might sneak up on him. He was paranoid like that. And he knew the paranoia had been growing for years.

Now, however, on this late evening, filled with dying wintry sunlight, with the shadows of The Ganger Mountains stretching out like long, rubber teeth over the barren rocky ground, there came a muffled *clank*.

Squib frowned. Had he really heard a clank? Or was the clank just a clanking figment of his clanking imagination?

The *clank* clanked again.

Squib felt a thrill of excitement and fear run charge through his veins. Here it was! Something out of the ordinary! *Forget them damn, damn bastard squibs with their guns, and rocket launchers, and stories of things going wrong on the underground tube-missile trains from Nechudnazzar and Raifnazzar, from Purple and Green and the distant far north city of Harmony. Forget all their bullshit and hero tales! Their jabbering of high adventure, and gunfights, and gangers trying to sneak into the Slush Pits for secret love trysts with surgeons willing to take sex in order to regrow an arm or leg or vagina! No, this was Squib's time, this was Squib's moment, this was Squib's adventure, man!*

He stood. He brushed down his neat black uniform. He took the heavy calibre rifle from its rack, and ran a pudgy-fingered hand along the smooth, cool, black stock. The gun was polished to a high gleam. Squib had put many man-hours into polishing that gun. Indeed, it was his third gun, having polished his way *through* two previous incarnations. That's how much time Squib had. That's how fucking bored he was. But then, boredom served a purpose. It made you ready for the action! Yeah!

More clanks echoed across the barren ground, and from behind a bank of rolling hills Squib watched with a growing erection as a huge, metal monstrosity rose, and rose. And rose. It was huge. Thirty feet tall! It could squash Squib with an ill-timed footfall! *It was fifteen times his height! Nay! Maybe twenty times!* In his imagination, and for the purposes of tales down the Squib Arms later, drinking Squib's Finest Ale and eating Squib Pie (don't ask), it could possibly be *a hundred fucking times taller than him!*

Squib puffed out his chest, clutched his gun tight, and opened the metal door with a long, slow creak. He stepped out into cool night air. The sun was dying over the horizon like a blood ghost. He felt a fresh wave of excitement rush through him. His cock pressed hard and true against his pants. He was ready. Ready for the challenge. Ready for the fight!

As the huge metal robot marched forward, inadvertently (and, Squib thought, *clumsily*) stepping on the metal fence with a *crunch*, so Squib waddled forward and lifted his well-polished carbine.

The huge machine clanked forward, swaying a little with each step, and Squib thought proudly to himself, *It's like a filmy. Like one of those famous ones like* The Squib, The Squib and the Squib, For a Few Squibs More, Once Upon a Time in Squibland, *and the seminal* Squib Wars. He preened, not even considering the Herculean task of attempting to kill a thirty-foot-tall metal monstrosity. After all, he was the hero, right? The righteous dude pouring furious and righteous anger on his foes. Or something.

"HALT!" Squib screamed, face twisted into the purest expression of anger and hatred, run through with a little streak of sexual fulfilment. "WHO GOES THERE? I WILL FIRE IF YOU DO NOT HALT!"

The GASGAM clanked and stomped towards the squib, seemingly oblivious to this little angry man, yakking like a little, annoying dog. A yakker snakker. The GASGAM had bigger fish to fry.

Like the building.

There was a click, as a missile slid sideways and into place on the GASGAM's arm, then a ROAR as the missile detached and slammed at the Slush Pit factory. Tiny holes opened up on the flanks of the building and counter-missiles launched in retaliation. Fire screamed through the heavens, and black, billowing smoke filled the sky. The GASGAM opened up with its heavy machine guns, strafing the side of the factory. Missiles slammed at the GASGAM, which knocked them aside without thought. Many exploded, but did little or no damage to the gunbot's impenetrable armour.

And all the while, Squib the squib danced like a maniac at the GASGAM's feet, trying to get noticed. He fired his weapon, and realised with horror he'd not fitted a magazine to the carbine. *Oh what an idiot squib you are! Oh how the other squibs will laugh at you down at The Squib and Jockey on Friday night! How they'll take the piss and pour beer over your head when you're laid out and unconscious with shame! You dumb little mutt!*

The GASGAM continued to attack the building. Rockets and bombs rained down fire and hell from the sky, but not a mark scathed the structure's exterior.

Amidst the turmoil, the chaos, the violence, there came twin *phwwts* as Pippa and her clone were ejected by the GASGAM, ejected and *projected* like missiles towards the building's roof. The GASGAM's calculations were perfect, and both Pippas landed lightly on the lip of the building, took a quick look behind at the flames and billowing smoke, the craters in the rocky ground and the exploding chaos around the GASGAM, then dropped onto the flat roof and hunkered down behind the rim.

Its quarry safely delivered, the GASGAM fired six

final rockets, which filled the sky with purple fire as they were destroyed in a screaming line by 25t Bitchcats, and turned to leave, job done, mission accomplished. It slid for a moment, as it stepped on an unexpected obstruction; there was a tiny *squeak*, and a sound of crunching bones, but this barely registered in its fast-scrolling million-core AI cell. The GASGAM strolled off towards the distant rocky hills, swatting pursuing rockets from the air like gnats.

Behind it, the gunbot left a smear of purple squib grease on the rocks.

PIPPA FELT A thrill of adrenaline and speed as she was launched from the GASGAM. Her ascent was a perfectly synchronised arc, and she landed lightly on the lip of the roof, having used up every joule of energy needed to carry her to her target. She dropped and checked her weapons, her yukana sword and an MPK machine gun provided by the GASGAM's competent in-built Quad-Gal Military stores, and glanced at her clone. She checked for cams, and spied the roof access. She signalled to her clone, who nodded in understanding, and under cover of fast-falling, bruised darkness they both ran in half crouches towards the Slush Pit entrance...

A DOOR SLID up in the wall of the factory. Ziggurat was there, bulky and hunched, one yellow eye and one green eye surveying the damage wreaked by the GASGAM.

"Sir, I thought they were under our control?"

"So did I," said Ziggurat, hobbling forward, a ridiculous figure, a figure of fun to be laughed at – or he would have been, if it hadn't been for the neat tool-roll of very sharp medical implements at his belt, coupled with an intrinsic knowledge of the ganger anatomy and a willingness to show no mercy, no matter how much his victim screamed. The soldiers from The Bad Army knew this. Which is why they gave Ziggurat enormous respect and a considerable, eager berth at every eventuality.

Ziggurat hobbled across scorched earth, and stopped by the splatter that was Squib the squib. He was wafer thin. He was, indeed, a pool of goo with crushed bones mixed in.

"Shall we bury him, sir?" asked one soldier.

Ziggurat looked up at the sky, then shrugged, which, on a hunchback, had double the effect. "No. Leave him for the buzzards. He can be easily replaced."

Then Ziggurat took out a small communicator. Matt black, with a single red light to signify transmission. He smiled, his curious lop-sided face twisting into deformity. He spoke into the comms.

"Pippa's inside. Be ready. Kill her on sight. Out."

CHAPTER NINE

PIRATES OF THE ORGIBBEAN

FRANCO SCOWLED AS the rope-ladder was rolled down to their craft and, with a host of perhaps eighty guns pointing at them from along the galleon's crusty, uneven rail, he took hold of the first rung and started to climb. The ladder flapped and slapped against the side of the ship, sea-spray splashed him, and the wind mocked him with a whining cackle. He passed huge letters carved into the flank of the pirate galleon. They read: *The Nice Lady*.

Hmm, thought Franco. *Somehow I don't think this is going to be all that nice an experience, and they don't call me Franco "Yo, Ho, Ho" Haggis for nothing!*

Franco reached the deck, fists clenched, and was decked with a club from behind. He groaned, rolling on the salty, sea-strewn planks, and felt his hands tied roughly behind him with coarse rope.

Tarly followed next, and was given the same treatment. The BCube containing a still-silent Alice was taken by Cap'n Bluetit and examined with only modest interest, before being tossed onto a chest brimming with gold and silver doubloons, necklaces of peals and all manner of glittering magpie treasure.

Four huge pirates – and Franco blinked, for they could only be described *as* pirates – stepped forward. They wore traditional costume: ballooning pants, heavy boots, slime-smeared jerkins of leather and wool; one even wore a red and white striped vest. They possessed all manner of bushy beards and shaggy, drooping moustaches, their hands were festooned with heavy rings like the finest of knuckle-dusters, and they wore brightly coloured headscarves wrapped, not surprisingly, around their heads. However. They were orgs, and so their pirate costumes were slightly ruined by their mechanical arms and legs, which hissed and fizzed and slid on greased hydraulic poles. Some had alloy machine faces, glittering with whirling gears and cogs. Some had augmented *bodies*, and were larger than any real man had a right to be, bulked out with metal armour and casing, but still wearing brightly coloured striped vests. The whole effect made Franco wince. It was like they'd ineptly copied an image from an ancient Earth filmy.

The four huge pirates carried a heaped net made

of thick metal strands, each fizzing and humming and burping. Occasionally it sparked. They acted as if the metal net was causing them some pain, and nimbly, despite their size and bulk, leapt up to stand in a swaying line along the galleon's rail, despite the huge ship shifting and rolling at the whim of the Teeth Ocean.

"A-HAR!" grinned Cap'n Bluetit, winking and chewing on a cigar. "'Tis an org Net, me hearties. Should slow down that there enemy org a right treat, so it should, a-HAR!"

The pirates threw the fizzing, popping net down over Queen Strogger, who had her head down, subdued, as if she knew her fate. It was as if she had lain down to die. She was captured; she knew it, they knew it. And if she was captured by the Pirates of the Orgibbean, then her fate was assured.

She was going to get a kicking.

Probably a lot, lot worse.

Ropes were looped around not just Queen Strogger, but the inflatable QGM boat, and the pirates formed two lines. "HEAVE!" they shouted, then "HEAVE-HO," and, working in rhythm, the two lines of pirates hoisted Queen Strogger, boat and all, up onto the brine-swilled decks of *The Nice Lady*.

Franco and Tarly, trussed up on the boards, got a gasping faceful of sea water as Queen Strogger was landed like the most undignified of fish. The org net engulfing her was fizzing and popping, and she was *writhing* at its core.

"At least we've still got our emergency supplies," said Franco, and gave Tarly a big grin and a wink.

She scowled at him.

"You there, stop talking!" bellowed an ugly org pirate with lumps and bumps all over his face. He leaned back, and Franco blinked as he realised the pirate carried a... a... a *whip?* It lashed across Franco's bare back with a *crack*. There was a moment of nothing, then pain like FIRE screamed across Franco's whole being and he let out a momentous howl that shook *The Nice Lady* to its watery bowels.

Franco struggled, slipping, to his knees, and scowled at the pirate. "You *bastard,*" he snapped, leaping forward and, his hands tied tightly behind his back, doing what he did best: brawling. He kicked the org pirate in the nuts. The pirate howled long and hard, eyes crossing as his legs closed reflexively and he fell to the decks in a foetal position. A fist whirred by Franco's head like a flapping partridge, but Franco swayed, stamped on the attacker's toes, and as the huge, seven-foot tall pirate bellowed and leant forward, Franco head-butted him good and hard on the nose, breaking it with a *crack*. A punch caught Franco in the back of the head, but he rolled with it, leg kicking out to break a knee-cap. Suddenly, he was a whirlwind of ginger beard at the core of pandemonium. Fists and kicks were flying, but Franco seemed to be dancing amongst the clumsy, oafish orgs, feet and knees making short work of many an unexposed groin, big flat head flattening any exposed nose that got in his way. Swords were drawn, flashing in the sunlight, and Tarly screamed, "Franco, behind you!" Franco whirled, as a blade whizzed down and cut the bottom inch of his beard clean off. There was a momentary pause as Franco watched an inch of ginger fluff waft gently down to the planks of the galleon, drifting from side to side as it fell. A scowl of fury took over Franco's face.

"Hey," he said. "NOBODY cuts my fucking beard!"

Another sword slashed down, and Franco leapt, and twisted, and the blade cut neatly through the ropes. Franco shook his hands free and lifted his fists as the pirates surrounded him. There were ten; no, twenty; no, thirty. Franco grinned at them all, then looked down at Tarly and gave a big wink.

"Come and get it, lads," he growled, puffing out his chest and cracking his knuckles.

The pirates charged in, and like in a comedy cartoon there were two THWACKS, and two pirates were lifted from their feet, heads up, sailing back and down, their feet following. They hit the deck, but *unlike* a comedy cartoon, their teeth broke and rattled across the boards. One sat upcradling his face, where his cheekbone had cut through the flesh.

And Franco was amongst them, straight punches and hooks thundering out, and it was easy, because they were the enemy, *all of them* were the enemy, and his fists pounded into temples and jaws and cheekbones, his fingers poked viciously into eye sockets, his elbows cracked exposed throats and his knees and feet stamped at groins and knees. The pirates's swords hissed around him, but they quickly realised the little ginger midget was dangerous, the little ginger midget was fast, the little ginger midget was *one* amongst many. Several arms and an ear lay flapping on the brine-washed boards before good sense told the dumb pirates to stop hacking at one another with their chunky cutlasses. Franco ducked a wild swing and planted his fist in a pirate's belly, then grabbed his balls within the loose soft clothing, and yanked *down* hard. On instinct, he rolled sideways as a club thundered over him, and the weapon connected with the pirate whose testicles he was clutching. There was a *crump*. Franco rose next to the club wielder, grinned at him for a moment, showing his missing tuff, then grabbed his ears and jumped, thus gaining enough height to head-butt the pirate, who groaned once and folded like a punctured sex doll. But Franco was over-confident, Franco was cruising and rolling and thumping and on a long enough time-line, luck always runs out. A club cracked his skull and he staggered. Another club cracked his ribs, and he spun, a right straight breaking the pirate's nose, which fell off, spouting gears and coils. Another blow caught Franco on the shoulder from behind, and pain flared from his collar bone, and then, *and then he felt himself descending, descending into the blood red world which he feared and welcomed, and which had haunted him since childhood, for it was the world of the berserker and he'd carried it like a demon, like a disease, since his very earliest memories...*

Franco spun, roaring, fists lashing out, but everything was just awash with a honey blur, and nothing was real anymore, and the fight around him was just a distant dream, held at arm's length like a mangy cat by the scruff. Franco danced, and punched, and kicked, and spun, and leapt, and he watched himself distantly, as if through a telescope filled with oil, but it was always the same, these things never worked out well in the end, for there was no thought, no construction to the fight, and because Franco was lost to himself, lost to his rage, lost to his anarchy, there was a huge injection of luck and it could not last for ever...

It first happened when he was at school. Franco had always been an optimistic child, a stocky, happy little boy with his maroon jumper and blue shoulder-pack, toddling along to the playground where his favourite friend Connor waited, so they could run around, jumping and skipping, being silly and playing the heroes from all their favourite filmys. Then there was the boy, and he was a Big Boy, and he was a Bad Boy. He was called Piston, because they said his punch was like being struck by a piston, but little Franco was too innocent for all of that and didn't fight. He didn't know *how*. He didn't understand *why*. Why fight when you could play? What was there to fight about when you were six years old? But Piston had other ideas, because

Piston was one of the Bigger Boys and Piston was one of the Badder Boys, he was a bully and proud of it, as bullies often are. So he found Franco skipping happily around the playground, and Franco stopped and stared inquisitively at Piston because that was the sort of happy kid he was.

Piston punched little Franco, straight on the nose, knocking him back to the alloyconcrete.

Franco cried, and did not understand. Why did the Big Boy hit him?

Why?

There was no reason, and it soured Franco's experience, and soured his school, soured his world, soured his life. He looked at people with a new apprehension, for now everything wasn't so innocent and everybody didn't want to play. People wanted to *fight*. But Franco didn't want to fight, because that wasn't his way. He had a peaceful soul, a happy, caring soul, one instilled with love by his Mummy and Daddy.

A few days later, Piston arrived again. Franco took a step back.

"I heard you've been calling me."

Franco shook his head, eyes wide.

"You called me a Pussy." Sniggers, from The Crew, the sort of weak-minded, weak-livered bunch who always followed someone like Piston around. The sort of children who enjoyed The Show, enjoyed The Pantomime, but always at another's expense. *Always* at the expense of the weaker kids. The natural victims. The natural targets. The *easy prey*. Easy meat.

"No," said Franco, taking another step back.

Piston charged at him, and this wasn't going to be a single punch, this was going to be something bigger; Piston was going for a bigger display of his physical prowess, and for a few moments Franco felt himself overwhelmed by the larger boy, engulfed, encompassed, and he was weaker and smaller, *but* there was something inside of him, something which way, way, way back, past his birth and upbringing and loving parents, something that was in his blood, some fire in his soul and it went *click*.

Franco grabbed Piston's ears, pulled them sideways with a crunch, poked his finger in Piston's eye and felt himself descend into a blood-red frenzy which he did not understand and could not control, and it was only when the teachers pulled him off Piston, both little fists red with the blood pissing from Piston's broken nose, that Franco wanted to say, *I didn't mean this to happen, I didn't want any of this to happen, I didn't want it this way!* But he was punished all the same, and Franco learned, then; learned that, despite all the learning, despite all the knowledge and history and empathy and supposed superiority, the human species, at its core, was a raw, bestial animal. You could dress it up however you wanted, with your academic progress, with your fucking philosophers and psychologists and superior technology. Humans were animals with a shallow veneer of empathy. Nothing more. Nothing less. And it only took a nudge to send them flailing helplessly and uselessly down that slippery slope back into the chemical soup of violent evolution which had moulded Man into a genetic entity of unbreakable iron. As the saying went:

You can't teach an old dog new tricks.

It saddened Franco. Always would. But it was the way it was. And Franco was the way he was.

And there wasn't a human in existence, given however much breeding and education and social engagement, who could ignore the baggage of those early years of evolution and competition – when the right buttons were pushed.

Not one.

Franco had learned, over the years, to fight the good fight. But every now and again, his ingrained berserker rage got in the way.

Sometimes it worked. Other times, it didn't.

And now, he heard the distant *slap* of wooden timbers on his skull, and his energy was spent, his rage was diluted, his anger was washed away by the rhythmical swills of sea-water splashing up from the Teeth Ocean and swilling the deck of his blood. He lay still, and dreamt he was swimming through a sea of treacle, and it felt pretty nice, actually, felt kind of warm and calm, and slow and oozy, and he looked at the red treacle between his fingers and wondered what all the shouting and cheering was about...

*   *   *

THE BUCKET OF water splashed into his face and Franco gagged. Another brought him semi-conscious, wondering whose bed he was in, and if he was going to start scratching again, and a third bucket brought him *round*. He could see wood. Old wood. Stained wood. He could smell salt. And sea-water. And other scents which were distant memories – like greased tarpaulin, and lantern oil, and... and...

What was that noise? That cheering noise?

Franco tried to turn, and realised he was tied to the thick wooden beam in front of him. And a dawning realisation pushed gently into his blurry existence as he looked up, and up, and saw billowing sails above.

A ship? A galleon? A pirate ship?

Aaah, shit. That!

I remember...

Just above him, on a tiny length of wood jutting from the mast, was a bright green parrot. It was staring at Franco, and he stared back, unsure what to make of the green bird, or indeed, his situation, for his head was thumping like an elephant tap-dancing on his skull, and his mouth tasted like the inside of an unhygienic whore's knickers.

"Pretty polly," said the parrot. "Squawk!"

Franco stared at it. "Fuck off," he growled, as if the bird was drawing attention to his covert position, when in reality, his position was about as non-covert as it could possibly get.

"Pretty Polly, pretty Polly, squawk, Franco get a beating, Franco get a beating."

Did I hear that right? Does it know my name? Or am I still in that fabulous Dreamtime Longtime?

"Pretty Polly, Franco get a whipping, whip it up, snap it up, cream it up, pretty Franco, Franco get a whipping."

"So you're called Polly, right?" said Franco, weakly.

"She sure is," said a face that loomed far too close, disgorging a mouthful of bad breath strong enough to make a strong man gorge.

Franco stared into the face. It was the face of a madman. But worse. It was the face of a mad*org* several plates short of a dinner service. Franco analysed the face: broad and round and friendly, with a shock of black hair, some of which was woven into dreadlocks, and some tied with dried strips of old meat – in themselves, worthy of a great stench. The whole creation was bound together with a shock of coloured ribbons. The face was middle-aged, sagging a little with fat, black rings under dark eyes like marbles in treacle and showing nothing of the emotions behind the glassy, dead-eyed stare. The teeth were bad, in the true tradition of the pirate stereotype – some crooked, some missing, some gold – so that when the *Cap'n* smiled it was like looking into a bag of burned voodoo trinkets. The face was finished with unwashed skin and dirty stubble, and a slightly lop-sided look, as if Cap'n Bluetit had been severely smacked across one side of the head with a cricket bat – which, Franco was pretty sure, he thoroughly deserved.

"Aah," said Franco, as the stench of the grave washed over him. "Have you ever heard of a device called a toothbrush?"

"And what be ye meaning by that, me old chum, a-HAR?"

"I mean your breath stinks like a dead skunk's piss sack. If you're going to play the villain, breathing all over your sorry victim, at least have the decency to have good sweet breath, not something that could be used to kill soldiers in trench warfare. Yeah?"

"A-HAR-HAR-HAR," boomed Cap'n Bluetit, unperturbed by Franco's weak attempt at slander. "You'll be joking on the other side of your bull-whipped torso in a few moments, me LAD."

"Pretty Polly, SQUAWK!" squawked Pretty Polly.

Franco groaned. *Why me? Why does this always happen to me? Why does this insane bullshit always happen to me? Why doesn't it happen to Pippa? I bet Pippa's sorted out all her bloody problems and is reclining in a soft bed, sipping Champagne and eating strawberries. The bitch. And Keenan! The lucky bastard. Absorbed into a machine God. Okay, I admit, he might be dead or have no individual soul, or summink, but at least he doesn't have to put up with retarded org pirate kings and their tattered parrots!*

"SQUAWK!"

"Listen," growled Franco, "I know I caused a bit of a kerfuffle, but then, that sort of thing happens when you go and whip a lad like that. I mean, it bloody hurt, it did! I bet it's left a right sorry sore mark down my back. I bet I look like raw steak! Prime steak, I'd be the first to admit, but raw prime steak, if you get my meaning."

Cap'n Bluetit went a little cross-eyed, then backed away, mumbling under his breath and leaving nothing but the tatty parrot in Franco's limited field of vision.

"I suppose it can't get much worse?" muttered Franco optimistically.

"Bets?" said Polly.

Franco heard the *crack* long before he felt the *burn*. But when the burn came, oh, it came bad, and then another *crack* filtered through the wave of red-hot branding agony and more fire torched up over Franco's flesh, and he heard a voice, a sweet female voice that he instantly fell in love with because she sounded like an angel, and he realised, it was Tarly, Tarly Winters, General Tarly Winters, and she said, "Sweet mother of God, *no!*" in a kind of hushed whisper that melted Franco's heart suddenly and without mercy, for she cared about him, cared for him, for his suffering and his pain and then another *crack* tore the air and the whip *sizzled* Franco's flesh. The pain slammed through him like a juggernaut, like a train-wreck, tearing his innards outwards and filling him with more pain than he'd believed possible. Through waves of red, and a sobbing sound he realised was his own voice, he heard Cap'n Bluetit's voice interject.

The Cap'n said, "Naw, that's not good enough, get the Cat o'Nine Tails, let's give him something to remember us by, eh lads, a-HAR!" and the next lash was like a meteor shower over Franco's shivering trembling body, and he felt his bravado leave him, and this was worse than being stabbed, worse than any bar-room beating, worse than being shot – and Franco had been shot lots (he had that effect on people) – and his rage was there, a bubbling terrible thing under the surface as the lash beat into his bloodied body and he heard Tarly whimpering and crying out for him, struggling against her bonds until a *thump* silenced the QGM General.

More lashes followed. Shameless tears rolled down Franco's face, as blood ran down his back and stained his knife-cut combat shorts red. His legs ran crimson, and his boots filled with gore until they overflowed.

When they cut Franco down, he collapsed.

"Lock him in the brig," snarled Cap'n Bluetit, showing a mouthful of coinage and rot. Then he turned to Queen Strogger, who held her head high, eyes locked defiantly with the org Pirate Captain's and refusing to back down. The net fizzled, but she ignored the pain.

"Do you know who I am?" she hissed, through glowing sparks and sizzling flesh.

"Oh yes," said Cap'n Bluetit. "You are the Queen of The Org States – Queen Strogger the Merciless. It's *your fault* us here reject orgs are condemned to a life on the salty brine, with your stupid rules and policies and petty bloody bureaucracy! We're going to hang you from the rigging and watch you dance a merry jig, me-HEARTY! A-HAR!"

"Oooh, Franco, you are so sexy, ve are ze sexy vixens who vould love to smother you vith butter and honey and lick it all off, ooh, ve are so impressed, you have ze best buttocks in ze vorld, first ve vould like to smear ze honey and ze butter over your buttocks and lick-y zat off first, then ve shall take you and roll you over, and then ze lick your manly hairy chest, ooh, it is ze best manly hairy chest ve have ever seen, then ve shall turn you back over and STRIP ZE FUCKING SKIN FROM YOU FUCKING BACK, AND RUB SALT AND VINEGAR AND MUSTARD AND CHILLIES INTO ZE RAW PEELED FLESH, AND SEE HOW YOU FUCKING LIKE THAT, ZE SCUMBAG!"

FRANCO OPENED ONE eye. The world didn't seem that bad, hey-hey? It was dark, yes, and it was cold, yes, and it smelled of rat piss, okay, he could live with that. But in the massive scheme of atomic war, and halo missile strikes on global cores, then HOLY JESUS, HOLY SHIT, WHAT WAS THAT, BOILING ACID DOWN MY BACK?

The world *throbbed*.

Franco groaned, and moaned, and groaned, and then a hand was on his brow in the darkness, and he felt lips near his mouth, and she whispered, "Shhh, you've got to try and be quiet, the minute they realise you're awake they'll come back and give you some more – I've seen this kind of scumshit negative-psychology stuff before."

Franco clenched his teeth together and fought the pain. It was a big fight, and he kind of got the feeling he was losing it. Fire rampaged up and down his back and he was surprised to find tears in his eyes. Franco hadn't cried for a long time. It wasn't something a rough, tough squaddie was supposed to do. But hell, they'd taken the skin off his fucking back. What was a man *supposed* to do?

"Did they hurt you?" growled Franco.

"Only a bit. A club to the head. Nothing like they... did to you. That was fucking brutal, Franco. One of the worst things I've seen done to a man. And I've seen lots."

"Should have felt it from this end," he breathed. "But at least I'm sure of one thing."

"What's that?"

"I ain't playing anymore," he said, eyes gleaming in the darkness. "What did they do with Strogger?"

"They're having some kind of ceremony. Then they're going to hang her from the rigging."

"Hang her? What? To dry, or something?"

"No, hang her by the throat, kicking and squawking, till she's dead."

"Oh. Ah. That kind of hanging. Then we must, y'know, get out of here. Help her."

"Can you move?"

"I'll try."

A pause in the blackness. A *gasp*.

"I feel like they removed every inch of skin from my fucking back."

"It certainly looked that way. You'll find most of it in your boots. And if you try and escape again... or fight?" Tarly shuddered. "They'll do it again. And again. And again."

"Right. I've fucking had enough of this shit!"

Franco forced himself to roll over, but the effort left his head spinning; he vomited. But it emptied his stomach, and the spinning receded a little, and he felt a notch better. A tiny notch, but a notch all the same.

Franco slowly moved onto his knees. Everything hurt. His back, obviously, but other pains intruded now. His knuckles, especially, from the sheer amount of punching he'd done in the scrap with the pirate orgs. There had been moments, in the pit of adrenaline, when he'd been punching *metal*.

"I need a weapon."

"There's a guard," said Tarly.

"Only one?"

"Yes."

"The fucking ignominy!"

That's a big word for a little squaddie."

Franco snorted a laugh. "I won't forget you sticking up for me, Tarly. You're a good girl."

"That's not really the way you should address your General."

"Hey," said Franco, reaching forward and kissing her. She paused for a second, then kissed him back. In the darkness, in the cold and the stench, this tiny moment of intimacy meant more than words, and more than worlds. They kissed softly, both of them covered in sweat and dirt, blood and brine. They kissed, and it was more intimate than sex, and warmer than a summer's day. It lasted forever, and filled Franco with an unbelievable strength, a belief in himself, an injection of *focus* that helped him to fight down the raw agony in his flayed back. He stood up and rested a hand against the wall – old timber, damp and slick – and now his eyes had adjusted to the dark, he looked around the floating prison cell.

Skeletons were chained to huge iron hooks. Franco looked down, but they hadn't even bothered to chain him, so confident were they that his severe lashings had broken him.

Franco glanced at Tarly. She was still tied with simple rope. "No chains or leg irons?" he said.

Tarly fluttered her eyelashes. "Well, I'm only a little lady, after all..."

Franco grinned. "I think it's time we gave these cunts a fucking wake-up call."

"I agree."

Franco moved behind Tarly, and with lots of fumbling, undid the tight knots. Tarly dropped the rope and rubbed her chafed wrists. Then she tenderly reached out to touch Franco's back, but he flinched. "Ow! Don't touch it, don't bloody touch it!"

"Okay, Big Guy. We'll get that sorted, just as soon as..."

"We've done some killing."

Franco kicked around on the floor, and found a length of old rusted chain. He hefted it thoughtfully, and wrapped it round both hands so an eighteen inch length hung between his fists. Then he lay back on the ground and glanced at Tarly.

"Right girl. Get him in here."

Tarly nodded and put her hands behind her back, then moved to the door and knocked on it with her boot. From the other side she heard a grunt, and saw a shadow loom through the tiny barred window.

"Hi sexy," she said, through the bars.

"You want something?" grunted the pirate. He was big. A hefty, hairy fellow, even for an org. She could hear the grind of his mechanicals. She recognised him as a hairy *Graham*-model.

"I thought you might like some company? After all, all those long and lonely nights on the rocking sea, it must get *awfully* lonely for a big, handsome, horny org like yourself?" His stench wafted through the door: faeces mixed with old engine oil. He grunted again, like a ferret in a tumble drier.

"Maybe," he ventured, cautiously, and they heard bolts slide in the door. Lantern light flickered by the window, and the door creaked open, allowing a soft yellow glow to ease into the cell. The org stepped through the portal. He was big. Very big. He grinned at Tarly, who tilted her head to one side and smiled coquettishly before leaping forward, her right fist swinging around to deliver an almighty smashing hook. The org grunted and staggered to one side, lantern swinging, as Tarly leapt and her boots hit him square in the face. But he was quicker than his size suggested, and he caught her legs and swung her against the wall. She hit hard, with a crash, and tumbled into a heap... as Franco reared up behind the big org and wrapped the length of chain around his throat. He put his knee in the org's back and pulled tight.

There was a sound like a steam engine breaking down. They staggered around, looking like some odd symbiosis, lit by the swinging, stroboscopic lantern light. The org suddenly charged backwards, thrusting Franco into the wall, slamming his raw back into the splintered wood. Franco muffled a scream – on the org's fist. He dodged the second blow, and the org hit the wall with a grunt and a *crack* of his knuckles. Franco powered a blow into the org's belly, then his groin, and then dropped and crawled between his legs, dragging his chain after him. Tarly ran, leapt over Franco and slammed both hands into the org's face; but he twisted, punching her to one side as Franco leant in and took the lantern like a lolly from a kid and, with a snarl, smashed it over the org's head. Oil splashed all over the pirate, and ignited; the org went up like Guy Fawkes soaked in happy petrol. He screamed, and tried to run for the door, but Franco lassoed his chain around the org's neck and dragged him back into the cell, where he fell to his knees, crawling around in aimless, burning circles.

Franco and Tarly watched the pirate org burn, grunting and panting, squawking occasionally, then finally collapsing into a smouldering heap. Smoke had filled the cell and the corridor outside, along with the crisp stench of frying pork.

"That was a risk," said Tarly, at last. "You could have sent the whole ship up in flames!"

"That was a risk I was willing to take," said Franco, voice level. Then he twitched, stooped, and picked up an old skull.

"What is it?" whispered Tarly.

"We're being watched!"

"By?"

"In the corridor!" he hissed.

Tarly turned, and Polly the Parrot met her gaze.

"Squawk!" it shrieked, "Prisoners escaping! Prisoners escap..." but was cut off as the skull bounced off it, sending its flapping green body spiralling down with a sudden thump.

Tarly ran forward and grasped the bird, pinned its wings to its sides and shook it vigorously. "Any more shouting, bird brain, and we'll be having parrot stew for lunch! Geddit?"

"Okay, okay," said the parrot, in a reasonable, level voice. "No need to be so rude. If you could just let me go, I promise I won't squawk another impromptu phrase..."

"Wait a minute," said Tarly, frowning and plucking at alloy feathers. "You're not a real bird. You're a robot!"

"Hey, I am *not* a robot!"

"What the hell are you then, a vacuum cleaner?"

"No!" The parrot preened, scowling. "I am a Special Robotic Friend."

Franco frowned. "Oh no," he groaned. "Not one of those little bastards again."

"You've heard of them?" said Tarly.

"You've heard of us?" asked Polly.

"Oh yeah," said Franco with a grimace. "You're made by Metal Mongrels Inc., aren't you, you little fucker?"

"No need to be rude," said Polly, frowning, which was quite a feat for a green parrot with dodgy plumage. "I am a DumbMutt v1.7, a much improved model, I can tell you! And ©hv3801 Metal Mongrels Inc. QGSMA Quad-Gal Safety Mark Assured (pending). I'm a quality piece of kit, I can bloody assure you!"

"Oh, no. No! Tarly, trust me, drop it on the floor and jump on it. The bastards follow you to the ends of the world, and they will never, *ever* let you fucking go!"

"Which model did you acquaint yourself with?" said Polly.

"You wouldn't know it. A fucking heap of junk with a bad hair quiff and a pretence at being a shite poet. Called itself Sax. A dogjunk heap of dogjunk dogshit, is what it was. The whole fucking thing was a mess!"

"Ahh, Sax, I know him well. We were upgraded together. He told me about you. About you, Franco Haggis, Quad-Gal resident DNA number 6753675347645376457532465 2. There were quite a few stories, ha-ha; bad stories admittedly, because that was all he could write, but oh, how we did laugh, SQUAWK!"

Franco scowled. "Yeah. Well. You're like a plague, you bastard little DumbMutts. I don't want anything to do with you, okay?"

The parrot shrugged. "That's okay, buster. SQUAWK!"

"Come on," said Tarly. "We have bigger fish to fry. Queen Strogger is in trouble..." she paused, then stared at the parrot. "What's happened to Queen Strogger?"

"Oh, it's okay, they're still arguing about where to hang her from. They always do this. When one pirate org says something, all the others have to say something different. It's like a backward pecking order, or something. Worse than children, they are. That's why I self-terminated their purchase regulation. I'm a free agent, so I am."

"That's okay then," said Franco, warily. "After all, last thing we need on a mission like this is a stupid Metal Mongrels Inc. DumbMutt tagging along. Eh?"

He stepped forward.

"Shall I let it go?"

"No," said Franco. "Give it 'ere."

Tarly handed the dodgy green parrot to Franco, who lifted it to his face. It peered at him inquisitively with bright little eyes. "Now, you listen to me," he said, scowling in the smoky gloom.

"Of course, your wish is my command," said Polly the Parrot.

"Eh?"

"You have invoked my ownership." The parrot's head spun around a full 360°. Then its mouth opened, and in a different voice, Polly the Parrot said, "*Congratulations!* on your purchase of the DumbMutt v1.7 special robotic friend. This special little friend will be your friend. A friend for life! Please find enclosed the instruction manual and ownership deed in a variety of Quad-Gal languages, Braille and scent-censorship tucked away in a tidy Plumage-Partition™." There was a pause. Franco went pale, and shook the bird, but his hands froze rigid around the little bird and he couldn't let go.

"No!" he howled. "No, no, not again!"

"Thank you, Franco Haggis, Quad-Gal resident DNA number 67536753476453764575324652. As you read this, a genetic sample has been taken from your fingertips and relayed digitally to the DumbMutt's brain. She is now yours. She will never leave your side. She is forthwith electronically registered to your unique DNA number and as such will follow you to the ends of whatever planet you inhabit [insert here] or travel to [insert here] or plan to travel to [insert here] FOR EVER. If you lose your DumbMutt v1.7 special robotic friend, do not fret, because she *will* eventually find you. If you vacate the planet, she has emergency funds to book passage on a shuttle to anywhere within the Quad-Gal bubble. In effect, your DumbMutt v1.7 (a much advanced model!) special friend will follow you to the ends of the Galaxy. Well done in this, the Smart Choice!"

"No no no!" sobbed Franco, and Tarly looked on, bemused.

"Why don't you just drop the little thing?"

"I can't! I can't! It's electric-shocking my hands! Get it off, get it off!"

Tarly tried to prize the parrot from Franco's hands, but it was as if it was spot-welded into position. Franco's fingers were more rigid than a steel exoskeleton. Tarly and Franco struggled with the bird, green feathers spitting everywhere, and the damn bird continued to speak, stubbornly, in the voice of a salesperson/engineer. "We do hope you enjoy your DumbMutt v1.7 special robotic friend. She will be a very special robotic friend. For life. Your special friend DumbMutt v1.7 comes with many exciting innovations and technical upgrades over the previous DumbMutt v1.6, which tended to burst into atomic overdrive and decimate entire cities. Don't worry! That doesn't happen anymore! Not often, anyway [please read legal addendum]. Your friendly special friend DumbMutt v1.7 is called [POLLY]. Please be kind to it. And remember. A robot parrot is for *life* not just for [insert applicable religious festival]. ©hv3801 Metal Mongrels Inc. QGSMA Quad-Gal Safety Mark Assured (pending)."

Franco was abruptly released, and he dropped the parrot like a steaming turd. It fell, and an inch from the ground ignited on a fiery jet and hovered in front of Franco, a big beam on its beaked face.

"Well done, Franco! The Smart Choice!"

"I didn't make no fucking choice," growled Franco, and waved his fist.

"Please take good care of your DumbMutt v1.7 [POLLY]-model. Your DNA has now been registered with the MMI central core database. Your deed will last: 999 years. Thank you for your custom. ©hv3801 Metal Mongrels Inc. QGSMA Quad-Gal Safety Mark Assured (pending)."

The parrot grinned at him.

Tarly placed her hand on Franco's shoulder. "Come on. It might be of *some* help."

"Yeah. Right! We can put it in a cannon and fire the fucker at the pirates!"

"SQUAWK! I know you're only kidding," said the parrot. "Just think of the adventures we will share! The places we will visit! The photographs I will take of your exploits, uploaded straight to the GGG FLICKER DATABASE! No secret shall go unshared! No sexual triumph unsung! You will be on public parade, Franco Haggis, from now until the expiry of my nine-hundred and ninety-nine-year contract! SQUAWK!"

"Come on," growled Franco, and Tarly followed him out of the cell. Then he stopped, and pointed at the parrot. "If you blow our cover in any way, or get us in any trouble *whatsoever*, I'll pull off your damn bastard wings and chuck you in the sea. You got that?"

"Oh, yes, oh, yes, squawk! Buster! Friend!"

"And don't call me *buster!*"

"Okay, buster!"

Franco peered from the top of the steps. Rain had started to fall, and the galleon's deck was slick with rain. Dark clouds flashed overhead. The pirate orgs were clustered around the foot of the mast, and there, tied to the rigging, was Queen Strogger, head down, the epitome of misery. The pirates were still arguing about what to do, lit occasionally by a blue *flash* from the org net imprisoning the old cyborg.

"What shall we do?" whispered Tarly.

"Rush them," said Franco.

"Franco, there's *seventy* of them, and two of us."

"I know. We'll outnumber them two to seventy!"

"You couldn't beat them last time, remember?"

"Ah yes, but now I'm armed."

"With a chain?"

"A chain will lead to a sword will lead to a gun. You watch. You'll see. I have hate on my side."

"And a lack of skin."

"No need to get personal, lass," he said.

"Wait! Look!"

Franco scowled. "Where? For what? Which direction?"

"That direction," said Tarly, smiling and pointing. It was another ship. Another *big* ship. This ship did not fly a pirate flag, the traditional skull and crossbones, as Cap'n Bluetit's galleon did. Could it be friendly? Could it, hope of hopes, contain org soldiers on their way to rescue their queen?

"Looks kind of... old and decrepit," said Franco, rubbing his nose. "What is it with this place? They spend all their money and efforts on upgrading their own bodies, and let everything around them fall into rat-shit? You'd think if they had no aircraft, their ships would be sleek and perfect. Not ancient timber vessels sporting bloody cannons – okay, I'll grant you, this one has a hyperdrive, but that's been nicked, not developed, I'd bet you both my rosy arse cheeks on it!"

"Shh. Watch!"

The pirates had also noticed the ship, and Cap'n Bluetit hurried over to the galleon's huge wooden wheel. He pressed a button and the wheel flipped over, revealing a control panel. His hands glided over the controls, as his voice boomed "Man the cannons! A-HAR!"

"They're going to attack," said Tarly as, deep down in the bowels of the ship, they felt the *thrum* of a massive power source, and the hyperdrive came alive. The galleon began to vibrate, the wood beneath Franco and Tarly's hands shivering as if transcribing a violent earthquake.

"ATTACK, ATTACK, ATTACK, SQUAWK!" squawked the parrot. Franco scowled at the robot bird, which shrugged, losing several small green feathers. "Gotta do it," it winked. "All in keeping with the character, right, buster?"

The galleon lurched forward, carving through the Teeth Ocean as the pirates ran to their stations, many pulling ropes and hooks, knives and carbines from wooden lockers.

The rain increased, and thunder rent the stormy heavens.

"They're going to ram it," said Tarly, as rain thrashed down at her and the galleon picked up ever more speed. Before them, the other large ship had started to turn, and they could see matchstick figures running around the deck, pulling on ropes, altering sails. But they had no chance of escape; they had no hyperdrive engine, for a start – an engine that could ram a modest sized spacefighter from sea level to void space in two minutes flat. If Cap'n Bluetit had opened the hyperdrive to full capacity, the galleon would have punched a hole through the enemy ship and then *through* The Teeth mountains beyond!

"Prepare for attack, a-HAR!" screamed Cap'n Bluetit.

"What's the plan?" said Tarly.

"Let them attack, then nick their ship?" suggested Franco.

"You have a wicked mind," said Tarly.

"Hey, they don't call me Franco 'Razor Brain' Haggis for nothing, you know?" He grinned, but the grin turned into a grimace as his lashed back reminded him why he hated the org pirates so much.

The galleon was bearing down on the smaller ship now, and at the last minute it slewed sideways and cannons *boomed*. Cannon balls decimated the ship, slamming through her masts and sails and rigging, leaving the side of the vessel peppered like an overenthusiastic pepper-pot.

"Board the bastards, a-HAR!" bellowed Cap'n Bluetit, and it could clearly be seen his blood was up, the rage upon him, and he was enjoying every damn second of it.

The galleon *A Nice Lady* pulled alongside the stricken ship, and boarding ropes were tossed aboard. The hooks *clunked* and orgs heaved, and the two ships pulled together with a deep, reverberating BOOM. The pirates drew their cutlasses and, swords and carbines in hand, leapt aboard what was now obviously an org merchant vessel. The merchants, a lower class of org mechanical than the ones invading, clustered together at the centre of the deck, hands in the air, unsure of what to do, whilst a few brave souls ejected blades and guns from the ends of their mechanical arms and a brief fight ensued. Blades clashed, sending sparks flying in the air, and carbines hummed and spat, kicking several orgs – pirates included – from their feet.

"Time to boogie," said Franco, leaping up and heading for the nearest pirate org still on his feet. He was holding a rope and watching the boarding with interest.

Franco tapped him on the shoulder, having to stand on tip-toe to do so. "Excuse me, my good man," he said.

The pirate org turned into a right hook that carried all the pain and hate of twenty lashes under the Cat O'Nine. Franco laid the org out in one blow, breaking his cheek bone and jaw along with a bone in his own hand.

"Ouch! Bugger."

Franco hurriedly pulled off the pirate's colourful jacket and hat, and dressed himself quickly, wincing as the fabric caressed his tortured flesh. He glanced at Tarly, through sheets of rain, and said, "What do you think?"

"A disguise?"

"Hey, they don't call me Franco 'Rubber Face' Haggis for nothing, you know! I does the job, and I gets the job done!" He fastened the org's belt around his waist and weighed the cutlass thoughtfully. "Time to go to work," he said. "You keep a low profile until we're free. Then hit that bloody hyperdrive and get us the hell out of here!"

"Aye, aye, Cap'n," said Tarly, face straight.

"Not even funny, bitch."

Fights were still kicking off aboard the mechant vessel in pockets of violent resistance. Carbines cracked. A bullet took the lobe off Cap'n Bluetit's ear in a spray of blood and he started screaming hysterically, unaware that the sniper was Franco, crouching over another laid-out pirate and putting his marksman skills to good use.

"A good shot, SQUAWK!" said Polly.

"Rubbish! I was aiming for his brain!"

Franco strode down the starboard rail, his cutlass slashing ropes. He did it calmly, methodically, and for a long time nobody even noticed what he was doing. In his mind, he counted. "Twenty-five ropes, twenty-six, twenty-seven... nearly there! A-HAR indeed!"

Franco turned, sodden from the downpour, and signalled to Tarly, up by the galleon's wheel and hyperdrive controls. There were still five orgs aboard the vessel, and possibly seventy aboard the attacked, ravaged ship...

Suddenly, somebody shouted, "Oi!" in the time-mannered tradition of anybody finding a ginger midget destroying your plans for loot and rape and pillage and slaughter. The org stood in front of Franco, and Franco remembered the lashings, and remembered they weren't playing any games anymore – if indeed, they ever had – and these pirate orgs were nasty scumshit, and out for the shit and the kill. He grinned and unloaded his stolen carbine in the org's face, blowing his metal nose out the back of his head to rattle off across the deck in a spew of shavings and blood.

Franco's grin faded, as the org refused to fall. *Shit,* he thought, *that's pretty tough, that is. Nose shot through the back of your head, brain a mush of mushroom soup in your skull, and you're* STILL *fucking standing! That's tough, my man. That's pretty fucking damn bitch hard!*

The org was still groping at the hole in his face like a man trying to unblock a toilet, when Franco reached him, bent, grabbed his legs and tipped him over the side. He hit the waters with a splash, and Franco hoisted his cutlass. Four ropes to go!

"You there!" shouted Cap'n Bluetit, who had turned, and was staring *incredulously* at Franco's handiwork, as if he could scarce believe somebody would do that to him and his ship. "I, I, I... you, you, you... stop it! Stop it, you hear! I say, stop it!"

Franco gave him the finger, and cut another rope. And another. And another...

"SHOOT HIM!" screamed Cap'n Bluetit, and at least fifty weapons turned on Franco, who squawked and ducked as bullets chewed the wood alongside his head.

"KILL HIM!" Another volley ate in the barnacle-encrusted wood.

"PULP HIM!" A third volley tore across the ship, bullets whining and pinging from a mad array of stolen projectile weapons spanning five centuries of piracy.

Franco crawled forward, popped up like a mole from a hole, and slashed another rope. More bullets screamed overhead, and, peering through a ragged hole, Franco saw the pirates running back towards the rail and their shortly-to-be-hijacked ship.

"A-HAR indeed," growled Franco, and gave Tarly the signal as he leapt up, probably in slow-motion, and bullets whined through the air, cutting past him and around him, and he was balanced on the rail with one hand, and his cutlass swung down with heroic precision, as Tarly hit the hyperdrive and the galleon moaned, and groaned, and shook, and shot off across the Teeth Ocean like a cat with a scalded arse.

Cap'n Bluetit stood on his new, stricken vessel, mouth agape, hands on hips, filled like a jug to the brim with disbelief. "I just don't believe it," said the pirate org. "I just don't bloody believe it!"

One of his subordinates sidled up to him. "You all right, Cap'n?"

"OF COURSE I'M NOT FUCKING ALL RIGHT!" he screamed, and slapped the dumb pirate across his metal skull. "THEY TOOK MY SHIP AND ALL MY GOLD AND MY COLLECTION OF FINE GANGER SILK UNDERWEAR! WOULD YOU BE ALRIGHT? EH? I ASK YOU!"

"Er, Cap'n, they're heading on a bearing of seventeen degrees, right?"

"AND?"

"Well, isn't that a direct heading for the, er, you know? The Mouth of the Ocean?"

"SO IT IS!"

Cap'n Bluetit smiled, suddenly, and looked around at his crew. "Get working, lads. We're going after my ship. A-HAR!"

*   *   *

FRANCO AND TARLY had overpowered the remaining rogue pirate orgs, and thrown them over the side for good measure, to sink under the weight of their metal. Franco watched them disappear under the waves, but his face went hard. "Fuck 'em," he said. "They made their fortune robbing and killing innocent folk. They gets what they deserves."

"Quite right, buster, SQUAWK!" said Polly.

Franco scowled at the bird, but said nothing, instead focusing on the bright horizon, filled with layered shafts of blue, magenta and orange.

"We did it," he said.

"We did," agreed Tarly.

They'd cut Queen Strogger down, who had sustained only minimal damage to her flesh and cyborg components. The only thing injured seemed to be her pride, and she made a vow to hunt down all pirates across The Teeth Ocean and destroy them utterly when she was returned to power on the Org Throne at Org.

The wind streamed through Franco's slightly reduced, square-bottomed beard. One hand on the controls, he piloted the galleon smoothly across the rolling Teeth Ocean.

"This is grand," he said.

"Indeed," said Tarly, and she moved in close to him, and snuggled up to him a bit. "You were quite heroic back there, Franco, to tell you the honest truth."

"Hey!" he said, and frowned, because he couldn't think of a name he'd been called which would perfectly sum up his current situation. "You know what, darling?" he said. "I could get used to this, a life on the ocean waves, just my good woman by my side, the wind in my beard, all nautical stuff inside my head; I think it'd be a reet good break from soldiering, I do."

"I'm hardly a good woman," said Tarly.

"Okay then, with my psychopathic assassin-killer QGM General by my side. How's that sound?"

"You don't mind that I'm a psychopath?" said Tarly, gazing into his eyes.

"Hey, what woman isn't?" grinned Franco, then held up both hands as she slapped him. "Joke! Joke! I beg a truce!"

Ahead, on the glittering ocean, a school of dolphins leapt from the waves, and in a surge of surf they ploughed on alongside the fast-powered galleon, smiling faces turned slightly to one side as if regarding the humans at the prow of this anachronistic, hyperdrive-powered vessel.

"Beautiful!" said Tarly, breathing deep the salty ocean air.

"Stunning," agreed Franco, as he watched the dolphins accelerate past the ship and disappear over the horizon. "But hot damn, I just didn't realise they could swim so fast!"

"They can't, SQUAWK!" squawked Polly. "You're heading for The Mouth of the Ocean!"

"The What of the What?" scowled Franco, thinking *oh yeah, here we go again, one more bloody damn and bloody problem to deal with, out of the fire and into the frying pan, an' all that!*

"It's an ocean whirlpool!" squawked the robot parrot. "It'll suck you in and suck you down and crush you into component atoms! You have to turn around, head the other bloody way! SQUAWK!"

"Hey, don't you worry you none," said Franco, flapping his hand as if to wave away a minor problem. "Is that *all*? A liddle widdle ocean whirlpool? This fucking hyperdrive could take us into *orbit*, baby! It'll be a super-hyper-match for some liddle biddle bit of bibble wibble water current any damn ocean could throw at us. You just watch and see. Now. See? *See?*"

He turned the ship around with a grind of gears.

Behind him, in the distance, under the magenta and red flashing horizon, the dolphins started screaming.

"Increase the power," said Franco, calmly, a man utterly and completely in control.

Tarly increased the power.

"Increase it some more," said Franco, although his voice had now lost its edge of calmness. There was a crack in the plaster. A beetle in the bath. A snake in his pants... so to speak.

"Increased to full," said Tarly, her own voice wavering a little.

"What? You mean to *full* full? A hyperdrive should get us bloody starbound, not flounder around in a puddle of piss like a fish with no fins!"

"*Yes*," hissed Tarly, "but this is a *hyperdrive* which has been stolen from a crash site and buckled together using zip-ties and spit, then cobbled to an ancient galleon using spit and spunk. It's on full power, mate. That's as fast as she damn well goes!"

Franco stared at his new horizon, which was a perfect reverse tracking shot.

"We're still going backwards," he said, voice level.

"I can see that," snapped Tarly. "What are we going to do about it?"

"Row?" said Franco, hopefully.

"You're all going to drown, SQUAWK!" yelled Polly the Parrot, helpfully.

"*We're* all going to drown," corrected Franco with a scowl.

"Not me, buster! I can fly!"

"Damn and bloody bollocks," snarled Franco, and ran towards the mast, where he started to climb like a monkey on acid. Below, the hyperdrive engine was whining and rattling as they fought the awesome pull of, well, gee, Franco could see it now *and lo and behold if it wasn't just the biggest damn ocean whirlpool he'd ever had the misfortune to lay eyes upon in his entire fucking existence!*

He climbed back down, and sidled over to Tarly.

"Er," he said.

"Is it bad?"

"It's bad, mate."

"Are we going to die?"

"Yep. We're gonna die."

"So, no paddling out of this one, then?"

"Nope. Don't think so love."

Faster and faster they went, backwards towards a vast ocean whirlpool more than four kilometres in diameter... and all to the distant, needle-scratching soundtrack of screaming, dying dolphins...

CHAPTER TEN
3CORE

PIPPA DROPPED INTO a dark corridor and crouched, yukana sword at the ready. For close quarters combat she found the sword more effective than any projectile weapon. Her yukanas were her *babies*.

Pippa's clone dropped behind her, and they waited in the gloom, tuning in to their surroundings, the feel in the air, the textures, the smell, the aura. Beneath their boots, they could feel distant, mechanical *thumps*; rhythmical, almost like a heartbeat. As if the Slush Pits were *alive*.

Pippa stood first, eyes narrowing as she stared off down the long, straight corridor.

"It's based on a grid," said the clone, voice low.

"Any idea where this Pod Vault prick-tease is?"

"At the centre, I think. The core of the facility."

Pippa gave a nod, and moved off slowly, the distant thumping unnerving her. It vibrated through her boots and made her feel a little sick. She reached a set of dark steps and peered down. Everything was lit by pin-prick red lights shedding a bare minimum of illumination, and giving the ubiquitous black metalwork an eerie red glow.

"Feels like the inside of a brothel," murmured Pippa.

"Been in many brothels?"

"You'd be surprised where I've been, sweetie." Pippa smiled. She was really starting to miss Franco, and right now, to have him with her, spade-like hands clasping a pair of Kekra quad-barrel machine pistols, she would have happily let him stick his tongue down her throat.

Pippa ran her hand down the stock of the MPK. It was matt-black, smooth, familiar, like an old friend, an ex-lover for whom she still had feelings. The gun felt totally solid and real in her hands, something she could rely on without doubt. No human was like that. She smiled, a nasty smile. *No clone was like that.*

Pippa padded down the stairs. She stopped halfway, hand resting against the wall. It felt soft and warm, even though her gloves. Organic, even. Pippa curled her lip in disgust. What sort of place had the gangers built? A living shell to clone other organic shells? The whole damn place was starting to disgust her, creeping up on her like a dark smoke, a mist oozing in off a river of sewage.

She reached the bottom of the stairs, easing herself to the edge and peering into the darkness. As her clone had said, the place was a grid, an ordered network of corridors. The thumping was subtly louder, as if great machines were hard at work.

Across from her, there was a door. She glanced back at her clone, who gave a little shake of her head. Pippa shrugged, and moved forward anyway. Her hand touched the warm metal, which gave a little as she pushed, then opened into a vast chamber. Warm air blew out, smelling of decay, of rotting garbage, old meat, decomposing vegetables, and Pippa stepped in and it was dark, but her eyes adjusted and she could see huge vats. They were low-walled, maybe waist-high on Pippa, and circular, each one fifty metres across. There were thirty of them, stretching off across the chamber.

Behind her, Pippa's clone closed the door and dropped to a crouch.

"What's in them?"

"You're guess is as good as mine."

Pippa moved forward and stood by the rim of one of the vats. It held some kind of green-tinged black chemical soup. Occasionally, a lump would surface, then disappear beneath the gently agitated surface.

"There's... stuff in here," said Pippa.

"I think these are recyc vats."

"Recyc vats?"

"Recycling."

"Recycling what?"

"You don't want to know."

Pippa saw a hand surface, bob for a moment in all its severed glory, then dip beneath the surface again. There came a *thrumming* noise and a sound like gnashing swords. The surface vibrated violently, then went curiously still.

"Interesting," murmured Pippa.

Her clone came up beside her. "Yes?" she said, with a narrow smile.

"That was a hand. What the *fuck* are they recycling?"

"Unused ganger shells," said the clone.

"What, dead people?"

"They're not people. They're blank bodies. They have no minds. They only last so long. You know how it is with meat – how easy it is for it to go... off."

From the far end of the chamber there came a clattering sound and Pippa's MPK snapped up, tracking, and it took every ounce of discipline she had not to slam off an ND. She blinked. Huge doors high up in the wall had opened, and she noticed for the first time the rails criss-crossing the ceiling, a mass of mono-track. Some kind of upside-down wheeled cart clattered into view, and swinging from it, like so many slaughtered beef carcasses, were...

"No," said Pippa.

They were men and women, even children, all naked. Their pale white bodies were unreal, ghost-like, covered with a viscous sheen. They swung gently as the cart clattered along the track, bringing them closer and closer to where Pippa and her clone crouched in hiding. They were clamped in tight steel vices with three prongs each, bloodlessly piercing their skulls. The ganger shells were drained of fluid.

"That's gross," said Pippa, standing, gun in her hands. "Just plain evil. What kind of fucking society do you have down here on Cloneworld?"

"And so it is, the base problem with humanity and all its self-centred pious hypocrisy. You think what we do is so bad? Look at your own history, Pippa, look at your own constant slaughter, your endless fucking examples of genocide! We clone ourselves, we copy ourselves – is that such a crime? Never, ever in our entire history have we rounded up millions of our own kind and exterminated them in ghettos, or camps, or fields, or hangars. And yet throughout your history books and filmys, this has gone on time after time after time. War crimes and slaughter – even whole fucking planets destroyed, billions of lives pulped into waste! So don't try and preach to me about our society being warped or evil. We're just different. And for humanity, with all its wisdom and technology and superiority, what is different is to be feared."

Pippa breathed deep. She looked into her own eyes, and saw for the first time that, despite their physical similarities, they were *worlds* apart. The clone was alien. The clone was more alien than anything Pippa had ever experienced – only emphasised by their identical appearance. They looked the same, and were genetically the same – but diametrically opposed in every single way. A living contrast. An existence of opposites. An *impossibility*.

Pippa gave a short laugh. "Fuck me. A potted history of humanity by a genetic thief. Remind me not to get on your wrong side, hey, love? I wouldn't like to wake up like one of your twitching corpses over there, that's for sure."

"You! You there! Halt!"

Pippa groaned.

It was an angry and officious little voice. It oozed temper. It was the sort of voice Pippa had experienced across the entirety of Quad-Gal, usually from behind bullet-proof glass, and usually whilst demanding some small pedantic payment for some unnecessary service by a bureaucratic government company that should have been dissolved due to lack of any real purpose decades earlier.

A platoon of small men emerged from a nearby doorway. They looked angry. Disturbingly, they carried guns. Big guns. Damn, the guns were nearly bigger than the men!

"We are halted," said Pippa, hoisting her MPK and pointing it across the space. She said, "I think they spotted us," as the squibs formed a line and, without further ado, opened fire.

Bullets roared across the chamber, and Pippa and her clone hit the ground, rolling behind cover and peering out to return fire. The squibs stood proud, faces contorted with anger, firing off round after round, roaring. Tracers streaked through the vast chamber. Pippa peered out, sighted, and fired off a volley. Two of the squibs were caught by her bullets, danced a jig on the spot and crumpled to the ground with little sighs, leaking blood. Obviously, the angry little men died as easily as anybody else, despite their awesome, ganger-supplied firepower.

The conveyor belt of ganger shells, clanking and trundling along high above, was suddenly caught in the cross-fire. Bullets tore into unprotesting, unprotected flesh, and the long line of bodies danced and jigged and jerked spasmodically. Pippa glanced up, and chunks of flesh and globules of thick green fluid rained down on her. She yelped and lowered her head, but the pulped ganger shells coated her. Smoke was filling the chamber. One came apart at the neck where bullets had chewed into its flesh, allowing the stretching skin to tear, no longer able to support the weight. The ganger shell, riddled with holes and leaking anti-rot, slapped onto the floor beside Pippa, making her curse and growl, then scrabble towards the right, through hunks of flesh and strands of pulped spaghetti skin. She shifted around the vat, pulled her MPK to her shoulder, and with a grimace that had more to do with hate than was strictly necessary, unloaded a full one-hundred-and-fifty-shot magazine into the ranks of the squibs, who were wearing big grins and, until that point, seemed to be enjoying themselves...

Two, three, four of the creatures were punched off their feet, flailing backwards, blood ejecting and mixing in a crimson spray. Pippa stood, still firing, moving right, *keep on moving, keep on shifting*, and her clone was firing in parallel, an onslaught from two different trajectories catching the squibs at the centre.

The squibs were ranting, anger-fuelled and foaming at the mouth. They charged, and Pippa and her clone mowed them down. They were punched from their feet, and Pippa coolly changed mags as bullets whistled about her face and head, and above her the empty ganger shells still danced as if in time to some bizarre, charnel-house rhythm. And suddenly –

Silence reigned.

Smoke filled the chamber. Smoke, and the stench of death. The squibs were caught in acts of grotesque impossibility, limbs twisted, bodies holed. Pippa moved forward a little, boots squelching in ganger shell anti-rot preservative.

She breathed deep, and glanced over at her clone. She looked like she'd been rolling in a butcher's bin of off-cuts. Pippa looked down at herself and cursed, lips curling into a snarl. She was soaked in... *whatever* it was. Covered with shreds of white flesh, and splinters of bone.

The trolley above clanked forlornly to a halt, only half its payload still attached. The angry little squibs had taken their tantrums out on the easiest available targets. *Some fucking soldiers*, thought Pippa savagely. *I've never met anybody so suitable as cannon fodder!*

"If they're the trained soldiers, I'd hate to see the new recruits," said Pippa's clone. She reloaded her weapon with a *clack* and looked around, nostrils twitching. "We've certainly announced our presence, then."

"They already knew," said Pippa, gently. She glanced up at the swinging shells. With a *click*, the bodies tumbled into the vat, splashing and bobbing, dead skin slick, shifting together just under the surface like so many submerged maggots in a stew. "I get the feeling this is some kind of test. Like those squibs were sent to test us. To gauge our abilities."

"Why would they do that?" said Pippa's clone, frowning.

"I don't know. And I don't like the implication. What I *do know* is that I need to retrieve this artefact – this 3Core. And all I can hope is it's worth all the damn fucking effort."

Pippa strode forward, away from the vat, which was creeping her out more than she could have believed. *I mean, I've been through some shit. I've suffered at the hands of machine gods, medical mutations, government-fed super-soldier super zombies, and a cleaner with her organs on the bloody outside and her heart on a chain around her neck! I've been stabbed, shot, nuked and had implants put in my spine so if I turn on my fellow Combat K operatives, my head will detach neatly from my shoulders! And for what? All for what? To get to some shitty little outworld outpost run by a collection of genetic clones whose idea of a prick-*

tease is to change shape and copy their best friends. I wish Franco was here. Wish he was here, with his sly humour and wisecracks. And I wish... I wish Keenan was here. With his steady voice, his order, his unflappability. Law in the midst of chaos. A calm centre at the heart of the storm.

"Damn it. Come on."

"What's next?"

"I don't give a shit. Whatever it is, I'll break its fucking nose." Pippa stalked ahead, stepping through the massacred squibs, boots squealing in their genetically modified blood.

Silently, her clone followed.

THE INTERIOR OF the Slush Pits was timeless. The temperature was constant, and the light – its tint and intensity – were even. Pippa felt like she'd stepped into a stasis field.

The clanking noises grew subtly louder.

Down more corridors they moved, one boot at a time, taking their time, checking every space for enemies. They saw the occasional squib, scowling at them from the gloom before running off and disappearing into the narrow spaces between the pipes and walls. Pippa's first impulse was to shoot them in the back, and she did blast a few, hitting them between the shoulder blades, watched them crawl along the floor before giving them a double-tap to the back of the skull. But in the end, she didn't have the heart, and simply let them run off on whatever errands they had in mind.

"You shouldn't let them go," said her clone, glassy eyes emotionless, hands steady on her MPK. "They'll report our position."

"But it's like shooting fucking oompa loompas!" complained Pippa. "If Franco was here, he'd be having a blue frothing rage at the sheer brutality of it! He believes in a fair fight. He was always a sympathetic little sap like that."

"A fair fight? I take it you do not," said her clone, calmly.

"No." Pippa frowned. "I believe in doing the job, and getting the job done. As a very old friend once said – get in, and out, and the motherfuck away. That's the only way you survive in this job. If, indeed, survive we do."

They continued through the near-subterranean gloom. They passed several more huge chambers containing vats of body parts, ready for a fresh recycling. Each time Pippa saw the vats, she shivered. It didn't matter to her that these were supposedly emotionless, brainless, mindless *shells*. It was one thing to shoot an enemy soldier in the back of the head, but quite another to watch streams of endless, helpless bodies churned into slush. And she realised: Slush Pits. The place where the dead went for organic recycling. *Nice*.

After journeying for what felt like hours, with the temperature rising to that uncomfortable level where sweat beads the upper lip and crawls like spiders down the spine, Pippa halted. The mechanical thumping had grown louder now, as they drew near.

The corridor ended in a door. There seemed no other path.

"We should double back," said Pippa's clone. "I don't like the sound of that."

"It's a machine, nothing more," said Pippa.

She stepped forward. On the door was small, white lettering. It read: GUN Workshop.

"A GUN workshop? They make guns here?"

"No," said her clone. "Genetic Urban Necrolatry."

Pippa frowned. "What's Necrolatry?"

"Worship of the dead."

"Sounds... unnecessary. And awful."

The clone blinked. "I suppose it's what gangers do – our ability to *change*. To die, and live again. Only, it's not really like death. It's like a snake shedding a skin. Death bringing about life. That's what this whole place represents. The Slush Pits are about *rebirth*."

Pippa gritted her teeth hard, and shut her mouth. Sometimes, it was just better that way.

She reached forward and pushed open the door. In the gloom, there was lots of movement. The room was long, with a high ceiling, and crates stacked high around the walls. Conveyor belts ran the length of the room, and between four sets of thick, wide, armoured conveyors was a machine – an industrial robot, to be exact. It was a ball, about the size of a large groundcar, maybe eight metres in diameter and made from dull, silver metal. It was plain to the eye, no fancy lights or markings other than an industrial stencilled stamp: THUMPER mkIV, in dark grey lettering. From the casing emerged four arms of steel, each with a different appendage for carrying out jobs in the workshop, and as crates came along different conveyors, the THUMPER, mounted on four large bubble tyres, rolled around at the heart of the conveyors carrying out various tasks. One pincered arm lifted the lids onto the crates and smacked them into place. Its second arm, a nail-gun, punched nails through the lids at high speed, RAT-A-TAT-TAT. The third arm was a hammer, and occasional crates were selected – to Pippa's eyes, apparently at random – and placed to one side on a huge metal plate, where they were smashed into oblivion (hence THUMPER, thought Pippa; oh, how those industry types like their onomatopoeias!). Once firewood, the square would flip down and the offending tinder swallowed by a big black tube. The final appendage was a large polished cone; the THUMPER didn't ably demonstrate a use for that one.

Pippa and her clone watched for a while, gauging the level of intelligence of the THUMPER mkIV. After all, if it was an AI model it might, at the very least, alert the authorities or cause some obstruction under some bizarre, corrupt and misplaced Health and Safety legislation. Pippa had seen it before. H&S Bots gone policy crazy and locking people up in restaurants and factories, thinking they were simply "upholding policy" but really "condemning people to horrible deaths." The H&S SafetyBot v2.9 had, on the 15th Julius one year, caused the deaths of three hundred and nineteen workers in an insurance office block because somebody spilt a cup of HOT-O-COFFEE CoffeeMax on the stairs. The H&S SafetyBot v2.9 had cordoned off the offending HOT-O-COFFEE CoffeeMax with steel struts, effectively sealing the stairwell. On a higher floor containing the SUPERZIPLIFT computers, an electrical fire had subsequently started, rendering all lifts immediately unusable and disconnected because of the H&S SafetyBot 2.9 in charge of "Lift Safety Policy." So, as the fire happily raged out of control, the two H&S SafetyBots had imprisoned everybody in this new cage, effectively sealing them *inside* the fire zone under the pretext of Health and Safety Policy. Two days later, when the insane inferno was finally wrestled under control and the H&S SafetyBots taken down by TAK squad laser bursts, three hundred and nineteen roasted corpses were found in states of immobilised shock. The H&S SafetyBot 2.9 had been fitted with a PG – a Paralysis Gun – to enable its necessary enforcing of Health and Safety Policy. The dumb bots had immobilised the screaming, panicking people trying to escape the fire. Effectively, frying them like bacon in a pan. Since then, the base unit H&S SafetyBot had been... *upgraded.*

And so, with lives so readily threatened by the crap machinery invented to protect them, Pippa and her clone were loath to step happily into the workshop environment without at least a few tests. First, they eased into the factory and stood for a while in the THUMPER's line of vision (using whatever visual sensory apparatus it used, as nothing was obvious from Pippa's perspective). The machine simply ignored their presence and continued fastening lids on crates – and Pippa shuddered to think what the crates might contain, but she was sure it was something organic, because the place stunk like a charnel pit in high summer after the Twenty Year Plague.

Genetic Urban Necrolatry?

Yeah, right.

Next, Pippa sidled over to a long rough workbench which lined one wall and picked up a heavy metal block. She weighed it thoughtfully, and glanced at her clone – who was tense now, as if sensing the THUMPER would kick off with extreme prejudice when it became the butt of Pippa's little test. With a grunt, she launched the metal weight, which hit the THUMPER square in the middle of its round body. There was a *BOOM* and the weight skittered off across the ground without leaving so much as a mark. Pippa, tensed with MPK at the ready, watched as the THUMPER studiously ignored the impact and continued thumping crates and punching lids into position.

Pippa allowed a pent-up breath to escape. It was safe. *Safe!* For once, SAFE! Maybe their luck was changing? Maybe *her* luck was changing? She smiled a grim, narrow-lipped smile. *Yeah. Course it was.*

"Come on!"

"I don't like this," said her clone.

"What's to like? Let's just get through this shit and move on. We can't be far from the 3Core now. If I'm any gauge of distance, another floor down and we're near the centre. Unless you were mistaken."

"Unless I was mistaken," agreed her clone.

They walked, warily – looking for enemy squibs – past a conveyor of huge crates, rattling and bumping, huge belly-slung motors humming. To their right, the THUMPER mkIV was thumping away, arms flailing, with a mechanised rattle like speeding chains. It towered over them, huge and ominous. Pippa stared at the machine, the pin-prick lights reflected from its dull metal casing. The feeling came to her before anything was actually out of place. She sensed rather than saw, as if discovering a crack in the world, like a bad egg with a rotten core, that something was subtly *wrong*; the THUMPER hammered a lid on a crate and Pippa *felt* the fracture with normality, with the world, with reality, with this GUN Workshop, with this situation, with this *machine*... and she was moving, MPK coming up, free hand drawing the yukana even as the THUMPER's claw *slammed* through three crates in a long lazy curve that could have demolished a house, and

Pippa dropped back onto her arse, a fast movement allowing gravity to save her life as the claw whistled past her head, parting her hair down one side. In pure reflex the yukana hissed up and rattled across armoured casing, and the MPK yammered in her fist, bullets spewing like hot metal parasites and pissing sparks up the THUMPER's dulled casing. Pippa rolled, an instinctive movement born of experience – keep moving, keep running – which was fortuitous, because from nowhere came the hammer, slamming down from the gloom and darkness, red lights highlighting a steel head twice the size of Pippa's own and capable of crushing her entire being with one massive splat. Indeed, it was probably capable of crushing a *tank*.

Pippa's clone, the instant Pippa's gun fired, whirled and unleashed a hail of MPK bullets. Sparks flew and spat, and the THUMPER spun around on its bendy hydraulics, bubble tyres hissing, and it shot towards her faster than something so big and ponderous should be able to move. The cone slammed towards Pippa's clone, and there came a WHUMPF as it ejaculated a gush of flame, and Pippa's clone squealed, sprinting, diving for cover. Fire splashed up the walls, and Pippa's jaw dropped open as the THUMPER – twisting, tyres squeaking like a large child's toy – turned, reversed, and spun towards her with a billowing arc of bright blossoming fire, sending demons racing up the walls. The stench of fire met her nostrils, and pure, hot razor fear filled her from cunt to scalp.

Nothing freaked Pippa more than fire. It was buried in her psyche like a cancer, an evil drug. Like a maggot eating her brain from the inside out. It was her torture. Her breaking point. Her event horizon. For Pippa, fire, the fear of burning to death, the stench of her own flesh roasting, filled her worse than any other terror. "Every person has a breaking point," Keenan once told her, as they sat curled on the beach of Molkrush Fed after the crash, the sea hissing against the shore. A warm wind blew in from the jungle. But Pippa crawled backwards from the flames, and looked up at Keenan, in his arms, a little girl again, a tortured little girl afraid of the flames.

"I didn't expect that," she said, pulling away from his kiss. Sand stuck to her golden skin. Her eyes sparkled.

"Neither did I."

"What is this, Kee?"

"What is what?"

"Stop being evasive."

He grinned. "I'm not evading anything," he evaded.

She slapped his thick bicep and leant forward, part of her fringe dropping across her forehead. Her hair was damp from her swim; her lips were rimed with salt.

"Do it again," she said.

"What, evade you?"

And they were kissing, touching, easing gently down to the sand. Pippa suddenly pulled away. "We might have to spend our lives here," she said.

"OK."

"Together."

"That's fine."

"That would be like... a dream to me." Only, now he was dead and gone, vanished into the flames, into the heart and soul of VOLOS, and she was alone, alone against the fucking VOID and in the fire she saw Keenan's face, in the fire she saw her own face, and the faces of a thousand tormentors, a million CLONES, and she was going to die, but even worse, she was going to

BURN.

"No!" screamed Pippa's clone, and sprinted, dived, slammed into Pippa so violently she was knocked across the floor, yukana sword skittering away under a teetering stack of crates. Fire ravaged her clone's back, the force of the flames' *impact* slapping her clean across the factory floor, where she hit hard and rolled fast, and lay in a heap, clothes smoking, tiny flames dancing up and down her spine.

Pippa growled, and rolled, and came up fast. The THUMPER towered over her, all four arms lifting and wavering, each with a threatening appendage. All four smashed towards her at once, and Pippa leapt forward, under its reach, as the four arms crashed and screamed through the conveyor belt, wrenching it from pulleys and steel struts, and the whole rattling giant ensemble came to a grinding, squealing halt. Pippa rolled under the creature, firing up into what she assumed, *hoped*, would be a less-protected underbelly. It wasn't. Bullets pinged and squealed, and ricocheted dangerously close to Pippa's face, sparks scorching her skin. Balloon tyres hissed and nearly crushed her head, and she rolled, slamming herself sideways with a grunt that was more rage than effort. Her eyes searched frantically in the gloom, lit now by several burning crates. There were no convenient hatches. No little banks of computer chips. Nothing! The THUMPER was industrial, built to operate in factories on and off-world, built to work on heavy industrial sites where a rogue AI CRANE or AI DUMPER might go meltwire AWOL and chew up half the bloody site. The THUMPER was built to be tough. The THUMPER was built to last.

"Shit," she snarled, and glanced to her clone. She wasn't moving.

There came a squeal of hydraulics, and suddenly the THUMPER careered off, ten foot into the sky, on struts still connected to the wheels, leaving Pippa suddenly exposed and vulnerable beneath the machine's not-so-vulnerable underside. She yelled in surprise as a stench of hot oil and grease – and the ever-present stench of organic ganger corruption – flooded over her, as if... as if the damn *machine* was powered by some kind of distilled human oil ejecting burned ganger fumes. Shit, *shit*, she realised. The ganger shells and fuck-only-knew what else was being used as fuel to power the Slush Pits! It was all one big horrible charnel house, a place for the dying, a place for the dead. An eco-nut's recyclable wet-dream. No waste. NO FUCKING WASTE!

The hammer swung between the THUMPER's legs, and Pippa narrowly missed being crushed. She scampered to one side and dived, rolling behind a section of the destroyed conveyor belt. Her MPK screamed, and bullets tracked up the shell of the THUMPER – causing no damage whatsoever. It turned on her, and she swore the bastard was grinning, despite having no mouth. It levelled another arm at her. What was it? She rattled her combat brain. What the *hell* had it used it for? Nailing shut crate lids? Surely that couldn't... be... a weapon.

"Fuck!" she growled, and was already running as the THUMPER started pumping out nails – a hundred nails a second. They howled and whistled through the air, decimating anything and *everything* in their path. Pippa dived long and low, sliding across the warm soft floor as nails struck – *thud thud thud* – down one arm. She squealed and let out a breath of hot agony. She looked down at her left arm, where five six-inch pins – thinner that a pencil, admittedly, but still long bastard slivers of steel – had punched completely through her bicep. She flexed her fingers, formed a fist, and every single movement burned her bicep with raw hot fire. "Motherfucker," she growled, and her head snapped left, and the pain fuelled her hate and she wanted it now, her temper was up and she wanted to kill! Nothing mattered anymore, not pain, not fear, she would destroy this fucking machine and eat its machine heart!

She stood. "You want a piece of me, you big

useless testicle? Come on, let's see what you're made of!" But it was quite obvious what it was made of. Steel. Steel impenetrable to bullets. Her MPK was useless. Like waving a plastic fucking gun.

She needed her sword. Her yukana. Forged from a single molecule, it could cut hull steel; before, she must have hits its armoured plating at an angle. She wouldn't make the same dumb-ass mistake again.

Sword. Under crate. Shit.

She stared at the THUMPER. It had hunkered down again on its tyres, and its four wavering tentacles had stretched out, the clawed one closing around a section of conveyor belt. *What's it doing? What's the slimeball actually DOING?* Pippa's question was answered painfully quickly, as the THUMPER suddenly wrenched back its claw and pulled a ten foot length of steel conveyor belt loose. Pippa blinked.

"You've got to be joking, right? Come on, give me a BREAK!" as the THUMPER started to swing the ten-foot length of jagged steel-links around and around, like the world's biggest, deadliest bicycle chain.

Pippa was backing away. She knew she was being foolish. Backed into a corner.

Door? If she could get to the door...

She glanced right. It had sealed shut. Convenient. She grinned like a skull in a tomb. After all, why would it ever be *that easy?* When would it ever go *that smooth?* If the bastard wanted to lure them into a trap like a rabbit in a snare, it had done a brilliant job.

Pippa slung her MPK on her back. It was useless against armour. She spread her arms wide, and watched the THUMPER approaching, bubbling tyres rising and falling over the crushed and torn conveyor system like some kind of deviated moon buggy.

The whirling conveyor section made a slow *whum-whum-whum* sound as Pippa watched, eyes focused, lips dry, waiting for the onslaught, timing its movements... would it go up, or down, or cut her completely in half?

The THUMPER disengaged, and at the very same moment Pippa's clone screamed "FUCKER!" and the THUMPER twitched. Pippa dived left, and the whirling conveyor belt scythed overhead, embedding itself in the wall, creaking and groaning. The THUMPER strode over to Pippa's clone as Pippa picked herself up off the floor, and the claw rose high in the air.

"No!" screamed Pippa, as the appendage slammed down through the clone's body, which convulsed violently, legs kicking under the impact. The claw rose again, slowly, drooling blood, and hovered over the clone's convulsing body. Pippa's clone lay gurgling and twitching, and Pippa stared with open hatred and glaring fury as the THUMPER turned towards her, its claw worse than any gun pointed at Pippa's face.

She was trapped. Trapped inside this smashed-up place with a psychopathic factory robot. What the hell was she going to do? How the fuck was she going to escape? *How* could she escape?

And the answer was simple.

She couldn't escape.

She'd have to kill it. Kill it, or it'd kill her.

"Son of a bitch," she growled, and wiped sweating hands on her pants. *Think, girl, think! There must be a way round its armour. There must be a service hatch. Despite evidence to the contrary, the fucker had to have a brain. Memory. Instruction sets. It was a construction model. Where would they put the access hatch?*

She needed her sword.

She *needed* her sword...

She ran, leaping up a series of crates to stand above the THUMPER, boots planted firm, hands on hips, hatred on her face. "Come on, you heap of cheap tin shit!" she screamed, and the THUMPER reversed, turning away from Pippa's wounded, dying clone and charging towards her, bubble tyres thumping over debris. The claw and the hammer whirled, clacking and yammering, and converged on the crates, and Pippa's position, shattering the wood as Pippa back-flipped from the crate to land in a crouch, eyes down, lips snarling. The crates had been sent flying, reduced to tinder, and there amongst the debris was her –

yukana.

Pippa rolled forward, coming up with the blade in hand and leaping as the hammer whirred over her at waist-height. It would have crushed every rib in her body, and more. The THUMPER's arms whirled about, and Pippa dodged more heavy blows and stepped in, ramming the sword into the Thumper in one straight, swift blow, right up to the hilt. The Thumper paused, a sudden, shocking stillness, and Pippa withdrew the yukana and rammed it into the Thumper *again*. It sparked and fizzled, and with a screech of metal on metal reversed fast, bubble tyres pounding the floor as Pippa took a step back and lifted her sword, dark eyes fixed on the machine, which, she assumed, had realised she could *damage* it.

"What's the matter, fucker, armour not as tough as you thought?"

The Thumper spun around and seemed to utter a low growl, almost below hearing. And Pippa realised it was *angry*. She'd stuck her little needle into its innards, and now it was *angry*. She laughed at the machine, and realised with a shocking chill that it *was* an AI after all, not just some dumb Bot with the intelligence of a brick. It had the ability to *think*. To analyse, and rationalise, and problem solve and, supposedly, empathise. *Yeah. Right. Like that thing gives a fuck whether I live or die!* But it did give a fuck. It wanted her dead. Wanted her dead real bad...

The Thumper sped at Pippa, who ran towards the machine and dived at the last moment, claw and hammer swishing through the air. Her yukana slashed left, then right, as she passed beneath the machine; huge chunks of rubber were cut from the bubble tyres, and as Pippa slowed she twisted, saw

the wheel struts, and lashed out again in a shower
of sparks. There came a *clunk* and the THUMPER
seemed to sit down with a jerk, collapsing off its
wheels. Pippa grinned and lifted her yukana, matt
black blade gleaming in the dull light of the red
pin-prick lights and the glowing embers of burning
crates. The arm with the cone lashed towards Pippa
and she knew what was coming, heard the *whoosh*
in its pipes, and she bit down on her fear like an
apple filled with maggots, and she grimaced, and
yelled, and charged forward, and her yukana met
the lashing arm with all her force, the blade sliding
and sparking up the scaled hose until she reached
the THUMPER's hull. The blade bit, and detached the
limb at its core joint. Pippa grabbed the protruding
bolts and climbed up onto the THUMPER's hull, and
standing, panting, streaked with sweat and dirt and
smoke from the fires, she lifted the yukana high
and rammed it down through the THUMPER. With
a shower of sparks, and a roar, as if Pippa swam
beneath the ocean during a vast earthquake or tidal
wave, the THUMPER's remaining arms settled on the
ground and the machine was still.

Pippa stood, panting for a few moments, then
dragged out her yukana and leapt down from the
machine. She ran over to her clone, who was lying
on her back with a hole through her body the size
of Pippa's head. At first glance Pippa thought her
clone was dead: she was soaked with blood, and
the wound was ragged and torn, edged with strips

of flesh and bone. Pippa reached forward, fingers nearly touching the wound but reluctant... what could she do?

Nothing, she realised.

Pippa's clone opened her eyes, and smiled through a sheen of blood speckles. "I... tried to help," she said.

"You did good," said Pippa.

"I was sent to... kill you. But you know something? In... in the end, I liked you too... much."

Pippa saw her clone's finger stretching out, flexing almost spasmodically, and she took the clone's hand and thought about all the bad things this creature had done, all the savage killings, the murders, the murders in *her fucking name*... and that was if she'd lied, because maybe *she* was the clone and the dying woman in front of her was Pippa. The real Pippa. The original. The template.

Pippa barked a laugh, but tears were rolling down her cheeks.

She was confused.

It was just too fucked up. Too mashed up.

And Pippa realised that here and now, before her on the ground, dying, dribbling blood like a baby dribbles spit, coughing up chunks of her own smashed lungs, a quarter of her body flushed out like bad piss... well, here and now, this wasn't an evil creature, wasn't a ganger, wasn't an enemy, wasn't somebody to be hated. At the end of the day, it was just a woman lying on the floor, dying.

Pippa squeezed her fingers.

"Thank you," she said. "For your help."

"What I said... said before... I..." she spasmed, and her eyes glazed over. Then she relaxed, and her tongue licked her lips. "It's a trap," she said. "All... a trap."

Then she died on the factory floor.

Pippa held her hand for a while, slack fingers in hers, and when she opened her eyes she thought her dead clone was crying. Until she realised it was her own tears, dripping from weeping eyes, flowing from her face to its mirror image. Pippa looked at herself in death, and shuddered. *Is this how I'll appear? Is this what it'll taste like?* And she had the unique experience of watching herself die.

She did not like it one bit.

Pippa stood, and rummaged through her clone's clothing for extra MPK mags. Then she took the second yukana sword and sheathed both weapons on her back, beneath her pack.

She looked up. Around. There had to be cameras. Had to be. She grabbed one of the spikes through her arm, readying herself for the agony, and yanked it out with a spurt of blood.

"Right, fuckers!" she screamed. "I'm coming for you!"

PIPPA'S MPK BLOSSOMED, yammering, hot fire ejecting from the glowing barrel. A line of squib soldiers went down in a fast line from left to right, punched from their feet, splattering blood up a wall of sand crates. Crouching, she paused as the smoke swirled and parted, her body tense, eyes narrowed. She stood slowly and stepped forward, searching. Another squib charged at her, screaming, and a single bullet between the eyes slapped him back, ending his fury with a nasty *crack*.

"Any more?" she said, voice calm.

Apparently, there were not, and she touched her arm delicately where she'd patched her flesh together with skinglue after removing the Thumper's nails. She took a deep breath, levelling the pain in her mind. *Control it*, she snarled at herself.

Pippa stepped gingerly between the corpses and stepped through the door into another narrow corridor. These were the worst – in the confines it was easy to get shot, easy to die – but Pippa's fury was carrying her on, pushing her on, and when it came down to it, when the shit hit the fan, she no longer cared, no longer worried about consequence, no longer gave a fuck about the 3Core and Quad-Gal and the invading junk army. That was just a backdrop, a distant play acted out for the benefit of the decadent and mocking gods. Pippa had nothing left to fight for, and even worse, nothing left to live for. Everything she had loved was gone, and that shrivelled her heart to a small black place and locked the gate.

You must be close. To the 3Core. They're throwing everything they have at you...

And she didn't care. Her whole life she had been a victim, and despite her hatred and violence and her ability to kill, she knew now – she had been the *victim*. A victim of bullies and an abusive father. A victim of hate. A victim of anger. A victim of pride. A victim of fury. And she was tired, so tired, and wanted to let it all go...

But could not.

She kicked open the door and bullets whined at her, slapping the wall beside her head, tiny splinters of hot steel stinging her skin. She unleashed metal fury, stepping, *leaping*, into a roll and coming up fast, eyes narrowed, lips pursed, MPK slamming in an arc that ended with a final *crack* as she took out the last enemy squib on the high bridge above her. He staggered, hit the rail, flipped over, and landed with a dull *thud* in front of her, unmoving.

Pippa stared through the gloom. There was, at the centre of the chamber, what could only be described as a huge *pod*.

Can it really be that simple? A Pod Vault? A fucking pod in the middle of a room? But then, she'd killed, what? Sixty? Seventy angry little gangers in the process? Did that make it an easy infiltration, or was she just jaded beyond belief after decades of slaughter? But it was all for the greater good, right? All for the bigger fucking picture.

I'm tired of death, she realised. *I'm tired of the kill. Maybe Keenan did the right thing after all. Maybe I should go back to VOLOS, the core of*

Sick World, the twisted, warped, corrupted Machine God... Maybe I should join Keenan? It has to be better than this.

Pippa moved forward, wary, MPK sweeping her surroundings. The Pod Vault was barely what Pippa would describe as a museum; it was a room, an armoured room designed to protect an item, a series of items, something precious. She stepped through the arched portal of the black pod and into the dark, oil-smelling interior. It occurred to her that it might be a trap; that the whole thing might just crush her, or swamp her in poisonous gas, or inject her with a thousand spikes. She no longer cared. Pippa had moved beyond thoughts of death. She was sick of the gangers, sick of the clones, she just wanted out of there – one way or another.

It was cool inside the Pod Vault. A single room with a gentle, glowing light. There were diamond shelves with various items ranging across their sparkling expanse. Pippa scanned the shelves, squinting a little, holding her breath. They'd travelled long and hard and fast trying to find an answer to the junks; could she really be this close to discovering the one thing which could save the Quad-Gal from their infectious invasion?

She murmured a tiny laugh.

Her eyes alighted on a small grey disc. Around the edge, in tiny, alien script were letters, or numbers – some form of identification. This had to be it. The 3Core. The junk's computer chip, once used to run their global mainframe, and which coordinated their civilisation and their battles and their society. The heart, mind and soul of their civilisation. The Junkala Soul. Quad-Gal Military could reprogram it, re-infect the spreading junks with a digital retrovirus. Turn them from warmongering creatures of accelerating destruction into... something not quite so corrupt.

Pippa reached out.

Her fingers closed slowly around the disc, and she lifted it to her face, and she *felt* the power emanating from the tiny object: something so small, so delicate, so fragile, and yet with the potential to do so much good. It had been hidden here, hoarded here, and Pippa was damn sure the gangers had no real idea of what it was, of what it could potentially *achieve*. They'd have taken over the Quad-Gal by now if they had any inkling of its *power*.

"Beautiful, is it not?" said the soft, slow voice.

Pippa whirled, crouching, yukana out and quivering, the *shring* hanging in the air.

At the entrance stood a small man, a hunchback, one shoulder lower than the other. His face was oval, his hair a straggled mess, his mouth upturned at one corner, his eyes mismatched in colour – one green, one yellow, a curiously mesmerising stare.

Pippa looked for weapons, but the hunchback was unarmed.

Pippa relaxed a little. His soldiers would be outside, of course. Waiting for her to step out. Ambush!

Hell.

"Do you know what it is?"

"I know it belonged to the junks. That is all. We have tried to decode it, but do not have the technology. Quad-Gal Military saw to that with their... *sanctions.*" He almost spat the last word, but then smiled lop-sidedly.

"Hmm," said Pippa, eyes searching for a way out. She did not consider the hunchback a threat. He was little more than a distraction before the real violence began. How many soldiers? How many guns? Shit, she was trapped like a bear in a cage. Well, she'd fucking dance all right. She'd dance and maim and kill until she could kill no more.

"How did you convince your clone to help you? We were amazed by that turn of events. She was genetically *programmed* to hate you, to bring you in, to kill you as a last resort."

Pippa gave a small shrug. "I did nothing."

"You changed her."

"I could not change her. She was me."

"She was a copy of you," said Ziggurat. "She was your clone. With a few... *modifications.*"

"Much as I'd like to stand here chatting," snapped Pippa, stepping forward, yukana lowering to the hunchback's throat, "I need you to step out of the way. In one piece is fine, but if you like, you can do it in several slabs."

"Tut tut," said Ziggurat, smiling gently. "You people do so underestimate me. But you only do it once."

Pippa hesitated. But she was deadly tired, emotionally distraught, mentally drained, psychologically bruised and just damn sick of the whole fucking ball game.

"I warned you," she said, and launched herself at the hunchback, yukana slamming down in a killing stroke – only Ziggurat wasn't there; he'd side-stepped neatly, right hand darting out, the palm of his hand slapping Pippa's chest over her heart and *accelerating* her backwards with such force she could not breathe. She sped across the Pod Vault's interior, hit the wall and fell to the ground. She rolled to her feet, hissing. Ziggurat traded his air of nonchalance for an expression of loathing. This was fine. Pippa was used to people trying to kill her. It was when they were nice she started to worry...

"A nice trick. What is it? A pulse accelerator under your palm?"

Ziggurat shrugged, discarding his robe with the same motion. Pippa blinked. He was now naked, his body twisted and scarred – *heavily* scarred – from either acts of torture, or a hundred battles with a blade. His small, shrivelled penis swung between his legs as he took a weird kind of wrestling stance, one shoulder low and stooped, the other pushed back by his spinal deformity.

"You going to kill me, or fuck me?" snarled Pippa.

Ziggurat smiled. "Show me what you can do."

"Come on, it's one thing trying to kill you, but I shouldn't have to look at your tiny dick at the same time. That's an unfair advantage," but even as she spat the insult she was leaping, sword whistling in five beautiful, precise strokes. Ziggurat, despite his deformity, moved with practised speed and an agility that stunned Pippa. He swayed, shifted, danced, and avoided each and every swing without seeming to make any effort. He was a dancer, he was a ghost. He was *untouchable.*

Pippa took a step back. A light sheen of sweat grazed her brow and upper lip.

"Shit," she said.

"Submit. We do not want to kill you. We want to question you. About the Junkala Soul. About how we can access its data. You can help us. We know all about you, Pippa. We know your Combat K history. We know you have the skills to decode this alien trinket."

"Fuck this." Pippa grabbed her MPK, rounded the weapon on Ziggurat and pulled the trigger hard. Bullets screamed, Ziggurat shifted posture and... Pippa blinked, then *howled* as the weapon was torn from her grasp, removing a layer of skin, and slammed across the Pod Vault's interior. The MPK hit the wall so hard it broke into three pieces, which skittered across the ground, shedding bullets from the blasted magazine.

Pippa charged, yukana whistling for Ziggurat's head. He brought both hands together with a clap like thunder, and Pippa smelled ozone, everything seemed to go red and black, and she was picked up and her yukana sword *bent and distorted into a twisted ball, and that was impossible, fucking impossible, and the pain exploded through her, and she was burning with hot hellfire as she was lifted, floated, accelerated, and she burned, and burned, and burned without flames, and tears ran down her scorched cheeks and she got one final glimpse, of Ziggurat, naked and grotesque, his green eye and yellow eye watching her, unblinking, uncaring* before the pain became too much and she fell down an infinite well of darkness and welcomed the bottom of the pit; welcomed oblivion.

CHAPTER ELEVEN

AN ORGY OF ORGS

"WHAT WE GONNA do, what we gonna do, SQUAWK buster? I didn't shack up with you guys to die a pointless death on a pointless bloody ocean, I thought you had a better plan than this, I thought you knew what you were bloody doing SQUAWK and here I'll be all lost and alone and lost at sea, and I'll burn me bleedin' motors out tryin' to fly all the way to dry land 'cos we're in the middle of bleedin' nowhere, so we are! What we gonna do? What we gonna SQUAWK do, I ask yer?"

"Shut up," said Franco. "You ain't helping the damn situation."

Tarly was pale. They were in the shit, and here, and now, there was no magical Quad-Gal Military to bail her out. No expensive computer like Alice ready to calculate a solution to the problem in the blink of an eye. Tarly Winters might be one of the richest women in the whole of QGM, she might command more respect and power than Franco could ever dream about in a trillion years, she might be at the very top of the ziggurat – but here, she was just as helpless as the next woman being dragged into a four-klick wide whirlpool.

"Do something, Franco," she said, clutching his arm.

Franco grinned, and puffed out his chest. "Hey, they don't call me Franco 'Bodge Monkey' Haggis for nothing, sweetness. Leave this one to me!" He pointed at the parrot. "YOU! PARROT! Find me a screwdriver."

"A sonic one?"

"Eh?"

"A sonic screwdriver?"

"No, duckweed, a bloody Phillips one! And a hammer. Can't fix nothing without a hammer."

"What are you going to fix, Franco?" said Tarly, looking over her shoulder at the impending whirlpool – and their impending deaths – in a sweeping, crushing, watery grave.

"The Hyperdrive," said Franco, proudly, scratching his beard and puffing out his chest once more. "You just stay here watch that, love," he said, as the parrot dropped a screwdriver into Franco's fist. He waved the screwdriver around, and without any hint of irony whatsoever, said, "I'll be back."

He disappeared below deck.

The hyperdrive was whining and belching, the power nozzles set on full power. Plumes of black smoke were emerging from the port side of the galleon, and Tarly and the parrot looked at each other.

"Pretty Polly," said the parrot, weakly.

"Fat lot of good you are, AI. You couldn't think your way out of damn Connect Four game. When we get *out* of this shit, I'm going to drop *you* in the shit."

"Hey, this ain't my fault, buster!"

Below decks, Franco was staring at the hyperdrive, hands on hips, a big frown on his face. He heard somebody on the steps and turned, seeing Tarly descend to stand beside him. He brightened, visibly.

"Ah! The Heckler and Steinberg 52pnm co-rotational Hyperdrive!"

"You know it, then?" Tarly looked uncertain.

"Er. No. But I've read about it."

"What did you read about it?"

"I read, er, that it was... a... good... hyperdrive."

Franco started forward, and Tarly shivered. Here was the most dangerous thing known to woman – a man with a screwdriver. Franco crouched by a huge panel and undid the screws holding it on. He dropped one, which rolled away and was lost in the galleon's interior gloom. He grinned back at Tarly. "That always happens," he said.

"We're going to fucking DIE!" she screamed at him.

"Okay, okay, don't hassle a dude when he's on a gig, reet?"

He held up his hand, flat palm outwards.

"Back up. Back up."

Tarly, with great exaggeration, took several steps back.

"A dude needs room to breathe, yeah?"

"Just fix the fucking ENGINE!"

"Okay, okay, don't hassle me."

Franco started to poke around inside the hyperdrive, which fizzed and popped. At one point, he was illuminated by bright white light. Then he tapped his teeth with the end of the screwdriver.

"Just as I thought."

"What did you think?"

"It's damn complex in there."

"Hmm. You don't know what the hell you're doing, do you?"

"Hey, just hang on there, trixie-knickers. Give me a few moments to codge... to codga... to think about it." He tapped his teeth again. "If I bypass the dytronium relays to the fusion hyperindex, then we should back a backpressure upsurge which negates the bipedal contrafugal..."

Tarly crouched in close beside him. "Do you feel that sideways pull?"

"Uh-huh." He nodded, meeting her gaze.

"That's us, spinning around the edge of the whirlpool. You've got a minute, fucknugget, then we'll be revolving so fast we ain't getting out of this shit-heap alive. *Ever.*"

"Don't pressure me, lass, don't pressure."

Franco reached into the hyperdrive and poked about with his screwdriver. There came an almighty scream, like worlds colliding, and the hyperdrive shut down. All lights flickered *off*. The engine was *dead*.

Franco grinned backed at Tarly. "Whoops," he said.

"You fucking, fucking, fucking idiotic, fucking, nim-witted dim-witted fucking stupid mind-frazzled drug-riddled numb-skulled brainless bowel-wrenching dog-fucking horse-fucking goat-fucking erection-obsessed fucking useless lump of fucking lard..."

As she'd been ranting, Franco reached into the hyperdrive once more. With a *whine*, the lights on the hyperdrive came back on. The galleon gave a *jerk*. The whole machine started to vibrate insanely.

Franco grinned. "Hey." He hooked his thumb in his belt and there was a swagger as he stood. "Get yo ass up there and give her full juice, baby, this baby's going home! Or, at least, out of the sucking whirlpool and over the ocean towards The Org States!"

Tarly disappeared, and Franco, holding his screwdriver as a cowboy would hold a six-shooter, swaggered up the steps – to be hit by a blast of wind as they were sucked around and around at the brink of the whirlpool. Queen Strogger was hanging onto the mast, her face grim, and the parrot was squawking and flapping, caught by random air-currents and the violent wind.

"What happened?" shouted Franco over the roar of the sudden storm.

"It came out of nowhere," growled Queen Strogger. "When you *fixed* the hyperdrive. I would suggest it could be centrifugal *blowback*."

Franco staggered across the galleon's deck. "Whatrafugal whatback?"

"The hyperdrive's short-circuiting. It's drawing energy from the ocean, from the whirlpool, from everything around it. What the hell did you *do to it, Franco?*"

"Well, I hotwired it, innit?"

Franco staggered across the decks and up the planks to Tarly, at the control deck. Wind and sea spray raged around them, whipping Tarly's ginger curls around her face. Her hands were hovering tentatively over the controls, as Franco's hands would have hovered over a particularly delicate clitoris.

"Give it some, love!" he shouted over the rage.

"I don't want to blow it up, you psycho!" she yelled.

"Bah and humbug," snapped Franco, slamming the controls. The hyperdrive shuddered and whined, and they took off across the Teeth Ocean as if somebody had shoved a rocket up their arse. The galleon slammed through the waves like a missile-powered ship – which, indeed, it was.

"See!" yelled Franco, triumphantly, and ran to the prow, leaning over and into the sea-spray with childish glee. "I did it! We're saved! I saved us! It worked!"

"Franco," yelled Tarly, grabbing his arm and holding onto him for dear life. "You've got to slow us down! We're going too fast!"

"What rot!" snapped Franco, his cheek flaps wobbling like a naked astronaut on re-entry. "This baby will hold strong and true! She's an incredible piece of ancient technology! She's as strong as an ox, as tough as a teletubby, as rabid as a pitbull..."

There came a distant creak. And a CRACK! The sort of CRACK! that indicated a major section of timber breaking in half. Franco went a little pale. "Er," he said, as the parrot flapped past him, squawking and losing its alloy feathers.

Franco and Tarly ran for the control deck together. They were way past the pull of the ocean whirlpool – a good fifty kilometres past it. But at what cost?

Franco hit the kill-switch and, with a whine and a shudder, the hyperdrive slowly wound down. The galleon hit the surface of the ocean with a *slap* and gradually slowed, huge waves settling around her bows like the skirts of an enormous lady after a vigorous ballroom dance on a cocktail of whiskey, speed and methedrine.

Gradually, the world seemed to return to a normal state.

Franco sighed a big sigh of relief.

"Well, that seemed to work out alright, didn't it?" He beamed at Tarly, then over at Queen Strogger, who was scowling at him, eyes narrowed, but in all fairness that seemed to be the expression she always adopted for dealing with Franco Haggis. Most people did.

"You put our lives at risk!" said Tarly, hands on hips.

"Bah! They were already at risk! We was gonna drown!"

"Yeah, but it's always the same with you, out of the bloody frying pan and into the bloody fire! You seriously put this vessel at risk of sinking! And what? So you could see if Charlie don't surf? You've got to think things through more clearly," said Tarly.

"Ach, stop whining. We've only just started dating and already you're nagging me like a carping fishwife."

"*What?*"

"I thought you was my good woman by my side as we rode the ocean waves. Now things ain't looking so rosy and oh, yes, soon you'll be wanting to trim my beard and iron my shirts and get my tuff fixed." Franco was a mite touchy on this subject, seeing as his last wife – an eight foot genetic super-soldier mutation called Melanie – had made him trim his beard and iron his shirts and get his tuff fixed.

"What the hell's a *tuff?*"

There came another **CRACK!** only this **CRACK!** was a damn sight bigger than the last CRACK! that CRACKED! through the galleon. The ship lurched, then sat its arse back in the water, and began – very slowly – to lift its nose in the air.

"Er, that doesn't look good," said Franco, looking around frantically.

"That's because we're sinking," said Tarly, voice a centre of stoic calm.

There came a long pause.

"Er," said Franco.

"I *told you* to slow down."

"Bloody nagging back-seat drivers!"

"Don't start! This is serious!"

"What, more serious than me getting us out of that whirlpool conundrum? I saved our lives, I did."

"Yes, and immediately dumped us in another bag of shit."

"It's not *my* damn fault the bloody hyperdrive broke the ship."

"The only thing broken is *your bloody logic.*"

Franco scratched his beard. They could hear a *glub-glub-glub* sound. Queen Strogger thumped over to them, and scowled. "We are taking on water. We are sinking. What's the plan now, Franco Haggis and Tarly Winters? An org is not the best creature to be lost at sea. The salt rots our components."

"WD40?" suggested Franco.

"Your joke is not appreciated," snapped Queen Strogger.

"Who said it was a joke? Listen, listen, ladies, ladies, it's not a problem, reet? We'll just... build a raft. Or something."

"Out of what?"

"Crates? Planks? Wood? I've seen the adventure survival programmes. All we need to do is lash together lots of wood using twine, or electrical cable, maybe dental floss, and then we can float our way to safety and freedom. See? Job done, problem solved, we'll all be saved." He beamed, as if the raft was already built.

"I estimate we have two minutes until we're under water," said Queen Strogger with the sort of patronising look Franco usually received from his drill sergeant. "Go ahead. Build a raft."

"Er. Right." Franco looked around, but the prow of the galleon rose further into the air with a splash and creak of timbers, until the ship was near vertical and Franco was left dangling from the rail, legs kicking.

Tarly kicked next to him.

And Queen Strogger, next to her.

"Any more bright ideas?" said Tarly, voice neutral.

"Go on."

"What?"

"Say it."

"Say what?"

"Say the raft idea was a shit idea."

"Franco, it's a great idea."

"Really?"

"Yeah, if we were stuck on an island with a timber merchant's and a hydraulic nailgun."

"Oh." He looked crestfallen.

"One more thing."

"What's that?"

"When the galleon goes down, it'll suck us under. You've got to cling to something."

"What, like Strogger?"

"I've got a feeling she's going to *sink*."

"Ah. Oh. So we're all going to die?"

"Yes."

Franco considered this. "Bugger," he said.

IT WAS A beautiful night. The stars were crystals scattered on sable. A cool wind blew over gently-lapping waves. The rhythmical *slap, slap, slap* of the ocean was enough to put any hedonist to a gentle, thumb-sucking sleep.

Franco clung to the top of the crate, starfish-style, and bobbed on the ocean. To his left, also spread-eagled on a crate, bobbed Tarly, and to his right, starfishing across *three* rope-lashed crates, was Queen Strogger, in possibly the most undignified position any queen had ever found herself – except, maybe, with her neck on a chopping block.

The water slapped.

They bobbed, like corks, on the ocean.

Polly the Parrot landed on the crate next to Franco's head, but careful to stay out of reach of his teeth. The parrot had seen what could happen to wayward and annoying Special Friends when a squaddie came too close with his gnashers.

"It's not that bad, SQUAWK!" squawked Polly.

Franco, aroused from sleep, mumbled and licked salt-rimed lips. "What isn't?"

"This. Being afloat. Lost at sea. Stranded. SQUAWK! Dying slowly of thirst. I mean, what's it been?"

"Three days," said Franco, weakly.

They had no water. No food. And the hammer of the sun pounded their limbs and bodies against the crate anvils. It was ten times worse for Franco, for the salt baked into his flayed back was agonising him every second of every day. And just when he thought the wounds were healing, another splash of brine splashed and slopped over him, bringing fresh salt and fresh, excruciating agony.

"You've got to admit it, it's pretty funny," said Polly.

Franco stared at the parrot with a beady eye. "What's fucking funny? Fucking funny will be when I get a fucking gun and shove it up your fucking arse. Then you'll be laughing on the other side of your beak. Only you won't, because I will have shot your arsehole up through your mouth."

"Charming."

"Never said I was."

"Squawk!"

"Will you *stop fucking doing that right next to my ear!* It's bad enough having no skin on your back, but if I have to spend another pissing day with tinnitus I'll give you something to worry about, lost at sea or no! You'll see, you mangy pile of stinking, half-feathered rectal scraping!"

"No need to be like that," sniffed Polly the Parrot. "I was only being friendly. Squawk!"

There came several minutes of savaging noises and squawking as Franco chased the hopping parrot around the crate-top with his mouth. It was not a dignified sight. Indeed, a spread-eagled Franco was far from the most dignified creature on any planet, never mind Cloneworld.

Eventually, weak after so much time without food and water, Franco finished his aimless chase, and lay there, drooling on the crate top. *I just can't believe it. Can't believe it's come to this! Chasing a parrot around a crate in the hope I can bite its bloody head off!*

"Hey."

Franco glanced over at Tarly. "What?"

"Another fine mess you've got us into."

"Oh, don't you start as well!"

Polly the Parrot, Franco's *Special Friend,* hopped about on the edge of the crate, riding the waves up and down, up and down, and occasionally dodging an errant splash of ocean brine. "What I don't understand," said the parrot, with a considered air, "is why you haven't eaten and drunk from the emergency rations packed in this very crate? I mean, you've been floating here for three whole days, dying slowly of hunger and thirst, and yet you are afloat atop a veritable minefield of nutrition! I find it most strange you haven't tucked into all the edibles I can scan beneath you. Most strange indeed."

Franco scowled. "Listen, dipshit, the reason we haven't eaten and drank our rations, reet, is because the crate lids are all screwed down! And lo! I do not seem to have a screwdriver about me."

"Yeah, but I can easily unscrew the lid," said the parrot.

"What?" said Franco, voice strangely calm.

"I can easily unscrew the lid," repeated the parrot, and smiled, a beaky smile, but a smile nonetheless.

"So let me get this straight. We've been lying here, dying, for *three whole days* and you never thought to mention it before?"

"You never asked," said the parrot smugly. "After all, a Special Friend needs to feel... *wanted*. And I haven't felt... *wanted* very much at all."

"Why, you little motherfuc..."

"Franco!" It was Tarly. She had a strained smile on her face. She turned her eyes on Franco's Special Friend. "Could you please, please, please, O great and wonderful parrot, please open one of the crates so that we don't die in the next few hours? Pretty please?"

"Sure thing, buster," said Polly, and dipping her head, used her now *rotating* beak to unscrew the crate lid. It spun like a power drill, and within minutes Franco was carrying out a strange balancing act as the hinged lid opened and he tossed hydro pills and packs of PreCheese to both Strogger and Tarly, who drank, gasping, and ate like hungry people.

"Good job you packed *some food,* at least," said Tarly, munching on PreCheese. It was like eating a block of lard with cheese granules. It wasn't very wholesome. It was downright disgusting!

"Hey, well, PreCheese covered in horseradish *is* one of my favourite foods when I'm stranded in an exotic foreign location!" Franco beamed, Tarly's irony lost on him, and he paddled his hand in the ocean. "Hey, this isn't turning out to be such a bad gig after all, is it?"

"Shut up," said Queen Strogger, who was scowling across the expanse of water at him as she chewed on a rancid lump of PreCheese. "I've never known a man land us in so much horse-shit!"

"Hey, that's a bit harsh," said Franco. "You can't blame *me* for the unfortunate sequence of events which have befallen us! Can you? Eh? I ask you?"

"We could ask Alice."

"Oh, that bugger come on line, has she?"

"It would appear so."

Tarly pulled the small black cube from her pocket. Green lights flickered across its surface, then a weary voice said, "Hello, gang."

"Alice!" beamed Franco. "Glad to have you back, lass! Sorry about the Hornet, by the way, and whilst you're here, you can just clear up a few little things about just what the bloody hell happened back there, and how it wasn't anything to do with me, oh, no, sir, and how I've been reet helpful and saved everybody's lives getting us off that ol' pirate galleon, and..."

"There's a boat coming," said Alice.

"What kind?" said Tarly, an edge to her voice. Last thing she fancied was being picked up by another pirate bunch of wacked-out crazy pirate orgs.

"It's flying a flag. A grey one."

"Does it show a cybernetic arm upthrust from a pot of grease?" said Queen Strogger, wearily.

"Yes," said Alice. "I believe that is the Royal Flag? Symbol of The Org States?"

"It is indeed," said Strogger, carefully.

"Hoorah!" said Franco, and danced a little jig, which sent his crate bobbing crazily about the ocean. "We're saved! Thank goodness for that! Time for a palace, and jewels, and rich food, and succulent women."

Tarly coughed.

Smoothly, Franco said, "And of course, by succulent women I was referring to the new succulent love of my live, Miss Tarly Winters, General for the Quad-Gal Military and all round succulent charm-monster."

The sound of powerful engines floated across the Teeth Ocean, and within minutes a huge grey steel vessel thundered into view. It was five times the size of the pirate's ancient rickety galleon, and was indeed a battleship, complete with massive mounted cannons, and machine gun turrets, and all manner of grim and pointy death-dealing devices.

"Hurrah!" repeated Franco, clinging on harder now as the sea became choppy with the battleship's turbulence.

It grew closer and closer, towering over them. Orgs stomped and clattered on the steel decks, and the ship slowed, turning to broadside the helpless heroes. A platform was lowered from the towering decks on hydraulics, and on it stood a massive, fearsome looking org. She was fully ten feet tall, a powerhouse of bristling steel weaponry, guns and electro-axes, laser-spears and stabbing weapons and advanced human upgrades. The only reason Franco could tell *she* was a *she* was because of the long blonde peroxide hair and the red lipstick applied crazily to the metal mask that was her face. It was not the most enticing or sexually pleasing image he had ever seen. It looked like make-up and a wig on a scorched MIG weld.

"Thank god!" shouted Franco. "It's so good to be finally rescued! We have your Queen here! Queen Strogger! We saved her life, saved her from the gangers!"

"Shut up," growled Strogger.

"She was in prison there!" shouted Franco, through cupped hands. "We saved her! Now, where's the palace, the hot food and hotter women! Eh?"

"Shut up!" snapped Queen Strogger.

"What's the matter, lass? Anyway, who is that?"

"It's my daughter. Princess Anklebolt III."

"Your daughter? Wow! Even better! What a coincidence!"

"Not really, I bet she's been out looking for me. Since I went missing. Since I, er, escaped."

"Wonderful! A happy family reunion!" Franco beamed around, as happy as a pig in shit, whilst Tarly watched on, a scowl touching her face as understanding dawned. Queen Strogger scowled, but then, that was only little old Queen Strogger, right? She always scowled like that and surely it was nothing to be worried about...

The ten orgs accompanying Anklebolt III pulled out heavy machine guns and pointed them across the short expanse of ocean. Bobbing on their crates, Franco, Tarly and Queen Strogger could do nothing.

"You are all under arrest," snarled Anklebolt III, hot-oil spittle ruining her finely applied lipstick. Clanking and slamming, more guns emerged from her own mechanised torso, from her shoulders and forearms, from her hips and even one from between her legs, like some crazy huge machine gun phallus clicking into place.

"Now that's a chick dick," said Franco, eyes wide. He held up his hands, an easy smile on his face, sure this was just some huge silly mistake and soon they'd be eating food and drinking wine and singing Old Kahuna hits on Solar Singstar and certainly with *no* machine guns pointing at their delicate floppy bits. "Hey, hey, hey, nice to meet you, Anklebolt, Strogger here has been telling me all about you, now I know you're looking forward to getting jiggy and providing us with sumptuous lodging and hot carafes of alcoholic beverage, so don't let me stand in your way, right?"

"Cuff them," snarled Anklebolt, and glared in hatred at Queen Strogger. "We have evidence, *mother*. We have the tapes! We know what you did, selling our precious org secrets to the gangers so they could build their army! You have betrayed your own people! You have betrayed your own race! You have betrayed the orgs! You are going to hang, *mother*.

You are going to be exterminated with maximum prejudice!"

"Er?" said Franco.

"*Shut up!*" hissed Tarly.

"Excuse me? Yes, you there, the big org with the gun dick. Yes, you, the fat one with a metal arse." Anklebolt turned her vitriolic glare on Franco. He grinned at her in a friendly, amiable fashion. "I'm sure there's been some huge kind of mistake here. Queen Strogger here, she was a *prisoner* of the gangers. I helped to *rescue her,* I did. I am a dashed and darned *hero,* I am!"

"Funny little man. Be silent! Strogger was a prisoner because the gangers betrayed her. But not after she betrayed us all. She sold every single one of our mechanical designs to the gangers. Now, they have intel on our every weapon, every shield, every device for human upgrading. They have been busy building an army. A vast army, of clones, and of cloned *orgs!* Yes, you heard me, funny little ginger man, the gangers have gathered a huge war host at the heart of The Teeth mountains – and they are preparing to attack! They have cracked the GASGAM AI units, and can now use air support, *air support designed by the orgs!* We will be wiped out. Annihilated, and all..." she pointed, "because of Queen Strogger."

"Ah," said Franco.

"Yes," said Anklebolt.

Franco thought about it. "So, they'd be clorgs, then."

"*What?*"

"Cloned orgs. Clorgs."

Anklebolt stared at him as if he was something particularly distasteful she'd found on the bottom of her steel boot. She waved a hand. "Take them to the brig. Chain them up. Shackle them! They will all stand trial at the Org Palace in Org."

"Hey, wait a minute!" said Franco as the platform drew closer, and several huge orgs started to spin lockchains. "Hey, wait, stop, why the buggering bugger are *we* being bloody arrested?"

"Accessories. To treason." Anklebolt smiled a horrible smile from her metal, upgraded face. "It carries the death penalty."

Chains soared out, snapping and locking like live snakes around Tarly, around Franco – even the parrot was captured with a wounded "SQUAWK!" – and they were hauled onto the platform, hauled onto the battleship. Finally, without a struggle, Queen Strogger was chained heavily and dragged onboard. The platform lifted, and they were all dumped on the steel deck.

"Take them below," snarled Anklebolt.

"Bugger," said Franco.

FRANCO AND TARLY were chained up together in a sterile steel cell. It had a small barred window overlooking the rolling Teeth Ocean. To the bars of the door, was chained Polly the Parrot. The Special

Friend was curiously quiet, except for the occasional, pitiful, mewling *"SQUAWK!"*

They were given cups of water, and plates of dried, er, "sludge," Franco christened it. It looked like engine oil on a bed of engine scrapings, topped off with a dollop of engine grease.

For long hours they stared through bars in a state of shock, not just at their more recent near-starvation, death-by-ocean, pirates and whirlpool, but at the total failure of the one bit of good fortune that seemed to come their way. It was worse for Franco than anybody else; after all, he lived day by day in the hope of constant hedonism. To have his future perceived pleasure at the Org Palace removed so swiftly, so mercilessly, so *unjustly*, by Princess Bloody Anklebiter, seemed somehow just *wrong*.

"There, there," said Tarly, patting his shoulder.

"We could just..."

"No."

"Aww, go on."

"No! Not here, not now, not like this. I want it to be romantic! I want us to fall in love, not have a quick wham-bam in a cell wrapped in chains."

"What makes you think it'll be any different when we're married?"

Tarly stared hard at him – after a while, he started to wriggle like a worm.

"What?" he said.

"You used the *M* word."

Franco frowned. "What, masochist?"

"No, *married*, idiot."

"Er. So I did."

"Did you mean it?"

"Er. Maybe. Depends."

"On?"

"On whether you like me that much."

"I do! You're special, Franco, real special!"

"And, er, whether you mutate."

"*What?*"

"Mutate. You know. Grow in height, have pus dribble from your oozing tits, that sort of thing."

"*What?*"

"Sorry. Long story. Last wife mutated. You know how it is."

"Er, I don't think I do."

"Still." Franco brightened. "As long as you don't mind a marriage prenuptial agreement."

"Why, have you got *that much money?*"

"No! I mean, if you mutate, then the marriage is null and void."

"Ah! I think I might be able to stretch to that arrangement. I can't see myself mutating any time soon."

"Yeah, that's what the ex-wife thought."

"So, does that mean..."

"Here, lass, let me do it properly." Franco, with a jangle of chains, got down on one knee. He peered up, like a man through a fog. A fog of love, naturally. Or maybe a fog of lust. Maybe just a fog of idiocy. "Will you, Tarly Winters..."

"*General* Tarly Winters."

"Will you, *General* Tarly Winters, do me the honour of becoming my wife?"

"I will!"

Franco stood, and they hugged, and the chain around his elbow whipped up and smacked Tarly a vicious blow in the face, nearly breaking her nose, and after she'd come round and they'd mopped up the blood, they laughed about it.

After all, being married to Franco Haggis, Tarly was going to have to have an amazing sense of humour.

"DRY LAND, SQUAWK! Dry land, SQUAWK!"

Franco swung for the parrot, but it flapped away with a rattle of chains and a smell of farting ozone.

The battleship docked, and from behind bars Franco caught his first glimpse of The Org States. A new country. A new continent. A new place to be tried and *hanged!*

"Damn and bloody bollocks," he said. And he meant it.

The huge battleship glided into dock, engines thumping and pulsing beneath their boots. This was the Port City of Mekal, just west of the capital city of Org. Franco noted that the orgs seemed to have little originality in their naming conventions; but didn't have anybody to discuss it with. Tarly was tired of his blathering, and just wanted to sleep, Alice was odd and distant, the former ship's computer giving simple one-word answers to any question put to her, and Franco was damned if he was going to stoop to speaking to the bloody parrot.

Franco gently shook Tarly awake, and it was minutes before Anklebolt III was there, hauling on their chains and giving them a hard time with a personal touch. All four were dragged unceremoniously into the hot sunshine, and shoved along a thick gang-plank to the dock. Thousands of orgs had turned out to see their princess arrive back safely on dry land with her newly captured cargo. Her mother. The traitor. The *Queen*.

The huge crowd roared in appreciation as Princess Anklebolt III appeared and waved her machine-gun arms. On a length of chain she dragged a miserable-looking Queen Strogger, suddenly small and weak and vulnerable. She half crawled, and was half dragged along the gang-plank, and Franco couldn't help but feel a large pang of sorrow. Right up to the point where he realised he'd been duped, and she'd betrayed her entire country; indeed, her entire species.

They descended the steps to the dockside, and the city of Mekal reared around and above them. The city itself was a forest of huge, crowding steel towers rearing into the sky, not one of them less than a hundred stories in height. There were thousands upon thousands of them, leading away from the docks and up the steep hillside, dominating the skyline and sending long shadows over current proceedings.

"What a brutal place," said Franco, rubber-necking up as he was pushed down the steps.

"Brutal," agreed Tarly, staring around. "Look, every single tower has a cannon on the roof. That's some serious bloody defences!"

"Yeah, from a time when they feared aerial assaults."

"It was built," said Queen Strogger, wearily.

"Whatdya mean, built?"

"The orgs terraformed their cities after QGM terraformed the world. We used great machines to change the landscape, to fold and bend the land so we could twist and dominate the land with terrible towers and fortresses. Machines are our lives. They are our *religion*."

"Get down there!" growled an org, a big fellow with knives for teeth, and Franco stared for a moment before remembering his manners. His *bad* manners.

"Shut your face before I ram your teeth up your arse!"

The org dragged his chains, and Franco fell over. It wasn't very heroic.

There was a huge, caged truck waiting for them. And it was being pulled by – Franco blinked – by a *robotic horse*. Franco eyed the beast warily. He did not get on with most humans, aliens, animals, or robots. Anything that could move, basically.

As he passed its snout, the great metal jaws made a lunge for him. Without thinking, Franco gave the creature a powerful right hook that sent its metal head spinning, spraying a mouthful of greasy horse spit over the org onlookers. They roared in anger, weapons bristling.

"Er," said Franco.

This was getting out of hand. As if his *whole life* wasn't already out of hand.

Princess Anklebolt III jostled Franco, Tarly and Polly into the truck. They grasped the bars and gazed at the hostile crowd imploringly. Finally, and with a savage display of filial love, Anklebolt III beat Queen Strogger to the ground with several hefty, mechanical punches, then dragged her up by the face and hurled her into the back of the truck, which rocked on protesting suspension.

The metal horse gave a metallic whinny and set off, metal hooves *clack-clippity-clopping* on the metal roads. They headed into the city. Amongst the towering towers. Amidst the metal *Hell*. The whole city was filled with the stench of old engine oil, of overworked machinery, of dying machines, of old grease and burning steel. Noise invaded the air, the *shring* of metal blades, metal saws, the *thump-thump-thump* of pistons, the clacking of gears, the spinning of cogs, the *thrum* of clockwork, and all these noises piled one on another, a million layered sounds from a million factories all working in a glorious crazy disharmony and filling Franco and

Tarly's head with a metal buzzing like that of a massive, productive *hive*.

"I didn't think it would be so... *mechanised*," said Tarly, clutching the bars.

"We are a machine race," said Queen Strogger, sitting in the corner of the truck. She looked terribly mournful; she had lost all the anger and fury and attitude Franco had come to know and, er, hate. "Our entire existence is built on the premise that the human shell is inferior – indeed, the ganger shell is *far* inferior – and it is a *necessity* to our species to upgrade, or augment, oneself with machine components. How else could you possibly hope to increase your speed, agility, strength and intelligence without external components hard-grafted onto a flesh–and-bone chassis?"

"Er," said Franco. "Maybe you don't need to?"

"What?"

"Well, you know, you could just... stay the same."

They hit a series of violent bumps in the road, and were jiggled about inside the truck, holding onto the thick metal bars for stability. They passed children in the street, who pointed, with metal arms and metal hands, some even with metal machine faces. Not one org creature, no matter *how poor*, had not been upgraded. It was a constitutional right. It was *given free on the damn National Health Upgrade Programme*. Even beggars had digital eyes. Even vagrants had machine cocks. Even footballers' wives had mechanical mouths – for talking, as well as for sucking lots of dick.

"Stay. The. Same." Queen Strogger seemed to consider this, for a long, long time. "Why," she said, eventually, old oil running down her wrinkled old chin, "would I want to do that?"

"Because," said Franco, "because, that's like, what you are, like. You're born. And you get what you're given."

"Ha! Fine words for a race whose greatest physical upgrade was an enlarged tit."

"What does that mean?"

"It means your physically weak and shitty shell was a poor chassis to begin with, but when you held the jewel of medical science in your blossoming palms, what did you do? Solve all the riddles of the diseases of your age? No. Make yourselves stronger, fitter, more agile? No. Find a cure for death? Hell fucking no. What you did, what your decadent and basically *stupid* species did, my little ginger friend, was find a way to make bigger tits. I have seen the history filmys. For a whole ten thousand years of your civilisation's advancement, more research went into tit enlargement than any other single field of medical research. I don't see how this could be a positive and fruitful use of your resources."

"Well," said Franco, and if he could have lit a cigar and puffed it, he would. "You know what they say."

"What's that?"

"Nothing's nice as tits."

"But, surely, medical advancement, improvement at a genetic level, finding the *tweak* which allows you to switch off neuron loss; all these are more beneficial?"

"Nope," said Franco. "Without *tits,* there would be no advancement of the species. Just like without *beer*, populations would wane and gradually die. That's my philosophy, anyway."

"Tits? Beer?" Tarly punched him on the arm. "You're a modern day fucking romantic, mate."

"I try," said Franco, puffing out his chest and wincing at his skinless back. "I do try."

Onwards they went through the metal city, the sun high in the sky, beating down and heating up their barred truck nicely. Past huge factories they went, where furnaces belched and sparks flew, and they could hear the rhythmical *clanging* of hammers on anvils, only on a much larger scale. They passed electronics plants, where computer-controlled arms whizzed and punched, clacked and jerked, and assembly lines rolled out with curious machinery Franco and Tarly had never seen. They passed huge plastic bins filled with mechanical arms and legs, face plates, chest housings, and then, lastly, a cylindrical tub – as wide as a house – filled with small slick units, each as big as Franco's fist. They pulsed, each one running with its own seemingly random beat, and the whole tub seemed alive, crawling, as if with black and red globular maggots.

"What, in the name of arse, are those?"

"Hearts," said Queen Strogger, sombrely. "Basic units, obviously. Nothing specially crafted, not like what resides in my chest cavity. I have a Cronenberg Mk VI. The best money can buy. It could power a *squadron* of orgs and still have juice left to run the lights of the city for a year."

"Why would you need so much power?" said Tarly.

"It's not about need," said Queen Strogger. "It's about possibility. And wealth. And setting an image. I *can* have it. Therefore, I will. Just how your ginger man there is the type to buy huge, excessively powered landcars when he could use a bicycle, or a two-cylinder eco-model. *I* am the Queen of The Org States. No matter what my shitty little Anklebolt thinks. I swear, I knew that child was trouble the day she was born; bit my finger off when she was six months old! Little tyke."

They started to climb out of the docks and up the steep hill, riddled with steel towers like spikes on a porcupine. Ahead, the org horse started labouring, puffing and panting, the noise of its motors rising in pitch.

"Sounds like it's gonna pop," grinned Franco.

"It has an inferior built heart," said Strogger. "It cannot cope with my great weight."

"You don't say."

They laboured up the hill, the horse wheezing like a geriatric whizz-addict. Franco felt quite sorry for it.

They passed beneath a steel archway, which lit up with advertisements for new upgrades and augmentations – everything from chassis components to "Scrotum Packs™" – and then flickered, and even as they watched from behind their bars, announced the impending trial and hanging of the traitor, Queen Strogger.

"How can it be a *trial* and hanging? Surely you only get hung if they find you guilty? Otherwise, it wouldn't be a trial, would it?"

"That's what it's like around here," said Queen Strogger, glumly.

"What bloody dumb and daft idiot implemented those rules, then?" snorted Franco.

"I did," mumbled Queen Strogger. Then scowled. "Well, it's different when you're the boss, innit?"

On and on they rumbled, through metal streets lined with metal orgs. Little org children, stomping along on hydraulic legs, threw metal bricks at the truck. They bounced off the bars harmlessly, but the principle of it upset Franco indeed.

"Little hooligans! Where are their parents, eh?"

"Orgs are released from their parents at the age of five. It makes them tough and independent. They have to fend for themselves in the rough and tumble real world. Learn to survive on their wits. Learn to be tough little orgs; tough enough to fight the gangers, anyway. It was a military decision."

"What a bloody idiotic, dumb and daft stupid rule! Who bloody implemented that one, then?" Then he saw Strogger's face, and grinned amiably. "Not had a good time of it, have you, love?"

"It would appear not," said the Queen, voice strained.

Now, org dogs came panting from the shadowy, hot-oil-and-scorched-steel-smelling metal side-streets. They were horrible, small, fat, ambling metal beasts. They pressed their wet slick noses against the bars of the rumbling truck as the captured heroes trundled past. They went, "Pant, pant, pant, clank-clank-clank."

Franco looked at them in distaste, and poked a snout away with his sandal. It snapped at his toes, and he retreated hurriedly at the veritable mouthful of JAWS-style sword-teeth. "Bloody hell! It could fair take your bloody foot off, that could!"

"And it would," said Strogger. "They're on a commission from the Foot Builders. Ten percent of the value of every org foot that gets replaced because of them. The org in question gets the foot half-price, too. Bargain."

"Ridiculous! There should be laws against that! Go on, buggeroff!"

He punched a dog on the snout, and it made a snuffling low-bass clanking sound, which sounded a little like "*Archie-Archie-Archie*" repeated over and over again, an oily, raspy, farting kind of noise. Franco wasn't sure whether the sound came from its mouth, or its arse.

Then, the most intense and horrible thing happened. From between Archie's stomping little metal org legs unfolded a huge pink alloy erection. Archie rubbed it over the bars, sliming a spunk-trail as it went, and Franco scrambled back with a squawk of utter disgust, eyes wide, face screwed into a ball of crumpled flesh, eyes locked on the obscene, pink, quivering, slathering dog dick.

"Why me, eh? What's it with me and bloody Combat K adventures and all manner of disgusting phallic interludes, eh? You dirty, dirty, 'orrible little motherfucker," he spat.

"Woof!" said Archie, panting with need and seeing in Franco a future possible fellow soul-mate. Or at least, a quick leg-hump.

Eventually, the stumpy little group of org dogs grew tired of running, and tired of rubbing their collective dog dicks on the bars. Shuddering, the group moved on through the steel city, leaving the metal dogs behind.

They rolled past endless towers of metal, past sprawling factories making org machine components, past weapons factories and landcar units, past *Merging Plants* which, Queen Strogger reliably informed them, was the place where flesh and machine met in a beautiful union. It all made Franco feel a little bit sick.

The hill grew steeper and steeper climbing up towards the Org Palace, sitting on top of the hill like a cork on a bottle. The metal horse pulling their truck puffed and panted, wheezed and farted, and generally sounded like a dying diesel generator waiting to keel over at any moment.

Looking behind them, Franco watched the admittedly stunning view of the hill dropping away, riddled with steel towers, to a bustling dockside where four huge steel warships sat at anchor, including the one which had brought them in. This was Queen Strogger's navy. Or had been, before she was... *usurped*. He rolled the word around his mind like a marble in a jar. Yes. Strogger had been usurped. Poor little love.

"The hill is this steep in order to test the mettle of anybody wishing to approach the palace," said Strogger. "It's also a test of wealth. Only the richest in our org society can afford the powerful legs and top-end power supply units needed to climb this hill. Thus, only the wealthiest are granted an audience, by default."

"And those that crawl?" said Franco.

"What?"

"Those that crawl? I'm sure some buggers crawl up here on their bellies. But then, you'd like that, wouldn't you? Pure subservience."

"I didn't make the rules, Franco Haggis. I just obey them."

"No. No. You're the damn and bloody Queen, for the sake of bollocknugget! Don't you see? You can change all this. You can change your society. Make it a more friendly place. Somewhere where humans and orgs could get along happily!"

"And how would I do that?"

"Tourism," said Franco, smugly. "I know lots of people who'd love to come down here and sample your world. There'd be some who would like to drink your molten cocktails, explore your dark back alleys, sample your org upgrades, you know, *experience* something different."

Queen Strogger considered this. "People would *pay* to do those things?"

"Oh yes," said Franco. "We're a mixed-up bloody race, is us humans, that's for sure. I bet there are even some weird and warped deviants who would like to *shag* your org folk. You know. As a kind of different experience thing going on."

Tarly looked sideways at him. "Yeah. Weird and warped deviants."

"Is what I said."

Queen Strogger looked thoughtful. "I will consider this. It is a possibility for the future."

"If you survive the hanging," pointed out Tarly.

"And the new improved ganger orgs don't wipe you out first!" said Franco, grinning with all his remaining teeth. "You know. The army you helped build? With your betrayal? Sort of thing?"

"*I was looking for a solution to the war!*" hissed Queen Strogger, suddenly. "Don't you understand, you bastad? I went to the gangers with that information to form a *truce!* I give them org secrets, they get extra weaponry, but then the gangers will blend with org technology and thus *become accepted into org society.* It could have been an end to the perpetual battles! I am sick of the War Charts, sick of getting lists of people who were once friends and have been killed in battle. I was trying to do something *positive for my people!* You see?"

"Mashed that up a bit, then, didn't you love?" said Franco.

"I didn't expect the clones to betray me!"

"And they locked you up?"

"Yes. The Mistress locked me up." Queen Strogger shivered. "She's an evil one, that Mistress. And although she looks like the gangers, she isn't one of them. She's different. She's... *alien*. She perpetuates the war between orgs and gangers. I don't know why. The gangers are doing something. They want the planet to themselves."

The org horse whinnied, and reared up as if in a final act of defiance, before collapsing on the ground before the org Palace gates. The gates opened with a ratcheting sound, clanking and grinding as ancient machinery kicked into gear. Wearily, the org horse climbed to its hooves and pulled them the last few metres.

A rank of towers, burnished with gold and jewels, surrounded a huge central courtyard. Each tower was layered with finely crafted marble and diamond tiles and spires, atop which sat heavy-duty cannons. The walls were white and gold, the courtyard cobbled with gold bricks, and a cool breeze wafted through the yard, free of the stink of oil and machinery drifting across the capital city of Org.

Princess Anklebolt III was waiting for them, with a group of ten rough-looking org squaddies (although to be fair, thought Franco, all the orgs look bloody rough). These wore combat fatigues and green tin helmets, bearing logos such as, "I Have Become Org," "Born to Pulp" and "Show Me Your Org Face." They carried very large heavy-calibre 8.62mm machine guns, which Franco ogled from behind his bars with gleaming eyes. Franco was unabashed about his love of milporn. He could happily stroke a gun all night.

Two squaddies moved forward, hydraulic legs clanking, and threw open the barred door to the truck. Franco jumped down and stretched, moaning, ignoring the ten guns pointing at him.

"Over there," rumbled a big meathead, and Franco gave a nod and moved to stand before Anklebolt. Tarly followed, also stretching, and pointed up at Polly the Parrot, fluttering on a chain twenty feet above the truck. An org grabbed the chain and pulled the stricken robot bird down to earth, where it shrieked and moaned and squawked like the annoying little bastard it was.

Finally, Queen-Strogger climbed ponderously from the truck, which rocked and creaked under her immense machine weight. She stood, hands on hips, and stared at her daughter.

"You've made a big mistake," said Strogger.

Anklebolt shrugged, and her metal teeth gleamed. "Mother. You always were impetuous. You didn't think I had the intelligence or perseverance to take your crown. Well, I have! You left a trail of evidence through the Org Offices so wide I would have had to *bribe* orgs not to implicate you in treason."

"Listen, daughter. This is not treason! I was trying to *save* the orgs! Stop the war! Secure us a better future... forever!"

"LIAR!" screamed Anklebolt, and her machine guns clicked and shifted and armed. Laser sites focussed on Queen Strogger, who stood with hands on hips, and now, to Franco, looked suddenly incredibly more menacing. "It has gone out over Org TV. You are finished. Every damn org in The Org States wants you dead and ground down into cat pulp. And as for your friends..." Anklebolt turned her fury on Franco and Tarly, who gazed back with wide eyes. "They will hang with you."

"Hey," snapped Franco. "What about a fair trial?"

"Did you help Queen Strogger escape from the gangers?"

"Er, yeah, so?"

"Guilty! Condemned by his own mouth! Condemned like the spineless rotfish he is! I'll see him crushed and pulped and spewed and cut, strangled and poisoned until he's deader than fucking DEAD! Take them to the gallows! Take them ALL to the gallows! Hang them! I want to see them dance and jig! I want to see them DIIIEEEEE..."

CHAPTER TWELVE
A PAINFUL UNIFICATION

PIPPA SWAM THROUGH fire. Flames teased her flesh, caressing her like a demon lover, and she cried hot, molten mercury tears, which ran down her cheeks, scarring flesh, and she would be scarred for life, forever, as she died and became soil and ash and flowed through the waters and down to the centre of eternity...

Slowly, Pippa opened her eyes. She coughed, and pain was everywhere: it invaded her, infused every atom, and all she saw was darkness.

"Welcome back to the world of the living." The voice was sweet. Too sweet. Sickly sweet. The sickly sweet of somebody who was used to getting what she wanted, when she wanted, *right fucking now.*

"What hit me?" groaned Pippa, becoming aware

of a low-level thrumming buzzing in her brain, like motors, like engines. Through her groggy demeanour she became aware of movement. They were travelling. They were *flying.*

"That would be *Ziggurat,* my faithful little human. He is a good boy, isn't he?" Pippa was aware of movement beyond her blindness, and she heard a purring sound, like a cat being petted. She reached up to rub her eyes, and noticed that her hands were bound tightly together with chains. *Oh, it's like that, is it? You bastards.*

"Yeah, well, what did he hit me with? A tesla coil?"

"Oh no. All Ziggurat's power is *homegrown.* He's like a camel, really. He stores energy in his hunchback, in his *hump* so to speak, then can fire it at will. As you found out when you attacked him, my pretty little Combat K princess."

The voice was friendly, chatty even, but Pippa could detect the power beneath, like a fault line below a stretch of desert.

Pippa rubbed her eyes. Now, she could see blurred colours. She felt sick, leaned forward to vomit into her lap. There came a slight tutting sound.

"Go and get a bucket, there's a good hunchback. And bring some wipes. We can't have her vomiting all over the TV Suite now, can we?"

Pippa groaned, and rubbed her eyes again. *So, the bastard dancing hunchback hit her with an electrical charge from his hump? Gods, she'd heard it all, now.*

"You must be the Mistress," said Pippa, voice calm.

"I am."

"You're the one in charge. The Big Boss. The Top Dude. The General in command of the gangers and the Bad Army?"

"Yes. I am also Prime of Core Government, to give me my official Clone Terra title. I run all governmental departments from The Monastery in Nechudnazzar. I have two subordinate Ministers who carry out, shall we say, Acts of Worship. They are Ziggurat, who you met recently and I *do apologise* for his lack of clothing. I, too, find it quite disgusting when he dances around in the nude. But he has to, you see, or when he *pulses* all his clothes set on fire! Then there's Teddy Sourballs. You met her earlier." Here, The Mistress's voice altered subtly in tone. "You were quite violent towards her, I believe. Left her cabled up inside a hijacked GASGAM."

"You hijacked it first," said Pippa, grinning and shaking her head.

"Yes, but we have the *War Effort* to consider. Because without the War Effort we won't get the new commission for CLONE TV."

Pippa's vision was swimming. She rubbed viciously at her eyes, and slowly the image grew in clarity until it seemed to *pop* into view. They were in a plush aircraft cabin. The droning sound was the plane's engines. Before Pippa sat a beautiful woman, with pale white skin and jet-black hair, neatly cut and running to her shoulders. But her eyes were solid black, like the eyes of an animal; like the eyes of a reptile. Beside her sat

Ziggurat on one side, thankfully clothed and grinning at Pippa from his lop-sided face. On the other was Teddy, looking nervous and agitated, her hands wringing together, her barbed-wire hair bobbing as she constantly shifted.

"I see they rescued you," said Pippa.

"No thanks to *you*, bitch. That GASGAM nearly crushed me!"

"A shame he didn't."

"I'll see you die, whore!"

Pippa considered this. "I'm always up for a fight," she smiled, face contorted into a mocking grimace.

"Ladies!" snapped the Mistress. "Not here. Not now. There are more important issues at stake. Such as the impending War Effort against the orgs. We will annihilate them! We will destroy them utterly! And all on LIVE TV!"

She laughed, hands rubbing together, fingers entwining and for a moment – for a *brief flicker of time* – Pippa could have sworn she saw those fingers *blur together,* as if the woman's flesh merged and joined like viscous liquid. She shook her head, rubbed her eyes again, and, as she accepted a glass of water and slurped it noisily, put it down to the after-effects of Ziggurat's joyful electrocution.

"Where are we going?"

"The Teeth, the mountain range you no doubt witnessed on your initial arrival on Cloneworld. It divides our two warring factions, keeping a low limit to casualties. Oh aren't QGM a wonderful father-figure? There to hold our hands and protect us! To stop one party becoming dominant and wiping out the other." Her voice went hard. "Well, we've fucked their ideas good and proper. We've overrun the GASGAM AA AIs, taken them over and secured the knowledge of Metal Meshing and Flesh Foundry from the orgs in order to further build and increase our army! The Bad Army! But now, with extensions and augmentations... let's call it The Bad Army-*Plus*."

"And that's why we're flying? You control *every* AI on the planet?"

"Yes," said the Mistress, licking a little spittle from her frothing lips. "Whilst the orgs have been messing about in their machine cities, improving their own augmented selves, we have been building aircraft! Weapons! Missiles! Then we *took* their knowledge and have applied it to the gangers. You saw the Slush Pits, right?"

Pippa nodded, drinking more water. Her brain felt as if it'd been fried in a pan, and her mouth tasted of copper. Her breathing was laboured. She was in a poor state to continue this battle... and yet here was this raving lunatic, who was quite obviously in control of the entire *planet* and planning a massive military offensive real soon...

"I saw them."

"What you saw were the old prototypes. A thousand years old. What we've built on The Teeth is *something special*."

"You have a factory there?"

"A factory?" laughed the Mistress. She looked to both Ziggurat and Teddy, who gave polite laughs of support. "We have built an *army training civilisation!* We have used some of the old terraforming machines, those which still worked and were dumped here by QGM Planet Designers. We levelled mountains. We built factories. A city! A city dedicated to war and extermination... and at the centre, oh beautiful thing, there is a new TV studio, CLONE TV CENTRAL! And in precisely six hours we will go live."

"When you attack?"

"You're a smart girl. I hope you'll help us."

"By doing... what?"

"You will see."

Pippa raised her manacled hands to rub at her nose, then her forehead. "Your new TV station goes live the day you intend to wipe out the orgs? Don't you have any sense of perspective?"

"Meaning?"

"TV is an entertainment platform. It should be for filmys, music, art; stuff that entertains, stuff you can enjoy!"

"What's more enjoyable than watching orgs die?"

"Death is not entertainment," said Pippa, eyes narrowed.

"It is for us," smiled the Mistress, and her little puppets laughed politely. "There can be no greater pleasure than watching an org taken slowly apart with a chainsaw! Live! No greater love than watching their limbs coming away at the joint, with lovely bursts of blood and machine parts! Live! It is quite... sexual, in its gratification."

"You're fucking sick," said Pippa.

"Why so? You humans have been glorying over war for a million years! Do you, too, not have your own vast TV networks, displaying images of intense genocide to your suckling children? You revel in it! Pippa, I thought *you* of all people would understand."

"Bullshit. What we do *is report the news!*"

"And so shall I. News of the final ganger victory over the orgs! Each battle filmed and broadcast on live feeds! Each org death, slaughter, bombing run, machine-gunned baby, all filling our wonderful screens! We will raze their cities and factories to the ground! We will decimate their entire fucking civilisation!"

The Mistress had risen to her feet, screeching now, and as Pippa watched the flesh *pulsed* around her face, lumps straining under the skin, like insects trying to break free of a ripe flesh cage.

The Mistress took a deep breath, calmed herself, and sat back down. She smiled at Pippa, who felt suddenly sickened by the warped evangelical vision of TV slaughter.

"And then, *then*... we will nuke them."

"Nuke them?" said Pippa, aghast.

"Every city! Every factory! After we have watched the battles, played out our moves with interactive buttons – *press the red button to see the org child's head blown off, press the green button to see the school bombed, press the blue button to see the org holy machine-gunned from the air...* yes, yes! We will have TV votes, interactive war, Pippa, interactive gore! And when we've had enough, we will hit every org city and installation with bombs so big we'll raze their whole continent to ashes!"

"You're insane," said Pippa, voice level.

"Why? Because we celebrate *real entertainment?*"

"No, because you'll pollute the fucking planet. Nukes! Don't you understand? You'll kill the *world.* You'll make it uninhabitable! Only retarded backwater oldlords use weapons like that now. what's the fucking point of a parasite if it destroys the host? You're a dickhead, Mistress. With your head up your flapping arse."

The Mistress had pulled something from her pocket and now held it up for Pippa to see. It was a small chip. The 3Core. She waved it, enticingly, a smile on her face.

"You want this, don't you?"

Pippa said nothing.

"I know *why* you want it. To stop the invading junks. To turn them from their paths of evil!" Her voice was mocking, a broad smile on her white face, and Pippa's brows furrowed into a look of hatred. *How can you mock something so vast, and evil, and grotesque? How can you mock the deaths of millions? And the prospective deaths of billions more?* If she'd had a gun, she would have blown the Mistress's teeth out the back of her skull.

"And?"

"If you help me, I'll help you."

"Explain."

"Our warheads. Our nukes. We had to raid antiquated junk computers to get the motherboards. They need tweaking, tuning, programming. I know you can do this."

"You want me to help destroy the orgs?"

"In order to save the entire *Quad-Gal!*" hissed the Mistress. "I have seen the junks. Seen what they can do." Her face flickered, bubbles rippling across her forehead.

"You were there, weren't you?" said Pippa, softly, as understanding dawned.

"I saw the junks. A *long* time ago. I saw Leviathan! I have seen things you could never comprehend."

"How..." Pippa made a clicking sound in the back of her throat. "How *old* are you?"

The Mistress shrugged. "A million. Nearer to two."

"Two million years old, and nobody's put a knife in the back of your skull? You've done well, bitch."

"Will you help? I have the codes. The codes to unlock this shitty little junk chip. But *you* have the programming skill. I know you do. I've seen your Combat K files."

"*What?* That's impossible. The encryption is incredible – unhackable, in fact. You would never get the clearance!"

"Of course I could," said the Mistress, smiling. "I have a lover, you see. A fine woman, a beautiful woman. We are the same, so to speak; entwined, like" – she laughed, gently – "like snakes. We are of the same ancient race. From before the junks. Before Leviathan, before VOLOS, before everything you knew. There's only two of us left now, passing down through millennia, and bearing a millennia-old *boredom*. But still, we entertain ourselves however we can. To alleviate the tediousness of your petty humanity and the petty alien races who surround you."

Pippa swallowed. Her eyes were wide.

And as she watched, the Mistress started to break apart, her flesh writhing, bubbling, growing more and more volatile as her flesh lost its cohesive bond, and even though she sat there, a human figure, she was made of *snakes*, pale white snakes, flowing and writhing in a seething mass but all the time looking a Pippa with a look of shock, and mock-surprise on her face, as if to say, "Oops! Look at me! Look at what I've gone and become!"

The snakes hissed, a background symphony.

"How did you get the clearance? How did you read my Combat K files?" whispered Pippa.

"My lover. My sister. My companion through the ages. You know her." The Mistress looked up, black snake eyes watching Pippa, red tongue flickering from her snakeskin lips. "She is called Tarly. Tarly Winters. She is a General for Quad-Gal

Military." She laughed. "Well. We have to pass the years *somehow,* wouldn't you agree? What better way than by infiltrating the most powerful military command in the Four Galaxies?"

"GUILTY! CONDEMNED BY his own mouth! Condemned like the spineless rotfish he is! I'll see him crushed and pulped and spewed and cut, strangled and poisoned until he's deader than fucking DEAD! Take them to the gallows! Take them ALL to the gallows! Hang them! I want to see them dance and jig! I want to see them DIIIEEEEE..."

"Whoa, whoa, whoa," said Franco, holding up both hands. "Wait one cotton-picking minute there, Metal Mickey. I ain't got nothing to do with your damn and bloody foolish internal war, I'm just here for... for..."

"Yes?"

"Er. For something." Franco's mouth went tight shut, and he looked right, *past* the org squaddies, to where a large mechanical gallows had been erected. It was built completely of black steel, held a dangling metal rope (with noose), and looked extremely ominous. Franco noted that several TV cameras had been set up, replete with org cameramen – all wearing bright bandanas and drinking from small flasks.

The org squaddies surged forward and four of them grabbed Queen Strogger and restrained, their hydraulics hissing, steam pouring from their mouths and ears. The others grabbed Franco and Tarly, whilst the last org soldier hauled in the chain attached to Polly, who squawked and fluttered, losing several more feathers in the process.

Anklebolt III stalked close, and leered at her captives. In a low voice of steam and hot oil, she said, "You have been tried. You have been judged. You have been condemned. Now, you will die..."

"We've got to get out of here," hissed Franco to Tarly, who gave a nod. Their eyes met. This was getting out of hand. They had to do something *now*. Unfortunately, that meant hurting people. But hey, they *were* about to be hung...

A big org was holding Franco's arms, standing behind him with a look of basic stupidity across its flesh and metal-melded chops. Franco, however, despite being modest in height, and despite having a pot-belly any sausage-eater would be proud of, was in fact a prize-winning pugilist, an award winner in the art of fighting dirty. He leapt up and slammed his head backwards, breaking the org's nose with a *crack* and slackening his grip, which meant his arms were now his own. A second org reacted, machine gun coming up, but Franco was faster, foot kicking out to knock the gun skyward, bullets whining at the sun, then a short step and a footballer's kick to the happy sacks. The org grunted as a look of acute agony crossed his face (no bollock upgrade *there*, then!), and Franco winded him with a punch to the belly, took the heavy machine gun from the org's hands and slammed the butt into his face, making him stagger back. At the same time, Tarly ducked and whirled, pulling her arms free of her guard's grip, and the org swung for her but she was fast, real fast, a fluid dancer as she dodged the punch and stepped on the org's own bent knee to boost her up, to where a karate chop to the windpipe made the org turn suddenly purple and splutter up a mouthful of phlegm and blood. Tarly took his gun, somersaulted backwards, and her and Franco put their backs together and stared at their enemies – who were stood, mouths open, wondering what the hell just happened. Both machine guns were aimed at Anklebolt's head. The Princess scowled at them with barely contained rage.

"This," said Franco, "is a QTM Longshave 8.65mm with Mad-Ejector Armour-Piercing cartridges. I've seen these fuckers eat through a tank's hull armour to pulp the unfortunate bastard inside. Now, I reckon you orgs have pretty tough armour, but I'm also reckoning you carry the firepower to put down enemy orgs. Ergo, these guns would kill Anklebolt III there before she could shout, 'Hang the traitors!' So, guys, put down your guns nice and calm like, and we won't shoot the dodgy princess in the fucking kebab-face."

There was a moment of hiatus...

"Do it!" screamed Anklebolt, flapping her hands.

The rest of the org squaddies bent slowly, putting their guns on the ground.

"Release Queen Strogger!" snapped Tarly, moving

close to Anklebolt and shoving the barrel of the gun under her chin. Anklebolt glared down at Tarly with a look that said if she ever got the chance she'd chew her face clean off. Tarly grinned back. She hadn't achieved QGM General without facing terrible odds and laughing in the face of terrible foes.

Queen Strogger was released, and moved to stand beside Franco and Tarly. "What now? The whole of The Org States think we are traitors. We've already been beamed across the TVs! There is nowhere for us to run, nowhere for us to hide!"

"We need to stop this ganger army," said Franco, chewing his lip. "We can't let you two groups of nutcases go back to war, even though I'm thinking you probably fucking deserve it. But first, we need to find Pippa."

"She's on another bloody continent," said Tarly, wearily. "And I'm damned if I'm sailing back across that bloody Teeth Ocean and facing down hordes of rampant, mutant, oil-dribbling metal-stinking pirates again; no offence meant."

Franco scratched his stubble. "Hey, Strogger! You said this city, and this hill, was terraformed, right?"

"Yes."

Franco grinned. "Good. I have an idea." He pointed at Anklebolt III, red with rage and trembling, her vast gear-driven jaws chomping like a rabid horse at the bit. "And you're coming with us!"

*   *   *

THEY MOVED THROUGH the palace like ghosts, Franco's gun barrel at the base of Anklebolt's neck. The palace was a shrine to old machinery, and everywhere stood pedestals containing old org body-parts: legs and hearts, tongues and hands, glittering from inside their glass cylinders like dodgy trophies. Anklebolt led them through many huge halls, some filled with vast tables containing org flowers, metal petals glittering, some filled with cutlery and tableware, steaming plates of org food on display, gold potatoes, alloy spinach, iron beef and augmented whole roast pigs, still on the spit over trays of glowing coals, their own hooves reaching for the spit handle to turn it, roasting themselves whole. It gave a new meaning to the concept of *reach around*.

"This is sick," said Tarly, walking close behind Franco, her gun weaving, looking around nervously. They'd tied up the solider orgs out in the courtyard, and according to Queen Strogger, the palace would be near-empty of personnel, for Anklebolt was so *paranoid* that she hated having anybody but the most trusted within her proximity. Quite rightly, for in the previous year alone there had been a hundred and seventy-seven assassination attempts on Anklebolt. One would have thought that gave her a good overview of her own popularity. Apparently, it did not.

"How far?" snapped Franco.

"The palace is a vast warren," said Anklebolt, and although she had stopped screaming, all present could see she was *steaming*. She was angry as angry could get. She was incandescent with slow-burning rage.

"SQUAWK! Watch out for traps!"

Tarly had released Polly, Franco's Special Friend, much to his muttering and consternation. Spending his escape attempt with a certifiably insane robot parrot was not Franco's idea of Good Time Frankie.

They moved through halls and corridors, extra-wide in order to accommodate big clanking orgs. All the time Anklebolt grumbled, and Queen Strogger marched along behind her wayward daughter. Together, they looked like a couple of horrorshow experiments. There was a kind of silent standoff going on between mother and daughter; they weren't talking, but ceaselessly glaring at each other. Their hatred was a palpable thing; like syrup on their metal teeth. Franco knew if they'd let them go at it, one would soon be dead and torn to raggedy pieces on the org palace floor...

Tarly nudged Franco. "Which one has more metal, do you reckon?" she whispered.

"Not sure," he replied. "I seen that Queen Strogger rise another ten feet tall on hydraulic legs and midriff. She's had a lot of shit added, that's for sure." He shuddered. "Not sure I'd like to be in *her* skin."

Queen Strogger turned, then, and scowled at them. "What're you two whispering?"

"Nothing," they both chimed.

Tarly checked behind them, weapon primed, and they moved on through the palace. Endless vast chambers passed them by, and then they were heading down wide marble stairs, into more chambers, down more stairs, into more chambers... Endless paintings, and tapestries, and marble and gold, depicting huge metal monstrosities and thousands of years of mechanical and digital augmentation, from base human form to the orgs Franco and Tarly had come to know.

Franco analysed the huge paintings grimly. "I'm surprised they've got any fucking skin left," he said.

Eventually, they left the opulence behind, and Franco realised with a start that they weren't just heading below ground, but into the *foundations* of the very hillside, a hill that had been created; terraformed. A city, a country, a *world* built by machines. *Fucking perfect,* he thought. *I mean, who better to populate a machine city, a machine country? Than creatures who have betrayed themselves, betrayed their own flesh. This is what happens when vanity is taken to extremes. This is what happens when you don't put a cap on supposed self-improvement. Guns up your arse and a cock that can fire missiles.*

Down they went, the opulence of the palace *degrading* as they went. Down more sweeping staircases, which narrowed as they travelled; through narrower chambers, darker now, many unlit, with only tiny shafts of light coming through the high tube-vents positioned far above. The dust lay heavy down here, and most of the furniture and antique machinery had been sheeted up. As they walked, Anklebolt and Strogger stomping along, Tarly and Franco padding after them, they kicked up swirls of dust which danced through shafts of light, swirling and twisting, dust demons intent on chaos.

Eventually, they came to a narrow doorway. Anklebolt stopped and turned. She stared at Franco, then at Tarly, then to her mother, who gave a nod. "Are you sure you want to go here? It's a very *very* dangerous place."

"Hey! They don't call me Franco 'Kicks Danger's Ass' Haggis for nothing, y'know? Get that there door open, and get us inside. I wanna see what terraforming secrets you have."

"But why?" asked Tarly, placing a hand on Franco's iron bicep. Despite the horseradish, despite the sausage, he was still a hunk. She squeezed his arm. He growled like a tiger.

"You'll see, babe," he said, and gestured with the gun to Anklebolt. "Now get it open. Before I shoot your machine face through the back of your head, you bloody psychopathic org freak."

Anklebolt stared hard at Franco, and he knew she was storing every little insult, every little put-down. But hey, so what? She'd been about to hang him an hour ago. It wasn't like her attitude to him could get much worse!

Anklebolt opened the metal door and, with a struggle, squeezed through. Franco and Tarly went next, shivering at the vast cold chill that swept out to meet them. Finally came Queen Strogger, looking nervously over her shoulder with a creak of metal and a hiss of ejected oil mist.

Nobody was there. No soldiers. No assassins. Maybe they were all glad to be rid of their insane royal family? Maybe they'd lost the scent? Or maybe they were busy appointing somebody new to the position of overall Ruler and God-like personage of The Org States. Queen Strogger snorted and slammed the door shut behind her.

What mattered now was stopping the ganger's Bad Army.

The new gangered *org* Bad Army. Bad Army-*Plus*.

And that wasn't going to be easy...

FRANCO STOOD ON a high bridge, overlooking a chamber scooped from the rock. It was so BIG he couldn't see the other end. Darkness seeped into his every pore, seemingly into his *soul,* and distant lights twinkled, like runway lights spied from an aircraft approaching through fog. Franco took a deep breath. He'd seen his fair share of vast underground chambers in his time – some even when he was sober – but this was perhaps the most vast and awesome *cave* he'd ever witnessed. The bridge under his sandals stretched away like a spider's thread through infinite space. Anklebolt started forward across the black steel umbilical, and Franco and Tarly followed. Tarly stayed close to Franco, her hand sometimes reaching out to touch his arm. He stopped after a while and turned.

"You okay?"

"Just... scared of the dark."

"*What?*"

"Hey." She shrugged. "Even psychopathic assassins have to have a flaw, right? With you, its beer and sausage. I pretty much guarantee you'd sell your mission pack for a crate of sausage and a keg of ale."

"Hmm. You got me there."

Queen Strogger followed on in silence, and Polly the Parrot fluttered off overhead, promising to "check things out," which Franco secretly hoped meant, "getting lost and dead."

The bridge wound on, and below them lights glittered like stars through oil.

They walked for perhaps a half-hour, through darkness, through gloom, through what seemed an eternity of *space*. Finally, Anklebolt stopped by a staircase, and Franco and Tarly, machine guns weighing heavily in their non-upgraded arms, also halted, the barrels *not quite* pointing at Anklebolt, but nevertheless locked and loaded and ready for action. Both Franco and Tarly were under no illusions that at the first opportunity Anklebolt would rip off their heads and shit down their necks.

"Why've you stopped?" barked Franco.

"Down there."

"Where?"

"If you had *org eyes,* you'd be able to see."

"It's the machines?"

"Yes."

Anklebolt and Queen Strogger exchanged glances. Then Queen Strogger said, "They have not been used for many thousands of years. What are you thinking of, Franco Haggis? I hope you do not intend to rearrange my city?"

"Oh no," said Franco, flapping his hand as if waving away a petty inconvenience. "Nothing of the sort." He pointed the gun. His face went serious. He felt serious. He felt seriously messed about. He felt like the sort of wounded, skin-flayed, false-fingered squaddie who might just shoot *everybody* if he didn't get his own damn way. "Now take us down. And no sudden moves or I'll fill you so full of lead you'll think you were a pencil. A fat one, obviously. And one with upgrades."

There were steps. Lots of steps. Hundreds of steps. *Thousands* of steps.

Anklebolt led the way, and Franco and Tarly started traipsing after her. Their assorted machine feet, boots and sandals slapped and thudded on the black iron steps, which spiralled, twisted and turned and shifted all the way down to the *ground.*

"*Pencil?*" said Tarly, after a while.

"Shut up."

"Yeah, but... *pencil?*"

"All I could think of at the time, reet? You want a better metaphor, you bloody come up with one."

"Touchy."

"It's this lack of skin on my back, and walking around in my shorts. Starting to get on my tits, so to speak."

Distantly, a "SQUAWK!" could be heard, reverberating off metal and fading to a metallic silence.

"Damn bird," muttered Franco.

It was a long way down. A *loooong* way.

Gradually the dim lights grew closer, and Franco and Tarly, without upgraded legs, were as weak as jelly and quivering like a nervous schoolgirl on a first date. Still, the view got more interesting as they descended. *Much* more interesting, as huge, vast shapes started to loom out of the black. Some were as big as skyscrapers, vast machines, all angular and matt black, with cables as thick as a landcar tunnel drooping in coils around angular, mechanical shoulders. Some had scoops and spades so big they could have... well, *created* this space.

Franco looked around him in wonder, and with a twinkle in his eye, as they descended yet further. They came upon trucks, so huge they could carry city blocks on their flatbacks. There were more diggers, and bulldozers that could have created mountains. Which they surely had.

"There," said Franco, pointing.

Tarly squinted. "What is it?"

Franco grinned, showing his missing tuff. "You'll see. Oy! Ankleshite! Take us across that gantry, there. You see it? Eh? There's a good girl."

They walked across the gantry, footsteps echoing across the bleak, titanic chamber. Tarly stared down, and blinked, and rubbed her eyes, then frowned. There were six vehicles, all lined up next to one other. Each was about the size of a very large steam engine – complete with twenty carriages. But they were matt black and corrugated, and at the front were what looked like two huge arms, each hundreds of yards long and ending in rounded scoops.

"Oh no," said Tarly.

"Oh yes," said Franco.

"They're *Moles*, right?"

"That's right, sugar-plum tree."

Tarly stopped. She put her hands on her hips. "Tell me, please Franco, tell me you're not thinking of *tunnelling* all the fucking way to Clone Terra! Tell me that insane thought hasn't gone through your tepid skull!"

"Hey, have you ever seen these babies go? They *blast* through the rock so fast they're a *blur*, mate! I saw a documentary on them a few years back. About QGM using them to infiltrate enemy wotsits, and all that. You know. Tunnel under enemy lines. Plant bombs. That sort of shit."

"I remember that documentary," said Tarly, voice level, eyes narrowed. "The Moles kept hitting pockets of gas and *exploding*."

"That's the monkey!"

"And sometimes, they'd hit pockets of oil, and explode!"

"Aye! That's the donkey!"

"Sometimes," she said, with a narrow smile that had nothing to do with humour, "they'd just explode."

"Ach, just teething problems."

"Franco, they're fucking *dangerous*. Like *taken-off-the-market* dangerous, like *responsible-for-thousands-of-people-dying* dangerous. You getting this into your thick skull? You observing a common thread here?"

"Ach, bollocks to it!"

"What's that supposed to mean?"

They were moving again, down more steps and sloping walkways, towards the Moles. Up close, they were *vast*. Tall as a building, long as city blocks, with two big digger-arms up front for tunnelling. They were a serious piece of earth-moving hardware. They were also, unfortunately, a bit of a death-trap.

"It means," said Franco, turning suddenly and facing Tarly, "that we're pretty much out of options. If you can think of another way to get to Pippa and shut down this bloody ganger army, then come on, spit it out!"

"Hey! Calm down!"

Franco sighed. Tarly smiled at him, and reached out, and took him in her arms. "What you need, mister, is a bit of good friendly loving."

"Better believe it!"

Tarly kissed him, and Franco was taken by surprise, but he responded, and their tongues entwined. *Wow, she can kiss, this lass! She's got a tongue like an electric eel, and hands like Mole diggers!*

They snogged, a full-on hardcore snog, and Franco couldn't help himself. He grabbed her arse, and gave it a good ol' big squeeze.

As they broke away, Franco smacked his lips. "You're a chick who knows how to set a man's tonsils on fire! You've got bite, baby! You're a wriggler!"

Tarly paused, lips moving soundlessly. Franco grinned, turned, and stomped down the final set of steps, his sandals slapping onto bare rock. He moved up to one of the Moles and pressed a hand against its cold flank. "Baby!" he muttered.

"Shit," growled Tarly, who for a moment had thought the game was up. She shouted out, "These machines, they've been down here thousands of years. You'll be lucky if this one fires up at all! You'll be lucky if it even moves a paddle!"

Franco wasn't looking. Which was good. Because at that point Tarly's skin started to ripple, to pulse, to show that her flesh was not *whole,* was not *as one,* but instead made from snakes and joined, bonded, by strength of will. Tarly Winters was a clone. Not a clone of any particular individual, but a clone of *humanity...*

Quickly, she gathered herself in *unity.* She pushed her snake flesh back together again; *bonded.*

"We'll see, we'll see;" muttered Franco, patting the Mole.

He turned, just as her flesh became one. Became *human*. Tarly gave him a dazzling, beautiful smile.

"We'll see," he grinned.

THE T5 JET came in through high cloud cover, dropping sharply with a roar of engines, and Pippa stared out of the window, heart pounding in her chest, and looked down over the vast range of mountains that divided the planet in two, known as *The Teeth*.

Peaks glittered, black rock beneath snow caps. A hundred mountains flashed beneath them, a thousand mountains, exhilarating and dangerously close.

The Mistress's War City opened up beneath them in a huge clearing on a rocky plateau, and it was vast, and it was terrifying. At the centre stood a huge raised compound – The Mistress's battle HQ. A Monastery, with high fortified walls and Big Guns. There were factories, a hundred at least, all churning out tanks and choppers, guns and jets. There were more *Slush Pits* like Pippa had seen back on Clone Terra. Only *here* there were *fifty* Pits, not one, and Pippa could only imagine how many clones were being churned out as soldiers for this new and terrible invasion. Around the high perimeter fences stomped GASGAMs – fifty, seventy, a hundred – and Pippa's eyes grew wide. The Mistress had not been exaggerating. She had repossessed them all; hijacked their cores, their programming, and bent them to her will.

Pippa observed infantry training. Thousands. *Tens* of thousands. Clones, but with a difference – for they had been modified, augmented, *upgraded* using the information supplied by Queen Strogger in the hope of gaining a truce. Instead, she had simply provided a new facet to the upcoming Reality War TV Show about to be aired on CLONE TV.

The jet soared down, and turned suddenly vertical, jerking Pippa in her landing straps. It sank slowly to the roof of The Monastery, and Pippa was led down a ramp and outside by Ziggurat and Teddy Sourballs.

A cold, winter wind hit Pippa hard, like a slap in the face.

"This way," the Mistress gestured, almost lazily, back in human form now, but still the images of her *snakes* haunted Pippa's mind with a shiver. She would never look at the woman – *hell, fuck it,* at the fucking *alien* – the same way again.

The Mistress reached the roof barrier of The Monastery. She gazed out, over her armies, over her factories, over her vast War Host. "There!" She pointed.

"Satellites?"

"Broadcast satellites. We're running test signals now, to every single TV set on Cloneworld, and to all our off-world booster cubes. We wouldn't want anybody to miss the biggest show ever made, right?"

"You're going to broadcast throughout Quad-Gal?"

"Of course. Everyone will have the right to see this, the biggest and best, the most original TV Reality Show ever made! Nobody has ever televised war like this before. Nobody has ever made it *interactive*. Just think, each viewer at home could be personally responsible for shooting that roomful of school children! They can hold an enemy org soldier's fate in their very own hands! Choose whether a ganger org can cut off his enemy's balls or not! Incredible!"

"Awesome!" said Pippa, voice dripping sarcasm.

"Come on! I will show you more!"

Pippa was led (forced!) down a number of ramps and stairs, all metal, leading through the heart of The Monastery. True to form, it was built from stone and contained alien prayer walls and bells. Somehow, though, to Pippa it kind of lost its relevance.

Outside, they climbed into a HJeep. Jets whined, and the Jeep lifted several feet off the ground and accelerated, a cold biting mountain wind ruffling hair as they hummed across the flat rocky parade grounds, down paths from The Monastery HQ to the huge training fields of infantry.

"To give the show *originality*," explained the Mistress, "we have cloned up battalions of different types of soldier. So there, for example, we have basic landbound grunts from various different nationalities of Quad-Gal. There, we have some standard Mongrel_grade, Simmo_grade and Jappo_ grade infantry units. We tend to breed in battalions of a thousand, give or take, depending on defect and re-feed numbers from Pits and Vats. We're finding different properties of the Slush Pits dictate different success rates in the mass cloning."

"Interesting," said Pippa, eyes scanning the fields from the back of the HJeep. "Wait! Stop!"

"Yes?"

The HJeep hummed to a halt, bobbing for a moment, and Pippa stood up and stared. She stared again. She stared a little harder. "Holy Mother of God," she said, "tell me my eyes are deceiving me!"

"No. What you see is true."

"It cannot be!"

"Oh, it is," chuckled the Mistress.

There, before their watching eyes, all stood to attention, with a Battle Sergeant screaming orders as they ran through drills, were *a thousand Franco Haggises!*

Each Franco Haggis was short, a little pot-bellied, with a shaved head and ginger goatee beard. However, whilst Pippa acknowledge *her* original Franco Haggis was, if one was truthful about the whole situation, something of a *slob*, here and now this battalion of Francos were smart, uniformed; their boots shone, their beards were combed, no horseradish stains marred their jackets, and their eyes shone with pride as they were drilled around the huge parade square with precision, and with none of the sloppiness Pippa had grown to love and loathe.

A stomp of a thousand boots, in perfect harmony, rattled across the parade ground.

"I don't fucking believe it!" said Pippa.

"Synthetic testing and probability controls show the Franco_grade infantry grunt is a very good infantry soldier indeed. He may be short and fat, but what he lacks in height and suppleness he clearly makes up for in raw aggression and lack of cowardice on the battlefield. This battalion is a miracle."

"It's a fucking abomination, is what it is!"

"We'll see how successful my predications are when the cameras start to roll."

"Mistress, you're a sick, sick lady, is all I can say. You've bred a thousand sexual perverts! You've bred a thousand versions of a known psychopathic lunatic! How could you do that? Did you think it *all the way though*, eh?"

"My choices will be vindicated," said the Mistress, smugly. She made a gesture, and the HJeep moved on. Pippa buried her head in her hands. *Oh, no. Oh, no. How can it be? Not one Franco, but a thousand of them! What's she going to show me next? A thousand Ronan Keatings? A thousand bloody Doctor Whos? A thousand Schwarzeneggar_grade soldiers? Shit. It'll be a damn miracle if I don't go insane!*

They sped off, and the Mistress showed Pippa the full circuit of her vast War Host before returning to The Monastery, where she was taken up a wide set of bare stone steps to a large room, filled wall-to-wall with advanced military hardware, all marked with the QGM logo. Military grade computers. Stolen! Nicked! For Pippa to work on. She sighed.

Ziggurat moved over and removed his clothes. The little hunchback sat on a simple wooden chair and regarded Pippa with his odd eyes, smiling.

The Mistress stood before Pippa. She held out the 3Core, which Pippa took, almost reverently. Here could be their answer to the junks, and the sweeping Quad-Gal invasion...

If she could just get it away from the hands of this mad, media-obsessed, multi-snake alien!

"One mistake, any attempt to escape, *anything*," said the Mistress, "and Ziggurat here will fry you. And not just a tickle like the last time. This time he'll burn you to coal. Understand?"

"Yes."

"You'll find the codes on the desktop. In the folder called CODES."

"How original."

"I want the 3Core unlocking. It will then control the modified GASGAM rockets. You understand?"

"I'll find my way round it," said Pippa, and watched the Mistress leave.

So, she wants me to program the GASGAM to take off and deliver nukes to every org city and war factory on the continent at her command? Well, I'll program them all right. I'll fucking program them good...

Pippa removed her thin leather gloves, plugged the 3Core into the console, took hold of the mouse and clicked OPEN.

CHAPTER THIRTEEN
MOLE HOLE

THEY STOOD IN the cockpit. Around them, Tarly felt the whole planet pressing in, pressing down, focusing its hatred at what was about to happen. A burrowing machine capable of going through mountains; an engine capable of travelling *through the core of the world*. This was not just a train built for *tunneling*, a small tool in the great terraforming canon of available weapons; it was something which could, possibly, undermine an entire planet.

They opened a door, which disengaged and slid open with a gentle *hiss*. Franco led the way into what could only be described as a train carriage, closely followed by Tarly, Strogger and Anklebolt. Just before the door closed on its thick iron-black hinges, Polly the Parrot nipped in, with a strangled "SQUAWK."

They moved through a tight underlit central corridor. To each side were sleeping compartments and store rooms. The Mole was designed to run underground, completely self-sufficient, for very long periods of time.

The cab up front had tinted windows. It had a small air freshener in the shape of a spaceship dangling from a rear-view monitor. Franco stood staring at the lifeless black controls. Each button looked like a blank eye to Tarly as she also glanced down, then back to Anklebolt. Polly had, thankfully, followed them to the cab and hopped up onto Queen Strogger's shoulder. The mad old org seemed not to mind. Franco scowled at the bird, mouthing silent obscenities.

"Alice?" he said.

"Yes?" said Alice, her voice dreamy from the small black BCube.

"Are you okay?"

"I feel... distant. Lost, almost."

"Hmm. Can you locate Pippa? Using her spinal logic cube implants?"

"I will try. For now, head west, then we'll update co-ordinates when I can pinpoint her."

Franco nodded, and rested his hands on the controls. "Okay," he said, "here goes nuffink!"

Franco might have been a shaven-headed, goatee-bearded, pot-bellied, psychopathic, nutjob fucknugget, but he was also a great sniper, a brilliantly deviant demolition's expert, and had an amazing affinity with *machines*. Many was the time Keenan had kicked him up the arse for tinkering with his Permatex WarSuit with a Phillips screwdriver. Many was the time Pippa had scolded him with violent expletives as he rose from a Hornet's EngineBay carrying a bag of spanners.

Franco and machines – they just got on.

Whereas Franco and people – they just had to agree to disagree.

Franco worked out the controls intuitively, and hit three buttons. The Mole's atomic reactor came back online, with a deep and distant rumble. Digits and bars flickered up on the HUD. Outside, the world looked very black.

"Ooh, there's power in this baby," said Franco, licking his lips.

"It isn't a racing car," snapped Tarly.

"*Nooo*, but it's all about the driver, reet, and not the vehicle. I mean, take your average woman driver..."

"Yes?" Tarly's voice was cold.

"Well, well, you see..." Franco's eyes glazed over as he saw the look on his beloved's face. "What is it?"

"Don't be giving me your *women are bad drivers* bullshit, or I'll kick you outside and stick this whole Mole up your arse."

"Hey, I was just saying..." whined Franco.

"Just drive!"

"Okay, okay, hey, I'm not the kind of driver who crashes into skips and supermarket shopping trolleys, though, am I?" He engaged the *iDrive* with a clunk and, grabbing a control throttle, eased the Mole forward. It trundled through the darkness with a dull roar and a whine of suppressed rage. Franco hit another button, and dazzling lights blazed from the Mole's snout, and Franco grabbed another lever and engaged the *iDiggers*. To each side, the paddles shifted and stretched forward with tiny clicks and clanks, and scoops and blades could be seen. They started to spin and gyrate, hypnotic in their implied violence.

"This is going to be fun," said Franco, and accelerated slightly, heading for the wall. Around them, machinery flashed past.

"If it doesn't work, or you screw it up, we're dead," said Tarly, fingers clutching the arm-rests of her chair.

"Ach, don't be such a pussy!"

They hit the wall, and the Mole's arms and scoops, blades and chewers *ground* into the rock and... they *flashed* into a tunnel. Darkness closed in. The Mole *vibrated*; rock-debris passed through an under-carriage chute to be spat out of the Mole's arse.

Lights illuminated a mash of churning.

Franco released his breath, and settled back. "See? I told ya it'd work!"

"Ha! You're a good bluffer, Franco Haggis."

"Hey, they don't call me Franco 'Cool Cucumber' Haggis for nowt, y'know? I'm a geezer. Part of the Smart Party!"

"Squawk! You're a lunatic, is what you are, buster!" squawked Polly.

Franco threw his robotic Special Friend an evil glare, gauging the distance between her alloy head and his right hook. Then he settled back a bit more and glanced at Queen Strogger and Princess Anklebolt III.

"You two not kissed and made up yet?"

"I would rather die!" sniffed Anklebolt imperiously, tilting her nose up. Which was quite something for a woman with a face like a bucket of bolts.

"That can be arranged, bastad," snapped Strogger.

"Oh mother, you were always such a bad-tempered bully!"

"Bully? You were going to bloody *hang me*! Me! You're good ol' mom!"

"The only good thing you ever did was set fire to the palace – with you in it."

"Hey, that was an accident with the chip pan!"

"Maybe if you spent less time frying chips and more time spending quality moments with your offspring..."

"Quality moments! There were bloody five hundred and thirty three of you, you little bunch of scrotes! Never a moment's peace! It was like giving birth to an alien fucking *zoo!*"

"Well, you should have learnt to keep your legs shut."

"*You* should have learnt to keep your mouth shut!"

"*I* only kept my mouth as shut as you kept your saggy, machine-fed pussy!"

"How dare you!"

"I dare, because I..."

Tarly pulled Franco to one side. "This thing has an automatic pilot, y'know?"

"What, the Mole?"

"Yeah, the Mole."

"So?"

"It means you don't have to man the controls. Not for a while, anyway."

"Yes."

"So."

"Yup." Franco scratched his beard.

"*So*... we could, you know, go for a little walk."

"Indeed we could."

"Or something."

"What kind of something?"

"You know." She winked and reached around, squeezing his bum. "Something."

"Oh! Ah! Ah! I see. Really? Now?"

"Yes. Really. Now."

"Lead the way!"

"I shall."

"Geronimo!"

"What?"

"Is just a figure of speech." He winked.

The sleeping chamber was surprisingly plush for what was, effectively, a rock-burrowing train. Franco and Tarly stood across from one other, nervous now, like teenage lovers finding themselves alone for the first time.

"Er," said Franco.

"Come here," said Tarly, and stepped into him, and her mouth was on his, hot and eager, and Franco responded with a surge of lust. After all, it had been a while. And even then, she'd been a zombie.

Tarly kissed him, hot and steamy. Her tongue ranged around the inside of Franco's mouth like an eel. Her hands were all over him, almost as if she had more than two. Franco reeled and was lost in the moment, and felt himself falling into their sex, and they were rolling together, naked, and she kissed his chest and belly and then lower, taking his snake in her mouth as she said, "This reminds me of something."

"Oooh, aaah, oooh, hope it was something nice."

"Oh, yes," said Tarly.

And then she leapt atop him, wriggled on top of him, and Franco's hands were all over her nakedness and she forced him into her, and Franco was crooning and moaning and falling into that hot honey otherworld of pleasure. In the gloom, as she writhed above him, her face seemed curiously blurred and Franco rubbed his eyes, but Tarly reached out and dimmed the lights as she fucked him, fucked him hard...

And Franco couldn't understand why he couldn't get the image of spaghetti out of his brain.

*   *   *

THEY LAY TOGETHER, entwined like snakes. Franco kissed Tarly's forehead, and she looked up at him, a sweet smile on her beautiful face.

"Did you enjoy that, lover?"

"I did!"

"You're special, Franco Haggis. A very special man."

"I know," he said, proudly, grinning, and puffed out his hairy, curly chest.

"What are your thoughts? On the clones?"

"I think it's a bit of a dirty trade."

"What?"

"It's a damn and bloody disgrace that you can be copied. I mean, is nothing sacred? It's like... like bloody shagging a bird, reet, and then finding out she's a monster! Or something."

"Disgraceful," said Tarly, her snake-like tongue leaving wet trails across his chest.

"SQUAWK! Emergency! Emergency! There's an emergency going on!" Polly was in the sleeping chamber with them.

"You move bloody quiet for a parrot," snapped Franco, leaping out of the bed and pulling on his pants.

"Just sounding the alarm, don't you know. SQUAWK! EMERGENCY! EMERGENCY! THERE'S AN EMERGENCY GOING ON, BUSTER!"

"Yes yes, we bloody heard you!" snapped Franco, and tried to slap the parrot as he hopped across the chamber.

Within minutes they stampeded into the Mole's cockpit, and Strogger and Anklebolt, who were *still having the same argument,* looked up, faces frowning.

"What's the emergency?" snapped Franco, panting. Outside, through the rockshield, they were still surging ahead, the mole's paddles continuously cutting and grinding through rock.

"I just wanted the Combat K ident code for Pippa," came Alice's sleepy voice. "So I can track her with more clarity through these miles and miles of strata."

"What?" said Franco, and glared at the parrot. "What's emergency about that?"

"It's important information, buster! Need it updating now, we do! Squawk!"

"You feckin' eedjit," said Franco, rubbing his groin. "Did myself an injury then, I did!"

Tarly closed her arms around him. "Yeah, but that's nothing a bit of loving won't put right."

It took three days for the Mole to dig under the ocean, on a solid bearing towards Pippa's location. At length, Alice called Franco and Tarly from what had been christened their "Love Nest" – a place from which they rarely emerged – and Franco slumped into the cockpit seat, face pale, hands trembling.

"Are you all right?" said Queen Strogger, staring hard at the Combat K squaddie.

"Yeah, yeah, it's this Tarly lass, she's got everlasting energy, I tell you! I feel like a bloody cow – milked."

Tarly sat down next to him, smiling and rubbing his leg.

"Hello, lover."

"Er. Hello. No, no! Focus! Alice, Polly said," and he eyed the bird evilly, "that you have more information. Or are you going to simply tell me a bit of rock went past?"

"No. It's Pippa. Her co-ordinates. She has moved."

"Where from? Where to?"

"She was lost in the depths of Clone Terra. Now she's moving – *fast* – towards The Teeth mountain range."

"Why would she go there? Do you think she knows about this plot by the gangers to build an army? And more importantly, has she found the 3Core?"

"I just have co-ordinates, Franco," said Alice, voice dreary. "Still, if she does land in The Teeth it will make our journey significantly easier. We are only hours away from the outer edges of the base bedrock."

"Hours?" said Franco.

"Hours!" smiled Tarly, rubbing his thigh.

"Gods, no!" said Franco. "I haven't got no energy!"

"Let me persuade you," said Tarly, taking him by the hand and leading him out of the cockpit.

He gave a feeble, backward grin. And disappeared.

Queen Strogger and Princess Anklebolt III glared at each other with daggers. Really. They had knives poking out of their eyes. And Polly looked on, oblivious to this biomechanical animosity surrounding her.

"Tsch," said Polly the Parrot, Special Robotic Friend. "Kids nowadays, eh? SQUAWK?"

IT WAS HOURS later. Franco, lying in bed, smoking a cigarette and drinking a glass of whiskey, felt the decline in power and sat up.

"Come here, lover," growled Tarly.

"No, no, listen! We're slowing down. Something's going on."

Franco got out and started to dress, in clothes he'd found in the Mole's stores. He pulled on a rough shirt and pants, and heavy boots, eschewing his usual sandals because he realised he was going into a possible combat situation, and after the loss of a little finger, didn't want to lose any other digits.

"Come back, lover!"

"No! Come on Tarly, shift your arse."

"Just once more..."

"Hey, just because they call me Franco 'Snake in His Pants' Haggis, doesn't mean I can perform for a whole *week* without a break. Anyway, we have more important business to attend."

"What's more important than servicing your snake?" grinned Tarly.

Franco stared at her. "You're behaving a bit weird, love."

Tarly shrugged, and climbed elegantly from the

bed. She stood, naked, tall and firm and proud, a perfect example of what a woman could aspire to. She was perfectly formed, she was athletic and yet demure, she was psychotic and yet exciting, and she did it for Franco in bucketfuls. She was a vixen. A Valkyrie! A *Goddess!*

The Mole gave a shudder, and slowed yet more. "Come on. We need to be ready. I bet there's a few surprises ahead of us!" Franco walked out through the narrow doorway.

Tarly smiled. "I think you may be right, there," she said.

"WE'RE REACHING THE surface. ETA three minutes," said Alice, as Franco appeared in the cockpit.

The Mole had slowed to a gentle rhythm of scooping and grinding, and Franco scratched his beard. "Alice, you sure now that this is where Pippa is?"

"To within fifty metres," said Alice, gently. "And now she's stationery. We're at the heart of The Teeth mountain range, slap-bang in the middle of Cloneworld."

"Are there any baddies?" said Franco, baring his teeth.

"My scanners show no other activities," said Alice, weakly. "Although I feel... *odd*. Like I may have been... *hacked.*"

"Great," muttered Franco, frowning. He scratched his beard. "So, it looks like Pippa found the 3Core then, and came here for a rendezvous?" He rubbed his chin. "Just... what a strange choice of destination. Unless she got some kind of message from QGM. Unless they're picking us up! Hey, maybe we're going home? Whiskey! Sausages! Brothels!"

Tarly coughed.

"Not brothels! Bars! Clubs and pubs and yippidy do!"

Ahead, the scoops slowed yet again. The Mole shuddered, engines whining. Then daylight broke, blinding them suddenly as the Mole surged upwards and *out* from the bedrock. Franco ran over and hit the controls, killing the engine. The Mole's lead carriage, vertical for a moment, toppled over and *thudded* on its suspension. The rest of the carriages remained beneath the rock, in an excavation of its own creation.

"Daylight!" beamed Franco, grabbing his machine gun and running for the door. "I do hope Pippa's all right, I mean, we didn't part under the best of circumstances, did we, but she did well, not dying after that fall, and I'm reet pleased about that, just hope she managed to get that message to Quad-Gal Military and there's a SLAM ship waiting to hot-drag us all from this ball of miserable crap!"

He opened the door. It had started snowing, a thick, swirling blanket toppling over the mountains. The world outside was white, and Franco slapped a button to unfold the steps. "Pippa!" he bellowed, tottering out into the fresh fall.

The world was white!

The world was beautiful!

The world was... full of soldiers pointing guns at him!

Franco blinked.

"Drop the gun, dickhead," came a voice from behind him, and Franco scowled, and turned, and stared hard at Tarly Winters – who was prodding him with the barrel of an org machine gun.

"Er?" he said.

"Gun! Or I'll turn you into ribbon fucking pasta!"

"Hey? What happened to *luvvy-duvvy-wuvvy*? What happened to *your little chickenhead*? What the bloody hell – nay! – the *bloody bollocks,* happened to *your little greasy piston of thumping delight?*"

"Just do it, moron."

Franco climbed down the steps and threw his gun to the ground. There were about a thousand soldiers waiting for him. He grinned. Not the best odds in the world, but he'd taken worse.

"I'm sorry, Franco!" Pippa ran across the snow, boots leaving imprints. She fell into him, and they held each other for a few moments, and Franco pulled back. He smiled into her face, a look of genuine happiness there.

"I'm glad you're okay," he said. "Did you get the..."

"Yeah. But they took it." Pippa gestured to the Mistress, standing, arms crossed, behind her.

Tarly walked across the snow as more soldiers ran into the Mole and bound Queen Strogger and

Anklebolt III with anti-org meshclips. Even Polly was captured, although she did manage to nastily peck a soldier on his hand; a quite vicious and bloody assault.

Franco scowled – his scowl getting even worse when he saw the face of Teddy Sourballs. "I don't bloody believe it! I thought I fucking killed you already! Come over here, let me do it again..."

"The benefits of living on Cloneworld," smiled Teddy, her face creasing into weird and wonderful ugliness.

Franco whirled back on Tarly, who strode casually, leisurely, to the Mistress. She draped an arm around the Mistress's shoulders, and grinned over at Franco.

"No!" he said.

"Yes."

"No!" His eyes were wide. "You're in this together? I don't believe it! I just don't bloody believe it!" He stamped his foot. Then he stamped it again! "And... you're... you're... you're hot bloody lesbians! Rabid Carpet Munchers! Gash Guzzlers! Marmalade Makers! You're... you're both... *Twat Bandits!*"

"Excuse me?" said Tarly, her eyes twinkling with a dark, inner humour. She waved her hand dismissively. "Oh, no. No, Franco, sweetie. It's nothing like that."

She turned then, and kissed the Mistress, and for a long moment it looked like a normal kiss, their tongues entwining, their hands enfolding, fingers interlacing, and they were enjoying themselves, revelling in the kiss, the sort of passionate kiss enjoyed by long-lost lovers finally reunited... and then something started to happen, something started to *change*, and big, wrist-thick strings broke away from both heads, peeling away, until their heads and faces were simply streamers of pale white snakes and the snakes merged and writhed and twisted together, sliming together, wriggling together in possibly the most intimate mating of flesh ever witnessed.

Franco gasped, and his jaw dropped.

Then his mind.

But there was more. It wasn't finished yet. The Mistress and Tarly Winters continued to *break down* into streamers of flesh, their clothes falling away like useless floating gasbags as their arms and legs and torsos all disintegrated into writhing thick snakes, each with its own eyes and flickering red forked tongues, and the two women *merged* and *grew* and turned to face Franco and Pippa and Queen Strogger and Princess Anklebolt and it was one huge seething mass of pink, almost a globe, without limbs, without hair, only lots and lots and lots of tiny little eyes and tiny hissing fangs...

Pippa looked at Franco, her face hard. "And you were shagging *that*?" she said.

Franco looked pale. His hands were shaking. "I wasn't just shagging it. I was going to marry it!"

Pippa tutted. "You're sick," she said.

"I'm going to *be* sick," he said.

"Lock them away!" came the low-level, sibilant hissing, and it wasn't a voice as such, but a *feeling*, transferred through the air on hundreds of tiny flickering breaths.

And a thousand armed soldiers, standing in a rough circle around the captured, closed in with ready weapons and hard eyes.

Franco covered his face and wept.

IT WAS LATE. Outside, it was dark. Pippa stood, and moved to the narrow window of the stone chamber. She reached out, opened it, breathed in cold fresh mountain air ripe with the perfume of snow. A few flakes drifted in, and she reached out, allowing one to settle on the warm flesh of her hand and melt. *That's me*, she thought. *Melting inside. Disintegrating. Breaking down into nothing. Dying.*

"What are you doing?" said Ziggurat, his voice soft, watching her intently. The hunchback never removed his gaze from Pippa. He never slept.

"I've done it."

"Reprogrammed the cards?"

"Yes, the GASGAMs can be loaded with the warheads. They will deliver your payload."

"Just remember," said Ziggurat, odd eyes narrowing. "This is for the greater good. This is for the Quad-Gal! To stop the junks. You understand, little lady? You remember that well?"

"I remember."

Franco, slumped in a chair in the corner, started snoring; Pippa stared at him. His hands and feet were bound tight, and he twitched occasionally. Poor Franco. Always the victim, no matter how much punishment he doled out.

"Wait here. Teddy will come and check the code."

Ziggurat disappeared, and Pippa glanced up at the twin-eye security cams. They followed her worse than any dose of clinging syphilis. She scowled up at them, and then at the snoring figure of Franco.

How can he sleep? How can he sleep now? How can he sleep through THIS? *How can the bastard sleep* AT ALL?

"Oy! Franco! Wake up!"

Franco snorted himself awake, and grasped blindly for his Kekra quad-barrel machine pistols, which weren't there. "Eh? What? Wassgoinon?" He rubbed at his nose, which was drooling a long trail of snot, and blinked rapidly several times.

"Oh. It's you."

"Nice to see you as well, dickhead."

"Sorry, Pippa. Don't be like that. What I meant was, we're in the shit again. Together. As usual. Ha-ha."

"I've don't it, Franco. Done what I always said I would not."

"You reprogrammed the GASGAMs? Into carrying warheads?"

"Yes. That *bitch* can detonate any whole city or org war factory she wants now. And all for a fucking TV program. Reality TV. It should be burned into infinity."

Franco stood, and stretched, and moved to Pippa. He patted her with his bound hands. "You had to do it. We need that 3Core. And talking of that junk chip, where is the little maggot?"

"There. In the console."

"Best grab it."

Pippa ejected the 3Core with a tiny *phzut*. She gazed at it, almost reverently. She offered it to Franco, but he shook his hands and head. "No no. You keep it. Look after it! We don't want to be leaving that little monkey behind!"

"So – you believe you'll be leaving the War Compound alive, then?" said Teddy Sourballs. She stood in the doorway, Ziggurat peering from behind her. She smiled then, a nasty smile on a nasty face beneath nasty barbed-wire hair. "Well. Allow me check your code first, shall I?"

She moved to the console, a cocky walk – especially for one who Franco had already slaughtered. He watched her with distaste. *The dead should bloody stay dead,* he thought bitterly. Then he brightened. *Maybe I'll get a chance to kill her again? Next time, I'll rip her damn head off and make sure!*

Teddy spent a good twenty minutes at the console, scrolling through the code, and then gave a single nod and turned to Pippa, who was standing, head hung low, feeling deeply ashamed of herself. After all, it wasn't every day you programmed a hundred nukes for a madman. Madwoman. Mad... snakeperson? Shit.

"You did well. Your code is... precise. You can tell that you once worked on missile systems."

Franco stared at her. "You worked on fucking *missile* systems?"

"There's a lot you don't know about me, Franco Haggis."

"Well how the *hell* do *they* know, then? It's Combat K classified, ain't it?"

"Supposed to be," growled Pippa. "Your bloody fiancée told them everything. Pulled the files. On you, me, Keenan, and God only knows who else. These gangers have all the intel they need. Tarly Winters is their direct line to the heart of QGM Intelligence."

"Yes. Well," said Teddy. She hit a key, and the code disappeared. All the screens went black. She moved to the rear of the console, pulled out a pistol, and put eight bullets into the heart of the machine. Smoke from the ruined case crawled into the air, as if ashamed. They could smell burning. "Just so you don't think you can change the horror you have wrought."

"Thanks."

"Now, my dears, it is time for *us all* to go to war." She smiled at Ziggurat, who stood naked, palms outwards, as if he expected trouble.

"When can we leave?" said Pippa, voice a low growl.

"You get your freedom after the war is done," said Teddy. Her dark eyes glittered. "*After* CLONE TV has made its show. *After* the orgs have been wiped clean off the face of Cloneworld! You see, the idea is all in the name. It's called Cloneworld for a reason. Us gangers, this is our planet. We don't want any filthy orgs polluting our water and air."

"You're just one big, happy family, aren't you?" said Pippa.

Outside, sirens suddenly started shrilling through the snow. Thousands of engines fired up, and Pippa groaned inwardly; the *attack* was now in progress. Even if they wanted to, how could they stop a whole invasion taking place?

"We must leave," said Pippa.

"No," said Teddy, backing away. "After the slaughter. After the wargames. After CLONE TV has had its moment of glory! After... *we have won.*"

Franco got the unwritten signal from Pippa. He'd worked combat missions with her for too many years not to know when impending violence was on the cards... he could sense her tension, and knew, just *knew* when she was going to explode. When she was lied to. When she was cheated. When she was betrayed. Times like now...

Outside, a thousand massive infantry SLAMs lifted off, jets roaring and turning the snow to mush. On the long road to the sea, convoys of tanks and mobile guns started off on churning tracks. Five hundred choppers fired their engines, and with rotors *whumping,* rose high into the snow-filled sky above The Teeth. Outside, the army moved. The army *flowed*... a huge black and green steel beast, with no head and no heart and no soul.

This wasn't battle.

This was extermination.

Pippa kicked herself forward, an abrupt movement, hindered by her bound hands, but fast enough to catch Teddy Sourballs off-guard. The woman stumbled back, Pippa hurtling at her – but Ziggurat got in the way. The small hunchback threw himself between them with a hiss, and Pippa bounced from his surprisingly solid frame, recovered, and snapped off five quick kicks to Ziggurat's body and arms. He took each blow with a stoic grunt, then lifted his head, grinning at her with lop-sided jaws.

"Want to play, little girl?"

"Want to die, little hunchback?"

"Well, I want to kill *you*," nodded the naked Ziggurat, spreading his arms wide. The *pulse* flew past Pippa's head as she went into a fast dive, and exploded against the wall behind her. Computer equipment, alloy panels and boards flew out in all directions, scattering sparks as they went. Smoke curled from the shattered equipment. The roar of the pulse deafened Franco, and he coughed on raw smoke.

Franco moved forward now: him to one side, Pippa, regaining her composure, to the other.

"What's his deal?" snapped Franco.

"Let me show you," said Ziggurat, and slapped his hands together, pointing them at Franco. Franco was picked up with a shout and tossed across the stone room. He plummeted through banks of computers and hit the wall, sliding to the floor behind a bench, groaning and trickling blood from his ears.

"He wasn't fast enough," said Ziggurat.

Pippa started to back away.

"SQUAWK!" squawked Polly, in the corridor outside. Her wings flapped, and she lost a green alloy feather. "Everybody's getting away! They're going to kill all the orgs! On live TV! It's not fair, SQUAWK!"

"Help me out here, then!" hissed Pippa, eyes still locked on Ziggurat.

"Bugger that!" squawked Polly, and flapped off through the smoke.

Ziggurat was moving forward, Pippa moving back on balanced heels. But she only had a few seconds before he closed her in, locked her down, and did what he was going to do...

"I thought you still needed me? In case things went wrong."

"Change of plan," said Ziggurat, lifting his hands up in the air. Bands of blue-white electric danced from palm to palm, and Pippa felt the hairs on the back of her neck and arms stand up as a truly awesome charge was built, fizzing and crackling, into something quite extraordinary...

Around the room, metallic items started to vibrate. A cold wind whipped in from the corridor down which Sourballs had fled. Pippa's hair streamed out behind her. Ziggurat was standing on the spot, naked, his whole body now *infused* with power, with raw energy, and he was drawing it not just from his hump storage unit, but from every power source in the room. In the Monastery!

"Time to fry," Ziggurat smiled, a narrow cruel smile, his green eye and his yellow eye fixed on Pippa without emotion, without compassion, without empathy.

Ziggurat was not a man who nurtured regret in his soul.

All he held was hatred.

And *power*...

His hands came together in a sharp vicious sweep, and Pippa hissed...

CHAPTER FOURTEEN
BATTLE TV

FRANCO LAY IN a hell-hole, his head spinning, copper blood in his mouth, wasps in his ears, fur in his throat, a steel timpani band thundering in his heart, which threatened to crawl up his throat and puke itself onto the stone floor. He coughed up a chunk of phlegm as big as his fist, and spat it on the floor, which twisted inside-out, turned into a rubber monster and tried to swallow him. Franco resisted the pull of the liquid floor, and his hands glooped upwards as he realised he was on his hands and knees, and that was a position he never wanted to suffer. Submissive. Taking it like a dog. No way! Franco fought through the sparks and crackling energy, and lifted his head above the parapet of fallen, battered computer consoles. Pippa was backing away from Ziggurat, who was capering like some comic devil, his little todge swinging for all it was worth.

Still swimming through treacle, Franco cast around for a weapon, and found a long shard of jagged crystal from inside one of the smashed computer systems. He tested it against his palm, and it drew blood. It was sharp as a razor. Franco grinned. *This'll do nicely!*

He watched for a moment, mesmerised by the growing charge as Ziggurat gathered his energy in order to *Holy Shit, in order to fry Pippa like a fried egg!* Franco's arm snapped back, and just as Ziggurat's hands came together Franco launched the makeshift dagger as hard as he could. It slammed through the air, end over end, and a split-second before Ziggurat's hands connected, before he sent the charge of dark energy blasting across the stone room, the crystal dagger pierced his eye, cleaving through to the brain.

His hands connected with a *snap* as he reeled back in sudden pain and disbelief, a shrill scream on his spittle-flecked lips.

"Aha!" shouted Franco, punching the air.

Big mistake.

The bolt of energy crackled and howled across the chamber, and clean removed Franco's arm at the elbow. For a long, long time Franco stared at the stump, his mouth hung open like a dead donkey's, and there was no pain, and no blood, and he just stared, uncomprehending, as the world howled around him and electrical static discharged, crackling, on every metal surface in the chamber.

Then reality *caught up.*

Pain lanced up Franco's arm in a smashing wave, like a storm sea against a brittle glass shore, and there was no blood because the limb had been removed by *hot blue energy*, cauterising the stump. Pain beat him like a hammer. Agony washed him in molten lava. Franco crumbled to his knees, his good hand cradling his elbow, as a scream bubbled up in his throat and spewed like vomit droplets into the air...

Pippa lowered her hands, blinking. Ziggurat was on his knees on the floor, swaying, sobbing, the dagger in his eye socket and blood running down his lop-sided face. Even as Pippa watched, he reached up to the length of crystal, touched it, screamed, and dropped his hands as if stung. Pippa's looked right, her head moving like pouring honey, and blinked at Franco. His arm had gone. Vaporised. He, too, was rocking like a baby...

Priorities.

Pippa climbed to her feet. She didn't remember falling to her knees. She walked unsteadily across the chamber, the air crackling around her, the hairs on her head rising in the static, and she broke into a run as she approached Ziggurat, whose single yellow eye watched her through waves of pain, and his hands came up – *No!* – but it was too late, as with a snarl Pippa leapt atop him, throwing him onto his back, and his hands scrabbled at her and she knew, *knew* the fucker would have disintegrated her into component atoms with his weird dark energy blast. Well, he wouldn't do it again. She fought past his struggling hands, and grasped the crystal deep in his eye socket. "Why hasn't this killed you, motherfucker?" she hissed, her mouth close to his, and she leant her weight on the make-shift dagger. She felt it ease in further, into Ziggurat's eye-socket, into the pulping brain beyond.

"No!" he screamed, "No! Have mercy! Please, have mercy!"

"Why? You never showed us any!"

"Let him live," said Franco, voice hoarse, and Pippa turned fast, head slamming round, eyes narrowing.

Franco was swaying, face pale, vomit on his shirt, his right arm gone at the elbow. His free hand was supporting the wounded limb as if cradling a newborn child, and he was panting, haggard, injured beyond repair. His eyes had a haunted look Pippa had seen before – like when somebody's worst nightmare had just come true, but realisation hadn't quite sunk in yet. And this was up there for Franco, she knew... up there with losing his eyes, or his legs. Ironic, considering he was trained in the detonations business, where loss of limbs was almost mandatory...

"Why?" she snarled.

"Leave him!" bellowed Franco, dropping to one knee, then pulling himself raggedly back to his feet.

Pippa shook her head. "I can't do that," she said, voice simple, eyes bleak. She yanked out the crystal with a *scloop* of punctured eye jelly and pulverised, mashed brain.

"He's defenceless," said Franco, groggy, swaying.

"Good," said Pippa, simply, and drew the sharp crystal across Ziggurat's throat. Flesh peeled back like neatly pared chicken, and the blood spilled in a thick gush, spreading across the floor as Ziggurat thrashed on his hump and Pippa held him down, her hands pinning his arms, her strength working against his spasming as slowly, slowly, Ziggurat died.

And then it was done.

Pippa stood wearily, and stared down at the corpse. She spat on it, then turned to Franco – rushing to him just as he collapsed. "Shit." She hauled him to his feet, and gave him a vicious hard slap across the face. "Stay with me, soldier!"

"Ha! I ain't going nowhere, bitch," he said, voice hoarse.

Pippa took the stump of his arm gingerly and examined the amputation. The blast had indeed cauterised his flesh, sealing the severed artery and blackening the stump as effectively as dipping it in a bucket of boiling tar.

Outside, more fighters and jets and SLAMs were lifting into the heavens. The stench of exhaust fumes came in through the bars. Soldiers were cheering. Engines revved, belching and screaming, metal on metal in sumps of oil. It sounded like Hell. It sounded like war.

"Come on!"

"Where're we going?"

"I have an idea."

They staggered from the stone room, Pippa stepping on one of Ziggurat's flopping dead hands, and into a narrow corridor. "They must be here somewhere," she muttered, and saw the doors leading off nearby. She moved to one, throwing back the thick bars. It was empty. The next held Queen Strogger and Anklebolt. They were wrapped in cunt_wire, immobile and scowling in the dusty gloom. Pippa stared at them, at the squirming, gleaming, constantly moving, *biting* wire.

"How do I get that off?"

"Ziggurat. He'll have a sonic screwdriver. That'll have the frequency."

Pippa leant Franco against the wall, and he waved weakly with his stump. "I'd give you a high-five," he coughed, "but looks like I ain't into that camaraderie-type shit anymore."

"What happened?" said Queen Strogger, eyes narrowed, lips drawn and gleaming, oil-smeared, chrome teeth shining. She was in constant pain, Franco realised. They didn't call it *cunt_wire* for nothing. It was a constant pain in the cunt... Even if you didn't have one.

"Ach! Ziggurat. 'Tis only a flesh wound. It'll heal. When I'm in Hell. Haha."

Pippa returned, holding what looked like a cross between a vibrator and a pistol. Queen Strogger read out various settings, and Pippa rotated the dials on the screwdriver's barrel.

She pointed it at them, and suddenly the cunt_wire went rigid, then flopped away. Queen Strogger and Anklebolt kicked their way free of the useless mass, like a nylon web, and stood, both with hands on hips, both with *attitude*.

"You in pain, soldier?" asked Anklebolt, her metal face mashing and shifting like cogs in a gearbox.

"Ach, don't you worry you none about my little arse." Franco was breathing heavily, face corpse-grey, eyes waxen and dull. "I'll be reet and dandy." His bravado knew no bounds. Nor did his stubbornness.

"Come here," said Queen Strogger.

"Eh?" said Franco, blinking, his eyes closing, then opening, then closing, then opening...

"I can help you."

"Er, you can?"

"Come here."

Pippa moved to Franco, and supported him as he walked over to Queen Strogger. In her torso, about where her belly button should be, an opening went *schlup*. To Pippa, who wasn't an expert in these things, it looked like a vagina. The puckered walls quivered, gleaming pink and wet. Pippa shivered. It just wasn't right...

"My Battlefield Repair Unit Upgrade," said Queen Strogger, looking into Pippa's eyes. "Trust me. I can help him. ORG INC. are the best machine inventors in the whole of Quad-Gal. We've had to be. Our religion depends on it."

Pippa gave a nod.

Franco struggled feebly.

"No! No! Not the belly-pussy again! I'm not that ill! Honest! It's just a scratch, mate, honest!"

Inside the quivering hole, Pippa caught a glimpse of complicated machinery, of spinning wheels and stepping gears. She swallowed, hard, as a stench of hot oil flooded out of the opening. Chains and weights spun and went CLANK. Franco was half dragged by Queen Strogger, half pushed by Pippa, and if he'd had his own way, had all his faculties about him, he would have turned tail and legged it.

The stump of Franco's arm was plunged into the gaping belly-mouth, and Franco screamed a high-pitched scream like a little girl who's fallen off her scooter and grazed both knees.

"Franco!" snapped Pippa, and he stopped, looking sullen. "You made less noise when Ziggurat blasted your fucking arm off! Be a man! Be a soldier! Show me why you're Combat K!"

"I'd rather be on a different planet," mumbled Franco.

"Be still," said Queen Strogger, not unkindly. "This won't hurt a bit."

"That's what they all fucking say!" screeched Franco, struggling hard now, but his severed arm was trapped in the old org's belly. Chains were rattling. Gears were crashing. From deep inside Strogger's body came several deep *clangs*. Then a ratchet sound. There were thuds, and a chugging noise like an old steam engine.

"*Noooo!*" wailed Franco. "Not ag*aaaiiinn!*"

CLANG SHUNK THAD THUCK SUCK CLANK CLANG CHUNK. There was a pause.

"Is that it?" said Pippa.

"Oh no," said Strogger. "That's just the beginning..."

CLANG SHUNK THAD THUCK SUCK CLANK CLANG CHUNK SHUNK THAD THUCK SUCK CLANK CLANG CHUNK CLANG SHUNK THAD THUCK SUCK CLANG CHUNK CLANG SHUNK THAD THUCK SUCK CLANK CLANG CHUNK CLANG THAD THUCK SUCK CLANK CLANG CHUNK CLANG SHUNK THUCK SUCK CLANK CLANG CHUNK CLANG SHUNK THAD THUCK SUCK CLANK CHUNK CLANG SHUNK THAD THUCK SUCK CLANK WHUMP RATTLE RATTLE *SHRING* CHUMP CLANG CHUNK CLANG SHUNK THAD THUCK SUCK CLANG CHUNK CLANG SHUNK THAD SUCK CLANK CLANG CHUNK CLANG SHUNK THAD THUCK CLANK CLANG CHUNK CLANG SHUNK THAD THUCK SUCK CLANK CHUNK CLANG SHUNK THAD THUCK SUCK CLANK CLANG. CHINK. CHANK. CHONK.

CHONK.

"Wahhhh!" said Franco.

CLANG SHUNK THAD THUCK SUCK CLANG CHUNK CLANG SHUNK THAD THUCK SUCK CLANK CHUNK CLANG SHUNK THAD THUCK CLANK CLANG CHUNK CLANG SHUNK THAD THUCK SUCK CLANK CLANG CHUNK CLANG THAD THUCK SUCK CLANK CLANG CHUNK CLANG SHUNK THUCK SUCK

CLANK CLANG CLANG SHUNK THAD THUCK SUCK CLANK
CLANG CHUNK CLANG SHUNK THAD SUCK CLANK WHUMP
RATTLE RATTLE *SHRING* CHUMP CLANG CHUNK CLANG
CHUNK THAD THUCK SUCK CLANK CHUNK CLANG SHUNK
THAD THUCK SUCK CLANK CLANG CHUNK CLANG SHUNK
THAD THUCK SUCK CLANK CLANG CLANG SHUNK THAD
THUCK SUCK CLANK CLANG CHUNK CLANG SHUNK THUCK
SUCK CLANK CLANG CHUNK. CHINK. CHANK CHONK
CLANG SHUNK THAD THUCK CLANK CLANG CHUNK CLANG
SHUNK THAD THUCK SUCK CLANK CLANG CHUNK SHUNK
THAD SUCK CLANK CLANG CHUNK CLANG SHUNK THAD
THUCK SUCK CLANK CLANG CHUNK SHUNK THAD THUCK
SUCK CLANK CLANG CLANG SHUNK THAD THUCK SUCK
CLANK CLANG CHUNK CLANG SHUNK THAD THUCK SUCK
CLANK CLANG CHUNK CLANG THAD THUCK SUCK CLANK
WHUMP RATTLE RATTLE *SHRING* CHUMP CLANG CHUNK
CLANG SHUNK THAD THUCK SUCK CLANK CHUNK CLANG
SHUNK THAD THUCK SUCK CLANG CHUNK CLANG SHUNK
THAD SUCK CLANK CLANG CHUNK CLANG SHUNK THAD
THUCK SUCK CLANK CLANG CHUNK CLANG SHUNK THUCK
SUCK CLANK CLANG CHUNK. CHINK. CHANK. CHONK.
RATTLE.

And then it was done.

Steam hissed from Queen Strogger's ears like
spurts of toxic poison, and Pippa stepped back,
releasing Franco, eyes wide, nostrils twitching at the
myriad of acrid, acidic odours.

Franco was suddenly released, and staggered back,
his arm held high in the air as a look of absolute
horror crossed his face.

"What's she done to me? What's she done to me? *Waaaahh!*"

"She's given you a new arm, Franco!"

Franco stopped. He lowered his arm. It was metal. He stared at it.

"Er," he said.

He flexed his fingers, and made a fist. Everything gleamed like silver. He rolled his wrist in both directions, then stared first at Pippa, then at Queen Strogger.

"Er?" he said.

"You have been repaired," said Queen Strogger.

"I ain't a fucking car..."

"FRANCO!"

"Er. Yes. Well. Thank..." he chewed his lip, face contorting. "Thank – you," he forced out between gritted teeth.

"You have been upgraded," said Queen Strogger.

"YOU FUCKING..."

"FRANCO!"

"Okay. Okay." He held up his hands. Well. One hand, and one metal appendage which looked like a hand. He took a deep breath. He looked at his face, reflected in his metal hand and arm. It was joined quite neatly to his flesh. There were only a few thin metal cables which broke through the skin of his recent stump. "I suppose I need to say *thanks*. Thanks for the, um, new arm. I'm sure I'll put it to a lot of good use."

Queen Strogger grinned at him. "I'm sure you

shall. I have also took the liberty of introducing various chemicals to your system."

"Chemicals?" Suspicion.

"Drugs."

"Drugs? Great!"

"Don't get too excited. Your human chassis is as weak as they get. I have given you antibiotics, and various anti-rejection agents to stop your own body fighting the cyborg additional. I've also pepped you up a bit; painkillers and stimulants and suchforth. Can't have you going to sleep on the battlefield now, can we?"

"Your concern for my welfare is much appreciated," said Franco through gritted teeth, voice dripping sarcasm.

"Good! Now then! Pippa! The way I currently understand this situation is that the Mistress and her sister, Tarly Winters, are waging war against the orgs. Their infantry and ships and weapons have set off to attack The Org States! Is this correct?"

"It is."

"We must stop them."

"I have a few ideas about that," said Pippa, smiling grimly.

THEY MOVED THROUGH The Monastery. It was deserted of personnel, and an eerie silence blew through the stone corridors. Outside the thick stone walls they occasionally heard shouts and yells and engines and rotors. But the army had moved on, moved away, headed off on its attack in the name of *LIVE TV!* on CLONE TV.

Queen Strogger led the way. She was purposeful now, head held high, mechanicals whirring and thumping in her cyborg body. Princess Anklebolt III followed, quite obviously subservient. Both orgs clearly understood – their whole world was under attack, and they had to work together to sort out the shit. Only afterwards could they resolve their petty differences. Which, surely, they would.

Franco and Pippa jogged along behind the two orgs who, despite their age and sheer mechanical size, made fast progress. Franco waved his metal arm about forlornly.

"Look what she did to me!" he hissed. "She made me... bionic! I have a bionic hand! I'm one fifth metal! I don't believe it! I just don't bloody believe it! I mean, of all the rotten stinking luck..."

"You're a moaning twat," snapped Pippa. "Most amputees would *beg* for what you've been freely given! You're a fucking ingrate, Franco Haggis. Be thankful you're still breathing the fresh mountain air!"

"TWAT! SQUAWK!"

"Oh great, the parrot's back. You big green COWARD! And hey, hey! Who're you calling an ingrate, anyway? An ingrate is it? But then, how could you understand *anything* about it, you're a bloody woman!"

"What's me being a *woman* got to do with it?" snapped Pippa. "You lost your arm! Now you've got a better one! Be pragmatic for once, will you?"

"Yeah but, y'know."

They'd stopped, Strogger peering up and down the deserted stone corridors. Then she set off, metal legs stomping across the cobbles, towards a steep spiral staircase. Anklebolt III followed. Behind Franco, out of reach of his bionic punch, fluttered Polly.

"'Y'know' what?"

"Just. Y'know."

"What the fuck are you talking about? I know Strogger said she was pumping you full of pills, but this is the Franco Haggis I remember from Mount Pleasant!"

"Don't mention that place."

"What, Mount Pleasant? The 'nice and caring and friendly home for the mentally challenged'?" Pippa grinned. "Go on. What's your problem now, dickhead?"

"This arm! This hand! It's just it's, my, well, *you know*, my *personal use* hand."

Pippa considered this. Only Franco could bring up the subject of *masturbation* on his way to a battle and impending death by bullets and detonation.

"Go on."

"Go on what? It's my, er, my *special hand*. Only it isn't anymore, is it? I mean, every time I do the dirty deed, I'll be bloody thinking about that there old Strogger machine thing, won't I?"

"Maybe it'll clean you up."

"Meaning?"

"Stop you being such a wanker!"

"WANKER!" squawked Polly.

"That's a bloody misrepresentation, that is!" snapped Franco.

"Yeah," continued Pippa, "maybe this will make the wild bad rag-tag Franco settle down, get married, have children. You know. The stuff any *normal* heterosexual individual is supposed to want to do."

"You ain't got no kids," sulked Franco.

"I ain't normal," said Pippa.

"I tried the marriage thing." He considered this. "First one became a zombie. Second *prospective* one became a... a kind of snake face."

"No way to talk about your fiancée, that," grinned Pippa.

"She's not my fiancée!"

"Did you break it off?"

"Er, no, but..."

"Well, you're still engaged then. Ergo, your fiancée."

"Just wait a bloody goddamn bloody bollicking minute!"

Pippa shivered. "I'd hate to be there on your wedding night. And just think of the mess when she *ate spaghetti!*"

"Here!" said Strogger, stopping before a huge wooden door. She raised her arms, and *split open*, a huge fat piston *whirring* out of her torso to smash the door from its hinges. It slammed backwards, destroying several shelves and leaving a pall of stone-dust hanging in the air.

"What is it?" mumbled Franco. "A sauna? A jacuzzi? A car factory? I can just hear the lads now, hear 'em with their mocking laughter, with their jokes and rib-poking. Old Claw Hand, they'll call me. And every time I pick my nose, I'll punch my nostrils through the top of my skull!"

"It's the armoury," said Pippa. She turned, face sombre, eyes gleaming through the dust. "Come on Franco. Stop moaning. It's time to tool up."

BROADCAST... CLONE TV LIVE TV! []
REALITY WAR PROGRAM, "WARGASM," EPISODE 1, CUE MUSIC, CUE CREDITS, ROLL CREDITS>>
WARGASMLIVE>>
(C)HG20201 CLONE TV/ LIVE TV!
CUE INTRO... ZOOM OUT, CROSS-FADE...
GOING LIVE IN THREE... TWO... ONE...

"And ho, ho, ho! Welcome folks to this, the first live SWITCHING ON of our new live reality TV show, WARGASM! brought to you by the one and only CLONE TV, here from our very own CLONEWORLD, 3rd Quadrant Quad-Gal Cluster 5567#. You can rest assured, folks, you ain't never seen anything like this before, ho, ho, ho, and oh, look, you can see now the Q-Wing Fast Jets are here, give them

all a wave as they zoom past on their way to their first bombing runs over our despicable and horrific enemy, THE ORGS! Ho, ho, ho!"

Above The Org States, over the vast western coast, a line of three hundred Q-Wing Fast Jets appeared, carrying underwing SlamBam ClusterBombs. They flew with perfect precision and unity, as befitted pilot squadrons of *clones,* who thought in exactly the same way and were, in fact, perfect imitations of only one man – the best fighter pilot Clone Terra had ever produced.

The Q-Wing Fast Jets appeared, a glittering arc of speeding triumph, and as they reached the coast of The Org States they peeled apart, heading on individual missions and bombing runs. Right down the western seaboard of The Org States, gun turrets came alive on every available rooftop, and heavy calibre machine guns started booming and pounding, hot casings ejecting as millions of bullets spun, screaming, through the skies, guided by flickers of green and orange tracer. The Q-Wing Fast Jets' guns thundered, peppering and shattering the orgs' high buildings. Across the six cities on the western seaboard of The Org States – namely Synch, Dog, Mekal, Outpost 12, Outpost 9 and The Rod – missiles and bombs sailed through the heavens. Explosions detonated across the skies, and through the cities. Towers toppled, screaming, trailing dust and smoke and flames to the scream-filled city streets. In the blink of an eye, a calm and moderately civilised world was plunged into chaos. In the click of finger and thumb, sanity became insanity, law became chaos, calm became storm, love became hate.

"And ho, ho, ho! Look at our brave ganger pilots go, raining down filth and pollution and hot retribution HELLFIRE on those dirty bastard orgs! But here comes the fun part! Soon, the CAM DRONES – a full ten thousand of the little beauties – will separate and link to individual remote handsets BACK IN YOUR OWN HOMES! That's right, folks, all you people out there in TV LAND will HAVE CONTROL OVER THE BATTLE! Have you ever heard such a crazy notion? Ho, ho! When you see this symbol flash up in the bottom left hand corner of your screen, you can access our LIVE TV! LIVE WAR! WARGASM! TV WAR MENU! You then have four options controlled by the buttons on your remote control!

"Now listen carefully, folks. This is so easy, even you stupid SOFA CHOMPERS and BLOBBERS and BURGER STUFFERS and FAST FOOD FUCKNUGGETS can do it! Let's say a Q-Wing Fast Jet is bearing down on a dirty scumbag school hall filled with screaming children – press your RED BUTTON to machine gun them all! Press your GREEN BUTTON to send a missile into the school! Press the YELLOW BUTTON to use the undergun flamethrowers – ho, ho, ho, just smell the dirty flaming chargrilled child orgmeat cook and sizzle! – and finally, and this is the beauty, folks, the BLUE

BUTTON *can be used for* OCCASIONAL SUICIDE ATTACKS!

"*That's right! We have a true special treat for all you folks here in* CLONE TV LAND! *We've got together with* QUEEN STROGGER, *that's right, the one and only* QUEEN *of the* ORGS! *And she's, heh-heh-heh, given us all their dirty machine secrets! So, we've bred up some lovely smushed gangers in the Slop Pits and Slush Pits and Dirt Boxes and Fat Vats, and then we've – and you're hardly going to believe this folks! – we've* USED THE ORG MACHINES ON THEM TO CREATE ORG GANGERS! *Now these happy volunteers are to be used in suicide missions, for those oh-so-hard-to-target targets such as inner city schools, compound hospitals, underground church halls, you know, those really hard to find places where civilians cluster and whimper like* BIG GIRLS! *Ho, ho, ho, folks! You heard it here first!* CLONE TV! WARGASM! WAR HAS NEVER BEEN SO MUCH FUN, BABY!"

OUT IN THE military training grounds, nearly all practically deserted, around fifty huge screens had been erected – presumably for use in training exercises, or maybe for light entertainment during R&R (not that anybody thought, in their wildest dreams, that the psychopathic Mistress would *allow* any R&R). Now, the screens were blazing with images blasted across Cloneworld from ten thousand AI remote CAM DRONES, programmed to cover *the best of the action, baby!*

The massive screens played out images of The Org States being bombed, strafed, detonated, smashed; all blasted across the screens; HUGE NOISE screaming from the speakers. Schools and hospitals and factories and tower blocks were bombed and crushed and smashed. Orgs ran screaming through the streets, only to be cut in half by machine guns (get that lovely blood spurt! just as the CAM DRONE darts through in a neat tracking shot). Orgs exploded, showering their surroundings with limbs, both natural and metal. Dogs and Archies were sent howling, peppered by bullets, spinning end over end into piles of rubble. It was Entertainment Evil on a huge scale. It was Insanity TV. It was the Massacre Movie of the Moment. It was Stupidity, squared to infinity.

"I just *don't believe it*," said Pippa, standing, mouth open.

A cold wind blew across the deserted parade grounds, bringing with it trailing wisps of snow. It smelt of ice, and desolation, and death.

"That's the craziest thing I've ever seen," agreed Franco, voice low. Then he looked over to Queen Strogger and Princess Anklebolt III. And although Franco had had his moments of antagonism with the two orgs, moments of confusion, and stupidity, of anger and hate and sheer frustration, the looks on their faces felled him as readily as any lump-hammer thud to the back of the skull.

Queen Strogger was crying, tears of black oil running down her metal-patched face. And it wasn't just her tears that conveyed her misery, but the look of total, utter hopelessness on her face. Because she knew, *knew* that at least partly, this was her own fault. She had brought the org secrets of machine-building and flesh-merging to the gangers, and they had imprisoned her, and built their own army of org clones, and no matter how skewed their motivations for TV war, Queen Strogger had been in a position to help. But she hadn't helped. And now, it had come to this...

"I cannot believe this is happening," said Queen Strogger, as guns and bombs, bullets and explosions blazed across the screens. Toddler orgs were smashed out of prams. Women-orgs screaming in the streets were smashed in hails of bullets, emblazed in unfurling petals of fire, peppered by payloads of burning hot shrapnel.

Pippa moved to her, carrying a brand new MPK from the Ganger Armoury. "You couldn't have stopped it."

"I could have tried!"

"Well, now we try," said Anklebolt III, moving to her mother. She took Queen Strogger in her arms, and gave her a big, metal-stinking hug. There came various *clacks* and *clangs* as the two cyborgs clumsily embraced. "I'm sorry, mummy, truly I am. For all the things I said and did."

Franco and Pippa exchanged glances. It was like watching two industrial refrigerators make up.

"And I'm sorry, little Anklebiter. I wasn't always

there for you like a proper mum should have been. What with all the five hundred other screaming, mangy orgs snapping at my ankles..."

"That's all right, mummy. That's all right."

"There there, Princess."

"Snuffle-snuffle, mamma. Love you."

"Love you too."

Both orgs were crying, and hugging each other, although from a distance it could have been mistaken as a violent wrestling match between two earth-moving diggers.

"We need to move," said Franco. "We need to sort out this shit." His face was still ashen, but even more so from the scenes on the TV. It was one thing to be involved in war – war for a reason, war for a cause, no matter how misconstrued or politically twisted. But it was quite another experience to witness war being used for the sake of pure entertainment. For TV ratings. Warporn, for all the wrong reasons, the bad reasons, the fucked-up-perversion-of-humanity-and-all-its-twisted-deviants reasons.

Franco was wearing full combats, boots, and a pack stuffed with two D5 shotguns and bombs. Lots of bombs. He carried Kekra twin-barrel machine pistols. And he chewed a cigar. He looked the business. No, he looked *more* than *the business*. He looked The *Fucking Business*. Franco was ready to put this war down, like a scabby, rabies-riddled dog snapping at his testicles, like the worst of annoying yakker snakkers. It was often said that war was evil.

This one *was*. And Franco knew exactly where to strike to make the bad go away...

"Okay." He looked around, and Pippa moved to stand beside him. "The Mistress has headed off in her War Balloon. Mad, I know, but then she's mad as a..." he smiled, "an eel in a bucket of snakes. And, like a snake, we cut off the head and the body dies real fucking fast."

"We can't stop the invasion," said Queen Strogger. "There's too many of them! Their firepower, their technology, they have control of airspace and all the damn GASGAM anti-aircraft AIs! And they have GASGAM loaded nukes to finish the job off! How could we stop all that? We're doomed!"

"Well," said Franco, eyeing Pippa. "I think Pippa has a few surprises up her sleeve with the programming on the nuke stuff. Teddy Sourballs didn't have such a keen eye as she thought. But first, we need a way through to the Mistress – we need to take her out, and we need to take out her camera crews. If we can disrupt her TV transmission, she loses the whole purpose of the invasion."

"There's soldiers, over there." Pippa pointed. They could see a battalion in the distance, still going through drills. They hadn't heard the men over the noise of the giant screens showing slaughter and carnage.

"Probably some reserve raw recruits," said Franco, rubbing his bristled chin thoughtfully. "I have an idea about that. But first, we're going to need vehicles. Pippa, you and Anklebolt head over to those WarSheds, see..." His voice trailed off.

A naked woman was walking towards them.

Tarly Winters.

"Uh-oh," said Pippa, taking a step back. "She's looking *real pissed*. She's your wife, Franco, why don't you deal with the bitch!"

Franco stared at Pippa. "I ain't married to her *yet!*"

"Well, she looks pretty angry to me. Maybe you forgot to buy the ring?"

More snow was falling, and Tarly's feet were leaving neat little footprints. Queen Strogger stepped forward, her legs and torso extending on their hydraulics and machine guns clattering out of her forearms and shoulders. Her teeth ground together.

"This bitch helped to bring this war to my people!" growled Strogger. "I want to deal with her."

"Er, yeah! Be my guest!" enthused Franco, who was never at his best when dealing with women at all, much less angry women – which happened a lot. Or at least, more than he'd like. Or could afford.

"Hi, love!" he said, giving a small half-wave as Queen Strogger, growling and hissing like a runaway train, strode out across the rocky parade square to meet her nemesis.

Tarly glanced at him and pointed. "I'll deal with *you* later!" she snapped, as Strogger broke into a thunderous, mechanical charge. At the last moment, her huge fist came up and over, and a massive hydraulic piston thundered out, slamming into Tarly Winters from above and burying her deep into the rock with a *BAM!* so loud the mountains shook.

Smoke curled from around Strogger's piston-fist.

Slowly, and oozing cooling oil and steam, Strogger reversed and retracted the piston, dropping tiny lumps of rock into the pit she'd just created.

"Well," chirped Franco, happily. "That's the end of that, then! Let's just say it was a happy divorce *before* the necessity of the wedding ceremony." He was unreasonably chipper; it was nauseating to witness.

Tarly rose from the pit vertically, unharmed, and her feet touched down on the rim. She grabbed the still-retracting piston, and twisted, flinging the huge, mighty Strogger a good hundred metres down the parade ground.

Strogger rolled like a marble, steel and iron and alloy parts grinding and crashing, sending showers of sparks into the air and cutting deep jagged grooves across the alloyconcrete.

"Shit," said Pippa, blinking, and hoisted her MPK. She flicked off the safety catch.

Franco glanced down. "Er. You think that'll work?"

"It's worth a fucking try, unless you've got a better idea?" snapped Pippa.

Franco hoisted his Kekras, and they unleashed a payload of screaming bullets on General Tarly Winters, bullets spinning and whining through the air, thumping into her flesh with *thump-thump-thumps* as she turned from Strogger's flailing, rocking body – like a turtle stranded on its back – lowered her head, staring straight at Franco –

And ran at them...

Franco shook his yammering gun, as if urging it to fire yet more bullets through willpower alone. Hundreds of bullets slammed into Tarly Winters, but were absorbed into her flesh, ejected from her naked back as if passing through molten wax, like maggots wriggling from a corpse. And all the while, her flesh *squirmed,* like snakes in a barrel, noodles in a honey-pan, larvae in a nest of rotting, rancid corpse-meat.

"*Shiiiiit...*" screamed Franco as Tarly came closer, and closer, and then she was there, grinning at him, and she swung her arm left, snapping Pippa's still-juddering MPK machine gun in two, and reached through Franco's gunfire to take his Kekras from him like toffees from a child. She tossed them aside, where they clattered across rock.

"Hello, Franco," she said.

"Er, you wouldn't hurt me, would you, love? After all, we *are* going to get married!"

"That's a cheap trick," growled Pippa.

Tarly turned on her. "Shut up, *bitch.*" She back-handed Pippa and sent her rolling off across the parade ground, blood spraying from smashed lips.

Franco held up his hands, and started to shuffle slowly backwards.

"Now listen, love..."

"I'm not your *love!*" squealed Tarly, and leapt – to be caught around the midriff in the pincer grip of Princess Anklebolt III's expanded mechanical hand. It was huge, like a set of giant pincers, each hinged gripper exploding to the size of landcar.

Anklebolt threw Tarly into a giant TV screen. The glass shattered, screeching, and the hundred-foot screen *imploded* with a detonation of electricity. Power surged through Tarly Winters, sparks ejecting like industrial fireworks *through her* as she jiggled in the centre of the screen, energy pouring through every atom. When finally the light show ended, Tarly toppled from the centre of the destroyed screen, hit the ground with a wet smack, and slowly stood up and rested her hands on her hips.

"Uh-oh," said Franco, and looked around in panic. He rushed over to Pippa, and helped the Combat K killer to her feet.

"I think you upset her," said Pippa, wiping blood from her mouth with a grimace.

"*I* fucking upset her? Why is it always me, eh? Why can't it be some other dumb schmuck?"

Tarly charged Anklebolt, looking ridiculous – like a midget attacking a giant. Again, the pincers came crashing down, but Tarly was ready and dodged the blow. Anklebolt's steel claws smashed through the rocky ground and lodged there. Tarly walked casually around Anklebolt's back, leapt up, and ripped something *free* from her spine. Anklebolt went suddenly rigid, and almost with a gesture of contempt, Tarly dropped a small cube to the ground and kicked it away.

She turned and looked at Franco.

He gulped.

Tarly started towards him.

"What's wrong with her face?" said Pippa softly, head tilting, eyes narrowing.

Franco blinked. Something *had* happened to Tarly's face during her massive electrocution in the giant TV. Now, it was open to her brain, or open to *something* slick and glossy inside; slick, and glossy, pulsing, and glooping. Fingers of snake tentacle wavered around the open pit of her face, like the half-burned petals of a predatory flower.

"That's pretty damn gross," said Franco, weakly.

"She's *your* fucking fiancée!" snapped Pippa.

"Will you *stop* saying that!"

"Distract her! I'll be back in a minute!"

"*What?*"

And then Pippa was gone, and Franco flapped around in a sudden panic, running to grab his discarded Kekras and turning back just in time to stare at his betrothed marching towards him, her face detonated open. He went weak at the knees. Suddenly, his biomechanical arm didn't feel like such a disfiguration.

Tarly stopped in front of him.

Franco could see through to the centre of her skull, the hole surrounded by wavering snake tentacles, each snake having its own set of eyes and an open maw and flickering tongue.

"I hope you ain't come for a snog," said Franco.

"No, Franco, my darling," said Tarly, and her voice was tinny, distant, as if she'd swallowed her voicebox and was speaking from inside her belly. "I've come here to kill you."

"That's all right then," he snapped. "Because if I had to kiss *that* then I'd *want* to be fucking dead."

Tarly squealed, a high-pitched buzzing noise: half woman's scream, half hissing snake. She leapt at Franco, who stumbled back, Kekra coming up to fire directly in her open face, her open *brain*, unleashing screaming bullets on hot streams of fire and gas that ate into Tarly, kicking her back to roll, and come up fast, and leap again. Again, Franco fired a volley into her snake-rimmed face, watching with horror as the snake tentacles wriggled and thrashed, the centre of her head seeming to *absorb* the bullets and spit them out the back of her skull. The white flesh was churned up, but no blood came out, and Franco was back-pedalling, panting, and he realised with a mental kick he needed his grenades, lots of fucking grenades! But the best he had was in his pack. On his back. With the shotguns. *What bloody good are weapons on your back, slackboy nutjob?* his mind screamed at him. *You're a gremlin-faced dumb-arse pot-bellied Combat K reject!*

Hey! he snapped back at himself. *I didn't realise my fiancée's face was going to explode and wriggle*

*like a can of industrial maggots on a fishing trip,
did I?*

Tarly forced her way forward like a climber
through a blizzard, leaning into the onslaught as
she approached, and Franco went paler than pale.
For the second time she snatched his guns. The hail
of fire halted, leaving a ringing sound reverberating
through the snow, and she lifted the guns to her
open face and... *ate them*. The snakes thrashed in
a feeding frenzy, and from the back of Tarly's head
came curls of hot metal shavings, ejecting with wisps
of steam and a high-pitched *zinging* sound.

"Er," said Franco, backing away even faster.

"That wasn't a nice thing to do to a woman you
shared such *intimate* experiences with," said Tarly,
snakes writhing.

"Er," said Franco, and in a rush, scrabbled with
his pack, yanking free a D5 and presenting himself
aggressively, as if to say, *A-har! You didn't expect
that, did you?*

"Tut, tut," said Tarly. "You're so predictable."

"And you're so *dead*, snake meat!" A BOOM echoed
across the rocks, and echoed back from the rearing
mountains. Franco peered through the smoke to see
how much damage he'd done – which was none at all.

"Foolish," said Tarly. "*That hurt.*"

"Yeah, well, it shouldn't have done – you already
look like a woman with her head torn open!" She
grabbed the gun with a fluid movement that left
Franco staring stupidly at his hands.

She levelled the D5 at him. "Let's see how you like it," she said.

"Now don't be like that, love," said Franco, lifting up both hands and cringing.

"SQUAWK!" Polly screeched at the last moment of her vertical dive from high above, and Tarly glanced up – to get the parrot Special Friend full in the face – hole – thrashing-tentacles – whatever. There was a metallic *whump,* and Tarly dropped the D5, both hands snapping up to the parrot now wedged in her head-hole, pecking like mad, its beak a flurry of violent activity as Franco dropped to his knees and scrabbled in his pack. He pulled out two BABE grenades – so named because they gave you a good *fucking*.

"Polly, get out of there!" screamed Franco, but he needn't have shouted. Tarly had grabbed the bird, and dragged it slowly away from her face – along with ribbons of her own stringy, writhing snake flesh.

Polly was flapping and squawking. Tarly threw the metal bird to the ground and ground it underfoot. The Special Friend flapped around listlessly, emitting *pops* and little blue sparks, and then was still.

Tarly looked up.

"Catch!" snapped Franco, and threw a BABE grenade into her open writhing face. There was a pause, but a short one because Franco had initiated a slam-fuse – then a *BOOM!*

Tarly went spinning backwards, black smoke pouring from her head, and Franco rubbed his hands together and grinned. "Job's a good 'un," he congratulated himself, and walked cockily to Tarly's prone, shattered body. He stared down at the blackened stump of her neck. He'd quite literally *blown her head clean off.*

"I fucking told you not to mess with me," said Franco, wagging his finger. "Everybody underestimates Old Haggis, so they do, but this time you got it, and you got it good."

Smoke drifted from Tarly's detonated head.

Her leg twitched.

Franco glanced back, to see Pippa emerging. She carried a yukana sword, and Franco shouted, "Hey, little lady, you won't be needing that anymore! I did the job, and did it well, with a good old bomb!"

"Franco!" she screamed, and something about the look on Pippa's face told Franco it was damn serious. And he was right. Hands grabbed his arms, and he struggled for a moment, wrestling with... with...

He turned. "But... you're dead!" he wailed. She obviously wasn't. Yes, she had no head, but more snakes had erupted from the scorched stump of her neck, wavering around madly, little black eyes staring at him with unabridged evil. "Get off!" he struggled. But Tarly was strong. Real strong. "Get it off me!" screamed Franco, fighting as hard as he could, but he was outclassed, and he knew it...

There was a *hiss*, a slap of flesh, and one of Tarly's arms came free. Franco gawped, uncomprehending. There came another hiss from Pippa's yukana as she cut Tarly's other arm off. Both arms were still holding onto Franco and he staggered back, a creature of four flapping arms, and howled a long, high howl as befitted any man put through such trials and tribulations. He tried to pull free the severed arms, which still gripped him and squeezed and shook. He screamed and slapped at them, and they quivered, and he tugged at them, and Pippa ran to him, cutting them again into four pieces. Finally, the pieces fell to the rocky ground and Franco danced back like a man on hot coals. "Eugh! Eugh! Eaurch!" he was saying.

"Keep away from them," said Pippa, and turned her attention back to Tarly. She was standing perfectly still, armless, headless, and Pippa wondered how many more bits she'd have to cut off before the bitch got the message. Suddenly, Tarly Winters... *shattered*. Or melted. Her body seemed to turn into a blob, sinking down towards the rocky ground in a fattening mass. From her clothing burst a hundred pale white snakes, and they wriggled in a high-speed frenzy, down between the rocks, down into cracks and holes and gaps, down through snow and ice and – Pippa blinked – in an instant, the snakes were *gone*. Tarly was gone.

"It it dead?" muttered Franco, grabbing his D5 shotgun and poking one of the cut arms with the toe of his boot.

"I... don't think so," said Pippa. "Gone, but not forgotten, yeah?"

"What a bitch," said Franco.

"You pulled her."

"I didn't know she was an alien!"

Pippa levelled a beady eye at him. "Yeah, right, that's what they all say. I'll go and help Strogger and Anklebolt. But you!" She pointed.

"Yeah?" he said, suddenly bright at the prospect of *not* having to marry General Tarly Winters.

"Go and see to the parrot."

"AND HO, HO, ho! Here we are above the battle, with the Mistress herself LIVE in her War Balloon! Hello, there, Mistress, can you tell me how do you think the war is going?"

"The War is going very well, Eamonn, and as you know we've sent in our Q-Wing Fast Jets and delivered a series of bombs across all manner of dirty, stinking org cities... we've had heavy casualties to various infantry battalions in the capital city of Org, but we're on our way there now, because that seems to be the orgs' focus of defence. Are you getting some good footage?"

"Oh, yes, Mistress! This is the most wonderful thing ever to happen on LIVE TV! Earlier, at the Heap7 Mountains, we had a swarm of ten thousand infantry bravely overrunning an enemy org position of several HUNDRED orgs! It was stunning! The slaughter was terrible, unfortunately, because the dirty, stinking orgs refused to lay down their weapons and surrender and be shot, but there's always atrocity in war, that's what I always say! Ho, ho, ho!"

"Yes, always atrocity in war. Now if you'll excuse me, I have to co-ordinate the HTanks, HJeeps and HCarriers as we advance on the capital city of The Org States."

"Yes, of course, Mistress, no problem, Mistress, and there she goes, our voluptuous and fabulous Mistress! Lets hear it for her from the studio audience, and I'm sure she'll be joining us later for the After-War Tactic Talks with Dermot O'Dreary..."

The War Balloon cruised through cold high-altitude air, the Mistress leaning on one alloy rail and gazing down at the landscape below. There, she could see five battalions marching across metal deserts, whole dunes of iron filings shimmering and sparkling in the cold sun's haze. And there, a hundred HTanks humming towards the Steel Forest to rain a hundred thousand shells into the tangled steel foliage to flush out the renegades. It was pointed out to the Mistress that surely they should concentrate on the main point of battle, the assault on Org itself, and she listened attentively to her Generals and then waved them away. She was not the sort of woman to take advice from subordinates – *any* subordinates! She found the tactics which had once worked in education worked equally well in warfare. After all, her point of view was the *only* point of view, wasn't it? Other people were there simply to make noise. Yes, *they wanted* to sound like they were giving opinions and a variety of alternatives, but all they were *really doing* was greasing their own CVs, right? It was simply the way of the world.

The War Balloon shuddered as a huge gun emplacement fired a shell at it. Her own guns turned on the AA weapon and thundered, raining down fire and bombs and pounding it – and a surrounding town, in its entirety – into oblivion.

To call the vessel in which she rode a *War Balloon* was to understate the vehicle. It was massive, a truly titanic Zeppelin made from brass and silver, each panel of the strange construct's decks shimmering under the cold light. The actual *balloon* part of the vehicle itself was a liquid metal orb with intrinsic anti-grav properties, and this main bulbous chamber – nearly a kilometre long – could therefore not be punctured in any way. The liquid metal simply rolled back into position when fired upon and stayed aloft.

She had named the War Balloon *Conqueror,* and smiled every time she considered the simplicity and gravity of the name.

"Mistress!" It was Teddy Sourballs, barbed-wire hair bobbing, rancid face screwed into a little ball of hatred and constant misunderstanding. "There are reports that we've taken great losses in the south, mainly at the armoured cities of Zeg and Zob."

"How many casualties?"

"Fifteen thousand infantry and three hundred tanks, at least."

"Did the cameras capture it?"

"No, Mistress. I've just despatched a platoon of CAM DRONES…"

"What? No fucking cameras? Am I *truly* surrounded by fucking retarded retards?" she raged, and clutched at her own hair, pulling out clumps. "What's the point of staging a live fucking war on live fucking TV, if we don't film the live fucking action and live fucking deaths? Hey?"

"No reason, Mistress," said Teddy, hanging her head miserably.

"Get *over to those fucking Order Consoles and sort it out!*" she screeched.

"Yes, Mistress."

"And Teddy?"

"Yes, Mistress?"

"Make me a cup of tea when you've done that, okay?"

"Yes, Mistress!"

FRANCO APPEARED, BEARING his screwdriver and grinning. "There. That should have spanked the monkey."

There came a grinding sound, then a *clank*. With a long drawn out groan, Princess Anklebolt III levered herself upright and clenched her fists. "That little bastad! If she wasn't already dead, I'd kill her!"

"We have more pressing matters," said Pippa, hurriedly.

"Such as?"

"The war's acceleration. The gangers are attacking the city of Org."

"How do you know that?"

"I've been watching it on the telly whilst Franco's been fixing your ass."

"Fair enough."

Franco packed away his toolkit and hefted a D5 shotgun. "Okay Pippa, you seem to be on the money. What's the deal? What's the plan? What's the gig, sweet lips?"

"The Mistress has kept a thousand jets here in reserve. So we need a thousand pilots."

"So, our own army, then?" mused Franco. He frowned. "Hey! Those guys, over there!" He pointed. "Must be damn near a *full battalion!* If we could get those guys to come with us, we'd have ourselves an army!"

"We can't use them," said Pippa, shaking her head.

"Why not?"

"Trust me, Franco. We can't."

"Ha! Snot and bloody bollocks! I'll convince them, you see if I don't! Just you watch me! Just you watch me charm their pants! Just you watch, there's still life in this fat, saggy old body yet. They don't call me Franco 'The Sexy Snake Charmer' Haggis for nothing, okay?"

"You didn't charm that last snake," said Pippa.

"Ooh, below the belt, below the belt." Franco hoisted his shotgun and set off across the battle-scarred parade ground. Halfway across he turned, and shouted, "Just you watch me! I'll stun you with my charm skills! You'll be stunned, you will! Stunned!"

"Not as stunned as you," muttered Pippa.

Queen Strogger settled down next to her, with a hiss and a clank. Pippa glanced at the old wrinkled org, and realised she really, really liked the old... woman. She'd miss her if she was gone, that's for sure.

"A clever tactic."

"What do you mean?"

"Who better to persuade a battalion of Francos than the template himself?"

"Do you think it'll work?"

"No."

Pippa looked into Strogger's ancient eyes. She felt a chill in her soul. "Why not?"

"It's been tried. A hundred times. A thousand times. It's an instinct thing. When the gangers tried it, in test after test, the clones always turned on their ganger template."

"Why?"

"Because a clone who knows it's a clone has the world's biggest inferiority complex. It's hard enough getting a kid to listen to its mother. Imagine if you were just a copy? Not even your own individual; just a *copy*. Not real. Not *human*. And then some bossy bastad turned up and started telling you what to do, because it was your genetic *master*. Would *you* listen?"

"Oh. Shit. I see."

"Good luck to him."

"Do you think I should go help?"

"No," said Queen Strogger. "From what I've witnessed, if there's one mad fucker who can pull this off, it's Franco Haggis."

THE BATTALION WERE going through endless drills without any form of drill sergeant when Franco drew close. His eyes narrowed as he watched their formations, their movements, their military executions. "Sloppy!" he muttered to himself. "I mean, just look at the way they're holding their guns! Like it's a length of severed flesh, or something. *No respect,* man." He moved yet closer, boots slapping the rocky ground. "And look at that! You call that a fast march? I've seen *dead people* march better." And he had.

The battalion wheeled about, stood to attention, brought their MPKs to shoulder height, and saluted.

"What a sloppy fucking salute," muttered Franco, scratching his head. "If a soldier of mine saluted *me* like that, I'd slap him around the whole bloody drill square!"

Closer, closer, closer...

"And just *look* how overweight they are! Carrying their bellies like they've *eaten* a pregnant baboon, or at least fifteen vindaloos and twenty-seven pints of Japachinese lager. A fucking disgrace, is what it is. Where's their CO?"

Franco looked around. Then he stopped.

Slowly, he turned to stare at the battalion, who now stood to attention once again, big bellies bulging over sloppily-pressed uniforms. Left unattended for just a few hours, boots were now unpolished and scuffed. Some shirts were done up like crazy pirate rigging. On a few of the men, Franco could even see the ragged string vests they wore under their army shirts.

Slowly, as one, the battalion wheeled to face Franco.

Two thousand boots stamped.

Franco's eye twitched.

With great care, he moved towards the soldiers – the *thousand* soldiers – who looked exactly the same as him.

"Ho. Lee. Jee. Zus."

The thousand or so *Franco Haggis* clones turned to look at the lone ginger squaddie as he walked up and down before them, muttering, looking at the floor, looking at them, looking at the floor, muttering, looking at them again, looking at the floor... and their eyes followed him wherever he moved. Without a sound.

Finally, he stopped, and put his hands on his hips, and stared at them.

"Reet," he said, and even as a thousand squaddies' sloppily-polished machine guns levelled at him, he did not blink, did not flinch, did not back down in the face of insurmountable odds. That's the sort of insane and stubborn bastard he was.

"REET!" he bellowed. "Looks like some bastard's been taking a liberty! Looks like some bastard's stole my genetic wotsit, and copied me, and I'm not that bloody happy about all that!"

Silence greeted him.

"Do any of you even *recognise* me?"

Silence.

Franco took a deep breath.

"I am your leader!" he announced.

Still, silence.

"I am your Master, your Template, the Spunk from which you have been copied like cheap and skanky third-rate porn magazines! You know, those really dirty ones you sometimes borrow, with all the pages stuck together."

Silence.

"I am your Boss. You will do what I say! I need you to follow me, over there," he pointed with his metal hand, and their eyes followed his metal finger for a moment before returning to his battered, bruised and scruffy exterior, "and we'll talk *then* about your shit-scruffy uniforms, your retrograde attitude, your ridiculously sloppy drill, and how the fuck you can manage to even *think about* calling yourselves soldiers!"

Still, silence.

Franco started to sweat a little.

One Franco Haggis stepped forward from the line. He stared hard at His Master. His Template. His Boss.

"Who," he said, and pointed, "the fuck are you?"

The entire battalion burst into uproarious laughter, slapping their knees, slapping each other's knees, giving high-fives and generally having a great old laugh at Franco's expense.

Franco beamed beetroot red. Then a scowl overtook his face. He looked far from even a hint of happy. "*I* am Franco Haggis!" boomed Franco Haggis, proudly.

The Franco who had stepped forward, turned to his mates, then said, "No, *I* am Franco Haggis."

Another clone stepped forward. "No! *I* am Franco Haggis."

Yet another: "No! *I* am Franco Haggis."

And another: "No! *I* am Franco Haggis."

A fifth: "No! *I* am Franco Haggis."

A sixth: "No! *I* am Franco Haggis."

"Wait! Wait!" Franco held up his hands. "I can see this is going to take a *fucking* long time, yeah? I get the joke, guys. I've seen the filmy. Heard the monkeytapes. But listen up, we have a situation and I need YOUR help. The Org States are under horrible, terrible attack! The gangers have invaded, and are slaughtering civilians in their beds..."

"Aren't we the gangers?" said one Franco.

"We sure bloody are!" said another Franco.

"Damn and bloody bollocks! Does that mean we're missing the fight?"

"Yeah, and the party afterwards!"

"With lots of fat chicks!"

"And PreCheese!"

"CubeSausage!"

"Horseradish!"

"Beer!"

"Guinness!"

"Alcohol!"

"Any alcohol! We'll drink the entire fucking country dry!"

More laughter.

Franco grasped his own head with his own clawed hands, and groaned. For the past thirty years, Franco Haggis had been a considerable pain in the arse to anybody with the slightest sniff of authority over him. He recalled incidents, hundreds of incidents, *thousands* of incidents, where he'd been vacuous, drunk, or deliberately obstinate and boorish. He remembered all the women he'd abused, all the COs he'd thumped, all the AIs he'd bad-mouthed, and all the beer he'd quaffed.

In terms of discipline, Franco Haggis was the *worst* a soldier could get.

And here he was, faced by a thousand of his own kind. And not just his own kind, but *his own personal brand of bastard*. Franco groaned. If he'd had a gun, he'd shoot himself. Then he realised he had – and for a few moments seriously considered it. Because, and this was a galling thing to admit, but gradually – like a new sun dawning over a virgin world – Franco Haggis came to realise, and accept, what a truly awkward *cunt* he'd been for all these years.

"Okay," he said, and flapped his hands. "Listen. Listen. LISTEN, YOU USELESS, FAT BUNCH OF IDIOTIC MOTHERFUCKERS!"

A thousand narrowed eyes snapped to lock on him. He realised, with a grin – and yes, it *was* the sort of grin you offer Death when he's arrived to kick your awkward arse all the way back to the Chaos Halls – realised he'd just insulted himself. And it was a fair and just insult. Franco Haggis *was* a useless, fat, idiotic motherfucker.

He sighed.

"You starting trouble, son?" asked one Franco, cracking his knuckles.

"'Cos if you are, you'll be getting some," said another.

"No, wait, wait," said Franco, holding up his hands again. Then an idea struck him. He gave a crafty sideways smile. Now – NOW! – was the time to use cunning, and crafty, foxy guile. After all, they didn't call him Franco 'Crafty-Arse Fox' Haggis for nothing now, did they?

"Go on, Fat Boy, spit it out."

Oh! To be insulted like that by yourself! So cruel!

"Having fun, are we?" snapped Franco.

"What's that supposed to mean? We've got a war to fight, y'know. We might only be reserves, but we're damn and bloody important reserves, you get what I'm saying?"

"Yeah, yeah, I know," said Franco, purposefully dropping his voice so the huge group had to shuffle a little bit closer. "But – well, you know how these battles and things go. You must have a good leader, with this Mistress-type tart, yeah?"

"She's a bit of all right," said one Franco. "Tits are a bit small, but we're not that fussy, are we lads?"

"Nooooo!" roared a thousand voices.

"AND WHAT DO WE ALWAYS SAY?" bellowed the improvised ring-leader.

"NOTHING'S NICE AS TITS, FRANCO!" they all shouted, and leant against each other, roaring with laughter, roaring and roaring until the *real* Franco Haggis was tempted to shoot the whole fucking bunch.

When the uproar had finally ended, and the collective Francos were wiping tears from their eyes and snot from their noses, the original Franco Haggis held up his hands for some semblance of quiet, which was only interrupted by the occasional fart or belch. Sometimes the two at the same time.

"Okay. This is how it goes. Has this Mistress-woman-type offered you an after-war party?"

The Francos looked at each other. A few shook their heads.

"Indeed, *has* this Mistress-type leader of yours offered you copious amounts of whiskey? Hot fat women with boobs you could use as inflatables if you were stranded at sea? Sexy, young, slick chicks in military uniforms with cans of custard and jelly?"

There was muttering now. And a few cross faces.

"Has this Mistress type leader offered you a full MONTH's R&R, with access-permits for free beer/whiskey/alcoholic-beverage-of-your-choosing throughout ALL THE BARS of Cloneworld? Hmm? Has she?"

"She damn and bloody well hasn't!" snapped one Franco squaddie clone.

"Well, lads," said Franco, puffing out his chest. "I can."

The Franco clone scratched his stubble. "Yeah. But. Isn't that, like, going against our morals kind of thing? I know we're a scruffy, hairy bunch, but we have our morals. They may be way down the ladder of such things, but when we says we'll do something, we'll do it. REET, LADS?"

"REET, FRANCO!" they thundered.

Franco ground his teeth and his mind worked fast. "Yes, yes, yes, BUT you are me, you are my clones, and I have much more information about this whole situation which I'm willing to share with you – about the unjustness of killing millions of innocent orgs in an unprovoked attack, the fact the whole shebang is being televised just for entertainment's sake – WAR as FUN, yes? And the fact that the Mistress is a snake-filled alien freak! And finally, FINALLY, I can offer you women and beer and sausage! What more does a fat lad need?"

The Franco seemed to consider this. They muttered amongst themselves as Franco stood, tapping his foot impatiently. At last the self-appointed ring-leader turned and beamed.

"We'll do it!" he said.

Franco beamed. "Thank the Gods of Chaos for that! Come on! Do any of you guys know how to fly Q-Wing Fast Jets?"

"Of course," said the clone, without any hint of

irony. "They don't call us Franco 'Ace Hot Pants' Haggis for nothing, you know."

Franco led the thousand Francos back across the rocky parade ground. They did not stride in any form of battle-organised unity. They were a straggling bunch of limping gimps.

As they walked, Franco said, "So, which bit did it?"

The clone grinned at him. His eyes twinkled. "Meaning?"

"Which moral angle of my fine oratory changed your minds?"

"Oh, that? We'd already agreed to come fight for you. That sexy lass Pippa talked to us a few hours before you arrived; convinced us what we were doing was wrong. We just decided to wind you up a bit. You know. Show you what a pain in the anus you really are."

"Ah," said Franco, scowling as he padded along. "Aah."

STROGGER AND ANKLEBOLT had gathered their available troops in a giant hangar where the reserve Q-Wing Fast Jets were housed. In the last hour, every Franco had tooled up, suited up, and was armed to the gills with enough guns and bombs to take out a small army – which was, indeed, what they intended. Strogger and Anklebolt, with occasional interjections from Pippa and Franco Haggis, outlined their objectives. Their primary aim was to bring down the Mistress.

Cut off the Head of the Snake. Take out the leaders, and the clones will follow.

Franco climbed up the ladder of his Q-Wing Fast Jet and, as the cockpit lifted, saw that several feet behind him, Polly had been inserted into a special little cubby-hole for Special Friends.

"She'll be your navigator," called Pippa from the adjoining Jet. "Make sure you don't get lost."

"She'll bloody make sure I go insane," growled Franco.

"Squawk! Gottle of rum! Gottle of rum!"

Franco waved his fist at Pippa, and they both donned helmets and climbed into their Jets.

Franco fired all systems, and heard the whine of warming matrix jets. The comms buzzed into life. "Brown Leader, this is Brown Five calling in. Do you copy, Brown Leader?"

Franco scowled. Brown Leader? Why the fuck did *he* have to be Brown Leader?

"Er, Brown Leader here, over."

"Brown Leader, this is Brown Two calling in. I have full systems on line, Brown Leader."

Franco glanced over to Pippa. She was Pink Leader. Now that was fine. That was great. That was *cool* for a sexy hot-pant-wearing military-type chick. And Strogger! Strogger was Silver Leader. Again, fine if the majority of your internal organs were made of mercury and iron filings. Anklebolt had the best though: she was Rainbow Leader. Franco had wanted the Rainbow Leader tag, but Anklebolt had give him a dirty look –

which can be quite impressive, with a face made of metal gears and cogs and shit – and Franco relented.

Franco gave the signal, and as a thousand Q-Wing Fast Jets lifted slowly, vertically, into the air, engines roaring, jet ports glowing, and then left the huge gaping doors of the hangar in their team formations and swept through the falling snow into a cold, bleak, dark storm sky.

"Time to sort this shit out, Brown Leader," said Pippa over the comm.

"Yes, over," said Franco through gritted teeth.

"You know what the lads have started calling you? Over," said Pippa, and Franco thought he heard a snigger as he lifted his Fast Jet higher, and winter sunlight glittered through his cockpit, splaying radiated patterns across his console. Up here, he felt suddenly wild and free. It had been a long time since Franco had been in a fighter jet. Slowly, the intricacies of the airborne weapon were coming back to him.

"Go on," said Franco, "although I'm sure it has a variation on the theme of excrement. I know these lads. They're, er, me."

"Mr Poo. Over," said Pippa, with a chuckle.

Franco shook his head, and grinned. Some things would never change.

"Mr Poo, over and out," said Franco, and pulled back on his control stick. The Q-Wing Fast Jet howled and lifted its nose towards the sky. Below Franco, Cloneworld spread out as a rolling, beautiful tapestry.

To the east he could see distant explosions, fiery trails, and the signs of battle against a tiny-detailed map.

Franco grimaced. All thoughts of comedy left him.

"Brown Leader, this is Silver Leader, over."

"Go ahead, Strogger, I got you, over."

"I've got a lock on – the Mistress is in a War Balloon. She's heading for the Org Palace. Her jets have taken out the main Defenso-Guns." There came a pause. Franco could sense Strogger's horror over the comm. "Franco. They've got a Disintegrator."

Franco licked his lips. A Disintegrator was *heavy duty* Quad-Gal Military hardware. It could remove land targets with one blast – HUGE land targets. Even whole *cities!*

"Where did the mad bitch get that from?"

"I don't know, Franco. But she's going to destroy the Org Palace! All my children are there!"

"What? All five hundred and thirty three?"

"Yes!"

For the first time since he'd met her, Franco heard the true woman inside the metal hulk of Queen Strogger. There was no machine there. Just pure humanity. And it spoke to the core of Franco's soul.

"Don't panic, Silver Leader. We're going in. Over and out."

Franco switched his comm to an open channel. "All Leaders. All Fighters. Lock your Q-Wings into Attack Positions."

"Yes, Brown Leader!"

"Agreed, Brown Leader."

"Let's kick some snake-arse, Brown Leader!"

"Time to sort this shit out," Franco muttered, cruising fast at high altitude, his wingmen behind him in a staggered V with him at the tip. Licking his lips, he activated the High Action Weapon Console, set his navigation computer – Polly – to the capital city of Org, and locked his Q-Wings into Attack Position.

The City of Org.

That's where the psychopathic egotistical narcissistic nutcase known as The Mistress planned her final, ultimate explosion...

Of course.

How else would she achieve the dramatic climax for her Live TV! show?

Franco put the Q-Wing Fast Jet into a dive, his squadron in close pursuit – and with grim smile, began the attack run.

CHAPTER FIFTEEN

CLONEWORLD

"MISTRESS! ENEMIES APPROACHING fast!" cried Teddy Sourballs.

"How do you know?"

"They've just shot down a hundred Q-Wing Fast Jets!"

"And what, pray, are the enemy flying?"

"Q-Wing Fast Jets!"

"*What?* How? Only *I* own Q-Wing Fast Jets on this godforsaken ball of shitty rock!" The Mistress was frowning, and ran to the barrier. She peered up into the bright, winter-sun heavens, where, even as she watched, several more Q-Wing Fast Jets were shot down, spiralling towards the ground in swirling balls of flame. Black dots raced through the sky, heading straight towards her War Balloon...

"I don't believe it!" she hissed. "It's that Franco and his battalion of Francos!"

"Mistress?" Confusion.

"It has to be! Why, the slimy little corrupt bunch of back-stabbing bastards! They've turned on me! They've gone against me, even though it was *I* who instigated their cloning! I created them! I am... their *Goddess!*"

"I don't understand..."

"General Banks!" screamed the Mistress. "Get clones to the Flak Cannons! Let's shoot the traitorous whores out of the sky!"

"Yes, Mistress."

A hundred Q-Wing Fast Jets howled overhead, guns thundering, and the War Balloon shuddered. The Flak Cannons yammered, flames blossoming from barrels as they filled the skies with shells. Ten Q-Wing Fast Jets were smashed like clay pigeons from the heavens, glittering under merciless sunlight, and went spiralling down to the city below, trailing smoke and shattered metal.

"Coming round for another pass," bellowed Banks.

"How's the Disintegrator?"

"Ninety-eight percent charged, Mistress!"

"Range?"

"Estimated time to firing range... three minutes."

"Good." The Mistress rubbed her hands, her fingers merging into one another, into snakes, then checked her monitors. The CAM DRONES were flitting about, filming, and she called back a hundred in order to film the action on the Org Palace – on, indeed, the whole city below. When she unleashed the Disintegrator, it was going to start at the palace and work outwards in concentric rings of slow detonation, leaving *nothing* behind. Then she'd fire the GASGAMs. Nuke every fucking city in The Org States!

It would be the best Reality TV show EVER MADE.

She would be a GODDESS of the MEDIA GALAXY!

The MISTRESS would, effectively, RULE the QUAD-GAL's entire MEDIA NETWORK!

The Q-Wing Fast Jets howled overhead, guns thundering, a manic-faced Franco in the lead fighter. Guns yammered and howled. Flak Cannons pumped thousands of shells into the speeding Fast Jets. The sky was a flickering haze of shrapnel and fire. Smoke billowed. Ships detonated. The War Balloon shook with multiple impacts... but it was no good. The War Balloon absorbed everything thrown at it. The War Balloon was indestructible.

IN THE AIR, Franco was fighting with the controls of his own Q-Wing Fast Jet. "God, this is an awkward bugger to control," he snapped, chewing his own teeth as he brought them around for another attack. Below, Pippa's squadron raked fire across the War Balloon as, below them, the Org Palace swung into view, at the heart of Org itself...

They had *minutes!*

Minutes before the Disintegrator did its evil work.

"Franco? It's no good! The War Balloon's too strong!"

"We need to take out the command bridge," snapped Franco. "Listen. You cut across the axis and try and draw their fire. I'm going in."

"What are you going to do?"

"I've got a bone to pick with this fucking *Mistress*," snarled Franco.

"Pink Squadron! To me!" said Pippa over the comms, and their ships lifted, slamming vertically towards the sun before sweeping around in a wide arc. "You've got one chance, Franco," muttered Pippa, but in her heart of hearts she knew, *knew* he'd never be able to pull it off. No pilot was that good. Or that lucky. It was a million-to-one chance...

Franco's Q-Wing Fast Jet came thundering around, Flak slamming along one flank and then powering off into nothing. Franco's squadron was close behind. He'd lost a few jets, but all in all they were still tight, still a unit...

"Listen up," growled Franco to his team. "This is what I'm going to do."

He explained.

They listened.

"That's impossible," said one Franco.

"If you've got a better idea...?"

"Well, bozo, it's your bloody neck you'll snap!"

"Then so be it!" snarled Franco. "Come on! Let's do it!"

Engines screaming, his two hundred Q-Wing Fast Jets came around on a wide trajectory and accelerated directly at the War Balloon...

THE MISTRESS GRABBED Teddy Sourballs by the throat. "They're going to fuck it all up!" she screamed. "Get yourself out there, lead a squadron of Q-Wing Fast Jets and engage them ship–to-ship!"

"What?" snapped Sourballs, her barbed-wire hair bobbing, eyes suddenly wide. She was an *English teacher*, not a damn fighter pilot!

"You heard me!" growled The Boss. "Do it! Now! Before I pull your bowels out through your stupid, flapping mouth!" The Mistress's face exploded into a shower of wavering snakes. Teddy Sourballs stared at her illustrious leader, her own mouth opening and closing as the Mistress's whole *head* became a wavering mass of slithering, wavering snakes. Like a pumped-up, drugged-up Medusa in tentacle-ridden overdrive. A Medusa whose snakes had usurped her face.

Teddy nodded, and rushed to the rear of the War Balloon's deck, shouting commands and waving her arms manically. Twenty clones joined her, and they climbed into Q-Wing Fast Jets and, engines howling, hammered from the relative safety of the War Balloon's decks.

Immediately, guns were thundering. The Jets spiralled between Pippa's squadron and the sky was filled with a chaos of fire and bullets.

In her cockpit, Teddy Sourballs was muttering, face a screwed up scowl, eyes narrowed, hands gripping the control stick tightly. *Send me out on a fool's errand, would you? Send me out on a damn suicide mission, would you? You're insane! You've let it go to your head! You call yourself the Mistress, the bloody* Head *Mistress, but what a lot of horse shit that really is! You think you're in Total Control! You think you're a Goddess! But you're not. You're an alien. And you hate the gangers as much as you hate the orgs — and all life that is not of your own species.*

Guns thundered. Bullets *thudded* up the cockpit's side, making Teddy flinch.

What am I doing here? Why am I doing this? I'm a long way from home. I'm a long way from sanity. I'm a long way from what I used to be... what happened to me? What happened to reality?

She gazed around. Hundreds of ships flew around her, guns blazing. Missiles fired, gleaming in the sunshine, to stream off after their targets.

Teddy seemed to dance a random, crazy path through their midst.

She was untouchable.

Immortal!

She laughed, a crazy laugh, high-pitched and whining.

I am no longer your slave, Mistress! You no longer command me, you no longer control me! I'm a free agent! As far as I care, you can stick your own stupid head right up your own fat arse and chew your own liver!

Suddenly, the Q-Wing Fast Jet veered left, dipping towards the city of Org far below. She glimpsed the War Balloon in her monitors, with the blue glow of the massive Disintegrator at its nose.

Teddy Sourballs laughed, a crazy laugh, and her hands were tight on the controls.

I'll show you who's the real Mistress around here!

"Squawk!"

"Do that at the wrong moment, muppet, and we'll both end up fried chicken meat!" snapped Franco. His hands were tight on controls. He held the Q-Wing Fast Jet steady.

"You're insane!" squawked Polly into her microphone.

"Shut up."

"You're mad as a rabid butcher's dog!"

"Shut up."

"You'll get us both killed and strung out!"

"Better that, than the entire city destroyed."

"Wanna bet, squawk?"

The Q-Wing Fast Jet came in fast, its entourage of Franco-piloted jets in a streaming V to either side, protecting Franco's craft with heavy duty firepower as he came around and slammed with a *boost* towards the War Balloon itself...

Aboard the War Balloon, General Banks took a

Flak Cannon in his own gloved hands and fired at the enemy craft, squeezing the trigger over and over. Q-Wing Fast Jets were slammed away in balls of glowing flame to either side of Franco, but still he came on, faster and faster and faster...

"The force is strong in this one," muttered General Banks, before giving a short, sharp scream and running away from the Flak Cannon, his arms curled protectively about his head. He now *understood* what the mad ginger squaddie was about to do...

It was a suicide mission.

The Q-Wing Fast Jets accompanying Franco peeled away in neat, tight arcs at the very last moment, guns still pounding, bullets and rockets strafing the War Balloon. But not Franco.

His head was lowered, eyes narrowed, and he came on strong...

General Banks sprinted past the Mistress.

"What are you doing?" she snapped, and he gestured vaguely behind him as he legged it for cover.

The Mistress turned, peering down the long flat decks of the War Balloon, past computer consoles, parked fighters and HTanks and HJeeps, and a thousand soldiers all standing at attention in straight defensive ranks, MPK machine guns at the ready.

"No!" she said in disbelief, face and head snakes wriggling. "It cannot *be!*"

Behind her, the Disintegrator started to vibrate. Huge blue pulses were emanating from the orb and the viral stacks. The humming of constrained, *contained* energy had grown exponentially until it was hurting the eardrums of every clone ganger aboard...

"It needs to be fired! Unleashed! *Now!*" screamed General Banks, from where he cowered behind an alloy bulkhead... but at that moment there was a titanic *crash* as Franco's Q-Wing Fast Jet hit the deck, ploughing into and through ten HJeeps in a massive shower of sparks and crunches, and the screaming stressed sounds of compressing, twisting metal. The Q-Wing Fast Jet turned as it slid, tearing down the War Balloon's deck and ploughing through a scatter of infantry who, still turning to run, were tossed aside like broken skittles. The Jet spun fast, slamming more HJeeps outwards as if slapped by the Hand of God. Its wings were torn free with banshee shrieks, and yet still it ploughed on, towards...

The HTanks.

"Ha!" snapped the Mistress, and put her hands on her hips. "You crazy fool! Let's see you go through *those!*"

The Q-Wing Fast Jet would detonate for sure.

FRANCO, HANDS JUDDERING on the control stick – which no longer controlled *anything* – watched several platoons of ganger infantry squelch and break as they were tossed upwards and backwards, over his blood-smeared, flesh-drizzled cockpit.

"SQUAWK! What now, idiot? If you hit those tanks you'll be squashed like a bug under boot!"

This is it, certain death! Unless...

The HTanks loomed like some big-ass baddy in a terrifying computer simulation. The parrot was right. Nothing was ploughing through the HTanks. In fact, the HTanks would absorb him, explode him, spit him out more readily than any machine-god planet core...

"*Aiieee!*" screamed Franco, thumping the [EJECT].

There came a clunk. A hiss.

And Franco was [EJECTED].

With a short sharp scream, Franco was fired vertically from the cockpit of the Q-Wing Fast Jet. The Jet spun again and connected with five HTanks, which exploded in a blossoming fist of raging blue fire and energy. Franco was hurled upwards, the roaring ball of fire tickling his arse until, with a soft *whump*, he was absorbed, like so many bullets and missiles before him, into the *liquid metal* of the War Balloon's *balloon*.

Everything was silent.

Everything was silver.

Franco spun like a top, arms and legs akimbo, his world engulfed by the silver mucus of the balloon. Slowly, the energy of his violent [EJECTION] was absorbed, and his spinning slowed. Then he realised with horror that he –

Could. Not. *Breathe...*

Franco started to swim, started to swim *fast,* but the mucus was far thicker than water and the *horror* and *stupidity* of his miscalculation suddenly struck Franco like a brick. It had been a *simple* plan. It had been a *good* plan. Plough the Q-Wing Fast Jet onto the deck of the War Balloon and, if the shit hit the fan, eject into the liquid membrane of the balloon itself –

Only. Only *now* he had no point of reference.

He couldn't breathe.

And he didn't know which way was *out*...

Franco struck out strongly, muscles burning, screaming at him, his sight and every other sense lost to the thick silver fluid engulfing him. His mouth was tight shut, nostrils quivering as the thick shit tried its best to invade his skull...

Bright stars began to flutter like flutterbugs in his brain.

He was fast running out of oxygen.

He was going to die.

Damn and bloody bollocks! To die like this! What a ridiculous way to go! What a stupid way to die! I thought I would go in a firefight, machine gun juddering in my sweaty fists, or grappling with big fat muscly men in vests, or away on some foreign battlefield with a BABE in my skull! Not here, like this, drowning in anti-grav piss!

And the Mistress, damn her! She will have won!

She'll disintegrate the Org Palace, then the city, then the whole fucking country!

Oh, the shame!

Franco spurted a bubble, which floated away.

Then another.

He swam on in panic, chest burning, muscles screaming, and just as he thought – *he knew* – he was about to suck in huge lungfuls of liquid anti-grav War Balloon balloon matter, he felt a stab against his right hand.

His flapped his hand in pain...

There came *another* stab.

He flapped his hand again! *Gerroff...*

Then something tiny, like a pincer, took his finger and *pulled*. And in Franco's oxygen-dwindling brain he realised *something was trying to help him, to guide him...* He swam in the direction of the pull, in which he was being drawn, and more stars were fluttering until –

There came a slow, languorous *pop*.

Like a greased baby eagerly ejected from his panting mother's womb, Franco slid from the balloon, covered in a thick silver membrane, and hit the deck with a useless slap. He sucked in great lungfuls of air, and opened his trembling eyes, reaching up to scrape the silver liquid out of his eyes.

Above him, there came a second *pop* and his saviour was revealed. It was Polly the Parrot, [EJECTED] a few moments after Franco from the crashing Fast Jet. It was his Special Friend. His Special Friend who had *saved him*, guiding him to safety with the tip of her metal beak.

Franco groaned.

Oh no!

Not again!

He sat up, as a hundred gangers surrounded him. They pointed MPKs at him, snarling, and Franco slowly climbed to his feet, crippled by the liquid anti-grav matter. "This shit is worse than treacle," he muttered.

"You there! Haggis!"

The Mistress was marching towards him, her face gone, a hundred snakes waving and spitting venom. Franco put his hands on his hips, a snarl on his face, and spat out a long quivering gloob of spittle.

"Yeah, bitch?"

"How... how... how dare you! I am the Queen of the Gangers! I am their Goddess! Their Mistress! I am about to destroy their enemies! Look!" And she pointed, to where the Disintegrator was practically dancing against its restraints. It was so filled with energy, with *charge,* that it looked pretty much ready to *burst*.

"You dumb-ass point is, venom-tits?"

The Mistress pointed to the clones, then to Franco, snake-hands trembling with suppressed rage and a need to strangle the little ginger bastard. "Kill him," she said. "Do it. Do it *now...*"

TEDDY SOURBALLS LOWERED her head, and accelerated, and behind her, her faithful squadron of gangers followed in close formation. She realised, in a moment of clarity, that this thing had to end. They had allowed the Head Mistress to rule them for too long – from School to Politics to Media to Global Domination. Absolute power corrupts absolutely, guaranteed, and the Mistress had wielded way too much power for way too long. So much power, she even *believed* her self-created legend.

You think us gangers have no pride?

You think we're just slaves to your fucking entertainment? To your Rule? Your Dominion? To your impending Quad-Gal Empire?

The gangers are nobody's slaves.

It crept up on us.

Like a bad dream.

But now.

Now, we're going to change that.

"General Banks?"

"Yes, Ms Sourballs?"

"Send out the message."

"Yes, Ms Sourballs."

FRANCO STARED AT the clones with a snarl in his beard. "Come on then, fuckers, one at a time or all at once, it's all the same to me!" He lunged, kicked one ganger in the balls, punched another across the jaw, breaking it, then took an MPK from a pair of stunned hands. He whipped the gun barrel around to face the Mistress's wavering snake-head.

"Anybody *moves* and I'll blow her, er, snakes clean off!"

Nobody moved.

The Mistress began to chuckle, a weird hissing, chuckling, gurgling sound, as if a hundred tiny snakes were making the noise; which, of course, they were. Suddenly, a huge snake head erupted from the centre of the Mistress's neck stump and, with a single, terrifying bite, chomped the MPK in half.

Franco took several steps back.

Behind him, the gangers likewise took several steps back.

The snake roared, and it was as thick as a human carcass, skin pale white like the bulging, rotten intestine of a disembowelled corpse. Maggot flesh gleamed. Black eyes stared hard at Franco – and at the thousand clone soldiers who, as one and without order, turned their guns *from* Franco and *towards* the Mistress.

Franco backed away further.

He sensed, somehow, that she was now the Common Enemy.

It's not every day your War Leader turns into a big snake.

"You fools!" hissed the snake, tongue flickering so fast it was a blur. The Mistress's legs staggered a little, as if struggling to hold the vast weight of the huge beast within. Around the thick scaled head, smaller snakes wavered constantly, like a hundred stalks of AI spaghetti biowire. "You think *any of you* can stand in the way of my Quad-Gal domination? Fools!"

Franco stared down at his half-chewed MPK, and dropped it with a clatter. He pulled free one of his faithful Kekra quad-barrel machine pistols and pointed it at the big snake.

"What you gonna do? *TV* everyone to death?"

"When you control the media, you control the Empire," said the Mistress and opened her mouth, opened it wide, slick skin spreading back over pale white jaws until only yellowish fangs could be seen – and then, from this huge orifice, poured snakes, hundreds and hundreds of white snakes, which hissed and slithered, rearing up to attack the clones...

The gangers yelled in sudden panic, turning to run. Bullets whine and slapped. Snakes struck out, biting, injecting venom...

A snake reared at Franco. He yelped, and shot its head off in a slurry of pulpèd snake-meat. More snakes flowed past, heads darting out to strike the clones. The poison was fast-acting, and many were dead before they hit the deck.

Suddenly *everything* was a crawling, slithering, bullet-yammering chaos. Franco's guns boomed and clattered, and he danced sideways, yelping, watching blasted snake heads go slithering across the deck. He suddenly realised what was happening: a diversion.

He glanced up. The Mistress, with her huge, thick, pulsing snake head, was walking unsteadily towards the Disruptor. It was ready to fire; damn, it looked like it was ready to *ejaculate!* And it'd take out the entire Org Palace in one blast! Strogger's entire family! Then, the city beyond... and who knew where it would stop? Neither the Disruptor, *nor* the

Mistress, would stop until Cloneworld was a barren wasteland. What did she have to lose? She'd got her Live TV programme. *And* she'd massacred the Orgs...

Franco growled and started after her.

Five snakes reared up before him, slinking out from beneath an overturned HJeep, heads snapping, jaws clacking, poison spitting. He fired with a yell, bullets whining, churning through snake flesh. The Mistress glanced back, but then she was there, at the huge weapon. Blue light danced in her black snake eyes. It reflected eerily from her slick, pale skin.

She reached out, just as Franco's last Kekra bullet removed the head of the fifth snake in a messy pasta splatter, and he yelled, "*Noooo*!" But she was there, and the distance was too great.

He tried anyway.

Sprinted with all his might...

"Pink Leader, do you copy?"

"Copy you, Silver Leader."

"How's Franco doing, over?"

Pippa slammed around in the Q-Wing Fast Jet but, at this speed and distance, the decks were just a blur. And then she saw... *them*: enemy Jets coming popping up out of nowhere. She armed her guns and gritted her teeth, but a little voice inside her head saw their trajectory, saw the pulsing blue glow of the Disintegrator – and she gasped in realisation and pulled up at the last moment, guns silent.

Teddy Sourballs ploughed her Q-Wing Fast Jet straight into the heart of the weapon. There came a hiatus of total silence, then a sudden explosion of blue light and a deafening BOOM that sent every Q-Wing Fast Jet in a two-klick radius spinning uselessly through the skies. Pippa grabbed her control stick, wrestling with the stalled Jet as the *pulse* kicked her up and away from the War Balloon and the centre of battle. Panic rose suddenly in her chest. Around her, every other Q-Wing Fast Jet was suffering the same fate, describing a high arc until, as one, they started to fall from the skies like a squadron of detonated birds...

"YOU WANT ANOTHER CUP OF TEA, MOTHERFUCKER?" screamed Teddy Sourballs, as her Jet ploughed into the Disintegrator. "WELL FUCKING SIP ON THIS!" and there was a deafening roar that ate through her, and consumed her in totality, and as she was blasted into a billion atoms of oblivion by raging blue fire, Teddy Sourballs died with a smile on her face. Now *that* taught her a lesson...

ONE SECOND, FRANCO was reaching out to grapple with the distant figure of the Mistress. The next, a Q-Wing Fast Jet appeared in the heart of the Disintegrator and Franco knew, fucking *knew* bad shit when bad shit was going down, and he hit the deck hard and fast, rolling towards a HJeep as a ROAR blasted across the War Balloon like a nuclear detonation, and blue light pulsed and raged, and the wind was a firestorm of hot ash and metal splinters. The War Balloon rocked and swayed like a tree in a twister. Franco covered his head and closed his eyes, but then thought, *that's the way dumb bastards die*, so he crawled beneath the HJeep as, above and around him, clones were torn off their feet, screaming, smashing along the decks like tumbling dolls to be spat out the rear deck like bomb-blasted confetti. HTanks were rocking in the shockwave, and a HJeep to Franco's left was picked up and thrown down the decks, crashing and smashing into other vehicles and stranded clones as it went.

Through the raging wind Franco stared at the Disintegrator. It was gone, as was the Q-Wing Fast Jet which had hit it. But the Mistress was still there – just.

She was no longer a body, just a thousand long, wavering strands of flesh, not even recognisable as snakes. It was like an unravelling of intestine. It was spaghetti gone sour. It was a squid put through a squid-mincer. And it was hanging onto the detonated Disintegrator as all around it the world roared...

Slowly, determinedly, Franco started to crawl across the deck of the War Balloon.

Got to stop it, he thought.

Got to kill it!

How could it survive that blast?

And how the hell was the War Balloon still flying?

His answer was soon answered.

The War Balloon *wasn't*...

There came more terrible roars, like secondary detonations. The War Balloon slowly, gradually tilted, until its nose faced the ground far below, and they were almost, *almost* vertical. Still the wind and blue fire from the Disintegrator rolled along the deck – from front to back. And as Franco looked up, he saw the problem immediately...

It was *melting* the balloon's anti-grav matter.

The balloon was gradually losing the one thing that kept it airborne.

"Why's it always me, eh?" muttered Franco, and continued crawling along the deck towards the remains, the *still-living* remains, of the Mistress, who was herself clinging onto the weapon console and reaching for –

The GASGAM nukes.

Franco groaned.

"What!" he screamed down the deck. The Mistress seemed to shudder. "Haven't you had *enough*? Isn't it *enough* that you're a pile of fucking torn-up tagliatelle? What more do you *want*? Carbonara sauce and a Caesar side-salad?"

Franco commando-crawled –

Then threw himself left, as a HJeep was picked up and bounced along the deck towards him. He rolled around, hands covering his head, as it left a three foot *gash* beside his quivering body and bounced off along the tilting deck to disappear, sweeping hapless clones off the deck with it.

On, Franco crawled.

Onwards, towards the Mistress.

Onwards, towards his bitter enemy...

And he realised. *Hey! The crawling's getting easier! At last! A positive bloody result! At last! Some beady-eyed god up there is trying to give old Franco a bit of a helping hand, a bit of lee-way, a bit of a hitch up the old ladder of positive progress...*

Until he realised.

He was crawling faster, because the War Balloon was *falling*.

Franco peered up, and peered down, and saw the capital city of Org getting gradually bigger down below. *There,* he could see the docks, where the friendly party led by Anklebolt III had brought him in after his adventures with the org pirates. *There* were the narrow streets, surrounded by thousands of needle-like steel towers, through which he'd been transported in a bar-walled prison truck. And *there* was the Org Palace – seat of power for the pretty much crazy-as-a-rabid-dog Queen Strogger and her weird and twisted offspring.

Franco eyed the steel towers getting closer, and closer, and closer...

Aah, he thought. *Aah. Shit. That looks pretty bad. That looks like maniac shit. That looks like a whole universe of fucknuggets...*

Daggers.

That's what they look like!

We're falling towards a thousand skyscraper-sized daggers...

Suddenly, Franco had less desire to kill the Mistress in her current tangled, distressed confetti format, and more desire to *get off the damn War Balloon.*

He forced his head right, and could see the barrier. He crawled along, past several struggling snakes also fighting to get... somewhere. Where? Back to their Mistress? Franco reached out, grabbed one, and with a *hiss* sent it spinning off in the raging hot wind. Blue flames ignited the snake, and at least Franco got a little satisfaction from watching the evil little bastard *burn.*

Come on, Haggis! Move your sorry ass!

He struggled towards the edge of the barrier and gripped it, and forced himself into a diagonal half-stance. There was a *clack* as Polly the Parrot landed next to him. She looked a little battered, and traces of balloon anti-grav matter still clung to her alloy feathers.

"Squawk! Well then, buster?" said the parrot.

"Can – you – contact – Pippa?" forced Franco from between gritted teeth.

"Squawk! Sorry. My comms are all shot to shit. You're on your own, buster!"

"Why? Where you going?"

"I'm bailing out, buster! When this baby crashes, it's going to take a quarter of the damn city with it! Have you ever *seen* anti-grav nitrex matter when it goes up? Kaboom!"

"KABOOM?" repeated Franco, staring hard at the parrot. "What the fuck am I supposed to do?"

"Can't help you there, buster! *Sorreee.*"

"Hey, I thought you were my Special friend? *This little special friend will be your friend. A friend for life!* That's what you said! '*As you read this, a genetic sample has been taken from your fingertips and relayed digitally to the DumbMutt's brain. He is now yours. He will never leave your side. He is forthwith electronically registered to your unique DNA number and as such will follow you to the ends of whatever planet you inhabit [insert here] or travel to [insert here] or plan to travel to [insert here]* FOR EVER.' You hear that? Words like, 'never leave your side' and 'a friend for life.' That's what you said, you traitorous, back-stabbing little bag of alloy shite!"

The parrot shrugged. "Hey. Times is hard, my man! SQUAWK! This one, you gotta solve yourself..."

And then Polly was gone. Franco waved his fist.

"Some damn bloody Special Friend you turned out to be!" he screamed into the raging hot wind, mixing now with the swirling cold uplift from the War Balloon's downward acceleration.

Maybe there's some control left? he thought, manically, self-preservation kicking him in the balls.

Franco Haggis struggled onwards, fighting his way past more rattling HJeeps and several clones, still hanging on for dear life. One by one, he watched them picked up and sent plummeting and spinning away.

He glanced up.

He was only *metres* from the tangled mess that was the Mistress. She was making a sound, Franco suddenly realised. A *hissing* sound. And with a grim scowl, he realised she was *laughing*. The tangled mess of massacred snake meat was *laughing at him...*

Franco scowled, and reached up, dragging himself up to the blackened, blasted control panel. He slapped at it ineffectually. It was dead. Deader than a dead dodo.

"Damn and bloody bollocks!"

"To think it would come to this," said the Mistress.

"What's that?"

"You got the 3Core. You stopped the war! But you'll *never* live to see any of the benefits! If the 3Core works – which it won't, because you don't know the *special* unlocking codes – *if it works* and the junks are pacified, their invasion halted, a better Quad-Gal for everybody... well, you'll still be dead, and buried in a pit with me for all eternity!" Her laughter rolled out, and Franco squinted, trying to see where she was laughing from so he'd know where to shove the next BABE grenade.

"Aah, get to fuck," said Franco. "At least if I die, I'll know you're dead too. So bring it on, that's what I say! I no longer GIVE A SHIT!"

"But of course you do." And her voice was perfectly calm.

"You know the unlocking codes?" said Franco, anger dissipating.

"Yes."

"What are they?"

"They are my very *genetics*, Franco Haggis. You need a sample of my DNA to get the 3Core to work. Don't you understand? *I* was the junk's mainframe – their biocomputer. A living, breathing *machine*. But I am so old, Franco Haggis. So terribly old and *bored*. The junks have come back, but the 3Core will stop them. If only you could live, to tell QGM how to cure them. How to use the 3Core! How to use my *flesh and soul!*"

"Too weird," said Franco.

"But you understand?"

"I understand."

Franco glanced to the right. The taller org towers were coming into view, and Franco winced. They were going to impact with the ground – really soon, and really fucking hard. There was no way he could survive. No way at all.

Have I had a good life? he thought.

Have I been a good person?

Well. You've done some bad things. You've killed some people. But in your heart, in your soul, you always tried to do what was right. Okay, so a lot of it was right for your own personal gratification, but deep down, deep down in the very core of your being, you are a Good Man. You have Heart. You have Courage. You have Spunk. And you have... Humanity.

Tears were rolling down Franco's cheeks. Through his beard.

I have Humanity, he thought.

*   *   *

Pippa wrestled with the controls of the Q-Wing Fast Jet, and like so many of her flying companions, thought she was going to die. She kept frantically stabbing at the starter, and as the ground rushed towards her a scream started to well in her throat... just as the engine whined, and burst into life and *power*. Pippa wrenched back on the control stick, and around her hundreds did the same, and the Q-Wing Fast Jets arced hard, spent exhaust fuel leaving cloud trails through the narrow city streets of Org... then up, up, *up* in crystal blue skies...

Franco!

Pippa wrenched on the controls, and saw the War Balloon in its long, almost painfully *slow* dive towards the city as anti-grav matter fought the planet, rumbling so deeply it made the very streets tremble.

Pippa slammed the Fast Jet around in a huge arc, and powered towards the War Balloon. *If she could just get alongside the falling War Balloon! Make a grab for Franco Haggis!* But she realised, suddenly, and with a dry bitter mouth, that rescuing Franco would be an impossibility. She would be too late.

Come on, soldier! Never give up!

She tore along, riding the waves of energy still pulsing from the dying Disintegrator. The Q-Wing

Fast Jet wobbled and screamed, wings rattling in the wild turbulence.

Come on, come on, come on...

Keenan was dead. She couldn't let it happen again, couldn't let her one final link, her one last FRIEND *die like this...*

If Franco jumped, she could use a wide-angle field net, she reasoned.

She could fire it! Catch him!

Pluck him from the sky like a stone caught by a child...

Pippa blinked, and eased back on her control stick.

It was too late.

With bitterness like acid in her mouth, Pippa turned her head – as the War Balloon impacted with the ground. It seemed to slowly fold in upon itself, compressing like a skyscraper, collapsing in slow motion, folds of silver billowing and collapsing like a metal blanket allowed to carelessly fall. And then the explosion slammed out in an expanding fireball of bright bright blue energy that left Pippa fighting the controls of the Q-Wing Fast Jet again, tears pouring down her cheeks, and she sent the Jet scurrying around in a wide arc, away from the awesome blast zone...

Pippa hovered the Jet, but did not watch. She *could* not.

Tears rolled down her cheeks.

Pippa wept for a man she loved, a friend, a companion, a brother, and a sexual athlete.

Franco had been on that War Balloon.

There was no way he could have escaped.

Pippa acknowledged the tragedy with a deep and hateful bitterness.

CHAPTER SIXTEEN

AFTERMATH

PIPPA DRESSED IN silence, in a long, flowing red silk dress. She tied back her dark hair, which shone with honey and oils, and smiled her thanks at the woman who'd attended on her as she'd bathed in a large, scented pool scattered with flower petals. The woman departed, and Pippa walked slowly in bare feet to the high windows. She opened them with pale, tapered fingers, and a cool breeze washed in from the city of Org below.

Her nostrils twitched at the familiar scents of the city: machine oil, hot metal, fried fish. She glanced right, to where the Org Palace stood, gleaming, on the opposing hill, and she could make out the fluttering of bunting and flags, and hear squawking, rasping, org *Metalliano* music; all the marks of joy, celebration, happiness.

This was the Day of Truce.

Pippa was invited to the party.

She slowly closed the high apartment windows and moved back to the huge bed. It was massive, to accommodate augmented org guests, and dressed with crisp white sheets. One thing Pippa had to admit – the orgs were hard workers, and there wasn't one element of her royal pampering that had been overlooked.

Long gauze curtains hung from ceiling to floor, diffusing the bright, low-slung winter sun. Pippa lay back on the bed with a groan, resting her aching, battered limbs.

It had been three days since... since the crash.

Her body was still a battered sack of shit, a skin-bag full of crushed marbles.

"Music. Classical. Old Earth Symphony."

Violins soothed her, and she reached out, took a sip of honeyed wine, and sank back to the folds of the supremely comfortable bed. Gods, it had been a long week. And an even longer life.

She was almost asleep, a doze of exhaustion, of regeneration, when she realised another person was present in the room. Pippa's eyes flared open and she went for her gun – but realised just in time who it was.

A woman.

Dressed neatly in body-hugging black. Black boots. Gloves. She had long brown hair, tied back with a simple clip. She wore several guns and a QGM PAD at her hip.

"You've got it?"

"Yeah."

This was Karella. One of Steinhauer's... personal operatives.

Combat X.

QGM's assassins. Very, very deadly.

Pippa handed over the 3Core, and sat back on the bed, hugging her knees. Karella watched Pippa for a while, as if gauging her, as if reading her innermost thoughts. Some said Combat X were psychic. But then, some said Combat X were immortal. Obviously, that was just plain bullshit. Pippa had killed one; assassinated the assassin. She gave a cold smile.

"I hope it was worth it," said Karella, her voice soft.

"Me too. Lots of good people died to deliver that fucker to Steinhauer."

"If it works, we'll be free of war."

Pippa smiled. "We'll never be free of war," she said. "That's why people like you and I thrive."

Karella nodded, and disappeared backwards, easing from the high window and closing it without a sound. A few minutes later, there was a knock at her door. A steward stood outside.

"The ceremony is about to begin, Lady."

"Thank you. I'll be there shortly."

THE MAIN HALL of the Org Palace was huge, and lined with *thousands* of dignitaries, nobles, politicians and merchants, people of money, people of royalty, people of *power* on the planet of Cloneworld and from Trade Clusters beyond. Here to witness this great occasion, to celebrate this landmark of history.

As Pippa stepped through the solid gold double doors, a troop of trumpeters struck up a loud, bright piece, and Pippa walked alone down the thick red carpet, feeling almost as if she was attending a wedding.

As a bride?

Yeah, right. I wish.

The Day of Truce. It would go down in Cloneworld History – the day when finally, *finally*, both sides, the orgs and the gangers, sat down and agreed on peace, agreed on trade, agreed on a *unity* from which both sides could prosper. They would share all secrets. They would integrate into a society, into a *Whole* where gangers were welcome in The Org States, and orgs welcome on Clone Terra soil.

Sure. Let's see how long this fucker lasts.

Pippa could not hide her cynicism, nor her bitterness. She'd seen too much bloodshed. Too much horror. Too much death.

She strode up the carpet, head high. On the platform ahead of her stood Queen Strogger in finest regal attire, her three Prime Daughters, including Princess Anklebolt III, looking supremely beautiful in blue and gold furs, their facial cogs and gears polished to a high sheen and inlaid with precious stones. To the right stood General Banks in his smartest military uniform, along with various Ganger Lords of power, there to represent CLONE TV and members of Core Government, including the newly elected *Prime*.

Music blared, and handshakes shook, and Pippa was offered a medal. She took it with good grace, and with a great sadness, descending like nuclear ash – for those not present to share the recognition. For those who had died in combat.

Suddenly, there was a commotion at the great gold doors. The trumpet music stuttered to an awkward halt.

Cursing and moaning, Franco Haggis staggered through the doors, tripped, and sprawled out flat. Muttering, he pulled himself clumsily to his feet, looked around at the shocked, muttering royalty and nobility, frowned, hoisted up his pants, and said in a loud, clear voice, as if speaking to somebody who couldn't understand his language, "I'M LOOKING FOR THE GREAT HALL OF QUEEN STROGGER, REET? DOES ANYBODY KNOW WHERE I CAN FIND IT? WHAT? *THIS IS IT?* OH GREAT! REET! I'M SUPPOSED TO BE HERE, I AM, YOU SEE THERE'S THIS AWARD CEREMONY THING, AND I'M A GUEST OF HONOUR, I AM, AND REET PLEASED ABOUT THE WHOLE KABOODLING THING…"

A steward approached Franco with hurried, clonking steps and a hiss of ejecting steam. He whispered in Franco's ear. Pippa could hear Franco's reply across the *entire* Hall, very loud, and very clear.

"What? Eh? What's bloody wrong with the way I'm dressed? No bugger said I had to wear a suit, if there's one thing I won't do, it's wear a bloody suit! I mean, just because my shorts are a *little* tattered, just because my sandals are *a little scuffed...*"

"Franco Haggis!" boomed Queen Strogger. "Please approach the stage."

Franco looked up. He grinned broadly, showing his missing tuff, and strode down the red carpet with chest puffed out, whilst the trumpets blazed his fame for all on Cloneworld to know, and hear, and wonder.

Franco took his medal.

He peered around, at the ten thousand faces who had watched his fumbled entrance and amiable acceptance of his Org Medal for Bravery. Franco waved at them all. Grinned. Coughed.

Then said, "Right, then. Where's the damn party?"

"YOU *STILL* SMELL funny," said Pippa.

"I can't *help it*. It won't bloody *scrub off!*"

"Come on, Franco! I thought you would have made a *bit* more effort! I mean, it's not every day you're awarded an Org Medal for Bravery. You could have put some pants on."

"You think the army shorts were a little overdressed?"

Pippa nudged him in the ribs, laughed coquettishly, and sipped her org Firepagne as she exchanged small-talk with local dignitaries. The three orgs moved on, legs clanking.

"Franco, sometimes I think you just don't take life too seriously."

"Oh, I take life serious enough, alright, mate! That's why I'm determined to enjoy every bloody moment!"

"Alice, do *you* think Franco takes life seriously enough?"

"What, after destroying my Fast Attack Hornet?" The small black cube in Pippa's hand flickered with coloured lights. Alice sounded perkier, brighter, *more alive.* "I think he owes me a *big drink!* Either that, or he's got a death wish. I haven't forgiven him yet."

"Hey, that was just a simple accident with a hole in my bucket. Could have happened to anybody!"

Alice chuckled. "If Tarly Winters hadn't hacked my core and sent my IQ plummeting into the tombworld depths, I would have spotted the danger before it happened. She wanted a disaster. She was playing us for fools."

"Yeah. Well. She's dead," said Franco.

"You hope," said Alice.

"Shut up," said Franco.

"Just imagine... she might one day come back to reclaim you as her prize?" grinned Pippa. "You *were* going to get married."

"Shut up," said Franco.

They stood for a while, both feeling out of place. Hundreds swarmed and mingled around the ancient rooms, which stood as testament to a thousand years of org history. Paintings as large as a house decorated the walls, and after a trip to the restroom, Pippa caught Franco studying one with some kind of winged org cherubs.

"Hmm," he said, drinking his Guinness.

"What?" said Pippa, eyes narrowing. Then: "Franco, how the *hell* did you get a *pint of Guinness* in this place?"

"One has contacts," said Franco, airily. "Hey, I'm a bit of a celebrity, y'know? After all, it's not every day a man survives a War Balloon crash by being encased in a dying alien's frisky snake body! Hey?"

PIPPA STOOD FORLORNLY on the remains of the detonation site. The War Balloon had impaled itself atop four skyscrapers, destroying them utterly. The following explosion had taken out nearly three square kilometres of buildings, but thankfully the denizens had seen it coming. It was hard to miss a slowly tumbling War Balloon of such epic proportions. Thankfully, there had been only a few ground casualties...

"Oh, Franco," said Pippa, miserably. She kicked around in the debris until she was waved over by Queen Strogger and ten org engineers.

"We've found something," said Strogger, pistons clacking, her old oil-breath washing over Pippa.

"What kind of something?"

"Something buried beneath the rubble."

"What is it?"

"We don't know. But it's making a racket."

The site had been carefully excavated until they found what looked to Pippa like a human-sized wad of old chewing gum. Hundreds of strands and fibres criss-crossed and wrapped around one another, in a kind of uneven and lumpy *ball*.

The engineers approached warily.

Pippa frowned.

There came a deep, metallic thumping.

"Let me out!" came the muffled cry. It was weak, but it was angry. Pippa frowned.

"Fuck me! It's *Franco*."

She leapt forward, and slapped her hand on the ball. "You hang on in there, Franco! We'll have you out in no time!"

That had been a lie, an exaggeration of epic proportions. Franco was encased in the hardened, explosion-baked remains of the Mistress. He was entombed in interwoven strands of cooked alien snake; this was what had saved his life.

Twelve hours later, after six thousand circular saw blades had been worn blunt, the shell was finally *cracked* and, like the rotten yolk of a bad egg, Franco tumbled out, shivering, dehydrated, weak... but alive, baby, *alive!*

Pippa grabbed him and hugged him, before he was wrapped in blankets and bundled off, complaining about needing a pint and a big fat woman to take his mind off their incompetent rescue attempt.

Pippa had grinned. Her questions could wait.

*   *   *

VOICES. LOTS OF loud, brash voices. Out on the carved metal balcony, Franco and Pippa exchanged glances over their fluted glasses of Firepagne.

"Eh? What? *What do you mean, it's not an official invite?*"

"Could sir please keep his voice down?"

"Why? It's a party, innit?"

"Sir, I assure you…"

"You bloody listen to me. If it wasn't for me and my good clone buddies here, you and your org friends would be all, like, detonated and flat and gone, y'hear?"

"I am sure if sir and his colleagues would just like to wait in the vestibule, whilst I garner authorisation…"

"I'm not bloody sitting in no vesty mule, and neither are the lads, eh, lads?"

"No, Franco!"

"No way, Franco!"

"Come on, us lads needs a drink!"

"Onwards!"

"Upwards!"

"Beer and sex!"

"Chips and gravy!"

They poured in. Like a wave. Like a tide. Like a tidal wave. Francos. Hundreds of Francos. Badly dressed. Drunk. Happy. And *gate-crashing the party, baby!*

Franco and Pippa looked at one another.

And burst out laughing.

"SQUAWK!"

"Look!" grinned Pippa, pointing. "They even brought your *Special Friend...*"

But Franco had already disappeared.

IT HADN'T TAKEN Franco Haggis long to recuperate in the Org Central Hospital. Admittedly, the Org Central Hospital looked more like a landcar manufacturing plant, and the ward on which Franco was being kept "for his own security and health" was filled with a wild and wacky gathering of weird old org scraps, but other than that – and the lack of alcohol and buxom young women – Franco was happy. Happy to be alive, anyway.

"Go on," said Pippa, pulling up a chair, scraping it across the tiled floor.

"Go on what?" said Franco, who was sipping something milky through a straw. There was a colourful paper umbrella in the cup. The drink looked suspiciously alcoholic.

"Spill the beans, dickhead! What happened up there? I thought you were cat meat, dead and gone."

"Did you miss me?" He reached forward and placed his hand on Pippa's thigh. Pippa stared at his hand. Stared hard. Nonplussed, Franco removed the offending article.

"Of course I did," she said, slowly. "You're the closest thing to a brother I've got, although

I'll readily admit it, if I had a brother like you I'd fucking hang myself."

"Charming! Well, what happened was this... I'm about to die a terrible horrible death, right, and the Mistress goes all funny on me, and tells me how she used to be a biological computer-type thing, harnessing the very soul of the junks themselves, their computer, like..."

"Wait. *What?*"

"She was an alien. A biological computer, gone mad, sort of thing. And the 3Core processor was *hers*, part of her, and we needed unlocking codes, and she was sad about the junks and them coming back and being nasty bad guys, right, so she told me where to get the codes and let me climb inside her. Then she wrapped all that horrible snake flesh around me, and I was encased, and she was one tough bastard, I can tell you. When we crashed, I could hear all manner of cacophony, and explosions and everything, but she gave her last remnants of life so that I could live, so I could be reborn from her egg, so to speak, and bring you the codes to unlock the 3Core and help stop the junks. To turn them good again. Like she wanted. It was her final, like, gift. To the Quad-Gal."

Franco beamed, and slurped on his drink.

"Is that booze?" snapped Pippa, as she internally digested Franco's insane diatribe.

"Sure is," he grinned, and tapped the side of his nose. "You gotta have contacts, reet?"

"Give it here!" Pippa grabbed the drink, and they wrestled with it for a few moments before she won. She turned and put it out of Franco's reach.

"Awww," he said.

"So let me get this straight... you were reborn from an egg made of snake flesh – so you're, like, kind of this newly made snake alien's new baby? That's just too weird, even for you, Franco."

"The important thing is we got the chip. And we got the codes. So now QGM can turn back the tide of the invading junks. Right?"

"We'll see," said Pippa, brow furrowed.

IT WAS LATE. Very late.

Pippa was a little drunk. She stood on a balcony looking out over the city of Org. A gentle wind blew the red dress around her, and it shifted gently, clinging to the contours of her slim, athletic body.

She realised somebody was watching her, and glanced up. Franco – the original Franco, the *best* Franco – was leaning against a pillar, a glass to his lips, eyes locked on her. She smiled at him, and he smiled back: a genuine smile, a warm smile, a smile of love and friendship.

Franco pushed himself from the pillar using his shoulders, and padded over.

"You okay, chipmunk?"

"I'm okay, Franco," she said, tracing her finger around the rim of her glass.

"I expect QGM will pick us up tomorrow, send us off on another crazy-arse mission. Eh?" He grinned at her.

"I expect they will," she said. Then she turned, and placed her glass on a low table made of machine gears. She turned back to Franco, and placed her hands on his shoulders.

"Er," said Franco.

"I want to try something."

"You do?"

"Yeah. I do."

Pippa leant forward, and kissed Franco. For once, Franco did nothing, just allowed the moment to sweep on over him, to hold him, to encompass him, to bury him in an eternal sweet dream.

When finally she pulled away, her eyes were closed.

Franco rubbed his beard which, admittedly, he'd trimmed, and was now looking rather smart, even if he said so himself.

"Why?" he said.

"Because," she said.

"I can live with that," he said.

"I know you can," she said.

Franco grinned. "Want to do it again?"

"I think I will," she said, and leant forward, and kissed him. This time, Franco's arms encircled her waist and he held her tight. So tight. As if this was the last embrace he would ever enjoy... as if the world and life and the entire Quad-Gal might end tomorrow.

Over the city of Org, a machine moon sparkled.

VOLOS

"Did it work?"

"It worked."

"So you've *opened* the core?"

"Oh, yes."

Steinhauer stood in the QGM Central Intelligence Computer Suite on the Heavy Accelerator, *Killer*. His new false legs – powered by ORG INC. technology – were working well, and that made him *very* happy. But even more so, the 3Core delivered by Pippa and Franco really *had* been used by the junks. And the organic codes given by Franco after his, frankly, insane story of aliens with snake heads had, indeed, been the right codes to fully unlock the chip.

"Is there information on the junks contained therein?"

The programmer glanced up at Steinhauer. His hands were shaking. In a small voice, he said, "There's everything. History. Politics. Religion. Science. Schematics for starships, their computer technology, artificial intelligence, *everything*."

"So we can begin," said Steinhauer, his voice little more than a whisper.

"Yes."

"I want you to call in every damn expert mind we have on the junks, on computer virus technology, the decoding of historical texts – I want every expert assembled here in twenty-four hours. You get that? Twenty-four hours!"

The programmer nodded and scuttled off to send out the most important messages of his career. Steinhauer clanked through to his office and poured himself a fine brandy, and pulled free a cigar. He took a sip, then a larger swallow, and slowly lit the cigar.

A chance!

They had a chance!

To end the nightmare. To end the invasion. To end the war.

Steinhauer sat for long hours throughout the night, thinking. At some ungodly hour there came a knock at the door to his office, and he buzzed the man in. The man was Combat X, small in stature, his eyes dark and fixed on Steinhauer with careful contemplation.

"A message, General."

"Go ahead."

"It's from VOLOS. He congratulates you on your – discovery. He hopes you can pacify the threat of the junks."

"Good. And the answer to my *specific* question?"

The Combat X assassin lowered his head, then looked up again, eyes bright, a half-smile on his lips. "VOLOS agrees. He is willing to release Keenan back into the welcoming arms of the Quad-Gal Military machine."

ACKNOWLEDGEMENTS

A big thanks to all those who supported me whilst writing this novel – you know who you are, and you deserve Big Kisses. Writing *Cloneworld* has been an insane, intense, ragged whirlwind of joy, sausages and whiskey – and I thank you all!

ANDY REMIC is a larger-than-life action man, sexual athlete, sword warrior and chef. His exploits have garnered him acclaim in the Guinness Book of Galactic Records, and he once worked as a biomod technician pioneering illegal nano-tek for underhand government agencies. His writing has picked up numerous esoteric awards for visceral hardcore action, clever plotlines, black humour and a willingness to push the boundaries of science fiction and sexual deviancy, all in one twisted whiskey barrel.

When kicked to describe himself, Remic claims to have a love of extreme sports, kickass bikes and happy nurses. Once a member of an elite Combat K squad, he has retired from military service and claims to be a cross between an alcoholic Indiana Jones and a bubbly Lara Croft, only without the breasts (although he'd probably like some). Remic lives in Lincolnshire and enjoys listening to Ronan Keating whilst thinking lewdly about zombies.

Cloneworld is his ninth novel.

Find out more about Andy Remic at
www.andyremic.com.

UK ISBN: 978 1 84416 650 3 • US ISBN: 978 1 84416 757 9 • £7.99/$7.99

The City: a planet filled with corruption, guns, sex, and designer drugs. Zombies roam the streets and are out for blood. The Combat K squad are dropped into this warzone to uncover what's turned this planet into a wasteland of murder and mutations. Soon their focus is on the Nano-Tek corporation itself...

UK ISBN: 978 1 84416 793 7 • US ISBN: 978 1 84416 792 0 • £7.99/$7.99

Sick World: a long-abandoned hospital planet, with possible information on the origin of the alien Junk scourge. As daylight fades, hibernation ends: the Medical Staff – the doctors, nurses, patients and deviants, a thousand-year gestation of hardcore medical mutation – can smell fresh meat, and Combat K face their toughest battle yet.

 WWW.SOLARISBOOKS.COM

Follow us on Twitter! www.twitter.com/solarisbooks

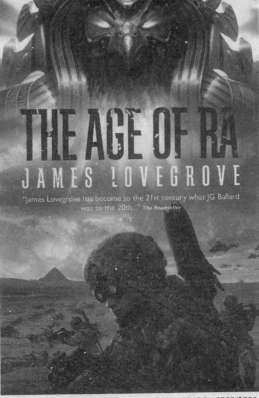

UK ISBN: 978 1 844167 46 3 • US ISBN: 978 1 844167 47 0 • £7.99/$7.99

The Ancient Egyptian gods have defeated all the other pantheons and divided the Earth into warring factions. Lt. David Westwynter, a British soldier, stumbles into Freegypt, the only place to have remained independent of the gods, and encounters the followers of a humanist freedom-fighter known as the Lightbringer. As the world heads towards an apocalyptic battle, there is far more to this leader than it seems...

 WWW.SOLARISBOOKS.COM

Follow us on Twitter! www.twitter.com/solarisbooks

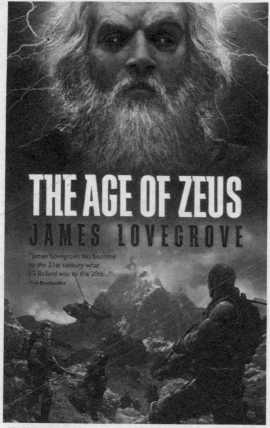

UK ISBN: 978 1 906735 68 5 • US ISBN: 978 1 906735 69 2 • £7.99/$7.99

The Olympians appeared a decade ago, living incarnations of the Ancient Greek gods, offering order and stability at the cost of placing humanity under the jackboot of divine oppression. Until former London police officer Sam Akehurst receives an invitation to join the Titans, the small band of battlesuited high-tech guerillas squaring off against the Olympians and their mythological monsters in a war they cannot all survive…

 WWW.SOLARISBOOKS.COM

Follow us on Twitter! www.twitter.com/solarisbooks

THE AGE OF ODIN

JAMES LOVEGROVE

"One of the UK SF scene's most interesting, challenging and adventurous authors."
- Saxon Bullock, *SFX*

UK ISBN: 978 1 907519 40 6 • US ISBN: 978 1 907519 41 3 • £7.99/$7.99

The Valhalla project is hiring former servicemen; no questions asked, for excellent pay; for Gideon Coxall, with one deaf ear and a British Army half-pension, it's like a dream come true. The last thing Gid expects is to find himself fighting alongside ancient Viking gods.

The world is in the grip of one of the worst winters it has ever known, and Ragnarök – the fabled final conflict of the Sagas – is looming.

 WWW.SOLARISBOOKS.COM

Follow us on Twitter! www.twitter.com/solarisbooks

THE NOISE REVEALED

IAN WHATES